PEACE OF THE PUZZLE

a novel

HAYLEY MORTON

First published by Haymeadow Stories in Australia, 2018.
www.hayleymorton.com

A catalogue record for this book is available from the National Library of Australia.
Morton, Hayley, 1977 -
Peace of the puzzle: a novel / Hayley Morton
ISBN-13: 978-0-9875466-2-3 (epub)
ISBN-13: 978-0-9875466-1-6 (mobi)
ISBN-13: 978-0-9875466-3-0 (paperback)

Cover Design: Karin Roberts, Art Tonic

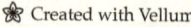

ACKNOWLEDGMENTS

This story has taken more than five years to reach its final form and has benefited from the input and support of a number of wonderful people.

My heartfelt thanks go to Erin M, Erin F, Chris, John, Eddie and Daniel for their willingness to read, either in-part or full, draft versions and provide some very useful and much appreciated feedback. Thank you to Rosie for the spark of inspiration when I was stuck, to the very flexible and adaptable Radhiah Chowdhury for her professional editorial services and insightful advice, Tamara for her patience in answering my various technical questions, and Karin Roberts of Art Tonic for the beautiful, mystical cover. Thank you to my husband Joaquín and all my family for supporting my desire to write and all the friends and colleagues who have shown interest in my debut novel and offered support in many and varied forms. Last, but not least, thank you to the immortal Alfred, Lord Tennyson. I can only hope he is not turning in his grave at my interpretation and use of his spellbinding masterpiece, The Lady of Shalott.

Dedicated to Jo for her friendship, support and all those girly talks; Helen Abbott for her insights and support during a difficult period; and my precious Joaquín, who appeared in my life at exactly the right moment.

Four gray walls, and four gray towers
Overlook a space of flowers,
And the silent isle imbowers
The Lady of Shalott.
No time hath she to sport and play:
A charmed web she weaves alway.
A curse is on her, if she stay
Her weaving, either night or day,
To look down to Camelot.
She knows not what the curse may be;
Therefore she weaveth steadily...
She lives with little joy or fear...
Before her hangs a mirror clear,
Reflecting tower'd Camelot...
She hath no loyal knight and true,
The Lady of Shalott.

— EXCERPT FROM THE LADY OF SHALOTT BY
ALFRED, LORD TENNYSON

Chapter One

THE DAFFODILLY TREMBLE IN THE WATER CHILLY

E lena watched Michael shrug off his black leather jacket, peel off his faded Levi 501s and tug his white t-shirt over his head. He ran a calloused hand through his reddish-blond, exaggerated pompadour, checking in the round bedroom mirror to ensure all strands of the seemingly messy 'do were perfectly placed, and smoothed his blond pencil-thin moustache. Although unfashionable, Elena thought it suited him. She had been smitten from the day they met. He reminded her of James Dean, albeit a shorter, more nuggety version with a moustache and freckled skin.

Michael pulled on his daggy old black-and-white striped flannel pyjamas and joined her in bed.

He could have made an effort and worn his new pyjamas.

Elena silenced her critical inner voice. *He'd made an effort with his hair, at least.* She fluffed her own long blonde tresses, arranging them on the pillow, glad she had permed her hair again. It filled out her face, making her seem less plain. The new grey eyeshadow, which she hadn't washed off before coming to bed, helped highlight her large blue eyes. She had worn makeup every day since overhearing the incredulous remark of a popular girl at school: *'Elena looks pretty with makeup on.'* She didn't normally wear it to bed, but tonight was a special occasion.

"Are you ready?" Her gut clenched. Even after two years' of marriage, this still made her nervous.

"Ready for what?" Michael stared at her with that familiar challenge in his eyes.

Elena's gut took a rollercoaster dive. He was in one of his moods.

"We agreed to ah… make love tonight."

"Did we?"

"Yes." She clutched her stomach, trying to stop the sudden gurgling rumbles. *Not tonight*, she pleaded silently.

Michael checked his watch. "It's already ten-thirty. I've got an early start tomorrow."

Elena swallowed a sudden lump in her throat and tried to hide her disappointment. It wasn't only when he had early starts that he didn't want sex. It was most of the time these days. There was always a reason to say no.

He was an ordered, regimented man who didn't like surprises, so a lovemaking date had seemed like a good idea.

"Do you remember when we first met? When you told me you couldn't wait until after marriage to make love?"

"Not really."

"I do. I remember you couldn't keep your hands off me." She recalled the torturous nights in his car, chests heaving with barely-restrained desire, his white-knuckled grip on the steering wheel as their desires fought against her fear of eternal damnation if she had sex before marriage.

"That was a long time ago."

"Seven years." It didn't sound so long, but Elena had to admit that sometimes it felt like an eternity. It felt like they had spent their whole relationship wading through molasses—backwards.

They stared at each other across the bed.

She reached across, giving his cheek a hesitant caress. "We could just cuddle." It came out sounding more like a question than a suggestion.

Michael gave her a small, twisted smile, took firm hold of her hand and moved it from his cheek to the bed. He gave it a quick pat before pecking her on the lips.

"Goodnight," he said, turning out the light.

"Goodnight," Elena mumbled.

Waves of disappointment washed over her. She tried hard not to cry though. It would make Michael angry. He hated emotional displays and talking about feelings. He was happy to talk about his passions—wine and butterflies—and he could be a charismatic conversationalist so long as the topic didn't revolve around feelings. After seven years, she still had no idea what he was thinking or feeling.

He didn't like physical affection, either. She knew not to kiss him often, and never in public. Sometimes she tried to give him a hug, but he would tense up and push her away. He didn't even like holding her hand. Sex was the only time they had prolonged physical contact, hence why she had resorted to setting up sex dates.

The truth be told, Elena wasn't that keen on sex. She knew it was supposed to be enjoyable, but her experience of it left much to be desired. Kissing and being caressed was enjoyable but intercourse seemed kind of rough. She had decided long ago that it must be more enjoyable for men than women since so many men seemed so driven to have sex.

Never having experienced affection from a man—her father and grandfathers were no-nonsense farmers of few words and even fewer actions—she was starting to believe that it was impossible for the male species to be affectionate. Yet that didn't stop her yearning for Michael to take her in his arms and give her gentle caresses while they talked about their feelings and hopes for the future, about things that really mattered.

A familiar, sharp pain in her belly caused Elena to scramble out of bed.

"Where are you going?" Michael called as she raced down the hallway.

"Bathroom!"

The stabbing pain reminded her of pains she had as a child. Her grandmother had called it a niggling appendix. Elena had spent many sleepless nights willing it to go away. The thought of abdominal surgery terrified her, so much so that as a teenager, she decided she couldn't have children, couldn't take the chance of needing a caesarean. Her resolve wavered once she reached an age where starting a family was an actual possibility, but the fear still plagued her.

The problem wasn't her appendix, though. It was a somewhat more elusive condition diagnosed at age nineteen in the absence of any other more concrete diagnosis: Irritable Bowel Syndrome. The nausea and diarrhoea that had made her anxious about leaving the house was under better control these days, but sometimes it still got the better of her.

Elena bent forward, clutching her belly while her bowels emptied in a violent explosion. The cold travelled from the hard terrazzo floor up through her bare feet and legs, spreading to every bone in her body. By the time her bowels finally stopped misbehaving, Elena's slight frame was shivering in the flimsy white lace teddy she had hoped would seduce her husband.

Michael's snores echoed through the little house.

Elena crept into the dark bedroom, fished under the pillow for her winter PJs, pulled them over her trembling limbs and slid under the blankets.

༶

MICHAEL LACED up his heavy-duty steel cap work boots, the chunky soles giving him some much-needed extra height. Elena was sure his short stature bothered him because he always chose boots with the thickest possible sole. In fact, he only owned two pairs of shoes: the work boots and a pair of black, thick-soled 1460 Doc Martens. She sensed his self-consciousness, but she had never asked him about it and he had never said. She had thrown out her high heels though, and always wore ballet flats so that she would never be taller than him.

Michael bent over the bed and kissed Elena's cheek. "See you tonight."

"Bye, have a good day."

She listened to him leave through the back door, locking and re-locking the door three times. Always three times. It was a minor obsessive-compulsive routine he carried out on every lock—house, car, letter box.

The car engine gunned.

Elena got out of bed and padded to the bedroom window, watching through a crack in the sheer white gossamer curtain as he

4

backed the State Water Utility ute down the driveway and drove off. She shivered in the cool morning air and jumped back into bed. It was Saturday, so she could sleep for another hour or two. Michael's job in the maintenance crew of one of Adelaide's sewage treatment plants meant he sometimes had to work weekends, but Elena, a research officer in the Department of Health, only worked Monday to Friday.

When Elena woke again, the sun was streaming through the window. She jumped into a hot shower, letting the water needle her stiff neck and shoulders. They were always stiff these days, and worse first thing in the morning. The last of the numerous physiotherapists she had consulted had seemed particularly concerned about that. In his view, she should be most relaxed after a good night's rest. She gave her shoulders a violent shake and turned off the water. Better not to dwell on it. She would end up more stressed and self-diagnose a serious illness for what was nothing more than tight muscles… tight, stubborn muscles which refused all professional attempts to heal them.

She dried her hair, threw on yesterday's jeans and a jumper and began her Saturday morning house cleaning ritual. Michael was very particular about cleanliness. She liked to keep things neat and tidy too, but before they'd bought their house and moved in together, sometimes she'd left the vacuuming or cleaning the bathroom for a couple of weeks. Now was different.

She ran the vacuum through the three bedrooms, hallway and lounge room, then scrubbed the original pale yellow enamel bathroom and light and airy kitchen. It was a 1948 double-brick Waterfall Austerity style home with rounded feature front brickwork in the suburb of Seacombe Heights. The rendered facade was painted a dark grey, but the paint was flaking with age, exposing patches of the original eggshell render beneath. When they bought it, she had been happy. It wasn't the greatest house, but it had seemed good enough. After more than a year of Michael picking to pieces every house they inspected, she had finally pushed him to make an offer. Now she wished she had waited for something more suitable, more comfortable. She disliked the boxy floor plan, every room separated by walls, creating a pokey house that wasn't conducive to entertaining. Not that they ever entertained beyond an occasional family dinner, but she hoped that would change when they knocked down a few walls.

There was plenty of room to extend out the back too, and she fantasised about a large open plan living-dining area and an extra bedroom to accommodate their future children. Elena was keen to renovate but Michael insisted they throw all their extra cash at the mortgage. Nevertheless, Elena often visualised what she would do when they could afford it.

Nose wrinkling in distaste, she ran a damp cloth over the curvy, Depression-era dark wood veneer bedroom furniture. Most of their furniture was Michael's from before they moved in together. She detested it—the 1940s red vinyl club lounge suite that stuck to your bare skin in summer, the retro drop leaf red enamel kitchen table. Sometimes she thought Michael had been born in the wrong era. She didn't mind his hairstyle and his vintage car was impressive. She felt special being a passenger in the shiny red convertible, especially in summer with the top down and the light breezes tickling her face. But the house decor was taking it too far. It made her feel out of place in her own home, like an intrepid time traveller who had run headlong into the past only to find herself stuck there, pining for the present which she had so recklessly abandoned.

Her mobile rang. It was her brother's girlfriend.

"Hi Carla."

"Hi, what are you up to today?"

"I'm just cleaning the house."

"Marcus and I are going for a bike ride this arvo. Want to join us?"

"I don't know…"

"Aw come on, the sun is shining, spring is finally here. It'll do you good!" Carla's bubbly personality was infectious.

Elena smiled, "Well, okay."

"We'll swing by around two o'clock if that suits you?"

"Sure, see you then."

"Bye."

As Elena dusted the frames on their bedroom wall, she studied the petrified butterflies beneath the glass. The kaleidoscope of bright, fragile wings seemed poised to take flight, but there would be no more flying for these lifeless shells, doomed to be pegged forevermore in their square, glass prison.

Michael's butterfly obsession had taken over their house. Reminders of that to which his heart belonged were everywhere:

framed pictures and preserved specimens on every wall, colourful adhesive motifs on windows, figurines on the dressing table, coffee mugs and tea towels, calendars displaying a different fluttering beauty every month.

She wasn't blameless though, having bought several of them as birthday gifts because he was so difficult to buy for. The only other gift she could think of was wine, and that seemed so impersonal. She'd started something that had no end and she shuddered as she envisioned their twilight years, every inch of their home cluttered with butterfly paraphernalia.

The housework complete, Elena made herself a cheese and tomato toasted sandwich and a cup of peppermint tea, popped her favourite CD—with a musical version of Tennyson's *The Lady of Shalott*—in the portable stereo and sat at the kitchen table to eat.

A small mesh butterfly cage swung on the standing hook next to the window. Michael thought putting them next to the window so they could get sunlight, fresh air and a view of the garden was a kindness.

Elena felt sorry for them, imagining their dismal, captive lives, seeing the world outside but not being able to play in it. She wanted to say butterflies should be free to flutter in the breeze, especially given the shortness of their lives, but she held her tongue, afraid of offending Michael. At first, she had found his choice of pet intriguing and unique. But a pet was supposed to provide long-term companionship. It was impossible to develop a relationship with insects which had weekly or monthly expiry dates. Even the longest lived of the species lasted no more than a year.

The haunting Celtic tones singing Tennyson's poem caught her attention. She had played the composition over and over during her university years but had forgotten about it when they'd moved into this house. She only rediscovered it recently whilst cleaning out a cupboard.

Listening again now, she saw the poem play out in her mind's eye and empathised with the poor lonely lady who had allowed her life to be limited by unfounded rumours.

> *No time hath she to sport and play:*
> *A charmed web she weaves alway.*

A curse is on her, if she stay
Her weaving, either night or day,
To look down to Camelot.
She knows not what the curse may be;
Therefore she weaveth steadily,

Yet something within her yearned to be free of her lonely existence.

Or when the moon was overhead
Came two young lovers lately wed;
'I am half sick of shadows,' said
The Lady of Shalott.

Elena was devastated when the Lady fell for Lancelot and thus brought the curse upon herself.

She left the web, she left the loom;
She made three paces thro' the room,
She saw the water-lily bloom,
She saw the helmet and the plume,
She look'd down to Camelot.
Out flew the web and floated wide;
The mirror crack'd from side to side;
"The curse is come upon me," cried
The Lady of Shalott.

It seemed unfair that just as the Lady allowed herself to hope and love, she was punished for it. Why was it okay for all the other characters to live freely in the world and find partners but it wasn't okay for the Lady? Elena wished she had the ability to write her own version, one in which the Lady survived to enjoy happy ever after with her Lancelot.

She gazed out the kitchen window, skipping over the unkempt, half-dead lawn invaded by soursobs which constituted the bulk of their backyard, and settled on the colourful flowerbed along the back fence. Their large, strangely-shaped block sat on the side of a hill, overlooking the city and the sea. It was flat to the end of the shed which abutted the eastern corner of the house, inclined steeply for some five metres, then levelled out again to create the wide flat ledge where she had created the flowerbed. During Autumn, she had tilled the soil and planted an assortment of dainty flowering ground covers, hardy geraniums, old-style stocks, hollyhocks, poppies and pansies. The Spring was late arriving this year—they were already in October and the nights were still cold—but the warmth of the daytime sun had yielded an explosion of vibrant colour and she gazed with pleasure on the soft beauty she had created.

The incline continued over the neighbours' fence, giving a clear line of sight to their gorgeous garden. Elena eyed with envy the wide expanse of manicured lawn, cobblestone paths leading to arches of blooming roses and golf bunker-shaped flower beds. Her backyard was a bare wasteland in comparison, but given time, she could make it look as good as the neighbour's. She couldn't wait to transform the entire backyard and have an uninterrupted vista of lushness from their backdoor to the neighbours… when Michael allowed it. He had grand ideas for the garden but refused to plant anything yet. Paying off the mortgage was more important than landscaping. He'd only allowed her to plant the flowerbed because most of the plants and seeds she had begged from Michael's mother, who had a beautiful heritage-style garden to match the heritage bluestone villa on her boutique vineyard outside of Gawler.

Sighing, Elena cleared the dirty dishes, changed into leggings and a sweatshirt, locked the house and retrieved her push bike from the shed. Marcus and Carla, puffing in unison, rode around the corner as Elena reached the end of the driveway.

"Hi, sis." Marcus kissed her cheek, "Michael home today?"

"Hi." She kissed Marcus and Carla in turn. "No, he's working today."

"Okay, let's go then." Marcus shifted the gears on his bike and started rolling back down the hill towards Brighton Road.

They chatted as they crossed Brighton Road and navigated the back streets, emerging at the esplanade.

Elena took a deep breath of fresh sea air. The breeze was cold on her face but as long as they kept moving, she wouldn't be too cold.

"I'm going to the body balance class on Monday night," Carla said. "Want to join me?"

Elena hesitated, "Er… I don't know."

Carla had talked her into joining a gym almost a year ago. Elena didn't like gyms as a general rule. The artificial atmosphere and lack of fresh air annoyed her, plus she suspected the trendy women were judging her inferior clothing and appearance. But with a friend alongside her, it hadn't seemed so bad—at first. Yet she couldn't shake off her discomfort within the gym, the feeling that people were staring at her, judging her appearance and movements. She caught unwanted glimpses of her beetroot face and bedraggled hair in the mirrors, standing alongside women clad in designer sportswear, whose hair and make-up remained perfect even at the end of a strenuous work-out. She detested those mirrors.

"Come! You haven't been for weeks."

"Yeah… but I'd have to prepare dinner the night before and Michael doesn't like re-heated meals."

"Then let him make dinner."

"Hmm," Elena replied. Carla didn't understand. Marcus loved to cook and shared all the housework. But Michael was different… and Marcus wasn't as fussy as Michael.

"So you'll come?"

She really did love the body balance class. "Okay, I'll come."

"Great!"

MICHAEL'S WORK ute rumbled up the street and turned into the driveway. He cut the engine.

Elena waited for him to come inside but he didn't. She found him at the top of the backyard, rooting around under the lemon tree in the eastern corner behind the shed.

"What are you doing?"

He straightened and turned towards her, his fist full of daffodils. The bulbs, planted by the previous owners, had been a nice surprise when they had poked their way through the soursobs in winter. Lemons, daffodils, soursobs and a row of large wattle trees along the western fence line were the only colour in the backyard. The previous owners must have liked yellow.

Her hopes soared. He'd never picked flowers for her before. "Are they for me?"

"No, they're for Mum. We're going for lunch tomorrow."

"Oh." Elena tried not to show her disappointment.

It was a sweet gesture on Michael's part. He had been more attentive towards his mother since his father's untimely death four years' ago. His mother now lived alone at the vineyard and they made the hour and a half drive every Sunday for lunch. Sometimes they would stay there from Friday night to Sunday night when there was work to be done — fence mending, pruning and the like.

She liked his mother, yet a small internal voice raged. *What about me?* Michael had not given her flowers since his initial efforts to woo her. As soon as they had fallen into a relationship, all romantic gestures had ended. He hadn't remembered Valentines' Day after the second year, and last birthday, he'd given her a first-aid kit! She needed to know that her happiness was important to him too; that she was worth his time and effort. Shame and dejection coursed through her as she struggled to overcome her emotions.

"Are you going to pick some for me too?" The words were out of Elena's mouth before she could stop them, a volcano expelling the first dark warning puffs of ash. She wished she could suck them back inside.

His steely face closed over. "I can pick you some if you want."

"Thank you," she replied in a teeny, tiny voice as realisation dawned that flowers would not make her feel better. Flowers would only be meaningful if he wanted to give them to her of his own free will, which clearly he did not.

Chapter Two

SHE KNOWS NOT WHAT THE CURSE MAY BE

"Hold the plank position, squeeze the glutes, flat backs... and remember to breathe."

The instructor's voice brought Elena's attention back to the present. She exhaled. She was forever forgetting to breathe; that was why she needed this class. A mix of pilates and yoga, it helped her relax and focus while increasing strength at the same time. As for flexibility, well that would be a long time coming. Even as a child, her muscles had been rigid blocks.

"Ok, push yourself up onto your hands, arms extended. Now move the hips backwards and up, coming into downward dog. Bend the knees if you need to."

Elena's knees were already bent. She couldn't have straightened them if her life depended on it. Her arms began to wobble.

"Uff," Carla grunted next to her.

"I agree," Elena puffed.

"Drop the head, let your neck relax."

The instruction made Elena aware her neck was sticking up like a turtle. She dropped her head, staring back between her legs and caught the lewd stares of three muscular men on the other side of the glass wall which separated the workout and weights rooms. As the men ogled the row of backsides pointed in their direction, Elena felt her shoulders tighten in anger. Her cheeks reddened and she shifted her gaze to the floor.

"Come down onto your knees and stretch the arms forwards. Deep breath, forehead touching the mat. Relax with each exhalation… and we're done for today."

Elena sat up and stretched her neck. It definitely did reduce her headaches and neck stiffness. If only she had access to a gym without having to share the space with blockheads like the men next door.

Carla grinned. "Great class!"

Elena smiled back. "Yeah."

"Same time next week?" Carla asked as they exited the gym.

"Sure, see you then," Elena agreed, despite her inner resistance. She shouldn't let the behaviour of others stop her doing what was good for her.

Elena hopped on her push bike and struggled uphill through the dancing twilight shadows. She didn't have her own car. Company policy forbade her from driving Michael's work ute and she wouldn't want to, anyway. She would only worry about damaging it. For the same reason she wouldn't dare drive Michael's personal car. A large, open-topped sleek beast of gleaming chrome and red Duco, it was one of only five 1939 Delahaye type 165 Cabriolets ever made by the French. She would never forgive herself if something happened to it while she was driving.

❧

THE SECURITY LIGHT flicked on as Elena walked the bike up the driveway.

"Ah, there you are."

Startled, Elena halted in the beam of light. She peered through the darkness, just making out the outline of Michael's body sitting under the back pergola, glowing cigarette dangling from his mouth.

"Oh! Hello. Why are you sitting in the dark? Turn the light on."

"I prefer the darkness."

Elena stored her bike in the garage, locked the garage door and took a step towards the house.

"Is the garage locked?"

"Yes."

"Are you sure?"

She took hold of the sliding door handle and pulled. "See, it's locked."

She bent and kissed him on the mouth, coughed as she inhaled his cigarette smoke, and headed towards the back door. "Brrr, it gets cold when the sun goes down."

Michael followed her inside, carrying an almost empty glass of wine. He sat at the table and watched her open the fridge door.

Both plates of food were still there.

"Haven't you eaten yet?"

"Yes."

"But your plate is still here."

"I'm sick of reheated food. I bought fish and chips on the way home."

Elena blinked but said nothing. She'd made his favourite roast on Sunday night specifically with tonight in mind. Normally he was happy to eat leftover roast.

After zapping her food in the microwave, she sat opposite him.

He filled a wineglass for her and refilled his own. "Peppertree shiraz," he said, nodding towards the bottle.

Taking a sip of the wine, she screwed her face up and forced herself to swallow. She never drank before meeting Michael. It still tasted like vinegar to her sometimes, but he was such a wine connoisseur and his family had owned a small vineyard for generations, so she made an effort to acquire a taste for the stuff.

Michael watched her eat in silence.

It unnerved her. Normally he sat outside to smoke or in front of the television.

She stifled a yawn as she downed the last of the wine. Already tired from the combination of a day at work, the gym class and the uphill ride home, the wine was having a strong effect on her. She forced her heavy limbs up from the table and washed her dishes.

"I'm really tired. I think I'll go to bed," she told Michael.

"I'll come too."

They brushed their teeth, changed into pyjamas and Elena collapsed into the bed.

Michael's strong hand grabbed her arm. "So, shall we do it?"

"Do what?"

"Have sex."

"Now?"

"Yeah, why not?"

"I'm so tired."

"You can just relax. I do most of the work, anyway."

Elena opened her mouth to protest, then closed it again. It was rare for him to feel like sex, so she should make an effort. "Okay."

As his hands roamed, she resigned herself to being undressed. Despite her tiredness, she felt the familiar anxiety at being naked. She was so skinny, her breasts so small and her skin impossibly white, almost translucent, with blue veins visible on her arms and legs. Even after all these years together, she was self-conscious, awkward, unsure what to say or do. He must really love her if he wanted to sleep with her.

His firm grasp pinned her beneath him, his kiss hard and hungry. She felt his need and his desire, and, as always, began to fear he would unintentionally bite her as his mouth and teeth ground into hers.

"If you didn't go to the gym, you wouldn't be so tired at night," he murmured in her ear.

"I suppose."

He had a point. If she were too tired for sex when he felt like it, they would never be able to start a family. Plus memberships were expensive. She could run or ride a bike for free. And she wouldn't have to be around those horrible men anymore.

Moments later she bucked in response to an excruciating pain in her right foot, pushing Michael off her as she reached for the foot.

"Again?!"

"Sorry," she groaned, trying to massage the cramp out of her foot.

She was prone to cramping, often at inopportune moments, like the first time she and Michael had made love after she had decided to renounce her religion.

"Are you sure you're okay with this?" he'd asked, searching her face for signs of distress.

"Yes, but you have protection, don't you?"

"Do we need it?" he'd asked, propped on his elbows above her.

She'd flushed. "I'm on the pill but condoms are still safer,"

"You don't have any diseases, I could tell if you did."

"How?"

"I just could."

But are you clean? Anxiety fluttering in her chest, she had refrained from asking in case it offended him. "Perhaps we should wait."

He had reached into the bedside drawer and retrieved a small silver package, then almost fell off the bed as she'd writhed beneath him.

"What's wrong?"

"Cramp," she'd moaned, mortified to have ruined the moment.

He'd scrambled, naked, to the end of the bed and grabbed hold of her foot. "Push against my hand as hard as you can."

It had taken a good five minutes before the cramp subsided, along with Michael's impatient questioning whether it was better yet.

Way to go Elena, she'd chided herself, *he won't forget this moment!*

Self-conscious, they'd embraced once more. Preoccupied with not placing her foot in a position that would cause the cramp to return, she had been unable to relax. Yet the experience had been more pleasant than she had anticipated. Pleasant, but somewhat anti-climactic, she'd admitted to herself, wondering why people craved sex and why religion was so against it. Physical closeness was enjoyable. Cuddles and kisses were lovely, but sex was supposed to create a closer bond between people. All that thrusting and grunting seemed to have the opposite effect on her. Even their marriage document hadn't resulted in an improvement, so why did religions see sex without marriage as a cause for eternal damnation?

"Has it gone yet?" Michael's voice brought her back to the present.

"I think so."

"Good." He grasped her arms and took up where he had left off.

Elena concentrated on trying to relax. Sometimes it felt like he had confused his work and personal life, treating her as a blocked pipe in need of clearing rather than the love of his life.

Michael climaxed and rolled off her without a word.

Elena felt a stab of jealousy. She had never experienced an orgasm and she suspected she never would. Michael's manner of lovemaking wasn't gentle enough for her. Or maybe she was the problem. Perhaps she was cursed by her past.

Michael pulled his pyjamas on, shoved his feet into his fleece lined Ugg boots, scooped a cigarette packet from the night-stand and left the room without a word.

ELENA'S CONTRACT at the Health Department ended in January. She had been helping her team investigate best practice in controlling infection outbreaks in surgical wards, but there was no funding for a third permanent position. Most positions were contract; such was life in the research world. Nobody wanted to interview her for the jobs she had applied for and she was becoming increasingly nervous.

On her last day at work, the Director of Population Health offered her a temporary position as his personal research assistant. His current assistant had quit, another in a long line of fed up assistants, if the office talk could be believed. Elena did believe it. Doyle was an imposing, demanding man whom she imagined wouldn't be easy to work for. But she needed a job, so she accepted it.

"It's only for a couple of months," Doyle reminded her as he signed the contract, eyeballing her over the top of his spectacles. "We have to advertise the permanent role. You can apply for it, but we can't just give it to you."

She nodded and scurried back to her new desk. His assistant was waiting for her, having agreed to spend the morning training Elena.

"Ok, let's go through the appointment book process and filing system. Everything must be colour-coded so he can see at a glance what it's about. Blue for HR issues, red for Non-Government Organisation contracts and proposals, yellow for financials, green for Population Health programs. Appointment book meetings must be colour-coded the same way, like this," she indicated a green entry for later that day and a matching green folder sitting in a rainbow-coloured pile.

Elena nodded, not trusting herself to speak. Her natural state was to be organised, but the level of detail Doyle required bordered on obsessive. Despite her organisational skills, she was nervous about making a mistake. He didn't give the impression of being patient or forgiving.

"He likes his coffee black and strong, one at nine o'clock, another at three in the afternoon. When he has a busy day, you'll need to go buy lunch for him."

"Er that's great but… what kind of research do you do for him?"

The woman flicked a strand of her black, bobbed hair out of her eye and snorted. "There's not much research, honey. This role is nothing more than a glorified secretary."

"Oh..." Her involuntary response sank into the surrounding silence. Elena didn't want to be a secretary, especially not to someone as imposing as Doyle, but it was still better than being unemployed.

"Well then, let me see," the woman continued, "'You'll also have to drive him to meetings in his government vehicle, take the car for washing and servicing, and run personal errands when he asks."

Elena's gut clenched. Since leaving home, she had only driven on rare occasions. She hated driving other people's cars, forever worried about damaging someone else's property.

"Where's my folders for today's appointments?" Doyle barked through his open office door.

The woman patted the rainbow pile and inclined her head towards the door. "Take them in for him."

Elena scooped up the pile and scurried in. "Here you go."

Doyle gave her a pointed look. "I'm willing to ignore the oversight, given it's your first day, but from now on I expect these to be on my desk by nine-ten sharp."

"Yes, of course. Sorry."

She missed her old job already. Her team had appreciated her assistance, whereas Doyle, it seemed, was quick to criticise and slow to praise.

Elena left the office that night, stressed and miserable. On the bus ride home, her mind replayed the day's events. Had she put all the files back in the right order? Had she remembered to give Doyle the message from the Head of Oncology? She should have prepared the files for tomorrow's meetings. What a fool she was. Now she would have to arrive early to ensure they were on his desk on time.

The bus screeched to a halt at her stop, causing her to stumble down the aisle. She grabbed at a seat pole to steady herself, cheeks reddening, and fumbled her way off the bus, careful not to look at her fellow passengers. What a klutz she was.

Elena paused for breath at the letterbox. That uphill trek from the bus stop to their house never got easier, no matter how often she did it. Her weak, asthmatic lungs contracted painfully and she coughed. She had hoped to grow out of the childhood condition but no such luck. At least it was only mild and she didn't often have to take medication for it.

Michael rose from his Art Deco armchair, downing the last drops in his wineglass as Elena, still flustered and coughing, opened the front door.

"What's up?"

Not waiting for an answer, he turned away and walked to the kitchen.

She followed him. "The new job isn't what I thought it would be."

"Why?" He put a white-gloved hand inside the butterfly cage and it was transformed into a flutter of colour. It amazed her how the butterflies gravitated towards him. She thought such a manly hand invading their home would scare them, but it didn't.

"There's no research component. I'm just his secretary, and he's so picky and arrogant. He yells at me if I'm late bringing his afternoon coffee." Heart racing and lungs constricted, she fought the sudden urge to cry.

Michael pulled his hand out of the cage and stroked a white butterfly perched on his index finger. "So what do you expect me to do about it?"

He regarded her with an expression she couldn't fathom; smug, disgusted and angry all rolled into one. She wasn't sure what kind of response she had expected but this definitely wasn't it. The verbal slap left her speechless.

I just need you to hold me until I feel better.

"I don't know," she mumbled, ignoring the whispered, childlike voice in her head. She couldn't impose her needs on him. If he wanted to comfort her, he would do it.

"Don't worry about it. Just do your job and forget about him when you come home." He shook the butterfly back into the cage and lit a cigarette as he went out the back door.

Chapter Three

SHE WEAVETH STEADILY

"Okay Mum, see you tomorrow," Michael lay his mobile on the workbench in the shed and picked up his smouldering cigarette.

Elena adjusted her weight against the air compressor. "What's up?"

"One of the hoses in the watering system is blocked again. I'll have to look at it before lunch tomorrow."

"So we'll go to the vineyard early then?"

"How else am I supposed to find the time to fix these things?" he exploded, startling her.

"I wasn't complaining… only asking." She tried to keep her voice even so as not to anger him further.

Michael ran a hand through his hair and sucked on the cigarette. "I have to talk to Mum about selling the property. I can't be here and there at the same time."

Elena felt a prickle of guilt. It was her fault he wasn't there to help his Mum more often. "Could we hire a handyman to do maintenance jobs once a week?"

"It's a small operation Elena, it barely makes enough to pay the bills as it is." His shoulders sagged as he stared out the shed window.

"You feel bad about leaving her alone, don't you?"

"I promised I'd look after the place." Michael blew smoke out the shed window.

"What do you mean?"

"Dad was always worried about Mum being out there alone if he died first, and what would happen to the property. It's been in his family for generations. I promised to take care of everything."

Elena was stunned. "So… after your dad's accident, when you moved back home… that wasn't a temporary move?"

"Bit hard to run a vineyard when you don't live there, don't you think?" His stare was cold.

"But you gave me the impression it was only to support your mother until she adjusted to life without him."

"You assumed that was the case."

"But… we continued looking to buy our own house."

"And I said you would have to live here on your own."

Elena remembered that conversation well. They had been standing right here in the shed, debating whether to buy the house. She remembered feeling blindsided, her body contracting in fear at the thought of living alone for the first time in her life. She remembered him brushing off her fears, telling her she would get used to it. During more than a year of house hunting—through the frustration of him backing out at the last minute, finding fault with perfectly good homes, flipping between wanting to buy close to the city and close to the Gawler vineyard—her living alone had never been part of the deal. But he had made up his mind so, despite her apprehension, she had agreed. Then his mother had come to the rescue, insisting he live with Elena.

Why hadn't he told her about his promise to his dad while they were searching for a property? Yet she couldn't berate him over it. Making such a promise and sacrificing his lifestyle to honour that promise showed deep integrity.

"I didn't know," she whispered.

His eyes narrowed as he tilted his head and blew smoke out the shed window. "Well, now you do."

Ashamed that she had ever been against him staying with Mum, she slunk out of the shed and wandered down the weather-beaten, unevenly paved driveway, feeling the heat of the sun soak into her bones. The house, too, showed signs of soil movement, with visible minor cracks in the outer walls.

Exposed patches of hard clay earth lay between occasional tufts of dry grass and bindi weeds in the barren front yard. In stark contrast, three heritage climbing roses ran the length of the waist-high white picket fence, their large velvety-red blooms in plentiful supply thanks to good winter and spring rainfalls. She inhaled their heady scent. This fence and the roses were one of the reasons she had fallen in love with the house.

She turned back down the driveway, passed the shed with Michael ensconced inside, part-obscured by a billowing haze of cigarette smoke, and climbed the stone steps to her flowerbed, picking up a trowel to dig furiously at the weeds until she became aware of Michael standing behind her.

He cast a disdainful eye over her garden bed.

"What a tangled mess!"

She was crestfallen. Where she saw beauty to rival any Monet painting, he saw an unkempt, unstructured eyesore.

"Can we start the front yard soon?" She refused to be baited by his comment.

"Can't afford it. Besides, we're never here all weekend to start big projects."

"Can we at least plan the design now?"

"I want clean lines. It has to have a structure."

"I like cottage gardens."

"What, like this bloody mess? It takes too much time to control it."

"But it's so pretty and colourful, and it's not *that* much work."

"No! It will be better with topiary conifers, a square of grass, neat hedges and a fountain in the middle."

"Can we at least keep the roses?"

"Maybe." He lit another cigarette.

"You shouldn't smoke so much, it's bad for you."

"Yes, Mum."

Her anger flared. "I'm only saying it because I care about you and I don't want to see you suffer. You need to watch your drinking, too. I know you love wine but everything is better in moderation."

"You're such a goodie-two-shoes. You should have dated boys from your church"

Elena was offended, but tried to hide it. "They never asked me."

"Even they probably thought you were too good for them."

Elena laughed out loud. "*Me*, too good for *them*? Look at me!"

"Yes, look at you, with that innocent look."

The comment stopped her short. She had been referring to her actions and choices, not her physical appearance. She had no idea people viewed her as innocent. She always thought they were judging her for her many imperfections, watching and waiting for her to stuff up, like a vengeful God on Judgement Day.

"Maybe you should go back, find a nice church boy," he laughed, more a bark than a laugh.

Elena stared at him in shock, "What are you saying?"

"I'm just saying you might be better off with a churchy boy."

"Don't you want me anymore?" she wailed, blinking back sudden tears.

"Bloody hell! I didn't say that, stop twisting my words." He stalked off, leaving her kneeling in the dirt.

Why hadn't she kept her opinions to herself? Every time she opened her mouth, she managed to anger him.

⁕

FROM HER VANTAGE point on the raised stone front porch, Elena watched Michael fixing the watering system in the vineyard.

"More tea?" her mother-in-law asked.

"Yes, thank you." Elena held out her tea-cup for a refill.

She sipped the tea, admiring the last of the hollyhocks' long stalks of hot pink funnel-shaped flowers interspersed with dried seed pods. The scent of lavender carried on the soft breeze and the heady-scented roses creeping over the iron porch railings made her feel they were in the English countryside instead of the driest state in Australia. This was Elena's favourite place; the garden, the porch, the old bluestone cottage created an old-world feel. There was something therapeutic about being amongst the rich colours and textures of nature.

"You know, Michael's father and I thought he would *never* meet anyone," his mother said.

"Really?" Michael was seven years older than Elena, but he had hardly been ancient when they met.

"I'm glad his father got to meet you before he died." She smiled at Elena, smoothing her blonde bob behind her ears.

Elena smiled back. "Me too."

Elena got along well with Michael's mother. She was a lovely woman who had always meant well. She suspected his mother meant that he was so reserved and fussy that she feared he would never find anyone he liked. Elena had been so lucky that Michael had thought she was good enough for him.

"I just wish he could have lived long enough to see Michael happily married," his mother continued.

Elena responded with an uneasy smile. *Was Michael happy?* She hoped so. She had asked herself that same question when they got engaged. Stressed that they had bought a house together but he had made no mention of marriage, she had worked up the courage to pressure him. The anti-climax of his eventual, somewhat reluctant agreement, and the way he had held her at arm's length and pecked her on the cheek when she had tried to kiss him had left her wondering. *Was this normal? Was it only in the movies that it seemed so romantic and joyous? I should be happy. I am happy... aren't I? Is he happy?*

The rollercoaster of emotions had continued with her own mother's squeal of joy when they'd phoned to tell her the news, followed by her father's gruff voice in the background.

"Took them long enough to get around to it."

"We wondered how much longer it would be before he asked you. So how did he do it?" her mother had asked.

"Um well... we just talked about it... and er... decided to get engaged." She had squirmed under the spotlight of Michael's gaze and her mother's probing, a situation she re-experienced as other peoples' well-intentioned inquisitiveness hit close to the bone.

"Well, time to get the chook out of the oven," Michael's mother stood up, drawing Elena back to the present.

"I'll let Michael know lunch is ready." Elena put her cup on the little wrought iron table, bounded down the porch steps, along the dirt path and up to the field he was working in.

He turned at her approaching footsteps, sweat running down the side of his face. "Hello."

"Hi. How are you going?"

"Nearly finished. Just have to join these two hoses."

"Good timing, 'cause lunch is ready."

"Okay, I'll be in soon." He turned back to the hoses.

Elena hovered, watching him.

"Did you have any girlfriends before me?"

His hands momentarily stopped before he continued "Yes."

"Did your parents meet them?"

"Why?"

"Because your mother said she was worried you might not find a partner."

"She always overreacts… here, hold these hoses for me while I fit the connector."

Michael was a master deflector. Whenever he was uncomfortable with her line of questioning, he would stonewall her with a curt response or change the subject and she was usually too timid to push him for an answer. But they had been together a long time now and she still knew so little about him. He was a wastewater operator who originally trained as a plumber in the years before the plant operator certification became popular, was a wine connoisseur, loved his car and was obsessed with butterflies. He didn't like public displays of affection or being in large crowds, and he had some minor OCD habits like needing to triple check doors were closed and keep everything spotlessly clean. But she knew nothing about his past or the experiences which had shaped his personality, his hopes and dreams for the future, what he was thinking, what he wanted from her as his partner. She still didn't even know whether he wanted to have children. His refusal to let her into his inner world frustrated her no end.

"Yes, but did your family ever meet any of your other girlfriends?" she persisted.

"No." The familiar finality in his voice signalled he would not stand any further questioning. To pursue the topic would only anger him.

He picked up his toolbox and headed down towards the house, ducking between rows of vines.

Elena trailed him into the house and sat at the heavy oak table while he went to wash up.

"Why don't we find you a retirement flat in the city, close to me?" Michael addressed his mother as he sat down to lunch.

Elena winced. His heart was in the right place, but his suggestion was brusque, no lead in, no discussion of how his mother was coping.

"No! I don't want to leave. All our memories are here."

"But it's lonely out here and it's too much work for you. You're not getting any younger, Mum."

"I've always lived here. This house has been in the family for generations."

"It is a bit isolated here. You might be safer in town with neighbours close by," Elena offered.

"Do you think I want to be alone? But what can I do? This is my life…," his mother bristled.

"You need to think about it, Mum. I can't keep up with maintenance here and do my job too."

His mother's shoulders sagged, her gaze bleak and pensive as she played with the peas and gravy on her plate.

Elena looked away. She wanted to comfort his mother, tell her it was okay, that they would find a way for her to stay on the property. But Michael was right.

His mother sighed. "Alright, I'll think about it."

※

ELENA'S SHORT-TERM contract as Doyle's assistant was repeatedly extended. With each extension, he reminded her it was only temporary, that he would need to advertise for a 'proper' assistant soon. Although she hated being considered incapable, a part of her didn't care if he didn't want to keep her. She had never wanted to be a secretary, anyway. But she needed to find another job.

In May, her wish was granted. An assistant research position in the team currently looking at electricity supply options in hospitals became vacant and Elena asked for a transfer. It was a level lower than her role as Doyle's assistant, but she didn't care.

Michael agreed she could take the pay cut because it was a permanent role. When she had first applied for a job in the Health Department, Michael had been delighted. "If you can get a permanent government job, you'll be laughing. You'll have job security for life," he'd said.

She had not given much thought to the pros and cons of contract versus permanent or government versus private sector. She had just wanted an enjoyable job. But Michael would know better than her.

He'd had a permanent government job since completing his apprenticeship.

Doyle stalked out of his office and brandished the contract in front of her.

"I've approved the transfer," he said, peering over his spectacles, "but if you go, it will be career suicide for you."

He'd been a bastard to work for, but this was a new low even for him, threatening to stand in the way of her future advancement because she was giving up his magnanimous offer of a perpetual 'temporary' position.

"Thank you," she murmured, her response tempered by the fear of angering him further.

ELENA LOVED her new role and, taking an interest in electricity for the first time in her life, she devoured scientific research on the topic with a voracious appetite, then enrolled to do an Honours thesis about the possible future of renewable energies based on the known history of energy generation. It might take her a few years to complete given she was working full-time, but she hoped it would lead to a long-term research career.

"What attracted you to a research career?" Robyn asked. She was another Research Assistant in the team, a divorced mother of two adult children, whose calm, reassuring presence Elena had been instantly drawn to. She wore long, flowing velvet skirts, chunky gemstone-encrusted jewellery and headbands in her curly red hair, all in shades which accentuated her kind green eyes.

"I think I kind of fell into it. I wanted to be an English literature teacher but I realised while studying my Bachelor of Arts that I couldn't teach teenagers."

"Why not?"

"It was bad enough sharing public buses with them, all that attitude and lack of respect. I would have been only twenty-one in my first job, barely older than the senior students. They would have eaten me alive."

"Was literature your passion?"

"Yes… but there was no way I could amass enough knowledge

and understanding in a few short years to become a good teacher. How could I have taught the work of great masters such as Tennyson, Shakespeare or Milton?"

"The same way every other teacher does. It's like any job, you get better the more you practice it."

"That wouldn't be fair on the students. They deserve the best teachers."

"So did you change your course?"

"No, I'd already completed two of the three years and maintained a distinction grade point average, so I finished it. I was also studying history and one of the lecturers said I should do an Honours thesis because I had a talent for analysis and research."

"Ah, that's where the research came in."

"Well, kind of. I didn't do Honours in the end."

"Why not?"

"I wasn't sure I was good enough. I went to a networking event for all the Honours candidates and there was a group talking about their plans to study political history. One planned to study the origins of and influences on the American political system. Another wanted to compare American and Australian political structures and hypothesise on the reasons for the differences between two countries both colonised by the British."

"So?"

"I was planning to explore how American history is portrayed through fiction."

"What was wrong with that?"

Elena shrugged. "It was such a lightweight topic in comparison. I knew they all thought the same. When I told the other students my topic, they were polite and asked questions, but I could see the glazed look in their eyes. I stood there listening to their political discussions, feeling like an imposter. I had nothing to contribute."

"Your topic sounds fine to me. I think you were a bit hard on yourself."

Elena shrugged again. "Well, it all worked out in the end. I got a Research Assistant Traineeship, and I've been here ever since. And now I'm back at University doing my Honours in a different subject."

Robyn regarded her with interest. "What's your star sign, honey?"

"Aries."

"Fire sign. Independent, intelligent, athletic, perfectionist tendencies, impulsive, fiery... Very much a perfectionist but you don't come across as impulsive or fiery," she mused. "What's your birthdate?"

"The twenty-first of March."

"Ah that explains it. You're a Pisces cusp: dreamy, adaptable, sensitive, intuitive, idealistic, easily led."

Elena squirmed under Robyn's gaze. Astrology had always intrigued her but she didn't know much about it. She recalled her father scoffing at horoscopes in the weekend papers. He was steadfast in his belief that nobody other than God knew the future and as a teenager she had accepted this as fact. But some of what Robyn had said rang true. She used to be athletic, but she had fallen into more sedentary habits in recent years. The gym had been a somewhat sporadic attempt to recoup her former health, but even that she had given up on now. She admitted to being a perfectionist and idealistic. Intelligent? That depended one's definition of the word. Impulsive, fiery, intuitive? Definitely not! Was she easily led? As a child, yes, she had allowed herself to be led by parents, the Reverend and teachers, always striving for their approval and doing what was asked of her without question. But that had been mostly out of fear. Her childhood Sundays had been spent inside a small stone church in Gladstone, South Australia, where the passionate, pulpit-thumping Reverend had exhorted the small gathering to love thy neighbour, turn the other cheek, serve others and obey every word of God in order to avoid the fire and brimstone of hell. His sermons had instilled enormous fear in Elena, combined with a niggling sense of confusion. God had been first introduced to her as a loving, forgiving entity who wanted everyone to be happy and to return to live with him in peace. But later, he was referred to as a jealous, vengeful, all-knowing being who would punish those who failed to live up to his standards by casting them into the burning fires of hell. There were no second chances once you'd kicked the bucket. What happened if you made an inadvertent error just before you died? Would he forgive you? Terrified of being found lacking, Elena had spent her entire childhood too afraid to breathe, lest she do something wrong.

But she was living her own life now and had made some hard decisions which were at odds with her parents and the church.

"Don't be afraid to let that fiery nature show, sweetheart. It's good to let it out sometimes," Robyn said, winking at her as she turned her computer off. "See you tomorrow."

"Okay, see you."

ELENA GOT OFF THE BUS, pulled her coat closely around her and trudged up the hill with the winter darkness closing in on her and an Antarctic wind chilling her to the bone. Michael was in the front yard pruning the last stem of the climbing roses, to which a few stubborn autumn leaves still clung. He'd hacked them back to bare sticks which now covered less than half the tall picket fence.

"What have you *done?*" she cried in dismay.

"What does it look like I've done?"

"But they were so beautiful."

"Roses need pruning Elena. If I don't, they won't produce flowers next season."

"Yes, but don't cut them so severely!"

Denuded stems protruded from the clay and clung to the scarred white fence—tiny skeletons in a barren wasteland.

"Oh shut up, you bitch," he barked, turning his back on her.

He had never spoken to her like that before. In stunned silence, she continued up the driveway to the house, hid in the lounge room and picked up the butterfly embroidery she was doing for his birthday, trying to ignore the pain his words had caused. If she hadn't said anything, he wouldn't be angry. But did she deserve his anger?

She knew she should be preparing dinner, but instead she rifled through their small CD collection and chose The Lady of Shalott album. When the poem track began to play, she paused with needle mid-air above her embroidery.

> *A charmed web she weaves alway.*
> *A curse is on her, if she stay*
> *Her weaving, either night or day,*
> *To look down to Camelot.*
> *She knows not what the curse may be;*
> *Therefore she weaveth steadily,...*
> *The Lady of Shalott.*

Elena rubbed a spasm in her neck. It was getting worse. Hearing a rustle, she looked up. Michael watched her from the doorway. Elena met his gaze, blinking back sudden tears.

"I'm sorry," he huffed.

She drew a sharp, surprised breath. He rarely apologised when they argued.

"But you over-reacted," he continued, "I'm just doing what needs to be done."

She managed a half-smile. "I'm sorry too."

He jerked his head towards the sound system. "What's *that?*"

"A singer who turned a poem called 'The Lady of Shalott' into a song."

"Sounds like cats fighting," he spat.

To Elena, it was the most beautiful sound in the universe. "I like it."

"Ugh," he turned away, a smirk playing at the corners of his mouth.

Chapter Four

THE SILENT ISLE IMBOWERS THE LADY OF SHALOTT

"The Government announced they are going to outsource the Water Utility," Michael informed her, his head inside the cupboard as he restacked the pots.

Elena froze, hand hovering mid-air while suds ran down the plate she had just washed. "What? When did you hear this?"

"Yesterday. They're desperate to reduce state debt. The maintenance gangs and treatment plants are all on the chopping block."

"Do you think it will actually happen?" She put the plate on the draining board and slowly washed another one.

Michael stood up and grabbed the washed plate, rubbing it furiously with a tea towel. "Not if I can stop them."

"What can you do?"

"I'm planning a strike with the union this week."

"Oh!" Elena placed the last dish on the draining board and let the water out of the sink. She watched him dry the dish and put it away, biting her bottom lip in concentrated thought. "What will we do if you lose your job?"

"Not going to happen," he muttered, pouring himself a glass of wine and stalking into the living room.

Elena was worried. She wanted to discuss it further but it was clear he had said all he was going to say for the moment so she kept quiet.

Michael went to the strike and soon after became immersed in meetings with the union and Government Ministers as a workplace representative. His moods oscillated wildly, one moment seething that the Government would dare to threaten his secure, comfortable job, the next disillusioned and uncertain over what he would do if he lost his job. Full of self-importance at being an integral part of the union sticking it to the Government, he became more talkative in the evenings, regaling her with stories of meetings with union officials and Government Ministers. He would recount with undisguised scorn how he had caught this official or that minister in their lies, how shocked they were that a mere plumber had outsmarted them.

Elena, pleased that he wanted to talk to her instead of ignoring her in favour of the TV screen, was willing to sit under the back verandah with him on cold evenings while he smoked, just to listen to him speak. But as the months wore on the conversation became a continual negative rant about stupid, inept people in high positions who should give him their jobs so he could show them how to run the State. She grew tired of it and retreated inside sooner, leaving him outside to smoke on his own. Not that he seemed to notice her absence. He was too busy talking to workmates on his phone, gesticulating wildly in a smoky haze while scheming to thwart the Government's plans and start a public service revolution. As soon as the first call came, she crept inside to work on her thesis or read a book. Sometime she watched him through the kitchen window, strutting the length of the back verandah like a little rooster, wine glass in hand, giving directives to 'his people' over the phone.

She was awake to hear him come in late at night, triple-checking the bloody back door was locked, then checking on his butterflies before coming to bed.

It worried her that they communicated even less now than before they were married. Marriage was supposed to have changed things. It had improved her relationship with her parents. Even though they had said nothing when she and Michael moved in together, she had felt the undercurrent of their disapproval, which had disappeared only once they were no longer living in sin.

She had even changed her name as part of the improvement process. She recalled the morning after the wedding when she had found Michael in his shed.

"Hey, do you mind if I keep my own surname?" she had asked.

Michael had blown a slow ring of smoke out the window. "Why?"

"Well, it's just that I've already been Elena Woodfyn for twenty-four years and it seems old-fashioned to expect women to assume their husband's identity, don't you think?"

"That's just how it is."

"But why can't a man take on his wife's name? Why does anyone need to change their name just because they get married?"

"I don't care, do what you want," he had said as he stood up and strode out of the shed.

She had sensed an incongruity in his reaction. Did he really not care, or was he offended that she didn't want his name but pretending not to care?

Worried that she had offended him, she decided it would be safer to assume his name, consoling herself with the fact that it might actually be a good thing. There wasn't much she had liked about Elena Woodfyn, anyway. Elena Woodfyn had been an unpopular loner in school, wasn't much to look at and nothing about her stood out from the crowd.

It was an opportunity to reinvent herself. She could walk down the street as Elena Mule and nobody would know she was the same Elena who had made stupid, selfish decisions and angered others; who had harboured harsh, offensive thoughts while others tried their best; who had allowed herself to be used, abused, and overlooked. Elena Mule would be a better person.

But even assuming his name had not brought her and Michael closer together.

❧

"IT'S DONE, the bastards have awarded a tender to outsource the treatment plants." Michael sucked the life out of his cigarette, pacing up and down the back verandah.

"What do you want to do? Transfer to the private company, take a redundancy package or join the redeployment queue and look for another government job?"

"I'm not giving up my tenure. Screw them, they can find me another job," he spat.

"What other government jobs could you do?" her question was tentative, for fear of offending him.

"I don't know, that's their problem. They can pay me to do nothing for all I care. This is all their fault."

"Why don't you take a redundancy? I'm sure you could find work as a plumber in the private sector."

"I'm NOT leaving the Government! Don't you know how bad conditions are in the private sector?"

"Why not take on the family business full-time? You could open a cellar door for wine tastings and your mother could sell her jams and preserves."

"Working on the land is too unstable. One bad drought and you're ruined. Plus the wine industry isn't what it used to be, thanks to cheap international markets."

Elena was secretly relieved he'd vetoed the suggestion, which would have meant moving permanently out to the vineyard. His mother was lovely, but Elena doubted their marriage would improve by living with her mother-in-law.

She wracked her brain for another alternative. "Then why don't you study something you're interested in? My job seems secure, so we'll still have an income, and the redundancy could pay off the mortgage."

He regarded her with scorn. "I'm not leaving. Do you know how hard it is to find a secure job these days? What would I study anyway?"

"Entomology? You could work with butterflies!"

"Just drop it," he replied, striding across the yard.

Elena watched his retreating form disappear into the shed. She hovered for some minutes, torn between being annoyed with him and wanting to run after him and beg his pardon for angering him. Eventually she went inside and sat at the computer to work on her thesis. Her mind wandered to the conversation with Michael. She forced it back to the task at hand. There was no use dwelling on problems she couldn't solve. Thinking would only create more stress. What she needed was less thinking and more doing.

The study door opened. "Oh, there you are," Michael said.

"Here I am."

They stared at each other. Elena waited for Michael to say something but he didn't. He looked uncomfortable. In fact, if she weren't mistaken, that emotion written all over his face was guilt. He felt bad about getting angry!

Elena gave him a hesitant smile.

His lips twitched into a crooked smile. "Well, I'll leave you to it, then," he said, backing out and closing the door.

He hadn't said he was sorry, but his demeanour had said it for him.

Elena smiled as she returned to her reading.

❦

MICHAEL WAS SUSPENDED in the internal redeployment centre, a no-man's-land full of lost souls whose jobs no longer existed. They rattled around the centre, reminiscing about the Water Utility's good old days, applying for vacant positions which didn't match their skill set and attending interview skills courses. As time dragged itself ever-forward, Michael became moodier.

"Surely studying is better than sitting in the centre all day," she ventured one night while he smoked under the back verandah.

"They're paying for me to apply for jobs, not to study insects!"

"But if there are no suitable government jobs, isn't it better that you study something? Anything is better than nothing, especially if it gets you out of redeployment."

"You're so naïve. I have to spend the time searching for work, not studying. That's the rule." He turned his face away from her, staring into the darkness of the backyard while sipping his glass of Coonawarra Cabernet Sauvignon.

It didn't make sense to her but, fearing further scorn, she swallowed the suggestion that he study out of hours like she was doing. She hated this never-ending existence of tiptoeing over eggshells, cringing as they cracked no matter how careful her step.

"It's Friday night, let's go out somewhere!" she suggested.

He raised his eyebrows, "Out? Why do you want to go out?"

"Because we're still young and we never go anywhere together. It might do us good to get out of the house."

"We do the grocery shopping together and we go to Mum's on Sunday."

"I mean something fun, entertaining."

"Like what?"

"I don't know… let's go to the cinema."

"Movies are free on TV."

She stared at him in consternation. "We used to go out for dinner sometimes when we first met. Why don't we do that anymore?"

"We get takeaway sometimes."

"It's not the same."

"No it's not. Takeaway is cheaper."

There's no point arguing with him, he always has an answer.

"I'm going inside to work on my thesis," she mumbled, turning away. At least she was progressing quickly with the research since nothing else was filling up her time. At this rate, it would only take her a year and a half from start to finish instead of the three years she had predicted when she'd started. *There's always a silver lining,* she reminded herself.

In the morning, she sat down to tackle the research again but made little progress thanks to the noisy chainsaw being used nearby. Unable to concentrate, she wandered outside and found Michael smoking in the shed. "Can we renovate the front yard soon?"

"I've decided to leave it the way it is."

"Why? It looks derelict!"

"Exactly! People will look at the front and think there's nothing worth stealing from our property. It's cheaper and more effective than a security system, plus we'll save on the water bill."

"But it's our home! I want a nice garden."

"You can plant things in the backyard. But don't go buying any high maintenance, invasive plants."

Elena's shoulders sagged. It seemed to her that Michael was intent of ruining her few pleasures in life.

"And we won't repaint the front of the house either. The more derelict it looks, the better," he added as she turned to go inside.

Her shoulders tensed with the effort of not responding. How could he be such an avid connoisseur of fine wine and French cars yet so abysmal when it came to aesthetics? She had been fooled into believing he had an impeccable, French-inspired sense of design.

As she left the shed, she noticed the ladder against a wattle tree on the other side of the yard. Half the tree was lying in pieces on the ground. The other wattles were already decimated, leaving bare branches and a few limp leaves hanging on for dear life. They had been in flower too, the vibrant yellow clusters giving some colour to the bland western side of the yard.

"What have you done to the *trees?!*" The words exploded out of her.

"They needed a prune."

"But they provide shade in summer."

"Can't let them get too big." He blew smoke in her direction. "Have to keep them in check. You don't know anything about gardening, do you?" He regarded her with derision as he walked past, picked up the chainsaw and climbed the ladder to resume pruning.

Blinded with anger, she wanted to shout obscenities at him, to throw herself on the ground kicking and screaming like a two-year-old. She wanted to grab one of those discarded branches and take a swipe at him, knock him off the ladder, and wipe that smirk off his face. Fuming, she felt the heat of her anger rising and her rigid body tremble. But, just as the anger threatened to spew forth, an internal jolt brought her back to reality. Anger was bad. She couldn't let it get the better of her. As she tamped down the anger, it was replaced with a heavy sadness as she watched him hack away at the poor tree. The sound of screeching metal against tormented wood followed her as she trudged inside.

She resolved to watch herself closely. If she let her frustration show or caused an argument, he might decide to leave her. An anxious thud developed in her chest at the thought. She collapsed into a kitchen chair and lay her head on the table.

This isn't the life you wanted.

Elena squeezed her eyes shut, straining to ignore the voice in her head. She was overreacting, she was too sensitive. Everything would be fine.

Michael came inside. She watched him lock and re-lock the back screen door three times before heading straight for his butterfly cage by the kitchen window. He donned the white gloves before putting a hand inside. Two butterflies fluttered onto his hand.

He stroked their wings as she made, then placed, a sandwich on the table in front of him. "Can you pat me like that?"

Michael gave a disparaging snort, "You're not a butterfly."

"I wish I were."

"Huh!" He smiled at her.

At least she had made him smile.

Life isn't so bad, she reminded herself, gazing past his shoulder and out the kitchen window. *When it seems terrible, all I have to do is look out to the highest point beyond our back fence and gaze on the neighbour's beautiful garden to remind myself of what is possible.*

❦

"THIS CAGE IS TOO SMALL," Michael grumbled, his gloved hand inside the door, waiting for a butterfly to land on him.

"We have space for a bigger cage in the lounge room, if you like?"

"I was thinking of building a big walk-in enclosure outside." His eyes sparkled.

"Oh...," Elena would have preferred to spend money on the garden or improving their house but he looked so excited that she didn't have the heart to disagree.

"The perfect spot is up along the back fence."

"But that will block the view of my flower bed and the neighbour's garden. I love looking out the kitchen window and seeing all the flowers," she wailed.

He shrugged. "There's nowhere else to put a big cage."

He set to work, designing and building an enormous, arched, mesh-and-plastic-covered enclosure which consumed the entire elevated back section of the yard. A two-door system mitigated the risk of enterprising butterflies escaping. He fitted a suspended water-mister to maintain the humidity, ventilation windows and planted shrubs and small trees, all researched to ensure the correct nectar would be available to the butterflies.

She had to admit he was a gifted handyman, and the result was impressive.

He came home from the supplier with an assortment of dainty, fluttering beauties in all sizes and colours. It was a truly magical sight as he released them into their new home. They flew free of their small transport boxes and spiralled upwards around Michael in an ever-widening kaleidoscope of swirling colour. He stood still, outstretched hands forming a cross with his body, until every last one had alighted on his frame. He moved his head ever so slowly, so as not to scare the butterflies sitting on his pompadoured hair, until he was looking directly at Elena. His eyes sparkled.

Elena smiled. She loved these rare moments of visible happiness.

When some shorter-lived varieties died, he made plans to breed his own butterflies. He researched ideal mating conditions, made minor adjustments to the enclosure and sat for hours watching for signs of egg-laying. Unsatisfied with the results, he bought caterpillar-rearing kits and erected a small greenhouse next to the butterfly enclosure, populating it with plants to please even the fussiest caterpillar. It was painstaking, labour-intensive and expensive. To maximise their chances of survival, he handpicked and cleaned each leaf the little critters ate. Every weekend and evening, Michael propagated plants, cleaned leaves, pinned chrysalis to a board, tended to his butterflies in their enclosure, inspected for signs of mating and egg-laying, and sat in the enclosure stroking the delicate beauties that alighted on him.

It was a labour of love that, at first, Elena had been glad to witness, but soon it began to annoy her. Not only had he destroyed her flower patch by constructing his Taj Mahal, but again his attention and affection were directed somewhere other than at her. She knew it was ridiculous to be jealous of butterflies, but she was his wife. Surely she deserved some attention too.

The Taj Mahal was only one example in her list of gardening woes. Her enjoyment in the garden had been destroyed as he continued to insist they leave the front yard a barren dust bowl as a security measure. He'd also cut the wattle trees down to the ground because they dropped leaves and pollen, creating too much mess. The only part of the yard which thrived was inside the Taj Mahal—butterflies couldn't survive without nectar. But the plastic was opaque so she couldn't even enjoy the view from outside. Every time she glanced out the kitchen window, the colossal plastic structure looked down on her from its vantage point, taunting her.

Elena turned her back on it and went into their bedroom, curling up on the bed with her copy of Vaclav Smil's *Energy in World History*, which she was re-reading in case she had missed some important information for her thesis. A few pages in, her breath caught as a pain pierced her chest. She sat bolt upright, her breath coming in shallow gasps. Trying to breathe deeper increased the pain. *Damn, it's asthma again.* She rifled through the night-table drawer, pulled out a Ventolin inhaler and spacer and forced herself to take short, quick puffs until the medication opened up her airways.

Only twenty-seven and I'm already falling apart, she thought, collapsing back on the bed. *Irritable bowel, neck pain and recurring asthma which caused a persistent cough and susceptibility to chest infections.* She shuddered to think what she would be like by middle age.

The back door opened and closed. Michael's footsteps echoed through the kitchen, moved towards the living room, stopped and then drew closer. She watched him come into the room.

As he took in the sight of her perched on the edge of the bed, his eyes clouded with desire.

Elena blinked in surprise. It had been a few months since he had last shown interest in her. *Why does he only want sex when I'm not feeling well?*

"What are you doing in here?"

"I was reading but my asthma is playing up so I just took some Ventolin."

Her limbs began to tremble, a common side effect of the medication. She lay back on the bed to wait for the shakiness to subside.

Michael leaned over her. "Feel like a quick roll in the hay?"

"I'm still shaky and weak from the Ventolin."

"I can get your blood pumping."

"Can we just wait until the side effect wears off?"

He snaked a hand under her t-shirt. "I can give you another side effect to keep your mind off it."

The shaking intensified as her body tensed. "Geez, Michael," she exploded, "How am I supposed to enjoy sex when I don't feel well? Show some consideration!"

The ember of desire in his eyes became an angry flame. He stood up. "At least I don't rape you," he spat over his shoulder as he stalked out.

His words sent her reeling back into the past, to a time just before Michael had entered her life.

Elena chatted as Isaac drove, paying no heed to where they were going. Since meeting on campus two months ago, their catch-ups had been sporadic because he was so busy with his legal studies. Isaac would call when he had a spare hour, pick her up and take her for a drive. Sometimes they would get takeaway to eat in his small cottage, then she would have to leave so he could study. But not before she'd swatted away his attempt to cajole her into sleeping with him. It was a dance they played out every time. Her attraction to him was strong, but they must wait until after marriage.

It still amazed her that the handsome Nigerian wearing a flashy orange shirt and lime green pants had noticed her outside the library. Few boys had been interested in her during high school. She'd been too much of a square, too plain, too shy, too odd. They had chased the pretty girls who partied on weekends and drank—in the local creek bed—alcohol stolen from their parent's cupboard.

When Isaac pulled over on a darkened street next to a parking lot, she was uncertain of their exact location.

He levered the driver's seat back and lay with his hands behind his head. "Put the seat back, babe."

She obeyed. Within seconds, he was on top of her, kissing her. The suddenness of his movement surprised her, but it wasn't unpleasant. It was nice to feel desired.

His hand groped under her top.

"Don't," she squirmed, moving his hand away from her breasts.

"Relaaax, you're too tense," he said in that exotic accent that made her weak at the knees.

Perhaps he was right, she was rather uptight. She exhaled and tried to relax. Making out was supposed to be enjoyable.

He pushed up her skirt and tugged at her underwear. She froze, gripped by the awful realisation that he planned to push her much further than she had imagined. A quick glance out the window confirmed they were alone in a dark, semi-industrial street.

"Don't," she protested as he pulled down her panties. A tiny squeak, it sounded weak and pathetic, even to her own ears. Her intention was to be firm, strong, to tell him to get off her. But she couldn't seem to get the words out. Nor could she get her body and mind to cooperate in order to push him away. In fact she couldn't move at all. Pinned to the seat by his weight and

still frozen with fear, she felt a sharp pain as he entered her, followed by a huge wave of sadness. Lacking both fight and flight responses, she folded back into herself in limp resignation, desperate to pretend it wasn't happening.

He stopped. Did he stop because she was so unresponsive, or had she blocked most of it out? She didn't know.

Isaac climbed back into the driver's seat and glanced across at her as she lay with her skirt still hitched around her waist. With a look of disgust, he waved a dismissive hand towards her panties.

"Pull them up before I do something I shouldn't."

But you already did.

Bewildered, she ignored the quiet voice of reason in her head and obeyed him.

They were silent on the drive home. Isaac pulled up outside the student building, leaned over and kissed her. "I'm busy this weekend. I'll call you when I'm free."

She nodded, got out of the car and crept up the path, expecting to never see him again.

The sound of laughter greeted her from the common room. Half a dozen students were watching a movie. She always went straight to her room at night. Tonight however she wandered, dazed and muddled, into the room and perched herself on the end of a threadbare couch.

"Hi Elena, how's it going?" one girl asked.

Elena forced a smile. "Good thanks, and you?"

"I'm well. The movie's just started, have a seat."

"Ok," she lifted her feet out of her black ballet flats, curled them under her long floral skirt and settled in to watch. The vibe from some students indicated they weren't impressed that she was invading their cosy little group, but she didn't want to be on her own just yet.

The movie was a welcome distraction, serving as a good focal point to return to whenever thoughts of Isaac threatened to overwhelm her.

They paused the movie to refill their drinks. Elena went to the bathroom. It had been a surreal end to the day, but she was ok, everything was fine. In fact, perhaps she had just imagined everything... then she saw the blood spots on her underwear and reality slammed into her. Doubled over, arms wrapped around her waist, she hyperventilated as tears coursed down her cheeks.

Calm down, someone might hear you! She forced herself to stop crying, straightened herself out and rejoined the group for the second half of the movie. She was desperate to hide in her room but the others might be waiting for her, so she had to show her face. She had years of practice at forcing herself to do unpleasant things: get good grades in boring subjects, walk through the school yard pretending she didn't care she wasn't part of the 'in' crowd and that she couldn't hear the taunts of the teenage cretin who'd taken it upon himself to make her life hell. 'Could Elena be any plainer? Elena the ugly brainer!'

If you're so strong, why didn't you stop Isaac?

She had no answer for the challenging voice in her head. She couldn't fathom why she could be so resolute in some aspects of her life, yet so incapable of defending herself in others.

Elena tried to forget the incident but it popped into her consciousness during unguarded moments and, as she replayed it, she began to believe it had been her fault. She could have fought him off, made it more clear she didn't want to have sex with him. But she hadn't. She had been too passive. She had no boundaries. She turned the other cheek indiscriminately. She was a bad person, a sinner. For the next couple of weeks she offered fervent prayers for forgiveness. She even confessed to Reverend Jones that she had been intimate with a man. He told her to pray for the strength to resist in future so she would be worthy enough to marry a Christian man and raise a family as was her duty. Yet she couldn't shake the small voice in her head that reminded her she was damaged goods. No good Christian man would want her now.

Then the polite, safe Michael appeared. He gave her flowers and took her to restaurants. They didn't have much to talk about but they both had quiet personalities so that was to be expected.

Michael pulled into the kerb and stared straight ahead through the windscreen, his hands gripping the steering wheel. "I suppose your religion doesn't agree with sex before marriage." *It was more a statement than a question.*

"Yes... I mean no... well I try not to...," *she stammered in a small, breathless voice.*

"Then you'd better go now." *He continued staring through the windscreen.*

"Ok, goodnight!" She fled from the car as if pursued by a banshee.

Safely inside, Elena contemplated whether she wanted to continue her involvement in the church. It was a question that had plagued her for a few months but she'd refused to give it serious consideration until now. Was she a true believer or had she just accepted her parents' beliefs? There were things that annoyed her about religion, in particular attitudes towards women, the restrictive undercurrent of the woman's role being in the home. At church, everyone was in a hurry to marry young and start immediate procreation. The prospect filled her with dread. She wanted to have children one day and spend time at home with them, but first she wanted a career. She wanted to expand her horizons, enjoy independence and spend time with her partner before they settled down to raise a family. She was still so young and didn't want to feel trapped in a lifestyle she may end up resenting. What kind of life would that be for her children, if she resented that they had come along so early and cut short her own youth?

Then there was the Eve stigma. Often Elena wished she was strong enough to argue that it was just a way for men to excuse their own weakness, using women as scapegoats. Didn't Adam have free will? Didn't he make a choice just as Eve had? Why punish all women with painful childbirth for something done by just one woman? Surely a just God wouldn't be so unfair. Furthermore, why even give Adam and Eve a choice at all if it was essential for them to leave the garden and have carnal knowledge in order to experience life as God intended? How unfair of him to punish them for something he had decided they must do to fulfil his plan. He should instead have celebrated their disobedience, their curiosity to know and experience things for themselves. He should have shouted them a round of drinks as a reward for enabling his plan to be put into action. The more she thought about it, the more ridiculous it seemed, and the more indignant she became, until she found the courage to throw off the shackles of religion and roared off into the sunset, safe inside the heavy, protective shell of Michael's Cabriolet.

Chapter Five

SHADOWS OF THE WORLD APPEAR

D ejected, upset and distressed had become Elena's normal state. So when Robyn invited her to a stress-remedy workshop using an energetic healing technique called Reiki, Elena was drawn to it like a moth to the light.

They spent an entire weekend with Reiki Master Rosa, learning how energy travels through the body and how to channel it through their palms.

Elena was dubious. "It's a bit too New Age for me."

"Did you study physics in school?" Rosa asked.

"Yes."

"Do you remember the law of conservation of energy? It states that the total energy of a system can increase or decrease only by transferring it in or out of the system."

"Yeah, I remember it."

"That's all we are doing, transferring energy between your system and mine."

"Yes, but *how* can you transfer energy using your palms?" Elena countered.

"Do you understand exactly how energy is conveyed to a house?"

"I have a fair idea thanks to my current studies but I don't know all the technical details. I couldn't wire a house myself."

"Yet you make use of that energy in your house. You have faith that when you turn on a light switch, it will work, even if you don't know how."

"Well, I guess when you put it that way…" Elena trailed off.

"Energy is constantly in motion. All living things use energy and require it to stay alive. So is the concept of meridian energy lines and chakras—or energy centres—in the body such a stretch to comprehend?"

"Huh. Yes. I see what you mean."

"If energy becomes stuck in particular areas, instead of being allowed to flow, it can create problems in the same way the energy of the sun, concentrated on a single area for a prolonged period, can burn something beyond recognition."

"Okay, I see how that could work," Elena conceded.

"Try it and see what happens. It can't do you any harm," Rosa encouraged.

Elena took part in group activities where she tried to feel the energy of other students, to note the subtle difference in temperature or sensation, but the only thing she felt was ineptitude as others attested they felt the energy that she could not. She began to think it might be a load of clap-trap after all, until Rosa performed an energy healing on her. As she lay on the table, an inexplicable range of sensations travelled through her; a gradual lessening of tension in her body, tingling sensations from head to foot, and a gentle heat that increased to a hot pulsing in the location where Rosa's hands hovered millimetres from her body. Other students joined in to practice on her and she felt such a flood of loving attention that it brought tears to her eyes. She fought them back, willing herself not to cry in front of these people and—correspondingly—all the feelings and sensations disappeared.

That night she practised on herself without success and returned to class the next day feeling like a failure. Rosa said Reiki was something everyone could do, that everyone could act as energy conduits, so why couldn't she do it? She struggled through the morning lessons and practice session, then, after lunch, went for her attunement session with Rosa. It wasn't explained what an attunement entailed, just that it was required to practice Reiki and needed to be administered by a Reiki Master.

She lay face down on the massage table and received what seemed like any other Reiki treatment she had received over the past two days. But when Rosa reached her heart chakra, she experienced a crushing weight inside her chest and waves of motion inside her body, like an ocean existed within her and tidal waves were lapping at her edges. The weight in her chest increased to a point where she worried she would not be able to take any more, then it dissipated abruptly, leaving her stunned and on the verge of tears again. Rosa gave her a hug and she wandered, dazed, out to the main room, sitting down next to Robyn and another lady, both of whom had already received their attunements.

The other woman gazed at her with a far-away expression and put her hands over her own heart chakra. "It was here."

Elena nodded, knowing they had experienced the same sensation. She smiled, grateful to share such a beautiful experience with someone else without having to put it into words.

Wonder of wonders, in the afternoon practice she felt something. While working on one student, she detected a tingling in her palms and heat at a few points on the woman's body. She raced home that night, eager to explain it all to a dubious Michael, and urged him to let her practice on him. It took a week before he agreed to let her try.

Nervous of his reaction and worried it wouldn't work, she forced herself to do it anyway, earnestly searching for energy hotspots. She wanted him to experience the same peace she had. As she focussed, a feeling of depression started to take hold in her. After going over his whole body, she worked a second time on his heart chakra. The longer she held her hands on him, the stronger the depressed feeling grew. Just when she felt she couldn't stand it anymore, she felt a shift. For the first time since she had known him, he seemed at peace. When she climbed into bed next to him, instead of the usual quick peck goodnight before he turned his back and went to sleep, he curled into her, placing his arm around her. Normally he only hugged her when he wanted sex, grabbing her with an unmistakable, firm deliberateness. He had never been this affectionate with no intention beyond being close to her.

She fell into an elated sleep but awoke the next day thinking about the strength of the depression she had sensed.

"You wouldn't do anything silly, would you?" she asked.

"What do you mean?"

"Well, when I did the Reiki, your energy felt so depressed."

He cast her a disparaging look, even while his eyes betrayed his sadness. "You mean would I off myself?"

"You wouldn't, would you?"

"Of course not," he sucked the life out of his cigarette, "I wouldn't give them the satisfaction."

"Who?"

"You know, *them*." His eyes glinted with a strange wildness.

She wasn't sure who he meant, but didn't ask for further clarification.

"I can give you Reiki whenever you want."

"No," his voice was sharp and final, making her wish she had kept her mouth shut. She was desperate to both help him feel better and to experience that closeness between them again but he had shut the door.

Elena worked on re-balancing her own energies every night. Focussing on her solar plexus and heart chakras provided a level of comfort she could not recall ever experiencing before. Robyn sometimes gave her a treatment too. She was still nervous about doing Reiki on others, though. She knew it worked, but what if she wasn't able to make it work? What if the other person felt nothing? It would be her fault if they didn't allow anyone else to give them Reiki again.

"The Government is forcing us to take redundancy packages," Michael informed her.

"What do you want to do?"

"I'm not taking a package. They stuffed up our industry. They can fix it for me."

She felt helpless, knowing there was nothing she could do. She couldn't even comfort him because he didn't want her affection.

"A redundancy might not be so bad," she tentatively suggested. "At least you won't have to sit in that horrible centre."

"I'm not taking a payout!" he exploded. "They can get stuffed."

She chewed her bottom lip while he smoked next to her under the back verandah. "But you don't have a choice."

"I'll fight them," he muttered, downing half a glass of Shiraz in one gulp.

The smoke constricted her airways and she coughed. She didn't want to leave him alone at a time like this, but she couldn't breathe.

"I've got contacts, I'll find something else," he muttered to himself, staring across the darkened yard as she went inside in search of her Ventolin inhaler.

Over the next few weeks, his anxiety levels ramped up as he wheeled and dealed with his contacts. They offered him a position as an Emergency Services call centre operator. He sat brooding in the shed, smoking one cigarette after another.

She stood by the door, wanting to talk to him but needing to stay away from the smoke haze lest it provoke her asthma. "How do you feel about working in a call centre?"

He screwed up his face as he lit his fifth cigarette in as many minutes. "Do you have any idea what dealing with the public is like? I'd rather be up to my armpits in shit every day than deal with them."

"You would have limited contact, though. You'd only have to talk until the experts arrive on scene."

He shrugged. "I guess. But I'd have to work weekends and evenings."

"I know it's not ideal, but isn't it better than being unemployed?"

He eyeballed her as he drew on the cigarette. "Would you be okay if I work late nights and you're here on your own?"

He'd touched a sore point. She knew she wouldn't sleep until he came home, but he couldn't give up a job opportunity just because she was scared of being alone in the house.

"I'll be okay," she replied.

"Are you sure?"

She had thought his concern for her touching but now the challenge in his voice was unmistakable. He was trying to use her as an excuse not to take the job.

"I'll have to be okay, won't I?"

Michael agonised over the decision but, by the end of the following week, his need to keep his Government security won and he agreed to the transfer.

He consented to buy Elena a car. With the new shift work schedule it would be impossible for her to continue relying on him to drive her around. After test driving a few zippy little models, she settled on a white Holden Barina.

The new car equalled freedom, it meant she could start and finish work when it suited her rather than fitting in with Michael's schedule. She could do the grocery shopping on her own instead of having to drag a reluctant, stressed Michael around the crowded shopping centre, and she didn't waste time waiting for buses. It was liberating to be so independent, to be in control of when and where she went.

Michael wasn't happy or at ease in his new job, though. The shift work played havoc with his body clock—and Elena's too. She struggled to sleep when he was on night shift, but she'd never admit that to him.

Elena hoped his mood would improve as he settled into a routine, but he stayed slumped in a state of depression. His wine intake suddenly increased too. Whenever he wasn't working, he was drinking or in the Taj Mahal; sometimes he drank inside the Taj Mahal. It worried her but her nagging made him angry so she kept quiet.

❧

ELENA HAD PLANNED to stay in her job at least until her thesis was complete but, when Robyn emailed her a link to a research role with Energy Network, the local energy distribution network company, she surprised even herself by deciding to apply.

Words spilled out of her mouth in an excited rush as she told Michael.

"What's wrong with the job you've got?"

"There's nothing wrong with it but I'm bored. I don't think there's anything else for me to learn there."

"Why do you need to learn anything? Just sit there, do your job and take your salary."

"But I need a challenge, a change. I don't know why right now, but I feel like I need to do it."

"Be very careful. EN isn't Government. It's a corporation. You'll lose all your entitlements." He fixed her with one of his piercing stares.

"But the advert says the infrastructure is still government-owned. Only the retail section was privatised."

"You better be certain about all the conditions before you sign any contract. Even if it is government-owned, you don't know that it would be as secure as your current job. You might have to give up your permanent status. What about your leave entitlements? You're almost eligible for long service leave. What if you lose that?"

An anxious fluttering developed in her stomach. "But the job sounds perfect. It's what I'm studying for and it's a lot more money than I earn now too." She didn't know how to make him understand that she needed to do this. She couldn't explain why, but, with uncharacteristic certainty, she knew it was right for her.

They continued to debate while she applied for the role and attended an interview. When they offered her the job, she confirmed she could keep her existing government entitlements. It was all working out perfectly. As she relayed the information to Michael, he raised an eyebrow.

"Make sure it's in writing. And don't say I didn't tell you so if something goes wrong."

She spent the next couple of days in an indecisive limbo, wracked with guilt that she wanted a job Michael wasn't pleased about. Yet she couldn't see how the job could be a bad thing. It was a chance for her to work in a professional role, to use the knowledge gained through her studies, and it was a significant pay rise. Everything about it felt right. As she signed the acceptance letter, she hoped for the best.

She wanted to do a good job, to show her new boss that she had made the right decision in hiring her. She wanted to be taken seriously as a professional. As a result, her anxiety levels increased. Some nights she woke up in a panic, wondering if she had made a mistake the previous day—she should have remained quiet in the staff meeting instead of voicing an opinion that the manager hadn't agreed with. Had she found all the significant existing research before presenting her findings on electricity load shedding?

Her new work environment was more corporate than the Health Department so she made more effort with her appearance. Gone were the long dresses and cardigans, in favour of business suits and shirts. She decided to cut her long tresses, too. A short hairstyle would convey sensibility and maturity.

The hairdresser was aghast. "Are you *sure* you want to cut it all off?" She lifted Elena's waist-length blonde ponytail.

"I'm sure, give it the chop."

"Okay." She regarded Elena through the salon mirror, scissors poised. "Once I cut, there's no going back."

"It's okay, I'm sure." This was part of the process of reinventing herself as Elena Mule. She should have done it years ago.

As the hairdresser cut and shaped her hair into a longish crop, Elena studied her reflection in the mirror. Come to think of it, her blonde hair was not so blonde these days. It was a more mousey, nothing-colour.

"Can you colour it for me too? I used to be blonde. I'd like it to be lighter again."

"But your hair is a lovely colour. It already has different shades and natural highlights. People pay good money to get this effect."

Why would anyone pay for a nothing-colour, she wondered? "It's too dull. I'd like it blonder."

"How about just a few highlights to start with? If you like it, we can add more next time."

Elena emerged from the salon a short-haired, blonde streaked version of herself. Removing so much hair at once made her realise how much weight she had been carrying around.

The colour was better too. She thought of the movie *Gentlemen Prefer Blondes*. If the history books were correct, the gentlemen had preferred Marilyn Monroe. Plus blondes had more fun, and she could definitely do with more fun in her life.

She bounded up to the Taj Mahal and smiled at Michael, "What do you think?"

He looked up from the butterfly perched on his arm and half smiled, half grimaced, "Ugh. What did you do?"

"Don't you like it?" She was crestfallen.

He shrugged. "It's okay. Bit of a dramatic change though."

The smirk playing around the corners of his mouth indicated his response might be good-natured teasing but she wasn't sure. Either way, she had hoped for a more positive response.

Chapter Six

THE CURSE HAS COME UPON ME

E lena worked longer hours in the office, telling herself it was because she wanted to do the best job possible. But, if she were honest, she preferred to be at work rather than home. At work people spoke to her, asked her for help, found her useful and thanked her for her efforts. At home, Michael barely gave her the time of day. Her usefulness was limited to cooking, cleaning and grocery shopping, and even those she wasn't able to perform to his satisfaction.

There was so little physical contact between them that, worried about the long-term effects of the contraceptive pill, she stopped taking it. But still she hoped for better times to come. She wanted to have her first child by thirty and taking herself off the pill now would make it easier to conceive when the time came.

When Michael wanted sex one night, it wasn't until afterwards that they remembered she was no longer taking the pill.

"Don't worry, I'll go to the chemist tomorrow and get the morning-after pill," she said, reassuring herself as much as him. She couldn't risk becoming pregnant now, it wasn't the right time.

Michael looked anxious. "Are you sure?"

"Yes, it'll be fine."

She called into the chemist on her way to work and endured a public interrogation by the pharmacist about her sex life and the need for protection. Back in the car, she removed the pill from the packet and stared at it. She wanted children, but Michael had refused to confirm that he was open to the concept. Here was her chance. It was possible she was pregnant. If she didn't take this pill, she might fulfil her dream of becoming a mother. But her fear of what might happen if she had a child with Michael was greater than her fear of never becoming a mother. She couldn't take the chance of Michael being angry with her. She couldn't risk having a child until Michael was one hundred percent committed to helping raise the child and supporting her through the birthing experience.

You can't ever have a child with Michael.

She shook her head to dislodge that last thought. What the hell was wrong with her? Of course she could have a child with Michael. He was her husband. It just wasn't time yet. She swallowed the pill and drove to work.

Michael called her mid-morning. "Have you been to the chemist?"

"Yes, it's all sorted."

"Oh... okay," he replied, subdued.

If she hadn't known better, she could have sworn he sounded disappointed, but it was just his normal, depressed state. He was getting worse—steadily working his way through his wine collection, eating too much and looking more like an overweight, exiled Napoleon than the James Dean she had first met. He'd even become slack with his grooming, his once pencil-thin moustache now a bushy mess and his hair flopping sideways instead of carefully arranged. But she couldn't talk—she'd gained six kilos after both the gym and bike-riding with Marcus and Carla had fallen by the wayside.

She called her brother.

"Hi sis, what's up?"

"Hi, all good here. How are you?"

"Work is busy but we're doing well."

"Good. Hey, do you guys feel like a bike ride this weekend?"

"Sounds good. It's been too long between drinks."

"Yeah, I know. Meet you at our place two o'clock Saturday?"

"We've got lunch with friends, so can we make it later, say around four o'clock?"

"Sure, it doesn't get dark until around nine so that should be fine. See you then."

"Great, see ya!"

In addition to helping her fitness levels, it would allow her to spend more time with her own family. Over the years, she had grown more distant from them because Michael preferred to keep to himself. She had held the occasional family gathering at their home but was careful to space them out, suspecting that Michael would kick up a stink if she invited people over too often. But having Marcus and Carla drop by before or after a ride didn't seem to bother Michael. Elena gauged his current level of discomfort to be less than when her parents or friends visited. In fact, he got along quite well with Carla who, as a Veterinary assistant, took an interest in his butterflies.

❦

ELENA SAT with Marcus and Carla in the bakery at Port Noarlunga, tucking into pastries after working up an appetite on the ride south of the city.

Marcus and Carla glanced at each other.

"We've got some good news," Marcus said.

"Yeah?" Elena waited for him to continue.

"We're pregnant!"

"Oh! I was expecting you to say you're getting married! Congratulations." They hugged and kissed across the small, square table.

"How far along are you?"

"Four months. The morning sickness has passed now—that's why we've been a bit absent the past few months," Carla replied, glowing with happiness as she patted the swelling belly which Elena hadn't noticed due to her oversized shirt.

"That's great," Elena smiled, right before she burst into tears. A confusing mixture of joy for their good fortune and overwhelming sadness that she and Michael were still no closer to starting their own family flooded her entire being. Her younger sibling becoming a parent before her was not something she had given any prior consideration.

Marcus and Carla looked at each other in alarm.

"Are you okay?" Marcus placed a hand on her arm.

Elena pulled herself together, wiping away the tears. "Yes, of course. It was just a shock that's all."

Yet, for the rest of the ride, she couldn't shake the feeling of dejection at being left on the sidelines, watching everyone else have the life she wished for but seemed unable to attain.

She arrived home later than expected.

Michael was waiting for her under the back verandah.

"Hi." Elena's kiss landed on his ear as he turned his head away.

"Where have you been?" Michael tossed his head as he blew smoke and glared at Elena, a challenge in his eyes.

Her heart sank. "We rode to Noarlunga and stopped for a coffee."

"You're always leaving me here alone."

"I've told you you're welcome to join us."

"Why would I want to ride a bike when I have a car?"

Elena didn't reply. They'd had this argument before. If she had dinner or coffee with Marcus and Carla, he refused to join them based on the quality of the food or coffee in their chosen venue. If they went to a movie, he stayed home because he didn't like the type of movie they chose. There was always an excuse not to do things together, but then he got angry with her for going without him.

He never wants you around until you're busy with other people.

Silencing her negative inner voice, she changed the subject.

"Marcus and Carla are having a baby."

"Yeah?"

Elena waited for him to say something else but he didn't.

"They're looking to buy a house before the baby arrives too."

"Where are they looking?"

"Further south. They can get a bigger house for less around Seaford or McLaren Vale."

"Your parents won't be happy."

"Why, because they want to live in the south?"

"No, because they're not married yet."

"Oh, yeah. Well, it doesn't seem to bother Marcus so much what they think."

She went inside to prepare dinner—a spicy noodle dish Carla had given her the recipe for. It was different to the roast lamb or steak and vegetables Michael favoured, but she hoped it would make a nice change to their culinary routine. Careful to reduce the spice content so it wouldn't be too hot, she fried the vegetables then added the soft-ened noodles. They began to stick together. Damn it, she'd cooked them too long. She would need some practice to get the technique right but hopefully it would still taste good.

"Dinner's ready," she called through the window.

Michael came into the kitchen and triple-checked the back door was locked behind him while she plated up the food, squashing the irritation which suddenly arose. *Why couldn't he just lock the door once, like a normal person?*

Elena put a plate in front of him.

Michael screwed up his nose and prodded the noodles with a fork. "What's this crap?"

Elena's heart sank. "Asian fried noodles."

Michael took a bite, "Ugh!"

"You don't like it?"

"Why can't you just cook like Mum does?" He pushed the plate away and got up, made himself a cold roast lamb sandwich and disappeared into the shed with it. Elena sat alone in the kitchen, eating her noodles. It had been foolish to try something different.

After cleaning up, she was at a loose end. The first draft of her thesis was with her supervisor for comment so she had no study to do. She used to imagine all the extra time she and Michael would have together once she was free of study commitments, but somehow it wasn't translating into reality.

She had a sudden urge to be alone.

"I'm going for a drive," she muttered as she entered the shed and unlocked her car.

She could have sworn she saw uncertainty pass over his features but it disappeared so fast she couldn't be sure.

"Okay," he said, with uncharacteristic cheerfulness. "Don't be long!"

She drove to the beach, remembering the early days when they used to drive along the coast together. She parked along the esplanade and watched the dark shapes of moving waves, listening to them crash against the shore.

'Chasing Cars' by Snow Patrol came on the radio. A single tear made its way down her cheek. She wanted someone to just lay in a comfortable, companionable silence with her, the two of them creating their own little world, forgetting everyone and everything else. She and Michael didn't have that kind of relationship. As far as she could tell, it wasn't something he even wanted. Or maybe he did but was scared to admit it? She didn't know. That was the problem. She didn't know what he wanted and, unless she could help him become more open, nothing would ever change. The thought depressed her.

ELENA'S JAW dropped as she approached the house. While she'd been visiting Marcus and Carla, Michael had dug out her beloved climbing roses and demolished the front picket fence.

She pulled into the driveway and braked, surveying the damage and fighting the urge to cry. Feeling eyes on her, she looked to the end of the driveway.

Michael stood in front of the open shed door, his eyes challenging her to say something.

She put the car in gear and drove into the shed, watching him take a swig of wine straight from the bottle as she drove past. *At what point had his appreciation for fine wine turned into a bottle-guzzling habit?*

"Why did you remove the fence?" She tried to keep her voice even as she walked towards him, deliberately not mentioning the roses.

"I gotta better 'un going up soon," he slurred.

"Like what?"

"A tall one, to stop them looking into our yard."

"Stop who from looking?"

"*Them,*" he said in an exaggerated whisper, putting a finger to his lips.

Fear gripped her. *Was he losing his mind?*

"There is no them. Why don't you come inside and lie down while I make dinner?"

"I'm not hungry," he turned and lurched up the slope to the Taj Mahal.

A WEEK LATER, Elena came home to find the new fence had been completed. He'd demolished her white picket fence dream and replaced it with a six foot galvanised iron eyesore.

"What do you think of our new fence?" Michael asked as she entered the house, that same challenge in his eyes.

I'll be damned if I'm going to let him see he's upset me, she thought. She shrugged, "I prefer the old one." She continued through the kitchen to the bedroom, trying to control the trembling in her hands.

Elena tried to ignore her mounting unhappiness and anxiety. She tiptoed around Michael to avoid his disapproval and found more distractions, going shopping with Carla and joining her and Marcus at the beach on weekends. The sunshine and company buoyed her spirits but when Marcus and Carla married in autumn and bought a house forty minutes' drive away, Elena found herself back to a more solitary existence. She started jogging but an asthma flareup forced her to stop.

When Marcus and Carla's bundle of joy arrived, a dainty little angel named Brigid, Elena was loath to give her up to other visitors in the hospital. She was such a beautiful bundle of perfection! Brigid mewed softly and snuggled into Elena's arms, making her wish anew for a child of her own.

Michael, never comfortable around children, declined to hold Brigid. *If only he would hold her*, Elena thought, *he would warm to the idea of having a child of his own.*

Elena was unprepared for the all-consuming dread which enveloped her when she realised that, in adjusting to a routine which revolved around Brigid, the new parents had even less time to spend with her. She missed having someone to interact with. She distracted herself by working longer hours again and met up with Robyn, whom she hadn't seen much of since starting her new job.

"What did you think of Atonement?" Robyn asked as they sat down to dinner in an Italian restaurant after watching the movie.

"It was good."

"Not as good as the book, though," Robyn replied.

"They missed bits out, but I still liked it."

Robyn wrinkled her nose. "I mean, you don't find out much at all about what the characters are thinking, especially Briony. The book gives her a good voice and you can witness her character developing as she gets older. The movie was so shallow in comparison."

"I guess so," Elena replied. She thought the characters were well played but perhaps she was being too lenient and using her prior knowledge from the book to fill in the gaps.

Robyn frowned in annoyance. "I wish you'd give your opinion sometimes!"

The outburst caught Elena by surprise. "Oh… ah, I'm sorry," she mumbled, lost for words. She did have opinions, didn't she? She had said she liked the movie. That was an opinion.

"Don't worry about it, sweetie. I shouldn't have said anything," Robyn brushed the incident aside with a flick of her wrist.

Elena picked at her carbonara while Robyn filled her in on the office gossip. Nothing much had changed. While the endless internal restructures played havoc with productivity, the people and issues remained the same. Doyle was still there, churning through assistants faster than credit on a teenager's mobile phone. Elena was glad to have left him behind.

"How is your thesis coming along?"

"It's getting there! Another two or three months and I think I'll be ready to hand it in."

"Well done. You've been working so hard."

"Thank you," Elena dropped her eyes to the table as tears welled. She always felt awkward when somebody praised her. She pushed her chair back, "I should get going, it's late."

"Okay sweetie, take care." Robyn stood up and came around the table to envelop her in a bear hug.

"You too."

Elena rushed back to her car and drove home. It was late and Michael would be waiting for her.

As she pulled into the driveway, she noted the living room light was on.

Michael was slumped on the lounge room floor in front of the murmuring TV.

"Hi," she said.

He didn't answer. She put a tentative hand on his back, catching a whiff of the boozy vapour surrounding him. He didn't stir. He was too heavy to lift and her timid attempts to wake him failed so she covered him with a rug, turned off the TV and went to bed.

In the early hours of the morning, he stumbled into the bedroom. His drinking worried her but she knew better than to comment.

Elena woke with a pounding headache. They were becoming more frequent and severe again and she could no longer shake them off by going to sleep. Painkillers were becoming her best friend. In desperation, and despite her needle phobia, she consulted an acupuncturist after work.

The elderly Chinese acupuncturist took her medical background and examined her neck and shoulders.

"Ah so bad! Muscles like rubber!" he exclaimed, pulling at a muscle across her shoulder blade. "Don't worry, we fix it," He patted her shoulder and shuffled over to a cabinet, removing packets of needles.

Elena tried to find something else to focus on but her senses were hyper-attuned to his every movement; the tearing open of packets, the tapping as he primed a needle. She tensed as he swabbed an area at the base of her head... and exhaled in surprise as the needle entered without pain. He continued inserting needles along her neck and shoulders, then attached electrodes to them to run an electrical pulse through. This, he explained, would help to move the stuck chi and break up the hard tissue.

She was terrified to move in case the slightest change in posture caused her pain. As he turned up the pulse, her muscles twitched involuntarily from the inside as if her body hosted dozens of tiny creatures trying to break free. An image of herself as a life sized voodoo doll flashed into her mind and she forced down the rising panic by focusing on slowing her rapid, shallow breathing.

The acupuncturist left the room. She heard him moving around next door, tending to another patient. The clinic was a production line torture chamber!

After what seemed an eternity, a timer buzzed and the acupuncturist returned. As he removed the last needle, she relaxed. Her shoulders did feel less tense. The change was only minuscule but it was change nonetheless so she made an appointment for the following week.

He patted her arm as she left. "Don't worry, young girl like you we can fix. You need strong neck and shoulders to carry babies."

Not the way I'm going, she thought, closing the door behind her. *There are no babies anywhere near the horizon for me.*

❦

ONE MINUTE ELENA was stirring a pot of homemade soup, the next minute she was crumpled in a heap next to the stove, her cheek pressed against the grey, diamond-patterned linoleum floor. She hadn't felt herself fall. It was as if there had been no time lapse between standing at the stove and laying on the floor. She wasn't hurt, yet she couldn't seem to pick herself up. As she gazed at the floor in dazed consternation, the linoleum diamonds morphed and merged, stacking themselves on top of each other to form walls around her. A closer inspection showed that the walls formed a rather imposing castle. She tapped at the solid wall closest to her.

That's a mighty strong castle you've built yourself there.

The crystal clear voice in her head was tinged with sarcasm. With a flash of insight she realised the voice was right. She had constructed these colossal walls and, in her usual perfectionistic style, had set about creating the biggest, strongest, most impenetrable castle possible. As she surveyed the interior, she saw that in order to make the castle more hospitable she had attempted some interior decorating but now she was cornered, wet paintbrush in hand, with no escape route in sight. She had chosen a colour that had appeared golden in the can but on the walls and floor it proved to be a disappointing, drab faecal brown.

After laying for some time in a despondent stupor, she acknowledged her own despair. She didn't like her life and she had a painful, sneaking suspicion that she was lonelier sharing her life with Michael than she would be if she were actually on her own.

She needed to talk to someone. But who? Having avoided complaining to anyone in her family, they would think everything was rosy so it wasn't fair to dump her issues on them now. She and Robyn still did things together sometimes, but there was a distance between them these days and Elena didn't share her feelings so readily.

She needed more than a friend—she needed a counsellor. With a burst of hope, she picked herself up off the floor, waded across the sticky painted surface to the study and turned on the computer.

Google displayed a list of local relationship counsellors. Elena scanned the list and stopped at the photo of a kind-looking woman. Hope Dangerfield—Navigating the danger zone, restoring hope. Services: Counselling, Reiki, past life regression.

She wasn't sure about the past life stuff but she knew Reiki worked and counselling was a proven mainstream method. Elena scribbled down the woman's number and agonised over whether to call. She put the number in the desk drawer.

That night, she developed another killer headache, took some Panadol and went to bed early. Michael joined her a half hour later, rolling into bed as she lay waiting for the painkillers to kick in.

"Hey," he gave a short, self-conscious laugh, "do you want to fuck?"

Elena winced. A tiny part of her felt she should be glad for his renewed interest but she couldn't believe he had asked in such a crude, impersonal way.

"I've got a headache." She squinted at him as he loomed over her.

"You don't have to do anything," he replied. "You can just lie there."

"I can't," she whispered in stunned disbelief, rolling away from him and burying her head in the pillow.

He grunted, rolled back onto his side of the bed and turned out the light.

୧୭

BY THE END of the week, exhaustion set in. Acknowledging that she needed help had been tough and she was still fighting with herself over whether to call the counsellor. It was all so humiliating. To top it off, Michael had been even more distant, spending all his time out in the Taj Mahal. Some nights he hadn't even come in when she'd called him for dinner so she had eaten alone and he had re-heated his food after she had cleaned up and left the kitchen. He hadn't kissed her good morning or goodnight. They barely spoke. Tears were always close to the surface and some nights she'd had to creep out of the bedroom so he wouldn't hear her cry. She had even dissolved into tears during a training session at work, hiding her face in shame at her own weakness.

She called Michael in for dinner then sat down to eat, resigned to the fact that he would wait until she had finished before he came inside. She was blinking back more tears when Michael appeared in the doorway.

"What's wrong with you NOW?" he exploded.

Her face crumpled in shock. "Nothing."

He paced up and down the kitchen, the thick soles of his black Doc Martens squeaking on the linoleum. "Look at you, you're such a misery guts. If it's that bad, we may as well end this now. Is that what you want? Do you want me to leave?"

Her world stopped. He had never, in all their years together, mentioned separating. She bent forward, hugging her arms around herself. He couldn't leave her. That would be the ultimate failure.

"No!" she sobbed.

"You're always miserable, I can't stand it anymore. This has to stop. I can't take it anymore! You need to see a divorce lawyer." He paced the room, gesticulating wildly.

"I'm sorry," she gasped, her breath coming in short, gulping jerks. "Please. I promise I'll change, whatever you want. What do you want me to do?"

"I hate your attitude towards me! You're so dismissive." He glared at her. He was barely taller than her but, when he looked at her that way, he seemed to tower over her.

He stalked out of the room, leaving her cowering.

Shocked by his last outburst, she was ashamed to admit he did have a point. She had become dismissive, even scornful, of Michael in recent years. After trying for years to help him show and receive affection, she had instead ended up becoming more like him.

Still shaking, she stood and cleared the table. The TV was blaring in the lounge room but she was too afraid to say goodnight in case the mere sight of her angered him. She crept past the open door and into their bedroom.

Through the open curtains, the twinkling lights of the city stretched out below their hill. Elena stood transfixed. *How many people out there were happy tonight? How many people felt as helpless as she did?*

Still awake an hour later when he came in, she lay as still as possible, hoping he would think she was asleep. She felt the beginnings of another headache as she drifted off to sleep and woke in the early hours of the morning with the familiar, insistent throbbing at her temples. Michael snored beside her. With vision blurred by pain, she stumbled to the kitchen and swallowed painkillers. Returning to bed, she tossed and turned, unable to fall asleep with Michael's snoring. If she was asleep before he started, she was fine but if she was still awake when he began to snore, it was almost impossible to block out the sound.

Michael left for work in the morning. It was Saturday so Elena lay in bed until the discomfort in her neck made her get up and stretch. She plodded through the house, shell-shocked, completing chores on autopilot. In the afternoon, she finally called Hope and made an appointment.

Chapter Seven

SHE HATH NO LOYAL KNIGHT AND TRUE

After dissolving into tears as she explained her situation, Elena sat on the sofa waiting for Hope to offer a solution.

Hope finished her note-taking and looked up. "I want you to spend a few minutes considering what you want to get out of these sessions, what your desired outcome is. Write it down."

Elena listened in dismay. Wasn't Hope supposed to tell her what the best outcome was and how to achieve it? She accepted the offered pen and paper and gazed out the window while she thought.

Hope left the room to make a coffee.

Elena began to scribble notes and glanced up guiltily on hearing Hope return. "I'm sorry, I couldn't confine myself to just one outcome. I know it's greedy of me but there's a lot of things I need to change."

Hope smiled, "You're not greedy. Let's hear them."

- To be strong enough to make the right decisions
- Happiness for both Michael and I
- To cope with Michael's behaviour without upsetting myself or angering him
- To understand Michael's behaviour and not take it personally
- To express my feelings without defensiveness or fear of upsetting Michael

- A direction in life, or maybe rediscover the direction I lost
- To be able to plan a future
- To help Michael help himself

"That's quite a list," Hope commented. "You need to understand that you can only help Michael if, and when, he wants you to. You can support Michael, but not until you've learned to support yourself first. So let's start by tackling your own feelings and learning how to manage them."

Hope taught her a tapping technique called Emotional Freedom Technique, which she practised with diligence over the next few weeks, tapping away at trigger points on her body. It gave her a sense of calmness similar to Reiki. She also kept a journal of the strong emotions she experienced during the week and their triggers. Sad, hopeless, insignificant, hurt and fearful were all recurring themes.

"Michael walked away while I was in the middle of speaking. He does it all the time. It's as if I don't exist." She winced at the memory of her words petering out into the void of his retreating back.

"Are you afraid of Michael?" Hope asked.

Elena considered the question. She feared making him angry, but was she afraid of him as a person? He wasn't a violent man, so she didn't fear that he would harm her.

"No, I don't think so," she replied.

Hope's gaze was thoughtful, "Okay, good. Because you know, don't you, that we attract what we fear into our life?"

"The law of attraction, you mean?"

"Exactly. The more energy you focus on your fears, the more power you give them." Hope turned to a blank page in her notebook. "Okay, now I'd like you to tell me about your past, your family and any significant events. Let's start with your family."

"Well… I grew up on a small farm outside Gladstone with my parents and younger brother."

"Was your childhood a happy one?"

"I guess so, same as most people. I went to school, rode my bike around the wheat fields, collected eggs from the chook yard, Mum taught me to cook and sew…"

"Did you have close friends?"

"I had a girlfriend in school and sometimes we played together during the holidays. There were a couple of girls at church so I saw them every Sunday. A lot of the time I preferred to read books rather than go out though."

"You went to church every week?"

"Yeah, my parents were really strict about that."

"Did you enjoy it?"

"Sometimes, but it scared me too. All that talk about Armageddon, pestilence and plagues, and being judged wasn't much fun. I haven't set foot inside a church since I was nineteen—except for our wedding. I preferred a garden wedding, but my dad was annoyed that we were not marrying in a church and proclaimed our union to be unfit in the eyes of God, so I capitulated."

"Tell me about your wedding. How did you feel in the lead up to it?"

"I was a bit stressed, but that's normal for a bride, isn't it?"

"For some, yes. What stressed you?"

"I guess having to do all the planning myself. My mum and mother-in-law helped, of course, but I had to make all the decisions about what we wanted because Michael wasn't interested. He told me to do whatever I wanted, but he has strong opinions about most things and he's a perfectionist so I was worried he wouldn't like what I chose. And he hates spending money. He said weddings are a waste of money."

"So why did he agree to a wedding?"

Elena squirmed and looked at her feet. "I guess I pestered him into it."

"Would he have preferred a registry office ceremony?"

Elena swallowed hard. "I think he preferred no wedding."

"Yet he married you."

Elena reddened. It was so embarrassing to have to explain her life like this. "It took me two years to convince him we should get married." She picked at a dry cuticle around her fingernail, avoiding Hope's gaze.

"The point of marriage is that two people agree they want to share their lives with each other. It's not about convincing someone they should be with you."

Elena's bottom lip trembled as she struggled to hold back her tears. "Some of us aren't that lucky…"

"Why did you want to marry Michael?"

"I loved him… and we were looking to buy a house together. I couldn't understand why he wanted to buy a house and live with me, but not marry me. I needed to know that he loved me enough to want to marry me."

"Did he demonstrate his love in other ways?"

"He called me every day."

"Okay. Did he tell you he loved you?"

Elena faltered. "Not really… I didn't say '*I love you*' either until after we moved in together. Neither of us were very comfortable saying it. But I finally plucked up the courage one day to tell him."

"How did he respond?"

"He laughed and told me the only cure for love was to run. I persisted and, over time, his responses ranged from patting me on the head to a mumbled '*I love you*' in reply."

"Was he affectionate?"

"Kind of, at first. But he doesn't like demonstrations of affection much. He's very reserved."

"I know that upsets you now, but were you okay with it in the early days?"

"Not really," Elena mumbled.

Hope paused, regarding Elena.

"Tell me how you approached the subject of marriage."

The painful scene replayed in Elena's mind as she recounted it to Hope. She saw herself and Michael descending the stairs to the old-world charm of Chesser Cellar. Michael didn't like to dine out much, but this old school restaurant with its boutique wine list was his go-to whenever circumstances demanded he venture out.

"We're showcasing a lovely organic Kalleske Shiraz tonight. Would you like a tasting?" The waiter leaned the uncorked bottle towards Elena's glass.

Michael raised his glass, "I'll try it. It would be wasted on her— she thinks all wine is vinegar!"

Elena's face reddened and she kept her gaze downcast until the waiter moved away.

After ordering their meal, Michael placed a small, blue velvet box on the table in front of her. Her heart jumped into her throat. When he had asked her what she wanted for her birthday, she had said a marriage proposal, surprising even herself with such uncharacteristic forthrightness. But she was desperate.

She opened the box with shaking hands to reveal a sparkling, pink stone nestled in a thin, silver band. Her breath caught in her throat.

"It's not an engagement ring."

Her heart plummeted into the pit of her stomach and her eyes welled despite her best efforts to control herself. Swallowing hard, she tried to smile, painfully aware that the only other couple in the dining room were watching from across the room. "Um, what is it?"

"The lady in the shop said it's a pink tourmaline." His look was hopeful.

"No, I mean if it's not an engagement ring, then what is it?"

Michael shrugged. "A birthday present."

"Oh! Well, it's my favourite colour… very thoughtful… thank you." She smiled, hating the telltale quiver of her lips, and closed the box, leaving the ring ensconced in its white satin blanket.

They conversed little throughout dinner, which was nothing new. Their whole relationship had been plagued by long periods of silence, interspersed with her nervous prattle and his occasional comment. But conversation failed her tonight.

"What's wrong?"

"Nothing." Her cheeks burned with humiliation.

The other couple cast covert, curious glances in their direction.

"You don't look very happy," he commented.

"It wasn't a ring I wanted," she mumbled. "I wanted you to ask me to marry you."

"Bloody hell! I can't marry you now. We have to focus on finding a house and paying off the mortgage. Plus I don't have the time, I have to look after the vineyard for Mum."

"Couldn't we just get engaged now? We don't have to plan a wedding yet."

"Marriage is just an expensive piece of paper. Forget about it."

She shrank down in her seat, ashamed and battling a mixture of guilt and self-loathing at her obvious selfishness, but also a sense of injustice that her feelings were once again being dismissed. Was it too much to ask that Michael consider how his words and actions might impact on her? How could he not understand that, under the circumstances, giving her a ring was cruel if he had no intention of proposing? Did it make her a bad person to expect that others consider her needs?

Teachings from her childhood Sunday School sprang to mind. Jesus said turn the other cheek, and that greater love hath no man than that he give his life for another. Should she give up everything she wanted in order to support Michael and help him find happiness? If he were happy, she might be happy too. Maybe she should practice gratitude for whatever gestures he was willing to make and not expect anything of him. If she didn't expect, she couldn't be disappointed. As a theory, it kind of made sense to her, so why did it feel so wrong that she was always expected to give up her desires for others? Whose needs did everyone else serve if not their own? When would someone take *her* needs into consideration?

No sooner had the thought taken hold in her mind than she remembered Michael had given up a lot for his mother. Was that how it worked? She put Michael before herself and, in turn, he put his mother first. His mother had put her family first for much of her life so she could be excused from paying it forward now. Yet Elena couldn't stop herself wishing for some consideration and affection from Michael. She was so confused, she couldn't think straight.

"Oh honey," Hope said, bringing Elena's awareness back into the room. "Where was your self-worth? You need to take responsibility for your own feelings and needs, not wait for someone else to do it."

Elena's cheeks burned. "I was. I needed him to marry me and I asked him."

"Begging someone to marry you isn't showing self-worth. If someone isn't able to give you what you need—and what you needed wasn't a marriage proposal, you needed an acknowledgement of your feelings, love and affection—then the thing to do is acknowledge they are not right for you and move on."

A few rogue tears trickled down Elena's cheeks.

Hope handed her a tissue and rubbed her shoulder. "I think we'd better call it a day. Keep practicing your EFT tapping this week, okay?"

Elena nodded, sniffling into the tissue.

❦

"I THINK Michael and I need to get away from our normal routine and spend some quality time together."

Elena and Hope had been working through a range of issues for a few weeks, exploring her childhood, her rape and her relationship further. It felt like they were making good progress, which gave Elena renewed strength to confront her current situation.

Hope nodded. "Sounds like a reasonable proposal. How long has it been since you last had a holiday together?"

Elena winced. "We haven't."

"What about your honeymoon?"

"We didn't have one. Michael wasn't keen to go anywhere. I guess having to endure a wedding was all he could handle."

"Because he was reluctant to get married, you mean?"

"That, plus he doesn't like socialising."

"Does he suffer from anxiety?"

"He's never said so. He doesn't tell me how he feels. I'm sure he's depressed, though."

"Depression and anxiety often go together. It sounds severe if he wouldn't make an exception for a honeymoon."

"Well, I felt guilty about spending money on a wedding, so I didn't push for a honeymoon either."

"I see… So what are your thoughts for this holiday?"

"I'd like to take him to Queensland to see the Cairns Birdwing, the largest butterfly in Australia."

Hope nodded. "I guess you'd better ask Michael what he wants, then."

Michael wasn't keen to travel, but she kept pushing until he warmed to the idea and consented to a short trip on the proviso that Carla watch over his butterflies.

They flew to Mackay, leaving Marcus and Carla with copious instructions on butterfly care. Elena had planned the trip on her own. At first she ran every suggestion past Michael, but after receiving non-committal, unenthusiastic responses, she stopped asking him. She had chosen Mackay as their first stop for the beautiful botanic garden, Eungella National Park, Highlands Rainforest Great Walk and the Bluewater Lagoon. There would be no beach time, though. It seemed such a shame to go to Queensland and not spend time on the beach, but Michael wouldn't like it.

It was the first plane ride for them both. Elena thought she would be okay but as the plane taxied down the runway, an intense fear gripped her—galloping heart rate, quivering limbs, shallow breathing, she had the works. She grabbed Michael's hand.

He shook her off. "Get a hold of yourself," he snarled.

She cowered in her seat until the plane levelled out.

Michael was an immovable, impenetrable block for the entire flight, his white knuckles clutching the armrest the only indication of his own fear.

On arrival, he complained about the unfamiliar hotel bed and the quality of the wine in the minibar. On the rainforest walk, he finally started to relax, pointing out wildlife and interesting plants. In response, Elena shed some of her pent-up tension. Back at the hotel, she ran a spa bath, hopeful Michael would join her. He refused, lecturing her about their unhygienic properties.

The next afternoon, Elena drove them to the Bluewater Lagoon. It was a beautiful, cloudless day. She had her swimsuit on and was eager to splash in the lagoon. Michael found a shady spot to sit while she swam.

She had been in the water all of twenty minutes when Michael's shadow descended on her.

"Are you done yet?"

"We just arrived," she protested.

"It's too hot."

She sighed and got out of the water, towelled off and they drove back to the hotel.

After Elena showered and changed, they wandered down the street, stopping outside a pub.

"I want a drink," Michael said.

"Okay. Shall we sit outside?" The cute wooden benches under a shade sail, surrounded by potted, flowering hibiscus looked inviting.

"No, it's too hot," Michael opened the door to the front bar and strode inside.

He surveyed the wine list. "Hunter Valley, Margaret River, even bloody New Zealand, but where's the South Aussie wines?"

"Sorry, mate, we don't keep SA wines," the barman said.

A thundercloud crossed Michael's features. "Give me your best Margaret River Cab Sav then."

"A Marlborough Sav Blanc for me, please," Elena added.

Michael took a sip as the bartender turned away, then spat the wine back into the glass. "What's this shit?"

Mortified, Elena hoped the bartender hadn't heard him. "It's what you asked for."

"I asked for their *best* quality." He pushed the glass away and sat, stony featured, as she sipped her wine.

"Aren't you going to drink it?" she whispered.

"No." He crossed his arms and sat back, glaring out the window.

Elena, afraid he might lose his temper and cause a scene, gulped down her wine while the glass of red sat accusingly on the bar.

The next day, they drove eight hours to Cairns, managing to get lost and having to backtrack more than once. Michael became more angry and frustrated, and Elena more stressed and tense. Arriving two hours later than expected, a fatigued Elena collapsed into bed, wishing for the holiday to end so she could stop trying to convince Michael—and herself—that the trip was a positive experience.

Michael was in the shower when Elena woke up. His phone, on the night table, beeped. She reached across the bed, picked up the Nokia and checked the message. It was from a Carol.

- Why won't you take our calls? Your son wants to meet you, don't you feel anything for him?

Elena re-read the message, perplexed. The woman must have gotten her numbers confused.

"What are you doing with my phone?" Michael stood in the bathroom doorway, staring at her.

"Er… you have a message but I think it was sent in error. It's from a Carol."

Fear flashed across Michael's face. He strode over, snatched the phone from her hand and read the message. "Shit!"

"What?" Elena sat up.

"Nothing."

"But…" she faltered as a gut-wrenching realisation dawned. "Who is Carol?"

"Nobody… just someone I knew years ago." He tossed the phone onto the coffee table and pulled on his jeans and white t-shirt.

"Why does she think you have a son?"

Michael paused while doing up his boot laces, his stiffened back towards her.

"Michael?"

"She was a one-night stand fifteen years ago, okay?"

Elena's jaw slackened. "You have a son?" she asked incredulously.

He finished lacing his boots and stood up.

"Why didn't you tell me?"

"It's no big deal. I've never seen him… Of course I pay her maintenance, though," he hurried to add.

Maintenance? How did I never notice maintenance payments from our account? Elena's head was in a spin.

As if reading her thoughts, he glanced over his shoulder at her. "The payments get deposited direct to her account through my payroll."

"Why don't you want to meet him?"

"He's better off this way."

"But you might regret it when you're older."

"Not as much as I'd regret losing you."

The words hung between them, their faces a mirror of shock. She wanted to say something nice in return but words failed her. Michael averted his gaze, pretending nothing had happened. She watched him move around the hotel room, gather his belongings into his pockets, and comb his hair. She had waited more than a decade to hear him say how he felt about her. *I should be ecstatic,* she thought. Instead she felt hollow.

It's too late.

She shut her mind to the pesky, taunting voice. It was never too late. It couldn't be too late. Failing to tell her about his son was a big deal, but it wasn't like he had hidden a whole separate life from her. And he had honoured the responsibility to provide for his son.

But not the responsibility to be involved in his son's life.

"Why is your son better off not knowing you?"

Michael rounded on her. "He just is, okay?!" The finality in his voice told her the subject would never be open for discussion again.

She dragged herself out of bed. They were going to Kuranda's Australian Butterfly Sanctuary today, and she had to get ready.

Chapter Eight

HE FLASHED INTO THE CRYSTAL MIRROR

"So how was it?" Hope inquired.

Elena slumped forward, weary and despondent. "It was stressful and we behaved the same as we do at home... and then I found out he has a fifteen-year-old son from a one night stand,... and he surprised me by saying he didn't want to lose me."

"My goodness! How do you feel about the son?"

"I'm hurt, of course. I can't believe he never told me. He's never had contact with his son, but now the boy wants to meet him."

"And what does Michael want?"

"To continue having nothing to do with his son, and he doesn't want to talk about it. He got really angry."

"Okay, then it would be wise to tread carefully on that issue, until emotions have settled down. What about him saying he doesn't want to lose you, how do you feel about that?"

Elena raised one hand then let it drop in a gesture of despair. "I thought I'd be happy, but instead I'm sad and confused. I feel like I have no energy left to keep trying, but I have to."

"Why do you have to keep trying?"

"Because we're married."

"What makes you think you have to stay married?"

Elena pondered the question. "I didn't get married to get divorced."

"Nobody does. What else?"

"I guess the religion I grew up in frowns upon divorce. Couples should do everything they can to stay together."

"But you said you don't identify with religion anymore, so why should that be a consideration for you?" Hope scribbled notes in her book.

"I don't know. I guess it's just ingrained in me. The perfectionist in me agrees that people should always give their maximum effort and commitment to whatever they do."

"Do you feel you haven't given this your maximum effort?"

"No," Elena sighed. "I feel like I've given it so much that there's nothing left to give." She paused as her own words sunk in.

"I asked him to come for couples counselling, but he won't do it. If he came, perhaps that would give me the boost I need to keep going."

"You can't force him. He has to choose it for himself. We all have to choose what feels right for us."

Elena tried to tap into what felt right for her; not what her parents, Michael or anyone else believed to be right. What did she feel was right? But every time she asked herself, she hit a blank.

Something else was bothering her, teasing at the edges of her consciousness. "Sex. There's something to do with sex..." she blurted out.

"Okay," replied Hope, "how do you feel about sex?"

Elena gazed out the window. "I think... I think I have always equated sex with love. I assumed that if a man wanted to have sex with me, it was because he must love me."

"It's not always the case. Sometimes sex is just sex. People enjoy it, but they are not in love with the person they sleep with. Sometimes the only emotion involved is lust. I'm guessing that was the case with Michael and the mother of his son."

A sickening sensation developed in the pit of Elena's stomach.

"How did you develop the belief that only men who loved you would want to sleep with you?"

"I've believed it for as long as I can remember."

"But *why* do you have that belief?"

Elena faltered, thinking of the men she had refused, those she had allowed, and the one who had taken the decision out of her hands. She had told herself that Isaac loved her despite her physical appearance. It had seemed the only plausible reason for doing what he did.

"Because I'm unattractive, so for a man to want to sleep with me, it had to be based on something other than appearance."

"Interesting. So you thought they were attracted to you as a person but not the physical you?"

"I guess so. Although that doesn't make sense either because I've always been a shy, boring person. I was just grateful they could see past everything that was wrong with me."

"They may well have been attracted to your personality, but that doesn't mean they were not attracted to the physical you. You are an attractive lady, Elena, and you're a beautiful soul. I can guarantee that how you see yourself is not how others see you."

Elena squirmed, tears welling in her eyes.

"Sometimes people who see themselves as unloveable embrace the illusion of love through sex. Low self-worth or guilt causes them to depend on the validation of others. But this only leads to disappointment, because it's based on an illusion, not on real love. You have to love yourself before you can allow others to love you."

Elena burst into tears, her body wracked by huge, gulping sobs, mortified to have lost control of herself in front of Hope but unable to stop. When the sobbing subsided, she collapsed against the sofa.

"Bravo, Elena. You needed to release that." Hope hugged her.

Elena nodded, not trusting herself to speak.

"So to round off our discussion, do you feel that Michael doesn't love you? That it was only about the sex?"

Elena sighed. "I'm not sure. Sometimes I think he does, but most of the time he doesn't behave as if he loves me. But if it was just a physical thing, why hasn't he left before now, given our sex life has been almost non-existent for years?"

"Maybe it wasn't just physical for him. He did marry you after all."

"But he didn't want to."

"Did you hold a gun to his head?"

"No... but I wore him down by asking so often."

"Do you still love him?"

Elena sighed again. "Yes, but not like a partner. Early on, there were things I loved about him, but I also felt obligated to stay with him once we had slept together, despite all the discomfort between us. I'd made a commitment by having sex with him and I had to honour it." She paused, scrambling to understand her own feelings and find words to explain them. "There are things about him I still love, but I'm not *in* love with him. I don't feel the connection I need in a relationship, and I'm so worn down with trying to develop a connection he doesn't seem to want."

"Did you ever have a good connection?"

"I thought so at first, but it was a physical connection. We never had common interests or much to talk about."

"Did you always let him control the direction of your relationship?"

Elena floundered. "Control?"

"Yes, control. From everything you have told me, it sounds like you were afraid to stand your ground. Apart from hounding him about marriage, did you ever challenge him when something didn't feel right, or when you felt hurt?"

"Well, yes… maybe a couple of times…"

"You can lose yourself when you try to fit in with someone else."

Elena opened her mouth to speak but the words refused to come.

"Sweetheart, you grew up being told how to fit in. You learned how to be part of a group at home, at school and at church, but you lost yourself in the group. When Michael appeared, he was a safety net since you thought men at church wouldn't be interested in an already-deflowered wife, and he was also your chance to rebel against fitting in. Yet in rebelling, you lost yourself again by letting him dictate the terms of your life."

Elena covered her face with her hands.

"You need to find yourself, Elena. As far as Michael is concerned, you have three choices: accept the relationship as it is, challenge the boundaries and prepare yourself for the inevitable fall-out, or move on. Whichever you choose, remember to keep working on yourself. Keep questioning your feelings, your responses, the situations you find yourself in. Ending the marriage is not a magic bullet for transforming your whole life."

Anxiety bubbled up at the possibility of separation. "I know I need to leave in order to preserve my sanity, but I don't want to do it until he is stronger within himself. He's under a lot of stress and I can't add to it by walking away. So I guess I'll just wait until it's the right time."

"It's your choice, but it's unlikely you'll ever feel there's a right time to end your marriage. In the meantime, perhaps we can work on changing your view of sex. It may serve you better if you can learn not to feel beholden to someone just because you have slept with them. Learn to take control of your sex life."

"How do I do that?"

Hope shrugged. "You could choose to have an interaction that is just about sex and nothing else, so you learn not to equate sex with love."

Elena eyes widened in surprise.

Hope smiled. "I can see you're shocked. It's just a suggestion— you don't have to do it. I see nothing wrong with casual sex now and then. If my husband wants to have sex with someone, I'm fine with that. As long as it's just sex and nothing else. But not everyone shares my opinion."

Elena's jaw dropped. Yet the suggestion brought to mind her colleague, Amin. "It's funny you should suggest that. There's a nice project manager at work who I have a good-natured banter with. A few months ago he started sending me flirtatious emails and asked me to have lunch with him. I said I was too busy but he kept asking so I agreed to meet him for coffee one morning."

Hope raised an eyebrow in silent enquiry.

"He told me he has a wife and children but his relationship with his wife has been bad for a few years. She seems depressed but won't seek help and she refuses to have any physical contact with him. He proposed that we have an affair."

Hope nodded. "How do you feel about that?"

"He said he won't ever leave his wife because his religion doesn't allow divorce, but he thought we could have fun together. I told him I was pretty sure his religion doesn't allow adultery either, but he said it was the lesser of two evils. It's a way for him to keep his family together while still meeting his own needs."

"That's his view, but how did it make you feel? What do you want?"

"It offended me that he thought my feelings and needs were not as important as those of his family but part of me was flattered that he found me desirable. I haven't felt desired by Michael for at least the past six years. And it was nice to banter with him. I've *never* done that with Michael."

"So what did you tell Amin?"

"I said I wasn't sure. I agreed to meet him for lunch next week to continue our discussion."

"Okay, go to lunch and talk, only do what feels right for you, and we will discuss it in our next session," Hope replied.

❧

ELENA WAS ALMOST beside herself with the pain. Nothing had a lasting effect on her neck and shoulders—not physiotherapy, manipulation, acupuncture, or the multitude of different pillows in which she had invested. The headaches were still frequent, and she relied on painkillers far too much.

The acupuncturist patted her shoulder, "Still so tight, missy, no good."

"Isn't there anything else I can try?"

"Yes, maybe you try yoga. Go to Jivan, my friend. He very good. Yoga and acupuncture together is what you need."

The suggestion piqued her interest. "I used to go to a gym class which mixed yoga and pilates. That was good for me, but I don't like the gym atmosphere."

"No problem, Jivan has his own studio in Kensington. Better than a gym." He scribbled a name on a piece of paper and handed it to her.

Breathe the Peace. Jivan Kumar. Kensington.

"Thank you, see you next week."

Elena fished her phone out of her bag as she walked to the car and googled the studio. Inside the car, she wrote the studio address on the piece of paper and the hours for evening classes.

She drove home.

Michael was in the Taj Mahal. She climbed up the steps and let herself into the enclosure.

"Hi."

Michael spun around. "Be careful! Make sure the door is closed properly."

"Sorry… How are you?"

"Fine."

"I went to the acupuncturist tonight."

"Oh yeah. How was it?"

"Okay but I'm still really tight so he recommended me a yoga studio."

"Yeah?" Michael gently scooped a red European Peacock butterfly off his leg and placed it on a hop leaf.

"I'm going to try the beginners class tomorrow night. I'll go direct from work."

"Mmm."

Elena hovered, waiting for him to pay attention to her. He didn't.

"I'll go get dinner ready now," she said, edging out of the enclosure.

He didn't notice her leave.

On autopilot, Elena made dinner, called Michael in, ate, cleaned up then went to bed, barely having uttered a word.

In the morning, she woke after Michael had left for his early morning shift, got herself ready for work, prepared a bag of clothes for yoga and left the house. She drifted through the work day, speaking to no one, then drove to the yoga studio. The studio was warm and cosy, with exposed wooden beams in the ceiling, high windows which let in beams of fading daylight and well-worn jarrah floorboards.

Elena hovered near the doorway behind a group of people removing their shoes.

"Hello, I'm Jivan. Can I help you?"

A friendly-looking man stood in front of her.

"Er… Hi. I'd like to try the beginners class."

"Sure. I'll need you to fill out a form for me first, if you don't mind."

Elena followed him to a counter, filled out the form and handed it back to him.

"So… Elena… Your neck and shoulder problems," he said, after surveying her responses to the medical checklist. "Were they caused by accident or injury?"

"No. It's just muscular stiffness. That's why I'm here. I've tried physiotherapy, manipulation and acupuncture, but it keeps getting worse."

Jivan tutted and smiled. "Well, let's see if yoga can help. The casual rate is fifteen dollars, or you can buy ten classes for one hundred and forty. Since this is your first time, I suggest you pay for a casual class tonight and see how you feel afterwards."

"Yes, of course," Elena scrambled for her purse and handed over the cash, then followed Jivan into the room.

"You can leave your shoes and bag on the racks here, and collect a mat, strap and blanket here. And if you set up at the front here, near me, I can see you more easily to help you with positions."

"Thank you." Elena smiled. He was such a nice man.

Her hamstrings felt ready to snap in downward dog and her hips were so tight that when she crossed her legs, her knees hovered around her ears. She flopped around on the mat like a dying fish, trying to emulate Jivan's graceful movements. He frequently made gentle adjustments to her postures and she was embarrassed by her body's many restrictions. But she loved the calm atmosphere and the unconditional acceptance which emanated from Jivan.

He approached her after the class. "How do you feel?"

"Much better than when I came in tonight! But I'm so stiff," she apologised.

"That will disappear with time. But I can tell you are very tight in the upper body. Perhaps you could benefit from a remedial massage. I offer them here, in between classes, so let me know if you'd like to try it."

"Yes, please. When can I come?" Elena replied, without thinking. *Why do I want a massage when physiotherapy hasn't worked for me?* She thought.

"I'm heavily booked this week. How does midday Saturday week sound?"

"Perfect, thank you."

"Great. I'll see you then." He smiled, placed his hands in the prayer position and bowed his head towards her. "Namaste."

"Oh… thank you!" she stuttered, embarrassed. Nobody had ever bowed to her before. *Should I say namaste too? Should I bow? Or do only Indians do that?* She raised a hand in an awkward half wave, half salute, tripped over her own feet as she turned away, and fled the studio.

MICHAEL WAS SITTING by the back door when she returned, one heavy boot slung across the opposite knee. An empty wine bottle lay on the ground.

"Hi." Her greeting was timid. She never knew what kind of mood he would be in when he was drinking.

"What time do you call this?" His even stare unnerved her.

"What do you mean? I told you I had a yoga class tonight."

"Well, it's a bit late to cook dinner now."

"Why didn't you cook it? I left sausages in the fridge."

"Your problem is you've got life too good. You've had too much freedom." He glared at her.

A surge of outrage overcame her. "Too much freedom! What era do you think we're living in?"

She had allowed him to call almost all the shots in their relationship, yet he still thought she had too much freedom! Well, she refused to give up her yoga class just to serve him dinner by 7 p.m. Already she knew yoga was the best thing she had done for herself in years.

Michael smirked at having baited her.

Aware that it might be the alcohol talking, she bit back a further remark and went inside to prepare a quick meal.

☙

AMIN WAS WAITING for her at the table of a restaurant close to work. He stood to kiss her on the cheek. She slipped into her chair, blushing as his eyes ran over her body. A sheer blind covered the window next to them.

Amin followed her gaze. "That's why I chose this spot. Nobody can see us."

She squirmed. Sneaking around like this did not sit well with her.

They made small talk until the waiter took their order. As the waiter retreated, Amin leaned forward. "So have you thought about my proposal?"

"Yes, but I'm still not sure if we should." Elena blushed. "I like talking with you and you're a nice person. It could be fun to enjoy physical contact given that it's missing from our marriages, but it doesn't feel right."

Amin sat back. "It's okay. We can talk, get to know each other better, and then see where it goes."

"Can I ask why you chose me?" It felt more like a job interview than the beginning of a torrid love affair.

"Well, you seemed similar to me. You're a nice person but in an unhappy marriage and I think you want to enjoy life too. I want to have fun, but not with just anybody. I can find plenty of women to have sex with, but it's about the person too."

Elena flushed with pleasure. He appreciated her as a person, wanted to talk to her and get to know her. Maybe his proposal wasn't so bad after all.

He insisted on paying the bill, handing over his credit card. "I can't do this all the time. My wife sees our card statement. But today I'll say I took a contractor out for lunch."

Her uneasiness returned. She would have preferred they each pay their own way and have no need to lie about card transactions, but she refrained from saying so lest she offend him.

They walked back to the office together and separated at the entrance, agreeing to meet for lunch the following week. But she fell ill with bronchitis the next morning and spent a week in bed, coughing up the gunk which lay heavy in her chest. It triggered her asthma again and she moved into the spare room so her coughing wouldn't keep Michael awake.

When her energy returned, she had a sudden urge to clean out the filing cabinet, removing years' of accumulated paperwork. She hated clutter. It satisfied her to put things in order.

Plus it means less to pack up when the time comes.

The whisper reverberated in her head as if it were a thousand whispers in cahoots.

She pressed her hands to her temples, feeling the throb of yet another headache coming on. The massage appointment with Jivan was this Saturday. Hopefully he would help her.

❦

JIVAN EXAMINED HER NECK. "Wow you're tight. You don't have much movement in your neck and your back and shoulders are like rocks."

He began a gentle massage from her lower back and worked upwards. Elena noted the immediate relief as Jivan worked, her body responding instantly to his touch. The man had magical fingers! He probably thought every muscle he worked on was still rigid beyond belief, but she already sensed the subtle difference.

"I recommend acupuncture too," he told her.

"I've been getting treatments from your friend for six months."

"Good," Jivan enthused "I'm glad you're doing that. The yoga will help as well. It's good for posture, flexibility and the nervous system. A lot of physical problems stem from the nervous system being overworked."

Elena paid careful attention. He sounded like he knew what he was talking about.

She was in love with the studio, with the exotic music playing softly in the background, the smell of incense, the warmth, the beam of sunlight shining through the high window and landing on her shoulder.

He shook her left shoulder. "Relax, let it loosen".

She breathed out and tried to relax.

"Relax!"

"I'm trying." She felt more relaxed than normal, but it wasn't good enough. What a failure! How could she hope to keep her marriage together when she couldn't even relax her own shoulders? Tears welled but she pushed them back down. She couldn't fall apart in front of this lovely man.

"Is something in your life causing a lot of stress?" he asked.

Her breath caught in her throat. "Um... well, my marriage isn't doing so well," her voice shook with emotion.

"Ah, you need to sort that out. We can't fix your body while there's all that emotional stress going on."

"I feel a difference already."

"Yes, but next week we'd be back where we started. We won't be able to sustain any improvements until you sort out the other issues."

Please don't send me away. This is the only place I feel safe and calm. I need to be here.

"I've been seeing a counsellor," she volunteered, hoping to convince him of her commitment to improve the situation.

"That's good. Keep seeing them until you find your answers."

"I don't want to be married anymore," she whispered, her voice catching on the last word.

Tenderness and sympathy radiated from Jivan as he continued to knead her shoulder. She had never felt so cared for. How could this beautiful stranger care for her more than her own husband? A few rogue tears escaped, falling onto her hands as they rested underneath the head of the massage table. She blinked, desperate to control herself.

"Then why haven't you done something about it?" he asked.

"Because I don't want to give up on him or make the wrong decision... I don't want to hurt him."

"You need to read a book called *Absolute Happiness*. I can't remember the author's name, but he knows what he's talking about."

"Okay," she sniffed. "Thank you."

"You're so full of guilt at the moment. We store emotions on a physical level so you need to sort that out before we can make any real progress with your physical body."

She was disappointed when the session ended. Jivan was different. She knew she was safe in his hands, knew that she could trust him. There was a calmness about him that made her want to stay in his presence forever.

He gave her a hug. "Good luck. Let me know when you've sorted it out and we'll try again."

"But can I still come to yoga?" Panic rose at the thought of being sent away.

"Yes, of course. The mental focus on the postures, the relaxation and the breathing techniques will all help on an emotional level, which will translate to the physical. It will help to stimulate the parasympathetic nervous system better than any massage could."

"Thank you." She left, feeling simultaneously loved and rejected, and wishing more than anything to stay forever ensconced in that room with him where she felt so peaceful and supported.

On the way home, she bought a copy of *Absolute Happiness* by Michael Domeyko Rowland and started reading it that night.

Michael entered the spare room to say goodnight. "What are you reading?"

She held the cover up.

He snorted. "'Absolute happiness'? What rubbish, there's no such thing."

"That's a bit negative," she retorted.

He smirked. "You're such a dreamer! Goodnight."

"Bye," she whispered, watching him close the door.

❦

SHE COULDN'T MAKE a decision about Amin and talking it through with Hope didn't bring her any closer to a resolution. On Friday, they met again at the same restaurant. He brushed his leg against hers under the table. She was torn between wanting to move her leg away and wanting to reciprocate the caress. Frozen in indecision, she left her leg where it was but didn't respond to his touch.

After lunch, he emailed her a link to a cheap city hotel. *They need a credit card to secure the room booking. I can't use mine, I don't want my wife to see it. Can you use yours?*

She stared at the computer screen while a debate raged within her. Why was it okay for her to risk her husband finding out when he wasn't willing to take that chance with his wife? Of course he had more to lose. He had children to think about. She was planning to end her marriage anyway, but he had no intention of doing so. A quick lunchtime dalliance in some seedy hotel was not attractive to her, but it felt so nice to experience affection from a man.

She typed a short reply. *I'll look into it.*

Over the next few days, she investigated the hotel website and a range of other options from backpacker hostels to a sordid motel in Gepps Cross which rented rooms by the hour, but she couldn't bring herself to book one.

Amin cornered her in the empty tea room. "Have you booked a room yet?"

"No, I don't think I can do it. I don't want to risk hurting Michael."

"See! You *are* a good person. You care about others," Amin replied, leaning over and kissing her on the mouth.

She froze. His kiss became more intense, more probing and she found herself responding. Then his hands were in her hair, on her neck, trailing over her chest. Her heart was pounding and her body responding in a way it hadn't for many years. When he grabbed her hand and rubbed it over his crotch, then slipped his hand inside her pants, her eyes snapped open.

"We're in a public place," she whispered, pushing him away.

He groaned, running a hand through his hair. "We need to find a room soon."

She closed her eyes, trying to slow her racing heart.

What the hell are you doing? This isn't your answer.

The voice had a point. That her situation had degenerated to this point made it obvious she had to end her marriage. An affair wasn't the answer. If she was so unhappy in her marriage, she needed to sort that out, not make it worse by involving a third person.

She stepped around him. "I have to go."

"Okay, we can sort something out next week."

There would be no next week but she couldn't bring herself to say so.

Back at her desk she fired off an email, telling Amin she couldn't see him again and breathed a sigh of relief.

❦

MICHAEL WAS in the Taj Mahal, enraptured by a dainty, pale blue beauty perched on his extended fingertip. Becoming aware of Elena's presence, he turned to face her, his expression changing to disdain.

"How was your day?" she asked, attempting to sound normal but feeling transparently false.

"Oh, it was fantastic, as always," he replied with heavy sarcasm.

She waited for him to ask how her day had been but he turned back to his pretty butterfly.

"A man at work asked me to have an affair with him," she said, the words jumping out of her mouth unbidden.

Michael froze for an instant, his face betraying only the slightest sign of surprise before being replaced with a blank expression. "Really? Poor man."

She had been on the verge of confessing the whole story but stopped herself, stung by his cruelty. There was no point.

"I said no." She stalked inside to prepare dinner.

They spoke little at dinner and Elena went to bed early. She was still sleeping in the spare room even though she was well over the bronchitis, telling Michael his snoring kept her awake.

Michael stuck his head in the doorway. "I have an appointment with a marriage counsellor tomorrow. A *real* counsellor."

"Okay," she replied hesitantly. He'd made no secret of the fact that he thought Hope was a quack. "What time are we going?"

"You're not going. I'm going on my own."

"Oh..." She fell into disappointment before scolding herself. At least he was willing to see someone. That was a huge first step.

"Goodnight." He closed the door.

"Goodnight," she whispered.

She read until 2 a.m, then tossed and turned for another two hours before falling into a fitful sleep and waking late after Michael had left for his appointment.

As she dragged herself through the household chores, she heard Michael's car purr up the driveway. He didn't come inside. When she finished, she went out the back to look for him and found him sitting under the back verandah, smoking.

"How did your appointment go?"

"It was okay," Michael shrugged. "He wants me to read this book." He held up a copy of *The Power of Now* by Eckhart Tolle.

"It has very good reviews," Elena enthused.

She dragged a sun lounge onto the grass, soaking up the warmth of the spring sunshine. She fell asleep and woke an hour later.

Michael was still reading.

"When do you next see the counsellor?" she asked.

"I'll decide after I've finished the book," he replied.

Panic bubbled to the surface. What if he didn't go back? "When can we go together?"

"I don't know."

"We need to go together so we can start sorting out our problems."

"Your problem is you focus on the past too much. You need to read this book. The past doesn't matter, you can't change it. All that matters is now."

She had flicked through *The Power of Now* in the Health Department library's mental health section when she had worked there, so she had an idea of what he was talking about. "Getting caught up in the past doesn't help us live in the present, but we need to talk about unresolved issues, otherwise how are we supposed to improve our present relationship?"

He dismissed her argument with a wave of his hand. "You don't get it. The past has no bearing on the present. Just forget it and focus on now."

Elena suspected he was using the concept as an excuse for not dealing with the myriad of issues that had accumulated between them. He would never apologise for anything he had said or done to hurt her because it was in the past. As soon as he again did something which hurt her, he would expect her to ignore it because as soon as it was done, it had become the past. But that meant her life would never change. Their relationship would never improve because he would keep behaving as he always had and absolve himself from any responsibility because his every action immediately became a past event. She wanted to argue the point but couldn't order her thoughts into words which would be clear yet non-confrontational.

Chapter Nine

OUT FLEW THE WEB AND FLOATED WIDE

It was dark by the time Elena arrived home. Michael was in his usual position under the back verandah, wine bottle beside him.

"Hi."

"You're always leaving me alone. Where have you been?"

"With Hope. We took longer than I thought."

"Dad wouldn't have put up this behaviour from Mum."

"What behaviour? Trying to improve myself?" she shot back.

"Don't speak to me like that. You'd be nothing without me. You wouldn't even have a job. I pulled strings with my contacts to make sure you got your job and this is how you repay me."

"What? I have a job because I'm good at it, not because I'm married to you." She heard the shakiness in her own voice and despised herself for it.

He sneered at her. "You don't have any idea, do you? Our whole life here exists because of me, not you."

For the first time, she wondered if he were delusional. "I need to be alone for a while," she mumbled. Hurt and confused, she walked back towards her car.

"Don't be long!" His contrived, sing-song voice couldn't counteract the sudden panic in his eyes.

She drove aimlessly, grief-stricken, not registering where she was nor considering her destination. What had made him say those things? Then self-doubt crept back in. What if he was right? What if he *had* pulled strings to get her that first job? She had had so much trouble landing interviews, maybe she *wouldn't* have got a job without his help.

Dazed, she found herself standing on the doorstep of Marcus and Carla's house.

"Elena! Are you okay?" Carla pulled her inside.

"Do you think I couldn't get a job without someone pulling strings for me?" she blurted, bursting into tears.

"What? No, of course not. Why?"

In a torrent of tears, the evening's events poured out of Elena. She fell into a numb stupor, with Marcus and Carla sitting either side of her.

"Why don't you stay with us for a few days, take some time out to think," Marcus suggested, putting an arm around her shoulders.

Elena nodded. Yes, time to think was what she needed.

Taking her phone from her pocket, she agonised over what to write to Michael. After erasing and re-writing a few messages, she finally hit the send button.

- I'm staying with Marcus and Carla 4 a few days. I need a break. We can discuss l8tr. Love Elena.

Michael didn't reply. Perhaps he was already in bed.

After a sleepless night on the air mattress in Marcus and Carla's study, Elena messaged her boss to say she would be in late. Michael still hadn't replied to her message. She waited until she was sure he would have left for work then drove to the house and changed into work clothes. She stuffed handfuls of clothes in a suitcase, not caring what she was taking and vaguely aware she was taking much more than she needed for a few days. In the bathroom she swept her toiletries into a plastic bag, then lugged everything out to her car and dragged herself to work. An email awaited her.

Elena,
I want you to come home. Running away will solve nothing. We have to talk about this present situation that you find so frustrating. I need you here. I will call you later.
Love Michael.

Her shoulders slumped and she covered her face with her hands.

She couldn't cope with speaking to him yet. But he had signed his name with love. Didn't that count for something? If he made an effort, she should too.

"Elena, are you okay?"

Sam, a young administration assistant from down the hall, stood in front of her desk.

She attempted a smile. "Yeah, I'm okay, just going through a rough patch."

"Do you want to talk about it?"

She hesitated. She didn't want to tell all and sundry her personal affairs but she didn't want to be rude to him either since he was being so nice.

"Thanks Sam, but there's nothing you can do. I think I left my husband last night so I just need time to sort myself out."

He sat on the edge of her desk and put a hand on her shoulder. "You shouldn't even be here. Why don't you go home?"

"No, I've got work to do. And I'd rather have something to keep my mind occupied at the moment. Thanks, but I'll be fine."

He nodded. "Okay, take care of yourself."

Elena hit the reply button.

Dear Michael,
I'm sorry but I'm not sure staying married is good for us. We don't know how to communicate to resolve issues and we don't have an emotionally supportive relationship. I feel like I don't even know you. Please give me time to think, then we can discuss it.
Love Elena.

That evening, the text messages started.

- Where are you?

- What are you doing?

- I want you to come home and talk to me.

Feeling harassed, guilty and emotionally exhausted, she turned the phone off and fell into a restless sleep. The next morning, she checked her inbox.

Elena
We have resolved issues before but I understand that they could have been

resolved more mutually. I believe you know me better than you think, but that is for you to decide.
I love you, Elena.
Michael

She cried silent, wretched tears. Their issues had never been resolved, she had always capitulated. She re-read the message. It was the first time he had said 'I love you' without being coerced. That he'd done so when she had nothing left to give only increased her wretchedness.

The day passed in a blur and she struggled to concentrate on the research she was doing on worldwide models of retail energy supply. In the late afternoon, her phone started buzzing.

- How are you?
- Did you get my messages?
- Why don't you respond?

She had to reply, it was awful of her not to.

- Is it okay 4 me 2 come by the house this evening?
- Why would it be a problem? You live here.

She blinked back tears. This was not getting any easier.

When she arrived, Michael was sitting under the back verandah, wine glass in hand.

She cringed, hoping he hadn't drunk too much. "Hi."

"Hello." He stood and kissed her cheek.

They made awkward small talk before she broached the subject of separation. "Michael, I can't live here with you anymore."

"Where are you going to live then?"

"I don't know. I'll find a flat to rent until we sort out our finances."

"No, you're not renting. It's a waste of money. Don't you remember how tight finances were when we first got this house?" He exploded. "Do you want to go back to that? We're in a good position now, with the house almost paid off. I've always made sure you had everything you need."

Not everything I need, she thought but held her tongue and tried to steer the conversation away from finances.

"I can't stay with you Michael. We're both miserable."

"Why are you miserable?"

"We've had this conversation many times. This relationship

doesn't give me what I want or need and I don't think it meets your needs either. We have no common goals. I want children but you won't even talk about the concept of us having them."

"If you leave me, you might not find anyone else to have children with, but if you stay, we might be able to have them. If you leave, you are stopping me from having children, too."

The familiar heaviness of guilt settled in her chest. On an intellectual level, she knew his arguments made no sense. After all, he already had a child who he could choose to let into his life. But emotionally, it was tearing her apart. She didn't want to be responsible for a decision that might impact his future prospects.

What if I can't find someone to have a family with? She shook her head. *Get a grip, Elena.*

"I'm sorry, I don't know what to say. But I can't stay with you."

He glared at her. "Who have you been talking to? Who infected your head to such a magnitude that you think I'm not here to help you?"

Weary and battered, she stood up and backed away, unable to cope with more accusations about her own ineptitude.

"I have to go. I'll talk to you later." Her legs shook as she walked back to her car.

She felt compelled to repair their relationship, even as she knew it wasn't possible, ping-ponging hourly between wanting to give it one last try, and wanting to flee as fast as possible.

The messages started again.

- *Where are you?*
- *What are you doing?*
- *When are you coming over again?*
- *I feel lost without you.*

She didn't want to ignore him, but didn't want to respond to his controlling messages. Yet the last message tugged at her heartstrings so she relented.

- *Hi, hope u r okay. Can I come over Friday nite 2 talk?*
- *I will be okay if you come back. We can go out for dinner?*

A public place wasn't suitable for the conversation they needed to have but he was making an effort so she couldn't refuse.

❧

THEY SAT across the table from each other, Michael attempting to sustain an upbeat, impersonal conversation.

Your marriage is on the verge of collapse and you're discussing the weather.

Elena opened her mouth to speak but nothing came out. Michael tucked into his steak with gusto while Elena picked around the edges of her chicken parmigiana. Her appetite had been non-existent since the night of her unplanned departure.

When Michael finished his meal, she laid her cutlery aside.

"Is that all you're going to eat?"

"I'm not hungry."

He paid the bill and took hold of her hand, leading her to a nearby park. She was dismayed to feel nothing. No joy that he had initiated physical contact, no affection for him, nothing but a heavy numbness. They wandered along the grass hand in hand while he updated her on the status of his butterflies and the latest dramas in his workplace. She made occasional appropriate murmurs in response, wondering how to raise the topic they were both avoiding.

"What's wrong?" he asked.

"I'm just thinking."

"Don't think. Be in the now." His grip on her hand tightened.

"I don't know Michael. This just doesn't feel right, we don't feel right."

"What are you thinking?"

"That we haven't even come close to sorting out any of the issues that caused our separation. I think you don't understand my reasons for leaving and I don't know how else to explain them."

His grip tightened further. "You said you wanted children. Come back and we'll have one now!"

Every fibre of her being recoiled in horror. A child wouldn't solve their problems. In fact, it would likely create additional problems. What a horrid environment to bring a child into! She shook her head. "No, I can't."

His shoulders sagged and he let go of her hand as they approached the car. She felt like the ultimate bitch. He was trying so hard to give her what she said she wanted, but what she wanted and needed, he could never give her. She didn't want to hurt him, but it seemed that she was damned if she did and damned if she didn't. Doing what he wanted would only continue hurting them both and dragging an innocent child into the mix was unthinkable.

※

THE NEXT FEW months were a waking nightmare. She wandered through the workdays with a lack of focus. Some days it became too much for her and Elena would call in sick, then spend the day languishing on Marcus and Carla's sofa. Elena's parents encouraged her to do whatever necessary to repair the marriage. They meant well, but the last thing she needed was that kind of pressure. It was partly her fault for not telling them earlier about her marital issues. She had been too humiliated to admit that her marriage was less than perfect, unwilling to even admit it to herself for much of the time. The longer she had left it, the harder it had become. Thus her parents had no prior knowledge upon which to base their views. But she didn't have the strength to explain it all to them yet. It was still too raw.

The only thing keeping her sane was Brigid. Her gorgeous little niece was always full of smiles and loved to receive cuddles from Aunty Elena.

Michael messaged her multiple times a day, alternately cajoling, affectionate, demanding and cruel. He accused her of being irrational, delusional and in need of serious help. He was convinced she had set her hopes on another man, when in reality she was so drained she couldn't even contemplate letting someone else into her life. Then he would tell her how much he missed her, how he needed her to help them through this rough patch. If she didn't respond to his messages, she felt terrible for ignoring him. If she did respond, she feared it gave him hope where she knew there was none. Guilt plagued her when she let her anger get the better of her or if her response was impersonal.

Never knowing whether his messages would be sweet or angry, nausea overcame her with every beep of the phone and she feared calling him. But she needed to collect more clothes and shoes.

"Hi Michael, how are you?"

"Fine. To what do I owe the pleasure of this call?"

"Er, do you mind if I come by the house on Saturday to collect more clothes?"

"I've burnt them." He laughed, a harsh, cold bark.

"What...?" Words failed her.

"Don't worry, I'm only joking."

She pressed a hand to her forehead, grimacing. "Well, it's not funny."

He snorted. "You need to lighten up."

"Whatever, I'll see you Saturday afternoon, okay?

"Until then..."

A few weeks later, she collected more items when he was still at work. Noticing she had been to the house, he accused her of breaking and entering and changed the locks.

Fearing that he would attempt to control her by moving their joint funds into his own account, she redirected her pay into a new account and withdrew half of what was in their joint account. His rage was unparalleled. But by the time she found a flat near the beach to rent and collected her few remaining possessions, he seemed more accepting of their separation. She hoped the worst was over and they could be friends.

Jittery about the prospect of living on her own for the first time in her life, she'd rented a flat in a secure complex. The security gates and intercom gave her some peace of mind but didn't remove the fear of solitary nights. She steeled herself for sleepless nights, but fell into a deep sleep on her first night and awoke eight hours later feeling refreshed and revived. Looking around the tiny, one-bedroom modern flat, she experienced the first spark of contentment. She was safe and she was free.

❦

"I'M CONCERNED you weren't strong enough to not take Michael's ranting so much to heart," Hope said.

Elena's shoulders sagged. All the counselling, journal writing, the EFT tapping, the self-help books, yoga and Reiki hadn't saved her from her own weakness.

"Don't feel bad, Elena. It's okay. But you need to build yourself up so you don't have such dramatic, immediate reactions to what people say or do. If you are secure in yourself, what others say and do won't matter. I believe you are a very strong person, but you haven't allowed yourself to own your strength yet."

Deflated, Elena picked up where she had left off reading *Absolute Happiness*, considering the concepts of blocked emotions and patterns stored in the subconscious mind, the negative conditioning of society around sex, and how experiences could create flawed beliefs about ourselves and our lives. The book made her aware of the need to release long-held beliefs that she was boring and uninteresting, and that life was never fun. She determined to allow herself to interact with people more and enjoy life now that she was free to do as she pleased.

It was also time to let go of believing she was unattractive. Based on this original view of herself, she suspected she had made choices— such as dressing like a frumpy old woman—that had led to her becoming less attractive. And her hair! It was long again, but she was still bleaching it almost out of existence. The stark colour didn't suit her at all. She laughed, remembering the first day she had bleached her hair and her impression that blondes had more fun. She had certainly proven that theory wrong. As her hair had become lighter, her life had spiralled into ever-deepening depths of misery. Neither had the 'gentlemen prefer blondes' theory worked out. Michael hadn't preferred her company as a blonde any more than he had when her hair was a mousy, nothing colour. In rebellion, she dyed her hair black and spiral permed it. *There!* She thought, surveying herself in the mirror. *Now I'm going to have fun, damn it!*

❀

SAM, the admin assistant at work, was bragging to colleagues in the tea room about his athletic prowess and cardio fitness as a result of a high-intensity gym program. Elena listened with interest. She wanted to be fit again but hadn't succeeded at motivating herself to do any exercise since her break up with Michael. She asked Sam about the program and went with him to the next class.

It was a brutal, gruelling hour of non-stop running, jumping, push-ups, sit-ups and more that left her gasping for breath and every muscle protesting. It also left her sporting a huge grin. She was alive again and loved pushing her body to its limit so, despite her distaste for gyms, she signed up for six months.

Sam shuffled into the office. "How you doing today?"

"I feel about as good as you look! I've got aching muscles where I didn't even know I had muscles."

"Yeah, it was a tough session, but the pain will go in a day or two."

"I hope so!"

He gave her an appraising once-over. "Hey, one of the gym guys is having a party Friday night. You wanna come?"

"Sure!" She hadn't been to a party in years.

On Friday, Elena surveyed her updated wardrobe of snug-fitting jeans, short skirts and spaghetti strap tops for something suitable to wear, and settled on a pair of jeans, silver ballet flats and a lace-trimmed silver singlet top. With her new hair and clothes she had to admit that the woman staring back at her from the bathroom mirror was quite pretty.

It amazed her how much the gym crowd drank for people so committed to their health. Elena knew she couldn't keep up with them, so she didn't even try. A couple of drinks were enough to make her tipsy—any more and she'd end up regretting it in the morning. Besides, she might lose control and do something stupid. But she drank enough to loosen up and join in a frenzied game of hide and seek in the pitch black yard, shrieking as she tried to dodge her pursuer.

She ran smack into someone. Sam put his hands on her biceps to steady her. "Whoa, are you okay?"

"Yes, sorry, I didn't see you," she giggled.

He laughed, his hands still on her arms. They stood in silent awkwardness for a few seconds then ran in opposite directions, searching for new hiding spots.

She woke late the next morning, muddle-headed despite having curbed her alcohol intake. Her phone chimed.

- *Wat u up 2 today? Sam*

She smiled, remembering the fun of the previous night.

- *Not much, thought maybe beach this arvo. U?*
- *Beach sounds good.*

- Want 2 join me? I'm close 2 the beach so if u come here then we can go 2gether.

- Sure, b there soon

They spent the entire afternoon at the beach. She oscillated between feeling relaxed in his company and awkward at the obvious sexual tension between them. It was only four months since she and Michael had separated. Was it too soon? She wasn't even divorced yet. Under South Australian legislation, she would have to wait twelve months before filing for divorce.

Yet deep within her was a need to know that a man found her attractive and to experience sex as enjoyable and relaxing.

After devouring takeaway pizza for dinner, they faced each other on her new sofa, legs entwined. Sam stroked her leg. A delicious shiver ran through her body as she enjoyed this strange, new sensation. She waited for him to make a move but he didn't.

"Would you like to have sex?" she blurted, astonished at her own audacity. A wave of emotions flickered across his features, from amusement to abashment, interest to wariness.

He hesitated. "I'm not sure. I don't get involved with work colleagues."

"And yet here you are," she replied. "It's okay, we don't have to. And if we do, it doesn't mean we're in a relationship. We can just take it as it comes."

Here was her chance to prove that she could have a sexual encounter without feeling beholden to commit to him, without sacrificing her entire life and soul for him.

He moved, suspending himself above her by supporting his own weight on his forearms.

She waited, eyes locked on his face.

He leaned down to place a cautious kiss on her lips then pulled back with a nervous laugh.

"What?"

He shook his head. "Nothing."

"Don't worry, you're not committing to anything. If you decide this isn't working for you, just tell me, okay?"

He nodded and kissed her again. He was a skilled, intuitive and experienced lover who knew how to draw sensations and responses from her body that she never knew existed. To her surprise, he seemed genuinely interested in pleasing her, too.

He left the next morning and she sat on the sofa, grinning. She had enjoyed the experience, and now she was alone again, and she was okay. In fact, she was more than okay, she was great!

The next day Sam invited her to lunch. They lunched again on Tuesday, then he invited her to his place for dinner and she stayed the night. When the weekend arrived, she realised they had shared meals and spent their nights together for the entire week. She had been careful not to assume he would want to spend more time with her but, wonder of wonders, he did!

From then on, they were hardly ever apart, seeing each other at work, lunching together, alternating between each other's homes at night. They attended gym in the morning, on weekends they drank and danced with friends and squeezed in occasional walks on the beach. In the whirlwind of activity, her sole moment of stillness was the haven of her weekly yoga class.

❦

"I can't see you anymore," Sam told her. They had been together four months.

Her breath caught in her chest and she reached her hand towards his. "But why?"

He withdrew his limp hand from under hers, staring at the floor. "This was only supposed to be a bit of fun. You're too nice for me."

Elena burst into tears of shock and dismay. How could someone be *too* nice? She didn't want to let go of him, of the shared experiences, the fun times, the great sex—but she was powerless to stop him.

For a few weeks, she operated on autopilot, in gutted disbelief that he had ended things so abruptly. However, it wasn't long before she moved on with her life, for she had enjoyed her time with Sam but she hadn't been in love with him. With time to herself to evaluate the relationship, she had to admit being with Sam had exhausted her. She had agreed to everything he wanted, leaving no time for herself. Life with Sam had been fun, but she wouldn't have been able to sustain it long-term.

Michael was ever-present in the background. He still sent her messages, wanting to know where she was and what she was doing, demanding that she visit him. In between all the angry, demanding messages, she would receive heartfelt messages that brought tears to her eyes.

She wished that she could let him know she cared about him but, afraid it would raise his hopes again, she crafted careful replies, which invariably elicited more hurt, angry tirades in response.

In his anger, he refused to negotiate a fair settlement on their house. He refused to sell and wanted her to agree to a payout which wouldn't stretch his finances. Elena hired a lawyer, loathe to do so but deeming it necessary if she were to stand up for herself.

Her lawyer was a hardened young woman whose only interests appeared to be verifying that they had enough assets between them to pay her fees, and in pressing Michael for a fifty-fifty split. Elena considered finding a less aggressive lawyer but decided she needed someone tough and hardened to counterbalance her own passive nature.

After receiving the first notice from Elena's lawyer, Michael messaged her.

- *You will receive some official documents from my lawyer. Don't be afraid.*

Her blood boiled. How dare he attempt to intimidate her under a pretence of concern for her welfare?! She chose not to reply.

His communications became more angry and threatening. She answered his call one night to an angry tirade.

"You have a university education so you have better prospects for increased earning capacity and should compensate me by giving me more of our combined assets."

"A university education doesn't guarantee greater earning capacity! There are plumbers who earn far more than I'm ever likely to earn," she reasoned.

"I supported you while you studied so I deserve more than you!"

Gob-smacked, she scrambled to gather her thoughts. "How did you support my studies? I worked full-time the entire period we lived together. We both contributed to household finances. You didn't even support me in kind by picking up more of the housework so I could focus on study. And don't get me started about emotional support!"

He ignored her question. "If I have health problems and can't work until retirement age, I could sue you for maintenance. I could take part of your superannuation, too," he threatened.

How had they reached this point and how on earth could she hope for a peaceful resolution now? Weariness overcame her and it took all her willpower to not succumb to guilt and offer him every cent of their combined assets in case one day it eventuated that he couldn't work.

"Neither of us knows what the future holds, Michael." She prayed he wouldn't be incapacitated. The thought of him bitter and alone, with no one to care for him, tugged at her heartstrings.

"But you'll leave me alone to find out, won't you?"

Her shoulders sagged. He was right.

"Maybe you won't be alone, maybe you'll meet someone else."

"I'm not interested in finding someone else."

"Don't say that," she pleaded, guilt returning with a vengeance. Was she condemning him to a lonely existence through her choice to leave?

"It's true."

She couldn't deal with this conversation. "I have to go now, okay? I'll speak to you later."

Chapter Ten

REFLECTING TOWER'D CAMELOT

E lena held the settlement cheque in her hand with a sense of immense relief. Michael had offered her less than a fifty percent share, but just enough that it wasn't worth fighting for.

"You're entitled to fifty percent. I recommend we file a petition in court," her lawyer had urged.

"Why would I pay more for a court case than the extra amount I would receive if I win?"

The lawyer had pursed her lips. "But it's the principle of the matter. I strongly recommend you petition for a fair settlement. There is no reason you should receive less than half."

Elena had wavered, questioning her instinct. Was this a case where she should be standing up to him instead of caving? Was she showing weakness by letting him control the outcome in this way?

Court will only benefit the lawyers and further poison relations between you and Michael.

The voice in her head was crystal clear, and she couldn't ignore it. "I'm happy with the amount. I don't want to drag it out in court."

Her lawyer had nodded, dismissing her. Time was money in her cutthroat, bill-by-the-quarter-hour world.

"Okay, I'll draw up an agreement and send it to his lawyer for signing. You can pay your bill for my time thus far on your way out."

Chiding herself for ever allowing a man to control her life, Elena admitted she had been on a similar path with Sam. His fun, outgoing nature had fooled her at first but, in hindsight, she saw that she had allowed him to call all the shots. She had given non-discerningly of her time, energy, and finances and made excuses for all the little examples of his lack of respect and consideration towards her, until he decided to give her the flick.

To ensure she didn't repeat the mistake she had to have a clear idea of what she wanted and needed in a partner. She made a list.

- Non-smoker
- Kind and affectionate
- Intelligent
- Someone who considers my needs and happiness
- Willing to commit to a relationship
- Able to manage own finances well
- Physically attractive
- Fit and healthy
- Likes to travel
- Enjoys the beach
- Likes to cook and eat good food
- Enjoys dancing and physical activity
- Interested in self development
- Sensitive lover
- Wants to have children
- Mentally and emotionally stable
- Will be open and honest with me

You've described Jivan. He's your ideal partner.

The thought popped unbidden into her head. In the short time she had known him, she could tell that he was intelligent, stable and a kind, gentle person. He was physically fit, interested in self-development and attractive—although if someone had asked her to describe him, she would have been hard-pressed to do so. He was short, with dark hair, dark eyes, a largish nose and café latte skin. Apart from his skin, it was hard to tell whether he possessed more of his mother's Spanish genes or his father's Indian heritage. She hadn't found him unattractive, but neither did she recollect staring at him in admiration. It was more the person inside the physical exterior she was drawn to. She sensed he was someone honest and open but didn't know if he matched the rest of her list, although she suspected that he did.

Pushing the thought of him aside, she berated herself for such a foolish notion. Jivan was streets ahead of her. Why would he be interested in someone like her? He might be her ideal partner, but she doubted she was his. She had a lot more work to do on herself first.

Her gaze fell on a copy of *Eat Pray Love*. During her darkest moments after leaving Michael, she had seen Oprah interviewing the author. Laying on the sofa, mentally and emotionally drained, she had flicked through the daytime TV shows until the interview caught her attention. She had bought the book the next day, intending to read it but never quite mustered the energy to do so. Then Sam had come along, leaving her no time for reading.

Picking up the book, she devoured a quarter of it before falling asleep with it in her hand. Elena related to the author's guilt-wracked choice to end her marriage, a whirlwind affair that came crashing down, and practising yoga to find inner peace.

Over the next few days, she read intriguing descriptions of life in an Indian ashram, meditation, finding a guru and the deliciousness of having an entire year to travel. India was both a fascinating and scary proposition. A desire to travel and explore new countries swelled within her, but Elena could only dream she would find herself in such a privileged position.

Putting the book down, she stretched her neck. The stiffness had improved since the end of her marriage. She was no longer plagued by headaches, the gym had strengthened her muscles and yoga was starting to loosen them. She had resumed the massage appointments with Jivan a month ago, benefitting from his gentle, perceptive techniques, but there was still much room for improvement. He encouraged her to continue with yoga, not that she needed any encouragement. His weekly class was the one thing she never missed.

She made friends with Jane, a bubbly new girl at yoga who was the same age as Elena. They were so similar in their outlooks on life and so comfortable together that people sometimes mistook them for sisters. They went bushwalking, bike riding together, and drinking and dancing on Friday nights, both on the lookout for a new partner, even though Elena was unsure she would find her ideal partner in a pub. More often than not, their Friday night adventures ended with Elena being pestered by guys she wasn't interested in. Or pursued by guys who seemed nice at first but turned out to be completely wrong for her—the one who was still in love with his ex-wife but wanted some 'adult fun', the one who turned out to be still married, and the friend of a friend of a friend who seemed decent enough when she'd had a few drinks, but in the light of day turned out to be slightly creepy.

"What type of guy do you want?" Jane asked as they trundled down to the taxi rank after another unfruitful night out.

"My list is long—kind, affectionate, financially and emotionally stable, fit, spiritual, non-smoker, not commitment-phobic…"

"Anything else?" Jane laughed.

"I know, I don't ask for much." Elena smiled. "A yogi. I want a yogi."

"Well, I'll settle for a sweet family man who loves and under-stands me."

Jane's comment gave Elena pause for thought. *Perhaps I am demanding too much. Perhaps love is enough.*

❦

"I'M INUNDATED with requests for school resources on energy genera-tion, distribution, and green energies but we don't have any," the Community Education Manager told Elena. "So I've been given funding to develop some."

"Okay. What do you need me to do?"

"I want you to research ideas for a picture book."

"Sure, no problem."

"Then you could write the book for us."

"Me, write a book?" Elena squeaked.

"Yes, I hear you have a degree in literature. You could research what works with kids, choose any aspect of energy you like and write a story."

Elena opened her mouth to decline. She had no experience in writing for children.

"Don't say no yet. Just consider it, okay?"

"Okay," Elena gulped. Mixed with self-doubt was a spark of excitement at the prospect of doing something creative and interesting to break up the monotony of a job which she now knew inside out. "I always wanted to write a novel one day but never considered writing for children."

"Perfect! I'll leave it with you, then."

As background research, Elena read various picture books with an educational focus. It struck her that many were dry and dull, some patronising in their attempts to be cutesy, and others had interesting stories but boring illustrations. Those which captured her attention were stories that took the reader on a fantastical imaginary journey while imparting educational facts at an almost subliminal level. Inspired, she started to develop a story about a superhero with special powers related to energy generation and distribution. The idea continued to germinate in the back of her mind as she went about her normal work. While she read books and articles, she kept her eyes peeled for ways of expressing processes that would be easy for children to understand. Sometimes random, disjointed ideas for characters and plot sprang from nowhere as she lay in bed at night. She made notes of these jumbled impressions until, bit by bit, a story developed and she was able to visualise the characters in her mind. There was no deadline and the lack of pressure opened creative channels in Elena that may have otherwise been hampered by the fear to perform.

꩜

THOUGHTS OF TRAVELLING the world continued to spring into her mind. After much deliberation and research, she booked a trip to Europe for the following August, an organised tour aimed at people in their mid-twenties to mid-thirties. It was more expensive than the Contiki version but promised to be more sedate. She'd heard mixed reviews about Contiki and couldn't imagine herself traipsing around Europe for a month with a group of drunken teenage revellers.

Knowing that travel abroad would never be an option with Michael, she hadn't allowed herself to consider the idea, but now she was relishing the freedom to imagine and plan as she wished.

At the end of a yoga class, she told Jivan of her plans.

"Good, good! I'm glad you're going to Europe. Good choice for a first travel experience. You know, I worked in Europe for a while, in my younger years."

"Really?"

"Yes, I worked all across Europe—France, Spain, Italy, Greece, taking whatever jobs came along. Wherever I worked, my bosses didn't want me to leave. But I was a free spirit, I was young and I wanted to explore."

He told her fascinating tales of his adventures, the characters he had met along the way, and advised her about places to visit and the tourist-targeted scams to watch out for.

"It's a bus tour, so the places I'll visit are already set. We're going to France, Spain, Italy, Greece, Germany and Switzerland."

"Oh." He paused then shrugged. "Not to worry. You won't see the real Europe, you'll get the sanitised tourist version, but you will still enjoy it."

"I didn't want to be alone my first time overseas. I thought a tour would be safer." She had been so sure that the tour was right for her, but his reaction made her doubt herself.

"Yes, of course, it probably is better… for you."

"I could change it. I booked a whole year in advance," she ventured.

"No, don't worry you'll have a good time. You'll love the clothes in Paris, the shoes in Italy. And the food! Gelato, paella, cheese, oh my God!"

Her soul burned to experience what Jivan had experienced and she allowed herself to indulge in a momentary fantasy of her and Jivan travelling together one day.

Elena pinched herself, not quite believing her life had already transformed into a much happier, more satisfying existence. She was fitter and stronger than ever, the asthma cough which had plagued her for more than a decade had disappeared, as had the irritable bowel syndrome. Work was challenging in a new, exciting way. The uncertainty and paralysing fear had been replaced by enthusiasm and a desire to explore. She stood at the threshold of a new beginning, with the freedom to spread her wings more than she had ever dared to imagine!

Chapter Eleven

LIKE SOME BOLD SEER IN A TRANCE

E lena stood on the Rundle Street sidewalk with Louisa and Jane, watching the retreating backs of her workmates as they headed home. It was only midnight.

"Come on." Louisa looped arms with Elena and Jane, tugging them along the pavement.

"Where are we going?" Elena hobbled along in her mid-heeled peep-toes, trying to keep up with Louisa.

"To meet my friends at Jive," replied Louisa.

Elena didn't know the club but allowed Louisa to lead them down Hindley Street into the west end of town.

A group of eight people sat on sofas overlooking the stage and dance floor. In the centre of the group sat a large, jovial bullfrog of a man with cinnamon skin, a long, thick ebony ponytail streaked with grey, and a small jagged scar on his left cheek. He wore relaxed fit blue Levis, a tie-dyed, button-down hemp shirt over his vast stomach, and Birkenstock sandals. He looked to be in his late forties.

"Hey sister," he said in a deep, gravelly tone, slapping palms with Louisa.

"Garri, bro, how ya doin'?"

"I'm Jane and this is Elena," Jane shouted over the loud music.

"Hello," Elena echoed as Garri shook their hands.

"Enchanted, ladies," he replied, staring at Elena.

Something about him made the hairs on the back of her neck stand on end.

"Name's Garridan but friends call me Garri—with an I."

"You sound Aussie but look like a New Zealander," Jane probed, twirling a strand of her bobbed black hair.

"Tongan," he replied, his luminous grin a stark contrast against his skin. "Well, my father is. I'm Aussie born and bred, like my mother."

"Is Garridan a Tongan name?" Elena quizzed.

"Nah, my Mum just liked unusual names."

He stood up. "What'll you ladies have? Drinks are on me tonight."

"That's kind of you," Jane smiled at him.

"Thanks bro. What are we celebrating?" Louisa squeezed his shoulders.

"The wonder of life!" Garri replied.

"Thank you," Elena echoed.

She sat on a sofa and tried to follow the conversation, but the music was too loud and the conversation banal, so she contributed little. She'd also had a reasonable amount to drink but just as she was contemplating heading home to bed, the group bounded onto the dance floor. It was the perfect moment to escape, but she loved to dance. *Just for a short while*, she thought as she joined them.

Garri shouted the group another round of drinks and Elena felt obliged to accept a vodka she really didn't need, trying not to spill it as she was jostled on the crowded dance floor. She had never stayed out so late nor drank so much over the course of a night.

The tension in her shoulders dissipated. She twirled, finding herself face to face with Garri. He was awkward and uncoordinated, heavy on his feet. She got the impression dancing was not something he often did. Or perhaps it was the effect of too much alcohol— whether on his part or hers she wasn't sure. Smiling politely, she continued to dance. Gaze fixated on her and sporting a clownish grin, he moved closer. Feeling uncomfortable, she stepped back, putting some distance between them but he moved forward, closing the gap. Then he leaned towards her.

Oh my God, he's going to kiss you!

Who does he think he is? She didn't know him, had barely spoken to him throughout the night, felt zero attraction towards him and had given him no possible indication otherwise. As the thoughts flashed through her mind, Elena came to a standstill and their lips met. She raised her hands to push him away, then paused. She didn't want to ruin his celebratory mood. Paralysed by indecision, she let him kiss her, though she struggled with an almost overwhelming sense of revulsion and a desire to put as much distance between them as possible.

Moments later, she found herself at the edge of the dance floor, perched on Garri's knee, legs dangling, feet not quite touching the floor. He was about a head taller than her, which would make him close to six foot—only marginally taller than the average man—but combined with his wide girth, the height discrepancy felt greater. *Geez, I must look tiny in his lap*, she thought. His solid, hairy forearms locked around her waist reminded her of her grandpa's suntanned arms when she had sat on his knee as a child. *How did this happen?* Elena asked herself, in a hazy, alcohol-induced fog. No answer came, and she continued to sit in a dull stupor, captive on his knee, hyper aware of the heaviness of his hand on her thigh while watching people bust their uninhibited, drunken moves on the dance floor.

"I should go home now," Elena said.

"Walk with me," he replied.

"Ok."

No, you'd rather go home now.

She ignored the voice in her head and allowed him to lead her along Hindley Street and up the incline towards Currie Street, holding her hand in a vice-like grip while he peppered her with questions. She noted a slight limp in his gait.

He put his arm around her but the disparity in their height and his limp made it an awkward uphill struggle rather than the romantic stroll she imagined he had intended it to be.

You're wandering around in the dark with a man who could be a murderer for all you know.

She shivered, as much from fear as the cool, early spring morning air. He removed his coat, placing it around her shoulders. She exhaled, unaware she had been holding her breath. A murderer wouldn't be so gallant as to offer her his own coat. But it was still time for her to go home and she had resolved to say as much when his next question stopped her in her tracks.

"How many children do you want?"

Michael had never asked her that question but this jovial character was asking within hours of meeting her.

"Two," she replied. "How many do you want?"

"Well, I was thinking one but I could manage two."

As they walked, her internal dialogue debated the pros and cons of dating him until she realised what she was doing. *What am I thinking? I'm not even attracted to him.*

They sat on a bench in the deserted Light Square and he turned his torso towards her, putting an arm around her shoulders. His right hand rested on her thigh. In the dim light cast by a streetlamp, she noted the letters PAND tattooed on his knuckles.

"What's PAND?"

He removed his left hand from her shoulders and joined the knuckles with the right.

PAND ORA<3

"It's my mother's name."

"That's so sweet!"

"She died eight years ago."

"Oh... I'm sorry."

The air was cold. Even with his enormous coat engulfing her, she shivered.

"What do you feel?" he asked.

She considered the question before answering. "I feel happier with my life than ever before... but I feel a little apprehensive right at the moment."

"Just as I thought," he nodded. "You're disconnected from your body."

"Huh? What do you mean?"

"Well, for example I feel the fresh breeze on my face, my feet in contact with Mother Earth. I feel my heart pumping in my chest."

She blushed. How foolish she was for not understanding his question was about physical sensations rather than emotions. He was obviously more grounded than her.

"Oh I see. Well, I feel cold and tired. In fact, I think it's time for me to go home to a warm bed."

"Are you sure?"

"Yes, I need to go."

They walked down towards North Terrace in search of a taxi, his heavy, hobbled steps thudding next to her dainty clip-clopping heels. His jacket flapped ridiculously around her, making her feel like a child playing dress-up with her father's clothes. She was glad it was now 5 a.m. and even the hardcore partygoers had deserted the streets so there was nobody to witness her fashion faux pas.

A lone taxi sat outside the Casino and, as they approached it, Garridan grabbed her hand.

"Call me."

"I don't have your number," she replied, handing his jacket back and ducking into the taxi.

He thrust his business card at her and gave a nonchalant wave as he turned away.

❦

ELENA WOKE in the early afternoon and pottered around her flat. Thoughts of the previous night popped into her head no matter how hard she tried to shake them off. Louisa was a friend of a colleague and they'd been hitting the clubs together with Jane for the past few months. But Elena didn't know much about her, so the fact that Garridan was her friend wasn't really a solid character reference. Yet he seemed a nice enough person and it would be shallow of her to ignore him just because she didn't find him attractive. In any case, talking with the guy didn't mean she had to date him. She picked up her phone.

"Hi Garridan, this is Elena. We met last night."

"Hi! Good to hear from you."

After a pregnant pause, he peppered her with questions: what she did for work, hobbies, how she knew Louisa. It was difficult to make out what he was saying, and she was mortified she had to keep asking him to repeat himself. His voice sounded muffled. *Was it the roughness of his voice or was there a problem with one of their phones?* She was relieved when they ended the call.

He called her every night for the next three weeks and amazed her with his incredible life story.

"I was a wild child. I think I was such a handful that my parents decided not to have any more kids. At sixteen I ran away to work on a deep-sea fishing trawler."

"Wow! Did you like it?"

"Yeah, turns out I was a born seaman. I started out as a deckhand but showed so much promise that within a year I was promoted to deck boss. A few years later, we ran into a huge storm and ended up shipwrecked in Tonga, of all places. I took it as a sign from the Gods I was supposed to be in the family village so I stayed there."

"What a coincidence! The village must have been a big change for you."

"Yeah, the lifestyle was totally different. I started playing rugby, and they wanted me to play for the national team, but I only wanted to do it for fun. They taught me to hunt but my main role was still fishing. I once caught the biggest fish the village had ever seen, and I always kept everyone well-fed, which pleased the matāpule—that's what they call the Working Chief. He took me under his wing and wanted me to marry his only child, the beautiful Tafotila, so I could inherit his position."

"Seriously?! So what happened?"

"Bah, village life was too boring for me. I wanted excitement. At twenty-three I returned to Adelaide and got caught up with the wrong crowd. I was working for the biggest pimp in town, driving prostitutes to their clients but eventually expanded it into a legitimate chauffeur car business, catering to a variety of clients from my original ladies of the night to teens attending school formals, interstate businessmen and even politicians."

"What an incredibly varied background you have!" Her own life seemed so dull in comparison.

"But the downside of being a self-made man is that the workload impacts on your health, so I sold the business. I needed a break and now I'm on the lookout for something new."

"And your father is still in Adelaide?"

"Nah, when Mum died, he returned to Tonga. Anyway, enough about me, what about you? What do you want in a partner?'

"Oh! Ah...," Caught out, Elena thought back to her ideal partner list and scrambled through a drawer to find it. "Well, he has to be a non-smoker. I hated watching my ex slowly kill himself. Plus I don't want my children to grow up around cigarette smoke."

"I quit smoking a year ago."

"He has to be kind, affectionate, intelligent, able to manage his own finances." She stopped herself before reading the requirement of physical attractiveness. She didn't want to offend him if he asked what attractive was for her. Besides, there were more important things than physical attraction in a relationship.

"Anything else?" he prodded.

"Fit and healthy," she ventured.

"Hmm, I'm not at the moment but, now that I'm not working twenty-four-seven for the business, I can focus more on my health, *mumble, mumble...*"

"Sorry, I didn't catch that last bit."

"I've just joined a gym."

"Great!" He was working on it and he was doing it because he wanted to, not because a partner was nagging him. That was a good sign.

"I want someone who has common interests. He has to like travelling. I've booked a trip to Europe for next year and there's so much of the world I want to see."

"Well, I've seen Tonga and parts of Australia. With the business, I didn't have much time to travel, but it's something I want to do more of."

"And I want to go to the beach, cook and dance together."

"I'm a water baby, you saw me dancing the night we met, and it goes without saying that I love a good feed," he chuckled, his deep voice rumbling down the line.

She laughed involuntarily. Now she was getting to the pointy end. She drew a deep breath.

"I want someone willing to commit to a relationship, who wants to have children and will be open and honest with me."

"We've already discussed children," he replied. "I didn't think I was ready for another relationship yet but when I saw you I knew this would be something special."

"Oh!" His confidence rendered her speechless.

"Is there anything else?" he asked.

Her eye fell on sensitive lover, but she shied away from saying it.

"The last one is very important. He must be interested in self-development. I don't want to be with someone who just coasts through life, existing but not extending themselves and growing. That seems a wasted opportunity."

"I agree. What have you done in the self-development space?"

"I've investigated alternative therapies like Reiki, been to counselling and read some fantastic books. Have you read *Absolute Happiness?*"

"No, but I've got *The Peaceful Warrior* and *mumble, mumble…* I'm Reiki trained too."

He suddenly became a lot more interesting to her.

"That's great! I do yoga now too, and I'm about to start a beginners meditation class at my yoga studio," she said.

"Yeah, I go to a meditation group sometimes, *mumble, mumble, mumble…*"

Every night, she struggled with his muffled voice. Embarrassed to keep asking him to repeat himself, sometimes she pretended to understand, hoping her responses were appropriate.

❧

LOUD MUSIC and laughter emanated from Louisa's house. Elena let herself in the front door, pulling up short as she came face-to-face with Garri. He wore a business suit and tie, his long ponytail and knuckle tattoos the only evidence of his more alternative persona.

"Wow, you're looking very smart!" Elena commented.

"Just arrived here myself after a business dinner," he replied, kissing her cheek. "What are you drinking?"

"A white wine would be lovely, but let me give Louisa her birthday present first."

Garri followed her into the living room and stuck by her side all night.

As the last of the revellers left, Garri handed Elena and Louisa glasses of a peppery shiraz. "One for the road," he smiled, putting his arm around Elena's waist and pressing her against his side.

Louisa did a double-take. "Are you two together?"

Elena blushed and opened her mouth to say no.

"We're hoping to be," Garri cut in.

Elena closed her mouth and ducked her head into his chest to avoid Louisa's gaze. *Am I?* She asked herself. *What do I want?*

Despite having moderated her alcohol consumption, Elena's head was fuzzy. She sipped the shiraz slowly while Garri and Louisa downed their glasses and refilled. As they continued to drink, they became raucous and crude. Elena ignored them, instead turning her attention to browsing Louisa's bookshelf until her head cleared enough to drive home.

Around three in the morning, Louisa lolled on a sofa in a boozy haze. Garri parked himself next to Elena on the other sofa, placing a heavy, possessive hand on her thigh. The book she had been reading lay next to her, and she was struggling to stay awake.

"Tired?"

She nodded.

He put his arm around her shoulders and pulled her head down into his lap, stroking her hair.

Embarrassed to be in such an intimate position, she attempted to rise.

In response, he pressed more firmly on her head, pushing her face into the soft rolls of his vast stomach.

She considered insisting that he allow her to sit up but she didn't have the energy, so she sank into his lap and closed her eyes. Her palm was on Garri's belly and she instinctively began giving him Reiki.

"Yes," said Garri after a few minutes.

"What?" She looked up in confusion.

His eyes met hers. "Yes," he repeated. He was giving her permission to give him Reiki. She realised that she should have asked permission first. Struck by his awareness, it was obvious he did know Reiki. It wasn't just something he had said to impress her. She relaxed and closed her eyes, drifting into a light sleep and awoke a short time later.

"Feel like dancing?" Garri whispered.

"Now?"

"Shh," he said, putting a finger to his lips and jerking his head towards Louisa who was sleeping on the other sofa. "I'll teach you a Tongan war dance, the Kailao. Normally the men do it but you can learn if you want to."

He sat her up, took her hand and led her into the backyard.

They regarded each other as their eyes adjusted to the darkness.

"Follow me," he instructed, picking up a nearby broomstick and beginning to twirl it around while stamping his feet, bouncing into the air and shouting words she didn't understand.

Elena tried to follow his movements but quickly became lost. She giggled.

He grabbed her arm and twirled her around, then kissed her.

He had caught her off-guard again, but this time she was less repulsed. His lips were wet and spongy, engulfing her like a precipitous cloud, but she could probably get accustomed to it if she had to.

"What are you two doing out there?" Louisa's voice interrupted the moment.

With a guilty start, they returned to the living room and Elena made her escape, driving home with the windows down so the blast of cool morning air would keep her awake.

Garri called her each night that week.

"Have dinner with me on Friday. I'll pick you up from work, we'll go to Henley beach."

"It's okay, I can meet you at the beach."

"It's no problem. I'll be waiting outside your office at 6 p.m."

"Well, if you insist."

"Bring an overnight bag with you."

Shocked, she opened her mouth to tell him it was too soon for that but instead uttered a meek agreement.

How was he able to make her feel like such a little girl, like she had no choice but to obey him? She knew it was ridiculous—of course she had a choice. So why couldn't she seem to exercise it?

A shudder ran through her slender frame at the thought of sleeping with him. She would not take a bag to work with her and she would tell him to drop her at home after dinner.

GARRI REFILLED her glass until she lost track of how much wine she'd drunk. *Thank God he's driving*, she thought. She struggled to make out what he was saying during dinner. That same muffled mumble was back, which ruled out a phone reception problem. It was either his gravelly voice or she had developed a hearing problem. As she asked him to repeat himself, she noted that he spoke out of the corner of his mouth, like a smoker speaking while exhaling, the words escaping in a billowing smoke haze, jumbled despite his efforts to control them. Perhaps that was the cause, an unconscious habit picked up from years of smoking.

They left the restaurant. She swayed in her heels as they walked along the Henley Beach jetty, grasping his hand for support while he limped beside her. It was dark except for the dim light cast by the occasional street lamp, and deserted apart from a young family of five walking towards them. Garri stopped in the shadow between two lights, turned her to face him, lifted her up to his eye level and kissed her. She heard the family talking as they drew near. *What must they be thinking at the sight of a tiny rag doll dangling in the arms of a somewhat out-of-shape island warrior?*

He pulled up outside her flat, watching her, waiting for an invitation. It would be rude not to invite him in for coffee when he looked so expectant.

"Er... would you like to come in for a cuppa?"

"I'd love to."

Before she knew it, they were making out on her sofa. For the third time, she had the uneasy, muddleheaded impression she was doing something she didn't want to be doing. A month ago she would have said it was because she didn't know him and was wary about getting involved with any man at this point in her life. But now she worried that she was being shallow, that the only reason she was not comfortable was because she found him decidedly unattractive. The more they spoke, the more he surprised her with his common interests and his desire to get to know her better. He was a nice man with an unfortunate outward appearance, which couldn't be held against him. God knew she had spent many years hoping someone would see past what she had considered her unattractive outer self. It would be hypocritical of her to dismiss him on those same grounds.

Her finger traced the jagged scar on his cheek. "How did this happen?"

"An old war wound courtesy of a pimp's heavies."

Her eyes widened, "What?"

"Don't worry, it's water under the bridge. I tried to protect one of the pros I chauffeured from their pimp. He had a real nasty streak. Didn't appreciate me interfering and sent his goons after me."

What a box of surprises he was.

"Would you like to stay?" The words jumped unbidden out of her mouth. Vaguely aware that she was speaking with an alcohol-befuddled sense of logic, she also figured she would need alcohol to get her through the experience—at least the first time.

"Are you sure?"

She nodded, not trusting herself to speak.

He ripped off his shirt, revealing a tribal tattoo over his right shoulder and the right side of his chest.

She ran a tentative finger along the faded, inky lines.

"Most Tongans tattoo on the leg and hip but I prefer the chest."

"What does it mean?"

"The sun is for leadership, shells for wealth, spearheads for courage and shark teeth for strength and guidance."

Elena opened her mouth to ask if there was a symbol for peace and love but he silenced her with a kiss.

Afterwards, listening to him snore next to her, she felt a little disappointed. She hadn't enjoyed the experience as much as she had with Sam, but it hadn't been terrible. It would just take some getting used to.

THE FOLLOWING WEEKEND, she pulled up outside Garri's Myrtle Bank house and regarded the ramshackle structure before her—the peeling paint, collapsing eaves, knee-high grass and a crumbling concrete path leading up to the verandah. A strong gust of wind would likely flatten the sorry, neglected home.

Inside was no better. The walls of the long central hallway bore the scars of many years of hard living and a dank mustiness hinted at moisture damage. Weary floorboards groaned in protest despite

Elena's lithe footsteps and a long, wispy blade of grass snaked its way between skirting board and wall.

She followed him down the hallway and around the corner to the kitchen, picking her way through piles of yellowing newspapers, crates of wine and other assorted items littering the pathway, trying hard not to show her horror. She couldn't get involved with someone who lived like this. It was the complete opposite to her neat-as-a-pin flat. But she tried to suspend her judgement, reminding herself that he shared the house with two other guys and had moved in only a few months earlier, after being left in financial difficulty when his last relationship ended. He had urgently needed to find cheaper accommodation. The situation had exacerbated his already dire circumstances caused by the enormous legal bills racked up fighting his ex-wife over their combined assets. Things had now improved with the sale of his business but he had yet to organise more permanent living arrangements.

Judging by the state of the house and the thick coating of dust over every surface, it had been in this state well before Garri had arrived on the scene.

Garri gestured for her to sit at the cluttered kitchen table. She cleared a small space to set down the cake container she was carrying.

"Sorry about the mess. It's a bachelor pad. My housemates are hopeless at cleaning up after themselves."

"Don't worry about it," she demurred.

"What have you got there?" He inclined his head towards the container.

"I made apple pie."

"Yum! I could get used to this." He leaned down to kiss her then returned to the stove.

She watched in fascinated disgust as a trail of ants snaked their way through the corner of the kitchen window, across the back of the sink and disappeared behind the stove top.

"Can you pour the wine for us?" He inclined his head towards the bottle of Chalk Hill Shiraz on the table.

"Sure."

Garri set the plates on the table. "I hope you like steak?"

An enormous T-Bone took up half the plate. "In general, I don't eat a lot of meat, but this looks lovely," she replied.

"Well, cheers," he said, holding up his wine glass.

"Cheers," she reciprocated.

"Don't be shy, pour yourself some more wine," he said, indicating her glass, which she had only a quarter filled.

"No, this is fine."

"I insist." Not waiting for a response, he topped up her glass.

After the meal, they moved to the dark lounge room with its dusty shag pile carpet and enormous flat screen TV.

Garri turned the TV on. *The Fault in our Stars* was just starting.

Elena preferred to read the books before watching the movies but she made an exception.

As the movie ended, Garri wiped the tears from her cheeks. "Haven't you ever been loved just for who you are?"

She hesitated before shaking her head. Michael said he loved her but she had never really felt loved when they were together. *Maybe if we had been dying, like Hazel and Gus in the movie, we would have stood a chance*, she thought.

Garri brushed a strand of hair away from her face and kissed her.

"Will you stay the night?"

Elena hesitated again, plagued by an uneasy feeling that, in Garri's mind, their potential relationship was moving faster than she believed it to be. But to say no would ruin this beautiful moment.

His room was a disaster—papers, money, and clothes strewn across the length of the floor. A large, unmade bed sat in the middle, a beat-up computer desk against one wall and piles of moving boxes stacked against an old, wooden built-in closet. The rest of the house could be explained by Garri's housemates but his room was his responsibility alone. However, before she could form a solid opinion on the matter, Garri gathered her in his arms.

From then on, they were always together. He gave her a key to the house. Everything was moving way too fast for her but, swept along by his flood of desire, she couldn't seem to regain her footing. She was uncomfortable about giving him a key to her place but felt compelled to reciprocate and the result was he often spent entire mornings lazing around in her flat after she had gone to work. He played online games on her computer, eating up her small data allowance, and left a trail of debris in his wake for her to clean up.

But he was considerate in other ways, often having a cooked meal ready when she returned from work, or taking her out for dinner. And he was much more affectionate than Michael, although sometimes overly so, leaving her bleary-eyed and befuddled from lack of sleep as she entered work.

Elena was even more glad she had signed up for Jivan's beginners meditation class prior to meeting Garri. It gave her two hours of peace and solitude every week. Yoga classes too became even more of a sanctuary and she felt a renewed sense of gratitude for the mental space it afforded her. Her attendance at the gym was the casualty as she struggled to fit in everything else Garri wanted to do, which didn't include exercise of any form outside the bedroom. Gone were the days of long walks on the beach. Garri's limp was the result of a shattered pelvis courtesy of the same goon who had left the scar on his face. Elena sensed that he hadn't told her the full story, but she refrained from pushing him for answers. According to Garri, he had been lucky to survive and required extensive rehabilitation. Damage to the nerves that ran down his legs had left him in chronic pain for many years and now he had arthritis in the hip. She could only imagine how disheartening it must be to have morphed from an active, fit rugby player to an overweight, sedentary man.

He talked of wanting to lose weight now that the pain levels were manageable, he wasn't working and had the time to exercise, but as yet he hadn't used his gym membership.

"Why don't you come to yoga with me?"

"I can't get into all those bendy positions." He sighed in resignation.

"You don't have to turn yourself inside out to get the benefits of yoga. You only do the poses that your body is capable of and the instructor can give you alternatives for those you can't do. It can be a gentle practice that builds up strength and flexibility without over-straining."

He shook his head, "That might be okay for people with minor injuries, but not for me. When I feel up to it, I'll go to the gym."

"But yoga has additional benefits like promoting mindfulness and helping the body sit in mediation for longer periods."

"My pelvis won't ever allow me to sit for long periods," he refuted, leaving her frustrated that he was so unwilling to consider yoga. He could walk, bend down, he could even carry things, although she suspected he put too much strain on himself by carrying heavy items to prove how strong he still was. It seemed crazy to her that he believed yoga to be beyond him but would carry a heavy piece of furniture on his own without a second thought.

"Okay, I'm going to yoga now. I'll see you in a couple of hours." She kissed him goodbye and closed the rickety front door of his house.

She pulled up outside the yoga studio and sprang out of the car.

Her phone rang. It was Garri.

"Hi, is everything okay?"

"Yes fine, sexy buns. Derek and I are going to the Rob Roy for dinner. Can you join us there after your class?"

Derek was the housemate he spent the most time with.

"I'll be in my yoga clothes."

"That doesn't matter."

"Okay, I'll see you there." She sighed as she hung up. The moments of tranquillity afforded by yoga and meditation were sandwiched between a continual flurry of activity—dinners, movies, amateur theatre shows and live bands in pubs.

Feeling eyes on her, she looked up.

Jivan was standing in the open doorway, staring at her. He crooked a finger, beckoning her.

Class was due to start in three minutes.

She half smiled, half grimaced in apology, turned the phone off and locked the car. "Hi, sorry, I'm coming."

He smiled back.

❦

ELENA FLOATED out to the car after class. She turned her phone back on and listened to the chorus of chimes. Three messages from Garri. They had changed the venue to the Raj on Taj in Unley, he had arrived at the restaurant, what did she want him to order for her?

- Be there in 15 and I'll look at the menu x

She would have preferred to go home for a quiet evening to seal in the benefits of the yoga practice. Reluctantly, she started the car and drove towards Unley.

When she arrived, Garri was in full flight, telling Derek another tale from his past. He often regaled their dinner table guests with outlandish stories of his high-sea adventures, island jaunt and underbelly lifestyle.

"Hi Derek," she said, bending down to kiss his cheek, and then kissing Garri

Garri paused only long enough to give her a quick kiss, then launched back into his story.

"When we came up alongside the ship, I realised something wasn't right."

"Have I heard this story yet?" Elena interjected.

"No. It's when I was on the fishing trawler. We were between Australia and Indonesia and we saw another boat sending a distress signal."

"Okay, no I haven't heard this."

"It was a medium-sized yacht, a bit tatty looking. There were four men yelling that their motor and radio were broken so one of our crew dropped a rope ladder starboard for them to come aboard. I didn't like the look of them. I was in the wheelhouse so I grabbed the pistol we kept there and snuck out the port."

Garri paused for effect.

"Then I heard the yelling. We'd just let pirates on the boat!"

"Pirates still exist?" Elena asked.

"Of course. Not they eye-patch-wearing type like in Peter Pan, but yeah, some men spend their life looking for lone boats that they can rob. Anyway, the pirates had guns, so I kept myself out of sight and waited. They tied up the rest of our crew who were on deck then two of them came towards the wheelhouse. I had a good line of sight and figured it was now or never so shot them both in their trigger arms."

"Geez, mate, that was risky. Why not just let them take whatever valuables they wanted and go?" Derek asked.

"Nobody messes with me." Garri placed his meaty arms on the table and leaned forward. "Once I'd done that, there was no time to waste. I came out, gun blazing and shot the other two. They were running for cover so I got one between the shoulder blades and the other in the leg."

Elena winced. "Did they live?"

"One died before we got them to shore."

Elena winced again.

He saw the look on her face. "I didn't have a choice. They were pirates. Who knows what they might have done to us?"

She didn't like being reminded of his rough past. He was different now—he would never shoot someone or get involved with the wrong crowd, but the fact that he seemed to revel in telling these stories bothered her, and a nagging uneasiness plagued her that, in the constant action of life with Garri, the awareness and focus she had been cultivating was slipping away from her.

On the way home from lunch one Sunday afternoon, Garri suddenly pulled off the main road, following an open inspection sign. They pulled up in front of a new home, sandwiched between older homes in a Norwood side street.

"Shall we take a look, sexy buns?"

"Okay, but I'm not ready to buy. I don't know what I want yet."

They wandered through the immaculate front bedrooms, Garri voicing his likes and dislikes.

"I can't contribute to the deposit," he blurted, "but I can chip in with the repayments."

She blinked in surprise. They had only known each other for three months and hadn't even broached the subject of living together yet. But how to respond without offending him?

"You don't have any savings?" she asked, sidestepping the real issue.

"Not really, the bitch took care of that thanks to the legal fees for our divorce settlement."

"Was it difficult to come to an agreement?"

"You could say that. She insisted on keeping the house, arguing that her family inheritance had paid the deposit but ignoring that I had contributed to the mortgage *and* supported her when she was out of work."

Elena's uneasiness grew. "What happened in the end?"

"By the time the court case finished, we had to sell the house to pay the lawyers. Neither of us got a bloody cent!"

Elena pitied him. Her experience in wrangling over property

settlement details was nothing compared to what he had been through. How lucky she had been!

"And I discovered my accountant had been siphoning cash out of the business and I had to liquidate it," Garri continued.

"Hang on, I thought you *sold* the business?"

"Yes, this time I did. But my first business was liquidated when it didn't have the cash to pay creditors. I started up again under a new name, working my arse off to keep things afloat."

"What did the accountant do with the money he stole?"

"I don't know." He shrugged. "I never found out."

"But wasn't it investigated? There must have been some kind of trail. Bank records, purchase records, *something?!*"

"The police started investigating him but I didn't want to take it to court. I was already spending all my energy and money on divorce matters. I didn't have anything left for fraud investigations."

"Oh, what bad timing! But were you allowed to start the business up again?" She didn't know much about business laws but she was sure some restrictions must apply.

"I wasn't allowed to become a company director again for five years but my father was willing to be the director. He was just a figurehead for ASIC purposes, though. I still owned and ran the business."

"What's ASIC?"

"The Australian Securities and Investments Commission. They regulate businesses in Australia."

"Wasn't what you did illegal?"

He shrugged again. "Technically, no... Anyway, it wasn't my fault the business failed. I was running a good business, I just trusted my accountant too much and he robbed me blind. I shouldn't be penalised for that. I knew the business was making a profit and had loyal customers, plus I had staff relying on me for their livelihood."

She understood his point of view. It wasn't as if he were being irresponsible in setting up another business to fail. He knew it was profitable. He should have paid closer attention to the bookwork the first time around but hindsight was a wonderful thing.

They entered the open-plan kitchen and living area overlooking the back yard. The agent was busy conversing with the only other couple in the house.

Garri put his arms around her. "Can you see us living here? Watching the kids play in the backyard while we cook dinner?"

It amazed her she had found a man who was so in favour of having children. Her heart overflowed with affection and she kissed him.

In response, he dragged her through the house to the main bedroom and inclined his head suggestively at the bed, "Whaddaya say to a quickie, sexy buns?"

"We can't! It's an open house. Anyone could come in!"

He shrugged and smiled. "So? It would give them something to talk about."

She shook her head and turned to leave, straining against him as he tugged her arm and laughed at her obvious embarrassment.

She wished he wouldn't call her 'sexy buns', wished he would pick a more respectful term of endearment. Sometimes he called her darling, but even that didn't feel right. It sounded false and contrived every time he uttered it. Perhaps her problem was she wasn't used to men addressing her with terms of endearment. Michael had never called her by a pet name. So she kept her disquiet to herself. Given time, she would get used to this strange new phenomenon.

ELENA LAY on Jivan's massage table, undecided on whether to mention Garri. She felt guilty. Not the all-consuming guilt that had plagued her towards the end of her marriage, but a niggling sensation that perhaps she was making a bad choice. Jivan might be disappointed in her for allowing herself to be swayed by someone else's desires before she had given herself enough time to focus on her own self-development. She couldn't imagine Jivan ever being so easily swayed.

"I've met someone," she blurted out.

"*Have you?*" He exclaimed, the strength of his outburst surprising her. "Why didn't you tell me?"

"Well, I wasn't sure. We only met a few months ago, and he's got a bit of a chequered past."

"The past doesn't matter. It's about the person now. If the person is right for you, their past won't matter."

She nodded. Did it matter to her? Was Garri the right person?

"Well, I've met someone too." His hands expertly kneaded her upper back muscles.

Her breath caught in her throat as a sharp pain stabbed her chest. She took a few moments to identify the sensation as jealousy. *What is wrong with me? I should be happy for him.* Forcing the unwanted emotion back down into the dark recesses of her being, she concentrated on formulating a suitable reply.

"Oh, really? So how can you be upset with me for not telling you I had met someone when you didn't tell me you had met someone either?!"

"Well, yes good point," She sensed his shrug, "but I wasn't sure either at first."

A silence ensued as Elena fought the urge to ask him about his new friend. It was none of her business but her curiosity won.

"What's her name?"

"Lakshmi."

"That sounds like a good Indian name." She'd had a hunch his preference would be for a partner from his own culture.

"Ye-e-e-s," he replied, drawing out the vowel in an endearing manner. They fell silent again.

"You're making good progress," he said at the end of her session.

"Yes, I can feel a difference. Sorting things out with Michael, the gym and yoga have all helped reduce the tension."

"Hey, do you remember when you first came here, how tight your neck was? I could lift your head away from the table then let go, and it would stay suspended there of its own accord!"

She chuckled, "Yes, I know."

"But now it's improving. I think we can space the massages out to every three weeks."

Chuffed as she was at her progress, she was also sad that the time between their private chats would grow longer. His yoga classes were supportive and relaxing, but there were always many students vying for his attention so she looked forward to her massages and their talks about yoga and travel. She loved to hear stories of his global adventures. But she knew she shouldn't be greedy. There were plenty of other people who also needed his help.

Chapter Twelve

FOUR GREY WALLS

They lay together on Elena's bed, Garri surfing Facebook on his phone.

"I think it's time I look for a bigger place. There's not enough room here for both of us."

Garri's head snapped up and he dropped his phone on the bed. "I was thinking it's about time I find somewhere else too. The share house was only a temporary measure to help me out of a tight spot. Where shall we look?"

Elena hesitated. "Er,… so… do you mean you would like to move in together?" she ventured.

"If that's what you want?" His eyes sparkled with delight.

She had meant the question to be a clarification, not an invitation. Plus, she preferred to buy instead of renting but she didn't want to buy with Garri. It was far too soon for that. She had to consider his existence in her life and accommodate him but if she bought a property, would Garri move himself in permanently? Would he contribute to expenses? If so, would that mean he had a right to part-ownership? She didn't want to end up in that kind of commitment by default but she was afraid to ask the questions in case it opened a floodgate. A safer option would be to keep renting for now but that meant finding somewhere bigger to rent in the interim.

He continued, not waiting for her answer. "I'm okay with it if you are."

Maybe it wasn't such a bad idea. They seemed to get along well. They'd had fun together the past few months. Renting together would be a good test and, if it didn't work out, they were free to go their separate ways once the lease ended.

She smiled. "Yes, I'm happy to rent together."

He gathered her in his arms then, a few minutes later, grabbed his phone.

"Which areas shall we look in, sexy buns?"

"I like the beach, but it might be better to be halfway between the beach and the city to reduce the peak hour commute. Plympton or maybe Cowandilla?"

"I'm thinking Unley or Kensington, somewhere just outside the city."

"They're expensive suburbs." She didn't want to waste money on rent that could be saved to buy her own home.

"It's not that bad, look." He searched for rental properties from Wayville to St Peters. Some were double her current rent but, with them both sharing the cost, they could afford to live in a beautiful, convenient area.

"But your share would be more than you're currently paying," she countered.

"It's okay. I've still got the business income."

"Huh? What business income? You sold the business."

"Steve couldn't afford to pay outright so he's... *mumble, mumble...*"

"What?"

"He's on a rent-to-own plan."

Why did nothing about his business transactions seem straightforward? Whilst she didn't have a head for business, she nevertheless had a hunch something was amiss.

"Are you allowed to 'rent-to-own' a business?"

"It's just a contract between the two of us. Remember I told you I couldn't own a business because of the liquidation? So how would I explain a large cash transaction for the sale?"

Her head was starting to ache. She didn't like it at all, but he had assured her one of the reasons he wanted to walk away from the business was because he didn't want any ties with his past. He wanted to operate on the right side of the law.

"Hey, sexy buns, if you want to stay beachside, what do you think of this?"

The ocean-front mansion on the screen was in Tennyson, arguably the most prestigious suburb for ocean-front living. The advertised property had five bedrooms.

"Do you want to split the rent with housemates?" She was dubious about getting into a share house situation just for the sake of living in a beautiful home. Her privacy was worth more to her than prestige.

"It's not for rent, it's for sale."

"Are you crazy? I can't afford that!"

"No," he said, choosing his words carefully, "but if we get a group of us together, we could do it. Louisa wants to buy soon. You can ask Jane, too. One of my housemates might even be interested—I think Derek is keen to buy something. Between five of us, we could cover the repayments."

Buying into a house with friends was even less appealing to her than renting with them.

"Even if we could cover the repayments, we'd still need the twenty percent deposit. I don't have that much cash and I'm sure Louisa and Jane don't either. Even between us we'd be stretched."

Garri was undeterred. "You have half the deposit already and between the rest of us, we should be able to come up with the other half. I don't have savings but I could chip in by paying a larger share of the repayments to compensate. Jane already has a house, so if she sells it, she should have enough for her share, and Louisa and Derek must have some kind of deposit."

He had an answer for everything, but still she hesitated. "If people don't put in equal amounts, that could cause problems when we need to sell."

He swatted away her feeble excuse. "We'll sign a contract stating what percentage we get of the sale based on how much we put in to begin with."

"If you're not contributing any deposit, but you are contributing repayments, where does that leave you?"

"We can work that out based on what everyone agrees is a fair amount. It's not a problem." His eyes gleamed with excitement. "Imagine living in a beachfront mansion!"

She wanted to share in his excitement, but felt only dread. "What about stamp duty? That would be huge! We wouldn't have enough to cover stamp duty and the deposit together."

"Some banks lend with only ten percent deposit these days. We could make it work."

She shook her head. "You don't even know if everyone would be willing to make a group purchase."

"So we'll ask them! There's no harm in asking."

"I dunno, I'm not comfortable getting into financial deals with people. I'd rather wait and buy a cheaper place on my own."

Garri tried to hide his disappointment. "Okay, sexy buns, whatever you want."

❧

"THIS IS AWESOME!" Garri enthused, standing in the middle of the downstairs open-plan living area of a renovated, two bedroom townhouse in a semi-commercial street in Dulwich.

Elena walked outside, eyeing the postage-stamp sized, paved backyard and the greyish brick walls with distaste. "The inside is great, but I'd prefer a little greenery. I miss not having a garden."

"We can buy some big planter boxes for you," Garri suggested.

"It might not be safe outside business hours when a lot of buildings are empty," she countered.

He put an arm around her. "Don't worry, nobody will hurt you while I'm around."

They stood looking back through the glass sliding door to the sleek, modern interior.

"Whaddaya think, darling? It's a good area and your share of the rent will be the same as you're paying now. Shall we do it?"

She smiled at his enthusiasm, "Okay, let's do it."

"Can you cover the bond and advance rent? I don't have enough cash at present."

"Oh!... Okay."

"I'll get Derek to help me move our furniture." His housemate Derek was a thickset, stocky, middle-aged man. Between the two of them, they were probably strong enough to do it but she worried about Garri putting weight on his pelvis.

"That's sweet of you, but it would be much easier and safer if I hire a removal company."

"I insist. You cover the bond and advance rent and I'll take care of the move."

"Okay." Elena smiled, holding her hands up in mock defeat.

They took another look around inside before approaching the agent for an application form and heading back out the front door.

Elena took one last look behind her. "It only has two rooms upstairs but I suppose we could turn the study into a bedroom if a child comes along."

"A child?"

"Yeah, if we have a baby."

"Are you sure you want my baby? It'll be a heifer and giving birth will probably tear you apart." He flashed a toothy grin, his eyes twinkling in amusement.

A molten anger exploded out of her before she could control herself. "*Really?!* You think that's so funny?" She turned and stalked down the driveway.

"Whoa, whoa," Garri came limping after her. "I was only joking."

Elena rounded on him. "Yeah, well you wouldn't be laughing if you were the one who had to give birth!"

"I'm sorry." Garri held up his hands to ward off the verbal blow.

Elena continued to her car and threw herself into the driver's seat while Garri trailed behind. As she watched him get into the passenger seat, she started to cool down.

"I'm sorry," she said, embarrassed by her violent response.

Garri just stared at her.

"It's not something to joke about, though."

"Sorry, I didn't know it would bother you," he replied, somewhat subdued.

"Don't worry about it," Elena muttered as she turned the engine on.

❦

THE SATURDAY BEFORE THE MOVE, Garri stayed at her apartment. They went for a walk on the beach and ate fish and chips on the sand while watching the sun dip below a pink-tinged horizon. She enjoyed these easy going moments with him.

The weather was still warm enough during the day for summer dresses, but as soon as the sun made its descent, the air became too cool for her pastel pink maxi dress. She shivered and Garri pulled her close, wrapping her in a warm bear hug.

She leaned into him. "I should have worn something warmer."

He tightened his grip around her. "I like that you wear dresses."

"Why?"

With a mischievous glint in his eye he shoved a hand up her dress and reached for her crotch. "Easy access!"

She squirmed, pushing his hand away.

"What's the matter? Don't fancy a quick shag on the sand?" he teased her.

Two people walking past snapped their heads around and peered in Garri's direction. The last remnants of light still provided enough illumination to make out their faces.

Elena blushed crimson. "Stop it, we're in public."

"So?" he shrugged, "I'm not afraid of an audience." He crept a hairy, arachnid hand towards the hem of her dress again.

She swatted him away and pulled her dress tight around her thighs, tucking her legs behind her. He laughed and leaned into her, trailing a finger down the side of her breast.

"No? You don't want to put on a show?"

"Stop it!" Horrified, she leaned away from him.

"Haven't you ever had a public shag?"

"No," she winced, wishing he'd just drop the subject.

"I have. In side-alleys near clubs, a golf course, the parklands…" He trailed off at her horrified expression.

"Oh I see I will have to tone it down. I think I'm a bit crude for you."

Yes, you are, she thought, regretting the decision to move in with him. But, more upsetting than his crudeness was the thought of him changing to suit her.

"I don't want you to change to suit me," she blurted. "You are who you are and if that doesn't fit well with me, then better we go our separate ways than have you try to be someone you're not. The worst mistake I made was staying with Michael, hoping that he would change, that I could help him become the person I wanted him to be. Now I don't want to be with someone unless who they are is right for me."

An anxious constriction made its way from her diaphragm through her chest and up into her throat, making her choke on the last few words.

Garri looked startled. "It's okay. I need to tone it down, anyway. With all the important business people I'll be contacting soon to set up a new business, I need to be more refined."

She wanted to believe him. "Okay, as long as you do it for you and not for my benefit."

"Don't worry, I'm not doing it for you." He hesitated. "That brings me to another point. I've been thinking about whether I want to have children."

"What?"

"I don't know whether kids is something I want or if it's something I was going to do because you want them."

"What do you mean?"

"Kids tie you down. I want to travel the world. That's a very different lifestyle—travelling with kids can be expensive. Wouldn't you like to travel with me and live in different places?"

"Yes, you know I would. But it's not impossible to travel with kids."

He shrugged. "But kids restrict where you can travel and what experiences you can have."

Her consternation increased. "I thought Tongan culture was all about family?"

"I'm only half-Tongan."

She hated how Garri so easily ripped the rug out from under her. How *dare* he wait until they had committed to moving in together before dropping this bombshell!

"You were the one who asked me how many kids I wanted! On the first night we met!" she exploded, fighting back angry tears.

His face became an image of solicitude. "Yes, I know, sexy buns. I'm just not sure I want that anymore. I'm not saying I don't. I'm just being honest with you. Things change, people's priorities change. I love you and I want to be with you, but I can't give you an answer about kids yet."

Her anger dissipated and she slumped in a deflated heap. His desire for children was the one thing she had thought was a given.

He picked up her hand, caressing the back of it with his thumb. "Can you just give me time to think about it? Is that okay?"

She stared at the dark outline of his face. The last of the light had gone and she struggled to make out his expression.

"Okay," she sighed. "Let's go home."

❧

"I've got a part-time job, sexy buns."

"Fantastic!" After months of non-stop eating, drinking and playing computer games, this was welcome news. She understood he had needed a break after years of hard work, but she was just about fed up with his slovenly behaviour. It was time to get back in the game before his brain turned to mush.

"What's the job?"

"Joe, a wealthy Italian importer, needs someone trustworthy to chauffeur the important international and interstate clients he entertains on weekends."

"Wow, how did you hear about that?"

"He's a friend of a friend who heard about my reputation within the industry. I'm contracted to work Friday and Saturday nights and the occasional Sunday."

"Great!"

"Yeah, and even better, he's paying me tax-free."

Elena's elation sank. "I thought you wanted to leave illegal activities behind you?"

Garri winked at her. "Tax-free is nothing to worry about, darling. Many people do under-the-table trades, and why shouldn't they? The government wastes so much of the working man's taxes. Why give them more if we don't have to?"

"Hmm." She didn't like it, but didn't dwell on her disquiet for long because her own job was consuming her thoughts of late. She had made considerable progress on her project, getting a completed picture book draft out for comment and reworking it a few times over. She had settled on a yellow lycra-clad cartoon hero called Bright Spark, an electrical charge in the form of a boy whose job was to explain how people could save on their energy bills and help the environment at the same time. Bright Spark took a child on an 'electrific' tour through the wires and circuits of their own home, showing how much energy was wasted and where it could be conserved. One of his super powers was the ability to convey humans through an electrical current by protecting them with his energy shield and shrinking them to the size of an electron.

The draft had received the thumbs up from their small kid sample and was now in the hands of a professional copy editor. They found a local illustrator whose quote was more reasonable than she had expected and the whole contract engagement process was quick and smooth. She discussed her ideas with the illustrator and he soon had concept drafts to her for comment. The pie-in-the-sky idea was morphing into something tangible and her anxiousness over needing to do a good job was being overlaid with a bubbling excitement.

Writing the book had unleashed a creative side Elena hadn't known existed. Her creativity radar was picking up all kinds of signals which had previously been out of range, like the fabulous Adelaide Fringe Festival.

Elena checked her watch. "The opening parade starts in an hour, we should leave soon if we're going to walk into the city."

"Ready when you are."

Elena grabbed a light jacket. The day was warm but it could get cool when the sun went down.

"Let's go," Garri grabbed her hand, leading her out the door.

They walked hand-in-hand across Fullarton Road and cut through the parklands surrounding the city centre. Dry gum leaves crunched underfoot, releasing a minty, honeyed scent.

I need to get out into nature more, she thought.

"We're so lucky to have a city full of parks and gardens," Elena commented.

"Yeah, and great bars and restaurants," Garri replied.

"We have great quality food but I'd prefer a picnic in the park on a sunny day over sitting in a crowded restaurant."

"You haven't experienced the best restaurants, then. A high-quality restaurant has plenty of space, good ambience and better food than you could ever pack in a picnic basket."

Elena didn't agree but she remained quiet. There was no point getting into an argument over it. Garri loved to dine out. Elena wasn't used to eating out so much. Her savings plan had gone out the window when she met Garri, although it didn't cost her as much as it could have. She paid when they ate alone but Garri insisted on paying whenever they were with friends, and there were often friends sharing their table. It made her uncomfortable though. She would have preferred they pay equal shares. His friends probably thought she was a kept woman.

When they reached Hutt Street, it was teeming with glittery, colourful Fringe Festival parade revellers and a surge of people heading to The Garden of Unearthly Delights. Despite her misgivings, Elena allowed Garri to lead her into the street. As they shuffled forward, getting jostled in the sea of people, someone in a gorilla costume charged past them, dodging and weaving, pushing people out of the way, almost climbing over them in his haste. As Elena watched the gorilla barrel his way through the crowd, an elbow connected with the spot between her shoulder blades, shoving her into Garri. Winded, Elena watched as a guy dressed as Batman pursued the gorilla, leaping through the infinitesimal gap between the people in front of her.

Garri gave chase, still holding firmly onto Elena. He dragged her along behind him as he shoved people out of the way in his single-minded determination to catch the guy who had pushed them.

"Garri, stop!" Elena tried to pull him back.

Garri glanced back in irritation before yanking her onward. Elena, not wanting to be a part of the madness, finally managed to extricate herself from Garri's grasp. She fell back into the crowd. "Garri, that's enough!"

He ignored her feeble calls.

Elena caught up with him outside The Garden of Unearthly Delights just as Garri collared Batman.

"Hey bro, you owe my woman an apology."

"Sorry man, I didn't mean to hurt anyone." Intimidated by Garri's threatening demeanour, he backed away with raised palms.

Elena cringed at Garri's own reckless behaviour. She hadn't seen this side to him before. Until now he had seemed gentle—sometimes crude but never violent. She resented being referred to as his woman. It made her feel like the possession of a Neanderthal thug.

She half expected him to beat his chest and declare, "Me Tarzan, You Jane."

"We, or someone else in the crowd, could have been hurt," Elena reproached him.

"Nah, I wouldn't let any harm come to you."

She opened her mouth to berate him, but stopped. If she examined the situation from his point of view, he was looking after her, demanding an apology from those who had treated her with disrespect. It was actually a bit cute, in a thuggish kind of way.

༻❀༺

ELENA GAWPED at the cover of her new Bright Spark book laying on the kitchen bench. She was unable to get her head around the idea that something she had written existed in all its printed glory. The graphics were amazing and the colour scheme so vibrant. The last four months had been a hard slog to get it ready for publication, but seeing the finished product, it had all been worth it.

"I read it to the daughter of a colleague today and it kept her attention, so that's a good sign," she commented to Garri, while cutting carrots for their dinner as Garri fried the schnitzels.

Garri put his arms around her. "That's because it's good, sexy buns. I'm proud of you. When you told me you were writing a book, I didn't think it would be that good... I mean, I knew you would do a good job, but I didn't expect it would be *that* good."

It was such a novel experience to be with a man who found her efforts worthy of praise. She still had nagging doubts about whether they were compatible as partners but at moments like this, she was grateful to have him in her life.

"I don't want to ruin your moment but I've got some bad news, sexy buns," Garri continued.

"What's wrong?"

"Steve can't afford to pay me for the business. He hasn't been keeping on top of chasing creditors and he's lost a few big customers. We're approaching a tipping point of more cash going out than coming in."

"So what now?" Elena was nervous. They were only seven months into their two-year lease. She was already paying all the utility bills. He had contributed for the first few months, but now, even when he offered to pay, he never quite got around to doing so before the due date and Elena would find overdue bills in the study. If she had to cover his share of the rent too, it would eat up most of her pay cheque.

"It's okay. It's just temporary until Steve gets the business back on its feet. I'll have to spend time with him, get him straightened out."

"What if it's too late?"

"I've got savings to cover the rent for a while."

Savings? She was glad he had a buffer, but he'd led her to believe he had no savings. Where finances were concerned, she never knew where he stood. She wasn't sure how much he earned from his part-time job, or what he owed on his car loan or credit cards. In contrast, he knew her income and the extent of her savings.

"But I need to know what I'm up for if I have to take over all your car and credit card repayments," she ventured.

"Don't worry, it won't come to that."

She wanted to know, just in case, but refrained from pushing him for more information. He had enough stress at the moment watching his well-respected business teeter on the brink through misman-agement.

What if the business had already been sinking and he'd chosen to leave rather than be at the helm when it went under?

She pushed the thought away. If she couldn't trust and support her partner then what good was she? Garri had never given her anything but support and praise and here she was suspecting him of dishonesty.

❦

GARRI WAS SITTING at the dining table waiting for her when she came home from work. "Hey sexy buns, I need to talk to you about some-thing." His cajoling voice followed her into the laundry as she kicked off her shoes.

An unexpected sense of foreboding stopped her mid-step. Taking a shaky inward breath, she returned to the living area.

"Hmm... what's that?"

"I heard from my father today."

"Really? Is that good?" Something had happened between Garri and his father. He wouldn't say what, but they hadn't spoken in four years.

"He's got leukaemia."

"Oh! I'm sorry," she said, hugging him.

"He wants to see me. I should fly to Tonga as soon as possible."

"Yes, of course. Do you want me to come with you?"

"I'd love you to come," he held her at arms-length, staring into her eyes, "but I think it might be better I see him on my own first, given how strained our relationship has been."

Something in his eyes didn't look right. *Is there something he's not telling me? But how could it be any more serious than one of humanities' greatest fears—cancer?*

"Okay, of course. When do you plan to leave?"

"Well, that's the thing. Last minute flights are expensive. The only seats available are business class and I can't afford to splurge right now."

"How much do you need?"

"The flight leaving tomorrow evening is two thousand dollars."

"Don't worry, I'll pay for it."   "Thanks, darling... He's in the hospital in Nuku'alofa so I'll need to stay in a nearby hotel instead of in the family village."

"Okay."

"... plus food money... I think *mumble, mumble...* should about do it."

"Sorry, how much do you need?"

"Four thousand should cover me for two weeks."

Elena gulped. "I'll transfer it to your account now."

Garri placed a moist kiss on her forehead, "Thanks, darl." He got up and dished out the pot of stew he had made for dinner.

"That means you'll be coming home when I leave for my Europe trip. Should I cancel it? I've got insurance."

"No, you go and enjoy yourself. You've been waiting all year for it."

"Are you sure?"

"Yes, I'm sure. Now eat," he said, handing her a bowl.

She took a bite. "Thank you, this is yummy!" It was still a novelty to have a man cook for her.

"You're welcome."

Garri cleaned his plate in record time and scraped his chair back. "I'm going to take a shower."

"Okay." She watched him plod upstairs. He was clearly worried about his dad, but she didn't know what to say. Everything she thought of seemed so inadequate.

She cleared the table and washed the dishes then climbed the stairs, hearing Garri opening and closing cupboard doors.

He looked up as she came in the bedroom. His half-full suitcase lay on the floor.

"Can I help?" she offered.

"Nah." He sank onto the edge of the bed and held out his arms. "Come here."

Elena squeezed him tight.

His hands wandered to her hips, her backside, then up the length of her back, crushing her to him.

Elena blinked in surprise. The last thing she thought he would feel like right now was sex. It was the last thing she felt like. In fact, she had been avoiding sex of late. For some reason, the thought of it left a bad taste in her mouth. But Garri needed comforting and he was going away for two weeks. She dithered between wanting to pull away and give in to his advances until guilt got the better of her and she responded to him.

Afterwards, he fell asleep, his arm draped heavy across her body, the hand grasping her breast. She eased herself away from his grasp but he stirred, groped for her and pulled her back towards him. She sighed and tried to fall asleep.

❧

GARRI MESSAGED HER ON ARRIVAL.

- *I'm here safe n sound. Hotel wifi isn't working so we can't Skype. Love u sexy buns x*

- *Have u been to the hospital yet? x*

- *2morro x*

- *Ok, rest up. I love u x*

After work, Elena was greeted by gridlocked city streets. An accident had blocked up all the southern and eastern parts of the city centre. Cursing, she inched forwards, stuck in the jam and forced to head north instead of due east. Thanks to city roadworks, the detour took her all the way to North Terrace.

As she came to a standstill just past the railway station, she turned her head and saw a man ducking into the casino entrance. She only glimpsed the back of him but the stature and long dark ponytail reminded her of Garri. From the back, it would be hard to tell the two of them apart.

A long horn blast from behind brought her attention back to the road.

"Yeah, yeah, ok," she said, putting the car in gear and lurching forwards.

Finally reaching home, she fixed herself a quick dinner then messaged Garri.

- How is my Tongan warrior?

He didn't reply. *Must be with his father*, she thought, and put the phone aside. She wandered into the study and surveyed his myriad of boxes still stacked precariously against the wall, containing papers which needed sorting through before being filed or disposed of. Some boxes were bursting at the seams, the packing tape lifted to show a jumble of tattered files. He had promised to sort it when they moved in but clearly preferred to spend his spare time playing military shoot 'em up games.

She couldn't face starting on the boxes tonight so she cleaned up the piles of never-ending paperwork on his desk. It amazed her how he could accumulate so many papers. She ordered them into overdue bills and receipts. There were numerous random scraps of paper with handwritten calculations, but Elena could make no sense of them. She placed them in a pile of their own. When she had filed everything, she felt a little better. Even if she could do nothing else to help Garri, at least she could create order in this small part of their life.

Her computer was still on the floor under the desk where it had been since moving day. Garri's executive sized, walnut corner desk took up so much of the room that her desk couldn't fit. It had instead become a haven for redback spiders in the backyard and she had been using Garri's computer when he wasn't using it—which wasn't very often. Elena clenched her jaw and averted her gaze. *No point getting angry. He can't remedy the situation from Tonga.*

Her phone buzzed. Garri was calling her via the Skype app.

"Hi sexy buns. The wifi is so bad here I can't video call, but voice calls are working at the moment."

"How was the flight?"

"Good. It's late here now, but I wanted to call you."

"Is the hotel ok, apart from the bad wifi?"

"Yeah, it's lovely."

"Hey, I saw your doppelgänger tonight in town."

There was a slight pause. "Huh?"

"You know, someone who looks like you—well, at least the back of him looked like you. He was entering the casino as I drove past."

"Oh! Well, how about that, hey? Sexy buns? Can you hear me?"

"Yeah, I hear you fine."

"I can't hear you, must have a bad line."

"I'm here, I can hear you."

"Not sure if you can hear me, sexy buns. I have to go now but I love you and I'll let you know what happens with Dad when I see him tomorrow."

"Love you too," Elena said as the connection was cut.

Over the next week, wifi issues meant contact with Garri was limited to a few messages and a Skype phone call one night. He was distracted and not forthcoming with information. He must be still in shock, she thought. After years of no contact, he was suddenly on speaking terms again with his father but also dealing with the reality that he could soon lose him forever.

- How is everyone? x

- Dad's not so good, he's weak from the treatment. Turns out he's had leukaemia a while but only told me because he hasn't beaten it as fast as he hoped. x

She opened the picture Garri attached. His frail, anaemic-looking father stared back at her from a hospital bed.

- I'm glad u 2 r patching things up but I'm sorry it had 2 be this way :(hugs 2 everyone. BTW Derek rang 2 check in, c if we needed anything. He's a good friend x

- Here's a pic of me with some of the family

The photo showed him with a dozen aunts, uncles and cousins, against a backdrop of lush green foliage. At least everyone was smiling and looked in good spirits.

    - Lovely, is that a new t-shirt? I haven't seen u wear it b4.

    - Nah, I've got clothes I left here last time I visited. x

                    ꗊ

GARRI WAS SITTING on the sofa when Elena returned from work.

She kissed his forehead. "Welcome home! How are you?"

"Tired, sexy buns but God it's good to see you!" He stood and hugged her fiercely.

"And your father, how is he?"

Garri sagged back into the sofa. "As well as can be expected."

She sat next to him. "Want to talk about it?"

"I can't at the moment. Just pray he recovers soon."

Her suitcase sat at the door, ready for her flight to Europe the next day.

"I feel bad going away while your father is so ill."

"I told you it's fine. Don't worry about it." He sounded snippy.

"I'm sorry, I didn't mean to offend you."

Garri sighed and pulled her towards him, kissing her forehead. "No, I'm sorry. I'm just tired and worried."

Chapter Thirteen

THE WEB WAS WOVEN CURIOUSLY

A s Elena walked down the gangway to the aircraft waiting to take her to Europe, her excitement was overpowered by an anxiety so strong she almost turned and ran back into Garri's arms. Doubts threatened to overwhelm her. *What am I doing? What do I know about travelling? What if the plane crashes or I have an accident or get separated from my tour group?* Trying to ignore the irrational fears and her hammering heart, she boarded the plane. She couldn't back out now! Everything was organised and paid for. She had waited so long for this chance to be completely unfettered and independent.

Almost thirty hours later, the plane arrived at Heathrow in the early evening. So exhausted that even the enormous labyrinth of terminals didn't raise her anxiety levels, she found her way down to the Underground in a daze and caught the crowded train that her map said would take her close to her hotel.

In the morning, the tour headed across the English Channel to France, beginning a frantic but fun month-long journey which left Elena no time to think of the possible dangers she may have faced on her travels. With only a few days in each city and a lot of time spent travelling between locations, they had time only to see the most popular tourist attractions. Elena lamented the inability to explore at her leisure and resolved to return one day to discover more of the varied European cultures steeped in history.

She watched the endless fields of sunflowers in the northern

Spanish countryside pass by the coach window, wishing they could stop to explore the scenery. Sting's *Fields of Gold* began to play on her iPod. She imagined the two lovers in the song dancing amongst the golden flowers and then, years later, watching as their children ran through the same field. Oh how she wanted that kind of experience! She wanted a tender, respectful relationship with a man, and children of her own.

As she gazed dreamily out the window, they passed a couple wrapped in each other's arms amongst the swaying sunflowers. She could have sworn the woman looked like herself. But the man looked nothing like Garri. He was much smaller, with short, dark hair. He was more like Jivan. She craned her neck, trying to catch another glimpse of the couple as the coach sped onwards.

With a guilty start, she realised she hadn't thought of Garri much at all during the trip, she had been too busy drinking in the sights and sounds of summertime Europe. She had texted him a few times but no more often than her parents or Marcus, and she hadn't replied to every message he sent. She could only message if there was wifi, which often the hotels didn't provide free of charge. Garri had called her one night, but she wouldn't have been upset to not speak to him.

Was being in the moment rather than thinking of home selfish? Was she a bad partner because she was enjoying being left in peace to sleep at night instead of dealing with his constantly roaming hands? She had to admit that sharing a bed with him was taking its toll. She liked that he was affectionate, but sometimes she wanted affection without the inevitable sex that defined *affection a la Garri*. She craved being able to sleep undisturbed instead of waking up to being groped in the early hours of the morning. It was like sharing a bed with an octopus. No matter how far away she moved, she was never out of reach of those tentacles. She thought back to all the years she had shared a bed with Michael, wishing he would take down the invisible wall between them and allow a little affection into the marriage bed. Now she wished she could have that wall at her disposal, although she was sure those tentacles would find a way to reach her no matter how high she built the wall.

She caught herself mid-thought and sighed in frustration. Now that she had the affection she wanted, it was too much. Would she never be satisfied? She resolved to practice more gratitude and toler-ance towards Garri when she returned home.

Their last week passed in a blur. The weather in Germany and Switzerland was cold despite it being still summer, and half the bus caught the sniffles. Elena caught the virus two days before flying home and boarded the plane exhausted, muddle-headed and blocked up. She walked into Garri's arms at the airport even more exhausted, then spent the best part of the next week sleeping during the day and roaming the townhouse at night until both the cold and the jet lag subsided. But the cold had irritated her lungs and she suffered the return of a persistent asthma cough.

Elena woke herself up coughing and reached for the Ventolin puffer. The clock read 3 a.m. but Garri wasn't in bed. She checked the study and bathroom then descended the stairs, crossed the darkened living room and flicked on the outside light. Garri, clad in his dressing gown, spun around as she opened the sliding glass door to the backyard, his eyes flickering surprise and guilt. Hanging from his fingers was a half-smoked cigarette.

"You startled me. I didn't hear you coming," he said, recovering his composure and turning away from her to take another drag.

"What are you *doing?*"

He shrugged.

"Why? You gave up smoking!"

He shrugged again. "All the sitting in my car on weekends is causing pain in my legs again so I need something to ease it. It's okay, it's not a *mumble, mumble…*"

"It's not what?"

"It's not a ciggie, it's a reefer."

She had thought the smell oddly sweet but wasn't experienced enough to recognise it. "Dope! How is that better than a cigarette?"

"It's natural, no chemicals like ciggies, and it's not addictive. I've stopped smoking joints before and I'll stop again soon."

"Cannabis is illegal."

"Medical marijuana is legal in some countries, you know. It's a soft drug. Lots of people use it, I used to use it for the pain."

"Yes, but it's not legal here! Why don't you take legal painkillers?"

"They have other health side-effects."

"Oh, but cannabis is so good for your brain, I suppose?" Her voice dripped sarcasm. An image of her ideal partner checklist flashed into her mind. The list of the things she hadn't already compromised was fast dwindling. He was still extremely unfit and hadn't used the gym membership he had boasted about when they first met. He didn't know if he wanted to have children, he spent his time shooting imaginary enemies on the computer screen instead of meditating or talking with her, and now he was smoking dope. Angry, she glared at him, stomped inside and threw herself back on the bed.

But by the morning, she had forgiven him enough to hold a normal conversation. It was difficult to maintain outward signs of anger with her guilt-wracked conscience always reminding her to 'do unto others as you would have them do unto you.'

"How is your father this week? Have you spoken to him?" She asked while preparing breakfast.

"No, I got a message from an aunty saying he's doing ok. Still in treatment but he hasn't gotten any worse."

"That's good news I guess. I'd like to meet him one day. Maybe we could Skype?"

"Maybe." Garri sipped a coffee while waiting for the toast to brown. "I've decided we can have a kid, sexy buns."

Elena spun around, butter knife in hand. "Really?!"

"Yes, after what's happened with Dad, it made me realise how important family is. You're my family, so if it makes you happy, I'll do it."

Her heart softened, letting go of the last of the anger she had been holding onto. "I'm glad you decided that, but if we have children, you need to actually want them, not just be doing it for me. If we have them and you don't want them, they will know. They will sense it."

"It's okay, sexy buns, I'm happy to do it."

"And I don't want to bring children up in a smoker's house—dope or nicotine."

"Don't worry, it's just a momentary relapse. I've stopped before and I'll do it again."

She hugged him. Just when she was having second thoughts about him, he did something to restore her hope and gratitude. She was so grateful this time that she couldn't even stay annoyed with him for not unpacking the boxes in the study as he had promised to do before she returned from Europe, even though she failed to understand how someone who worked so few hours each week couldn't have found time during the past eight months to unpack one room. Instead of badgering him, she set about sorting it herself. She unpacked his books into the shelves. He had some interesting titles like *The Peaceful Warrior* and *A New Earth* but he never seemed keen to discuss them with her. In fact, most of the books appeared brand new. No dog ears, no creased covers or tattered edges. The pages still sat flush together the way new books did before they had been pawed by an avid reader. She looked at her bookshelf, full of well-read books. *Perhaps my books should be more like his, pristine and well-cared-for,* she mused.

More like ignored, with the hidden gems left undiscovered between the covers.

She pushed the pesky, judgmental voice away and moved on to sorting his files into the cabinets.

His desk was full of his paraphernalia: little boxes of paperclips, bull dog clips, staplers of various sizes, pens and markers of every colour in plastic holders, and document trays full of a random assortment of papers which followed no logical filing sequence. She fought down her growing annoyance at the way he spread himself around and consumed space without a thought for her.

Don't sweat the small stuff, she scolded herself.

Garri came in as she stood gazing over his little empire.

"Thanks, sexy buns It's looking good."

She pointed at her computer on the floor. "My computer won't fit on your desk and there isn't space for even a small second desk."

"I know, darling, but I need the whole desk."

"Why?"

"Joe has offered me a business proposition. He has his own system for Forex trading but doesn't have enough free time. I've got the time, so he wants to train me to do it. You didn't think I was just playing games in here, did you? Soon I'll be hosting Joe's clients here for meetings and I need everything at hand."

Elena knew little of Foreign Exchange Trading, but enough to know it was risky. "Is it wise to gamble like that?"

"Don't worry, it's a fail-proof system, easy money… and you can use my computer when I don't need it."

She sighed. The sight of her computer shoved under the desk annoyed her. "I may as well get rid of mine and buy a laptop. Then I won't need a desk."

"Are you sure, sexy buns?"

"Yes, I'll find someone to give it to."

"Derek will take it. He needs a new computer, but he can't afford to buy one."

Derek was a good sort, always willing to help them. "Okay, let him have it."

Garri gave her a wet, sloppy kiss and settled in front of the computer to play World of Warcraft.

Elena chose a good book in which to bury herself, trying to ignore the intense stiffness that had taken hold of her left shoulder and the referred pain running down her arm. She gave it a violent shake, to no effect. Just as well she was seeing Jivan soon. He would sort it out for her.

※

FOR A WHILE, life was good. Garri's father's condition was stable, they dined with friends, took country drives on weekends, and even joined a new meditation group together, one that Garri thought would be better than Jivan's group. Elena had her doubts but agreed to try. She was self-conscious around the more experienced meditators like Garri, who had meditated on and off for years. The facilitator, Rosemary, was a friendly, quirky Irish woman with bright purple hair. Her strong, foul-mouthed persona created an atmosphere at odds with Elena's idea of a peaceful meditation sanctuary, but she ran some fascinating guided meditations and Garri enjoyed it so Elena continued to attend.

At the end of each session, people shared their experiences. For the first few months, Elena contributed little. She felt inadequate for not experiencing the fantastic images that others described. Garri always seemed to drop into meditations with ease and regaled them with descriptions of himself as a sword-wielding mediaeval knight or a Native American warrior. He was always fighting for the underdog, meting out justice or saving damsels in distress. Rosemary would nod sagely at his descriptions and tell him he'd seen himself in a past life.

Elena still wasn't sold on the reincarnation theory. On one level it made sense that existence was a circle of life, death and rebirth. All religious texts talked about being 'born again'. Most religions interpreted it as symbolic rather than literal, but why not literal? If you believed in the entire world being drowned except for those on a wooden, floating zoo, then why not believe in literal rebirth? It made as much sense to her as anything else religion offered on the topic of life after death. What she didn't understand was how anyone could actually *know* what their past lives were. How could one differentiate between a vision of a previous life and the product of a vivid imagination?

She sounded out Jivan after yoga class. "Do you think reincarnation is possible?"

"Yes, of course. That's how the universe works. We are born, we live a life, gain experiences and knowledge, then we die and get to do it all over again. We have experiences to teach us lessons and if we fail to learn the lesson, we get it again in the next life, and the one after and the one after that."

"But how do you know that?"

"I just do. We can see the cycle mirrored within a single lifetime. We all know people who repeatedly attract the same situations, issues or types of partners. Those around them shake their heads in wonder that the person can't see their own pattern. But the person living the experience doesn't see what the onlookers see because they haven't learned the lesson yet. The universe keeps sending us the same situations until we learn the lesson."

Elena absorbed his words, mulling them over. "That kind of makes sense," she offered.

"You can see your own past lives if you want to," he said, stacking the yoga blankets back on the shelf.

"How?"

"You can buy books that help you with techniques, or go to people who do past life regression work. I meditate with the intention that I want to see a past life. I've done it a few times." He sat on the bench to put his shoes on.

"Really?" Elena sat next to him and reached for her shoes.

"Hmm, but the last time I saw myself being killed, so I stopped doing it. A very unpleasant experience." She felt him shiver beside her.

"What else did you see?"

"One time I saw myself as a peasant, another time as part of a Native American tribe."

Fascinated, Elena wondered if she would ever be able to see her own past lives. Jivan was such an interesting person, full of insights and self-confidence. But it was nothing like Garri's blustery bravado. With Jivan, it was an unassuming, matter of fact, 'I'm laying my cards on the table and you can decide what to make of them' approach. Jivan was passionate about many things and held strong views, but he never tried to either force them on her or cajole her into accepting them. There was no need within him to convert everyone to his world view.

On the drive home and as she entered the house, Elena continued to think about Jivan.

"Sexy buns?" Garri's voice called Elena out of her reverie.

"Hmm, yes?"

"I was just wondering why you don't often give your opinions or express how you feel?" He sat next to her on the sofa, clanging his mug onto the coffee table.

"Um…" Thrown by the question and unaware she was still doing it to such an obvious degree, she gave it some thought before responding. "I guess I've spent so many years burying my feelings because I believed I wasn't allowed to have them, let alone express them. Especially anger, fear and sadness. It's a conditioning that began in my childhood and was strongly reinforced by my ex-husband who made it clear he didn't want to hear my thoughts or feelings. I still struggle with identifying what I'm feeling. You'll notice that sometimes my answer is that I don't know, but I come back to you later once I've identified and processed it."

"That makes sense." He nodded.

Sometimes she also refrained from saying how she felt in the interest of keeping the peace. If it wasn't something important or life-changing, there was no point making an issue of it. For instance, all the damage he caused to both of their possessions, largely through lack of attention: scratched furniture, broken appliances, and the day when he'd misjudged the carpark and scraped the length of her car along a concrete pillar. Elena hadn't been able to hide her frustration but had succeeded at least in keeping her mouth shut. It was an accident and he had apologised. The perfectionist in her had wanted to keep it pristine, but she recognised a car's purpose was to take her places, which it could still do with scratches. She sighed in resignation. His life was full of unnecessary dings and, by default, hers was now too.

He may be like a bull in a china shop but he paid attention to detail in other ways, like massaging her shoulders while they watched TV and surprising her with exquisite beribboned packages of her favourite Haigh's chocolates—a selection of truffles, cherry bars, chocolate-coated nuts or peppermint frogs. She loved that he would do it for no reason other than because he had thought of her and wanted to please her.

❧

ELENA STRUGGLED to focus on Rosemary's guided meditation. Something about the ocean, swimming with dolphins, and tall, thin, pale Pleiadeans—whatever they were. But her mind kept wandering to a different scene. Eventually she stopped fighting it, tuned Rosemary out and focussed on the image in her mind's eye.

She was standing in a big, open room on the top floor of a solid sandstone building. A short, dark haired man in a white linen suit sat on the ledge of an arched window, gazing back into the room. She found his calm observation of her embarrassing and looked away. When she raised her eyes to meet his again, she observed the resigned sadness in his eyes. He leaned backwards and her heart leapt into her throat. She wanted to tell him not to jump but she couldn't speak. She wanted to run to him but her feet felt glued to the floor. Just as he began to fall, she realised that he resembled Jivan, which was enough to uproot her, but she reached the window too late. As she leaned out the window, their eyes locked. His piercing eyes questioned her. She jumped onto the ledge, hesitated as she saw how high they were, then took a deep breath and threw herself after him, arms outstretched. They fell in slow motion, reaching for each other... and then she was jolted into the present by Rosemary's voice calling them back.

Darn Rosemary for interrupting at the crucial point! Now the outcome is beyond my reach. Did I reach him? Did we soar through the sky together towards new adventures, or plummet to the ground, to a messy ending?

Elena listened to the others recount their experiences and then it was her turn. She didn't mention the identity of the man and hurried through her description, hoping her embarrassment was not evident.

"The message for you is to just do it! Don't let your fears stop you," Rosemary advised.

Elena nodded. *But do what?* she thought?

She was still mulling it over as they drove home.

"I have some bad news," Garri said, drawing her out of her reverie.

"More bad news?"

"Steve's lost the business."

"I thought you were helping Steve sort it out? Why didn't you intervene earlier? You had time to chase overdue accounts yourself."

"The clients believed it was Steve's business, so I had to let him run it."

"But while he still owes you money, it's your business too. You are relying on it as much as him."

"To be honest, it wouldn't have looked good if I interfered. Plus I've been occupied with the Forex set-up."

In her view, his livelihood was more important than appearances and it was smarter to put effort into a proven business which was paying the bills rather than gamble on the Foreign Exchange Market.

"So what are you going to do if it's too late to save the business? What will you do for income? Take on more chauffeur jobs?"

"No, my legs can't handle more time sitting in cars. Don't worry, it won't be long until I'm making shitloads through Forex."

She didn't like him putting all his eggs in one basket but he was so confident about it that she couldn't squash his spirit.

Chapter Fourteen

HER BLOOD WAS FROZEN SLOWLY

O n New Year's Eve, Garri and Elena dined on the beachfront with Derek, Louisa, Jane and her new partner Dale. The restaurant owners adorned the group with festive, plastic lei which matched Garri's lurid pink Hawaiian shirt.

He's like a chameleon, Elena thought, *one day a serious corporate suit, the next a laid-back hippie, and other times what could best be described as luridly camp.*

Cafe del Mar tunes serenaded them until the midnight fireworks, then Garri ordered a bottle of Penfolds Bin 389.

"It's not Grange," he apologised to the group, "but it's still a very nice drop."

"It's not necessary, mate. There are plenty of good quality wines for less than forty dollars," Derek protested and the rest of the group voiced their agreement.

"Nonsense. It's New Year's Eve, I'm enjoying your wonderful company and I want to treat you all to a good vintage."

Elena sneaked a glance at the wine list and gulped. *Ninety dollars a bottle!*

As the wine flowed, Garri entertained them with stories from his past.

"I broke up a fight on the rugby field one day. At the end of a game, Tonga versus Samoa, tensions were already high when one of our players tackled a Samoan player and they ended up in a brawl.

Next thing we know, it's turned into a free-for-all. I come running up from full back and there's a pile of six players all laying into each other."

"Rugby players aren't small," Louisa said.

"That's an understatement. We were all big buggers... anyway, I start pulling men off each other, roaring at them to get a hold of themselves and copping a few blows in the process. One of the guys I pulled off tried to run past me back into the melee so I cuffed him by the back of the shirt and threw him backwards. I'm breaking up the last two players and this guy king hits me from behind. I'm seeing stars but I stumble to my feet and deck him, knocking him out cold."

Dale and Derek whistled under their breath.

Garri grinned, his chest puffing in pride.

Elena was silent. These brawn before brain stories didn't impress her. She caught Jane's eye and they exchanged a look.

Something teased at the edge of her consciousness. He'd told her something about playing Rugby in Tonga when they first met.

"I was under the impression you didn't play in the national league," she blurted as the memory surfaced.

Garri blinked in surprise. "Yes, of course I did. But only for one season. All that seriousness took the fun out of it for me."

"Ah, okay."

As the clock struck three, Garri bundled a sleepy Elena into a taxi. When they reached home, he insisted on carrying her up the stairs and collapsed onto the bed with her still in his arms. She was tipsy and very relaxed, so relaxed that she responded to his kisses without having to fight the instinctive resistance that had become commonplace in response to his advances of late.

A strange vision flashed across her mind and her body stiffened. She saw herself as a prisoner of war, held within a large stone building that might have been a castle judging by the lofty ceiling and thick stone walls. But she couldn't inspect the building for herself because she was tied to a hospital gurney in a row of gurneys that ran the length of one wall. Women on other gurneys were in various stages of labour or in the process of being impregnated by men in wartime uniforms. The sounds of fear and pain bounced off the walls, crowding together, creating a sense of claustrophobia in the otherwise spacious room.

Elena watched in terror as a white-coated doctor advanced on her with a scalpel, focussed on her bare, swollen belly. She gripped the sides of the gurney, her breath coming in shallow, shaky bursts as she waited for him to cut into her abdomen without the aid of anaesthesia. The double doors to her right swung open and soldiers wheeled another gurney into the room. Her panicked eyes met those of the soldier standing guard outside the door. His lips curled in an amused, heartless grin. She had considered calling out to him for help, but his obvious mirth at her distress caused the cry to stick in her throat. Horrified, she couldn't tear her eyes away from him. As they stared, eyes locked on one another, she recognised him as Garri. He didn't physically resemble him, but she knew that the soul behind those eyes was Garri. Just before the door closed, the soldier smacked his fist into the palm of his other hand. A word was tattooed on his knuckles—PANDORA.

The whole scene flashed across her mind in an instant yet it seemed she was living out the sequence of events in slow motion. Paralysed by shock, she was aware of Garri still moving on top of her in the real world but, disconnected from her body, she felt nothing. As her consciousness returned to the room, Garri climaxed and rolled off her, reaching out to pull her into his side. He had no idea anything was wrong.

Elena didn't know how, but she was convinced, with every fibre of her being, that she had seen the two of them in a past life.

Rolling away from him, she scooted as close to her edge of the bed as possible but his tentacles found her and drew her towards him again.

She shivered.

"What's wrong, sexy buns?"

Traumatised, she lay still, wishing he wouldn't touch her while she tried to process the whirlwind of emotions the vision had brought up.

"Nothing, I just need to sleep."

Sleep was the furthest thing from her mind but she didn't have the words to explain herself. He would be offended if she pushed him away so she waited for him to fall asleep before she inched her way out of his arms and curled up in the foetal position, re-running the images through her mind as she tried to make sense of them.

Completely at his mercy in that lifetime, he had shown her none. She couldn't get her head around the fact that the man next to her was the same person. It was even harder to comprehend how she could now be so certain that people existed across multiple lifetimes, that they were souls which travelled across time and space. Yet know it she did. Her dubiousness of reincarnation was a thing of the past.

She now also understood why she had harboured an irrational fear since childhood of having to undergo stomach surgery, why the thought of appendicitis used to keep her awake, panicking she would have to have her stomach cut open. It explained why she feared child-birth and a potential C-section. Her soul bore a deep scar inflicted by a doctor who was more interested in experimenting than in her wellbeing.

It also explained why she became so incensed whenever Garri taunted her about the potential pain involved with her giving birth to his future child. Despite his initial contrition, he had continued to drop hints and seemed to delight in warning her that his child would likely be a hefty bub. Garri had laughed at her pain and distress in a previous life and he was still laughing at her prospective distress in this lifetime.

Elena had the urge to break up with Garri, to run as far away as possible, and she started planning her exit strategy before catching herself in mid-thought. Just because something bad had happened between them in the past didn't mean she had to let it ruin their relationship now. They were different people now. Garri was more gentle and caring. Even Jivan, after meeting him, had said he seemed a gentle person. She trusted Jivan's judgement.

The next day, despite still being freaked out, she recounted her experience to Garri. He stared at her with a sadness in his kind brown eyes. He had believed in reincarnation long before she had ever considered it a possibility so she knew he didn't think she'd lost her mind. It was as much an unpleasant shock for him as for her. If she were in his place, the information would be distressing to her too. She wondered if she should have kept her mouth shut, but she knew she couldn't keep something like this to herself. If they couldn't talk about stuff like this, there would be no hope of developing the strong, honest connection that she needed and wanted with a partner. She'd had no choice but to tell him.

Elena tried to forget the experience, but her newfound knowledge didn't want to leave quietly. She picked up a health and lifestyle magazine left in the work lunch room and an article recounting the author's experience of a planned natural home birth going wrong jumped out at her. The message of the article was the need to make plans but detach from the outcomes so we can more easily adapt when things do not go according to plan. What a woman could control was her reaction to the circumstances of the birth, reducing the trauma and emotional stress caused by her inability to make the experience what she had wanted and planned. For Elena, it was a pertinent example of the yogic philosophy of detachment which brought fluidity, ease and grace rather than mental and emotional anguish from holding onto what could have or should have been, but wasn't.

After digesting the first half of the article, Elena decided that she couldn't continue to allow this particular fear to run her life. If she wanted children, she had to accept the risks that came with the territory. All she could do was remain focussed on providing herself and her child the best possible experience rather than focus on what might go wrong.

The weight of the fear she had carried for many years lifted from her shoulders. She returned to the article more serene and a little closer to being willing to commit to having a child with Garri. The serenity lasted only as long as she took to read the next sentences.

'It is important for a woman to be emotionally supported and relaxed. She, her partner and medical staff need to work together to provide a loving, peaceful environment for the baby's arrival, regardless of the circumstances.'

There was the real crux of the matter. She wasn't confident Garri could support her in the way she needed to be supported, or to help create the loving environment so important for such a significant occasion as the entry of a new soul into the world. Garri's presence didn't feel right for her and her child. She feared he would treat labour as light-heartedly as he treated everything else, not recognising the sacredness of the moment nor the sacrifice she would be making to bring a life into the world.

If she analysed the situation rationally, Garri was a decent person who was always willing to help his friends, saw it as his role in life to stand up for underdogs, and he loved Elena. Why was that not enough for her? The more she thought about it, the more confused she became and decided this was something she must keep to herself until she had answers. If she spoke to him about it now, it would be yet another revelation to hurt him when she couldn't even explain herself properly. He had enough to worry about with his father's illness. Plus she didn't want to risk having his arguments confuse her further. He could be very persuasive when he wanted something and she knew herself well enough to know she would cave in to his assurances even if she wasn't convinced. She mustn't say anything until she had her thoughts clear in her own mind.

❦

As ELENA ENTERED the house after work, Garri looked up from the PlayStation. "I've chucked in the chauffeur job, sexy buns."

"Why?"

"My legs are giving me too much grief from all the sitting. Even the cannabis isn't helping like it used to."

"Please, go to a doctor!"

"I'll go tomorrow. Don't worry about the job. I'll have more time now for the Forex training and soon I'll be ready to start trading."

Elena bit her lip to stop a negative comment escaping. He had been training full-time for four months. She didn't understand why he wasn't ready to start working yet. "Ok, but take care. Sitting for hours in front of a screen isn't good for your legs either."

"At least I can stand and stretch at home when it gets bad. I can't do that in a car."

She worried as he did the rounds of doctors and pain specialists, with no reported improvement of his symptoms. Life spiralled out of control as Garri lived on painkillers and spent long hours sleeping. When not sleeping, he was glued to the PlayStation or computer, shooting at graphic targets to keep his mind off the pain.

He no longer had time for her. He used to at least pause his games to kiss her and ask about her day when she came home from work.

Now all she received was a distracted hello while he continued spraying bullets at his screen victims.

⸻

ELENA COULD HEAR Garri on the phone in the study. "Of course I'm not avoiding you!"

His voice softened to a murmur and Elena crept closer to hear.

"Ok, I'll see you tomorrow."

She entered the study. "What was that about?"

Garri spun around, startled. "Just a friend."

"Why do they think you're avoiding them?"

He ran his hands down his face with a weary sigh and turned back to the computer screen. "My old business still owes money to a friend who helped me set it up. He's mad as hell and wants his money back."

"Oh my God! What else can go wrong?"

"He's a bastard, I shouldn't have let him get involved in the first place," he complained. "It's all about money to him. He lent me the money at a steep interest rate because he knew I couldn't get a bank loan and had no other options. Then he hounded me to pay him back. I was working like a dog to raise the cash as fast as possible. He couldn't even give me time to get everything established properly."

Elena massaged her spasming neck and shoulder muscles. "But you didn't pay him back."

"I managed to pay half before I sold the business but it just about killed me. He wasn't supportive at all."

Elena made a few small noises she hoped sounded supportive.

"Regardless, it seems he helped you when nobody else was willing."

"True, but he lent the money to the business, so he needs to chase Steve for the remainder."

"Was Steve aware of the debt when he took over the business?"

"He's denied it but I'm sure I told him!"

A sense of foreboding descended on her. "Is there a written contract?"

"Yeah, I've got it somewhere."

"You need to sort this out before he ends up paying for a situation he didn't create."

"I know, I'll sort it." He slammed papers around the desk.

"I hope so."

"Just leave it, will you! I said I'd sort it." He turned back to his computer game, slamming the mouse on the desk.

"I'm going for a walk." She left the room in a huff, mad but not prepared to push him further while he was in such constant pain.

The door slammed on her way out. She flinched at the sound, pushed the guilty feeling away and stalked over to the parklands bordering Fullarton Road. She picked up a thin, dry branch from under a tree and slashed at the grass as she walked, trying to swing the tension out of her shoulders.

His financial situation was an increasing source of contention. He still refused to give her information she needed to create a budget, reiterating that he would let her know when his savings ran out and he needed her to take over his share of the rent. But it wouldn't be just the rent. It would be whatever he owed on his credit cards and his car loan. Then there was car insurance and registration, health insurance premiums, the gym membership he still hadn't cancelled. The list was endless but he seemed to think she would have an equally endless supply of cash once he had exhausted his own savings.

Elena dropped the branch and rolled her shoulders. Her entire back felt like a block of wood. She kneeled in the brittle, end-of-summer grass and pushed herself up into downward dog. That would stretch out her back.

"Uff," Elena collapsed onto the ground, clutching at her foot. *Damn cramps!* They had disappeared after she left Michael but reappeared a few months ago.

She massaged the foot until the cramp finally subsided and, feeling sorry for herself, hobbled home.

❧

"Do you feel like doing something this weekend?" Elena asked Garri.

He shook his head, eyes glued to the computer.

"It's nice weather. We could go for a walk."

"My legs hurt."

"A drive in the country?"

"Nah."

"We could see if Louisa or Derek want to catch up for brunch."

"Cheaper to eat at home."

"Yes but we hardly ever eat out now. It can be my treat," Elena offered.

"Thanks but I'd rather stay home."

In the past he never would have knocked back a meal offer, especially if it involved catching up with friends. He had become such a recluse. Even his interest in sex had reduced. The only thing he hadn't given up was the dope. She worried that it would only cause him further harm and impair his ability to recover, but he said he needed it to cope with the pain, so giving up would have to wait until he was better.

His change in personality worried her. He was reminding her of Michael, although really, the dope aside, Elena was happy to have earlier nights and quiet weekends and his libido had been too much for her, anyway. The change in lifestyle suited her, bringing her closer to the person she had been before she had met Garri. She even stopped dying her hair black, feeling a desire to return to her more authentic self. But her relief at rediscovering that part of herself was tinged with guilt that it had come at Garri's expense.

With more time and energy to invest elsewhere, she started working on a second book. The first book had met organisational requirements and was well received by kids and teachers alike. Now the business wanted a picture book explaining how energy was distributed to houses, how turning on a switch made lights work and how children could stay safe around power points. She attacked the challenge with gusto and, after speaking to some technicians to ensure she had her science correct, had produced a first draft in record time. The editing, illustration and publishing stages were faster and easier now that the team had experience in such matters and it wasn't long before she held her second book in her hand: Bright Spark's Safety Tips.

She was also drafting manuscripts of her own and even writing poetry. A floodgate had opened and the ideas were pouring out of her.

Elena saved the poem she was working on, stretched, laid her laptop on the sofa and wandered upstairs to the study to check on Garri.

"Feel like a bite to eat?" she asked.

"Not really."

She hovered by the door. "How is your dad doing? You haven't mentioned him in a while."

"Not good. I spoke to him yesterday, actually. He's stopped responding to treatment and unless there's a sudden change, the doc is giving him two to three months max."

Elena hugged him. "Oh my God, I'm sorry." She felt so inept. His father was dying and all she could manage was, 'I'm sorry'.

"There is one more option, a new treatment they could try."

"That's great! He *is* going to try it, isn't he?"

"It's expensive… the family can't afford it…"

"Oh…"

The silence stretched out for an eternity.

"I wish I could pay for his treatment…," Garri broke the silence. "You know, I thought I'd never get another chance with Dad and now that I have, I can't do a damn thing to help him."

"How much will it cost?"

"Sixty-five thousand."

"Whoa!"

He turned his pleading eyes towards her. "Would you be willing to lend us the money, sexy buns? We'll pay you back as soon as we can."

Her heart stopped. "It's a lot of money."

"I know. You don't have to say yes. I told Dad I'd ask you but it's your decision."

That money was her life savings, for her future house… but a life was worth more than a house and Garri needed her support, especially now that he had rekindled his relationship with his father.

She fought the sense of foreboding which descended on her.

No! Say no!

What the hell was wrong with her? Family was more important than money.

"Ok… but I can't transfer such a large sum. I'll have to get a bank cheque for you."

"Thanks darling. Dad will really appreciate it." He kissed her.

❦

AN UNCONTROLLABLE TREMBLE took over Elena's entire body. With jerky movements, she made her way along the city footpath. As the bank drew nearer, she stopped short. Her heart contracted in her chest and dread flooded her entire being. She struggled within, trying to force herself forwards while her body seemed possessed by a force intent on stopping her. But she couldn't back out now. She had promised Garri the money. He was relying on her. Perhaps the message in her meditation about Jivan was meant for this purpose. She should make herself do it despite her fear. Continuing the internal pep talk, she entered the bank.

It took forever to have the cheque drawn. She suppressed the urge to ask the teller to cancel her request. Eventually, cheque in her shaking hand, she headed for the office. It burned a hole in her pocket all day and she handed it over to Garri that night with a lingering sensation of dread coupled with relief that she had made herself follow through with her promise.

Garri took the cheque with a nonchalant thank you and a peck on the cheek as if she had just handed him a cup of coffee and the morning paper.

❦

ELENA DRIFTED off on her own tangent again. Once she let go of her need to 'do it correctly' by following Rosemary's guided meditation, she saw herself in the Botanic Gardens, sitting cross-legged on the grass next to the lotus pond. Jivan was walking towards her. When he had appeared in her previous meditation, she hadn't been able to make out his features clearly, but this time there was no mistaking him. He sat cross legged opposite her and offered her a red rose. She accepted it, surprised, pleased, embarrassed and unsure of his intention. Was it a friendship offering or something more? They sat in silence, she awkward and uncomfortable, he emotionally removed, a patient observer waiting for her to engage in conversation with him. But afraid she might say the wrong thing, she remained silent, tongue-tied, fidgeting with the rose petals. Jivan stood and backed away, his piercing eyes fixed on her, a sadness in their depths. Not a single word had been spoken between them.

Deep waves of sadness and loss washed over Elena. She wanted to call out for him to stay but she knew attempting to change his mind would be futile, so she remained silent, watching him back away. When he was out of sight, she looked down to see she had completely stripped the rose bare of its petals.

Look what you've done, you silly girl. Now you've lost his beautiful presence and you don't even have the rose to remember him by.

Her inner voice was relentless in its judgement. Mourning the destruction of his precious gift, she wallowed in her sorrow for what seemed an eternity. When she looked up, he was walking towards her again. In near disbelief, she watched as he again sat across from her and held out a second rose. She accepted the rose with a tearful smile and suddenly their limbs were entwined, together their bodies forming the shape of a pretzel which rocked with a gentle seesawing action on the grass.

Elena emerged from the meditation so stunned that she didn't even have the presence of mind to consider whether she should share the experience with the group, instead blurting it out when it was her turn.

Rosemary inclined her head. "You two have a special connection."

Elena was pleased, embarrassed and confused in equal measure. She wasn't even sure Jivan considered her a friend or if she was just another client to him. Yet she had to agree that she felt a special connection, even if it were only one-way.

She was secretly glad that Garri, who had stopped meditating, wasn't there to hear the discussion.

There had been little change to Garri's condition. Some days the pain was bearable, other days painkillers were his best friend. He said the pain was affecting his memory, although Elena suspected it was more the cannabis than the pain. He remained at home, saying he was working on the Forex trades for Joe. Elena was becoming increasingly nervous. Whenever she tried to find out the exact state of his affairs, she always received the same vague answer—he was watching the market and making small trades, enough for pocket money now but later the big bucks would roll in as the profits increased.

It enraged her that he wouldn't give her details.

She walked in the door and dropped her bag on the sofa.

Garri looked up, mixing the last of the Milo into a cup of hot milk on the kitchen bench. "How was meditation?"

"Good. Everyone says hello and they hope you can come back soon."

Garri nodded and sipped the Milo.

"What have you been up to today?"

"The usual, doing some trades. I did do some calculations of the profits we will make once we've hit the ideal trading conditions."

"Really." Elena, feeling the energy drain out of her, collapsed onto the sofa.

"Yeah, it's huge!" His eyes sparkled. "I'll be raking in six figures and I'm going to buy houses at the beach, in the hills and a penthouse in the city. That will come in handy when we want to go into town for the night."

Elena ran a hand across her brow. She'd heard this all before. Planning for when he'd 'made it' was his new favourite pastime.

"We don't go out at night anymore."

"Yeah... but we will when I'm feeling better again."

"So you want to live in the city centre?" Elena wasn't so keen on that. It was greener and more peaceful in the suburbs.

"No, the penthouse will only be when we need somewhere to crash for the night. We'll live at the beach in summer and in the hills during winter. Imagine the log fireplace, the fog outside."

"So you don't want to rent them out?"

"No, I want them all at my disposal so we can move location whenever we feel like it."

"Huh."

"I'll need an SUV to live in the hills, a sedan for the city, and a convertible for the beach—maybe a Maserati."

Elena listened with half-hearted interest. One house, reliable cars, stable incomes, no financial issues and the ability to travel would satisfy her. But if he wanted more and was able to make it materialise, she wouldn't argue.

"When I refine my strategy, I'll be making enough to support both of us so you can focus on writing."

She smiled, liking the idea of being free to write. But she wouldn't be comfortable relying entirely on him. She was too independent for that.

"Yeah, I'll take care of everything and I'll give you a few hundred dollars a week spending money."

Her smile disappeared. It sounded like she would be owned by him, under his control and at his mercy.

"Of course, you'll need me to manage your affairs once you start earning money from writing, too."

"Why?"

"Because I've got the business background. You'll need my help to be a success."

Her skin prickled and her left shoulder twitched. Did he think she couldn't succeed on her own? She didn't reply, not trusting herself to speak lest it cause an argument.

She mulled the idea over for the next few weeks, wondering if she were being unreasonable. Offering to provide for her, if circumstances allowed, was very generous. Was she being too proud and stubborn in wanting greater control over her own financial life? Should she be more grateful? They were questions she didn't have answers for.

☙

"How is your dad?" Elena asked over a late Saturday breakfast of bacon and eggs.

Garri put down his fork and looked at her, eyes wide with excitement. "I spoke to him during the week. The treatment has worked wonders and the doc says he'll be in full remission soon!"

"Why didn't you tell me? That's awesome news!" Elena enthused. Between the cannabis and painkillers, Garri's memory was getting so bad. He never updated her about his father's progress without her prompting. "Maybe we can all Skype one weekend when he's feeling better, I still haven't met him."

"He'd love to meet you too, sexy buns, but better to wait until he's feeling and looking himself again."

"I don't care how he looks."

"Yeah, but he cares. Give him time."

"Okay. What about Steve and the business loan, is that sorted out yet?"

"Not yet. I'm meeting him and the creditor again on Wednesday night, so I'll be home late… hey there's something I need to tell you."

"What?"

"I had a little setback with a Forex trade."

"What happened?"

"Joe told me to trade some of his clients' investment funds and I lost half of it. I wasn't concentrating because I'd taken painkillers. I shouldn't have been trading at the time but it seemed like an opportunity too good to miss."

He had tried to explain the Forex process to her but all the talk of trading currency pairs and aiming for strong win:loss ratios to offset the poor risk:reward ratios gave her a headache, so she didn't ask for details.

"Do you think you can make the money back again?"

"Of course. Even the most successful Forex traders have more losses than wins over a given period."

Elena shook her head, not understanding how more losses than wins translated into success.

"But the clients aren't happy," Garri continued, not looking at her. "They're threatening to send thugs over."

Elena was disquieted. "To do what?"

"Teach me a lesson."

"God! Be careful."

"Don't worry, I can take care of myself. It's you I'm worried about."

"What?!."

"These guys play dirty."

"Who are 'these guys', the *Mafia*?" Elena snorted, amused and alarmed in equal measure.

"Yeah."

"What?! I was joking."

"I'm not."

"How does Joe know the Mafia?"

Garri gave her a stern look. "You have to keep this to yourself, okay? Joe is a Mafioso."

"You're working for a Mafioso?! You told me he was an importer."

"Yeah, he imports stuff but it's mostly a cover for their various drug operations," he lowered his voice conspiratorially. "Who did you think I get my cannabis from?"

Elena stared at him, slack-jawed. "I thought he was importing borlotti beans or Limoncello!"

"Just promise me you won't answer the door if you don't know who is there."

Elena blinked. "Of course."

"And if you have any problems, use this," he reached on top of the kitchen cupboard to retrieve a small pistol.

"What the hell? Why is there a gun in the house?!"

"For protection. Do you know how to use one?"

"No! I don't want to know! Put it away."

Ignoring her protest, he loaded the gun and showed her how to aim it.

Elena's head was in a spin. She didn't want a gun in her house and she didn't want to be around a man whose activities might require the use of one. What on earth had she gotten herself into?

Chapter Fifteen

BEHOLDING ALL HER OWN MISCHANCE

G arri was in the bathroom. His phone, sitting on the table, rang. The screen displayed the name Rob.

Elena picked it up.

"Where are you?" a hard voice demanded before she had even opened her mouth.

"Er, this is Elena, Garri isn't available at the moment."

There was silence on the end of the phone. She could hear heavy breathing.

"Hello?"

The line went dead.

Garri came out of the bathroom, saw the phone in her hand and the look on her face and came barrelling over. "What is it? What happened?"

"Rob called but when I told him who I was, he hung up. Who is Rob?"

Fear flashed through his eyes before he recovered himself. "He's a client whose money I lost in the trade. Don't worry about him, I'll sort it." He took the phone off her and went into the study, closing the door behind him.

For weeks thereafter, she was jittery, but Garri made no further mention of Mafia or guns and eventually issues with their personal finances returned foremost in her mind. Garri's memory failed every time she asked for information about his financial position. She put together a spreadsheet of her income and expenses and those expenses of his which she knew about, then asked him to fill in the blanks. After hounding him for weeks, there were still noticeable gaps.

"Why haven't you completed all the fields?"

"I can't remember the figures just now."

"But you must have documentation. Even if your memory is bad, there are ways you can find out the answers. For some of them you just need to check your bank statement."

Tears of distress swam in his eyes. "I'm sorry, sexy buns, I've told you I can't remember. I don't know where the paperwork is but I'll find it and let you know. I just can't concentrate on this stuff right now."

For the first time, it crossed her mind that his memory lapses might be a convenient decoy. She had long suspected his financial position was worse than he had let on. She was now covering all their rent, bills, and groceries. Plus, before realising how tight their financial situation would become, she had booked them to go to Kings Beach on Queensland's Sunshine Coast this summer. She had already paid for the flights and reserved the accommodation. There would be cancellation fees if they didn't go. Either way, it would cost her. Their situation wasn't dire yet. A portion of her house deposit remained, but she didn't want to keep dipping into that. It was to buy a house, not fritter away on a lifestyle they couldn't afford.

"We will have to find a cheaper rental when the lease expires," she ventured.

"I can't cope with moving, sexy buns," he replied, his distress intensifying.

"It's ludicrous to continue living beyond our means, though! You won't have to do anything. I'll hire a removal company."

Garri dissolved into tears.

Startled, she let the subject drop. She would support him through this rough patch, but his stonewalling her every attempt to bring their life back into order was making her increasingly uneasy. Her frustration grew with each passing week, reaching a peak one afternoon when Garri found a photo of her taken four years earlier. Her face was tired and worn, her eyes reflecting the deep sadness of those times.

"Wow, I looked so old! I think I look younger now than I did then."

Garri shuddered. "Ugh! If you had looked like that when we met, we would never have been together."

Initial stunned disbelief morphed into a surge of anger. It took all her willpower to resist the urge to remind him that he was no oil painting; that she—repulsed by him on a physical level—had forced herself to see beyond the physical. The whole foundation on which she thought their relationship was built crumbled under the weight of that one, off-the-cuff remark. She was left with the sickening suspicion that she had made a serious error of judgement in letting him into her life.

"I don't think we can stay together." The words leaped out her mouth while her befuddled brain scrambled to catch up.

He sagged back against his computer chair. "Why?"

"It just doesn't feel right. We're not connecting in the right way and I don't feel like I want to support you anymore..." she replied, staring at a spot on the floor in front of her "... because I can't trust you." She trailed off into a whisper, wincing at her own words, amazed they had actually come out of her mouth.

She felt like a royal jerk, despite being flooded with relief that she'd finally found her voice. Garri left the room. She heard him descend the stairs and throw himself on the sofa. Forcing herself to go down to him, she intended to offer more of an explanation.

Her resolve faltered at his reproachful glare. Perhaps she wasn't being compassionate enough during his time of need. She had always been super sensitive. Maybe she was reading too much into his words and actions, assigning intentions that weren't there.

"I'm sorry. It's been a difficult time for both of us. Maybe we just need to spend quality time together. Let's see how we go on the Sunshine Coast."

"What's the point? You've made it clear you don't want me around."

She shook her head. "That's not what I meant. I need you to cooperate with me so I can balance our budget because I refuse to live beyond our means. If you can do that, everything will be okay."

"I'm trying. I'll get you the info as soon as I can. Besides, you don't need to worry because I feel well enough to work again."

This was welcome, if unexpected, news.

"The pain is gone?"

"No, but I haven't needed many painkillers the last few weeks and I've cut out the reefers."

She breathed a sigh of relief. "That's great! Will Joe give you back the part-time chauffeur job?"

He shook his head. "I'll have to find something less sedentary. A mate needs a business manager for his restaurant. I know he'd give me the job. I'll talk to him this week."

His confidence amazed her. She was the opposite, always wondering if she was good enough, even if she knew she could do the work.

"So you'll come to Kings Beach?" she asked.

He shrugged, still offended. "I'll think about it.

THE JOB OFFER from his mate didn't eventuate but he found a sales job in a city mobile phone store where his charisma and gift of the gab would serve him well. Garri initially told her it was a temporary job until he got a break with Forex, but within two months he was talking about opportunities for moving into managerial roles in the company.

After more than a year of uncertainty, things were finally looking up. He'd even admitted to falling behind on his car loan and credit card repayments and organised payment plans to catch up. Yet not all was rosy. The issue of the outstanding business loan continued to shadow them and Garri often received calls from, and met with, the creditor in an attempt to sort it out. He still struggled with energy levels too, and when she again broached the subject of them moving, he flat out refused.

"I can't cope with moving."

"Why not?"

"I'm struggling to adjust to the new work routine."

"But you said everything was good."

"It makes me tired," he replied dropping his head in his hands.

A sense of dread flooded Elena. "So you don't want to keep working?"

"I'll work, but I can't move house."

"But we can get help to move. You don't have to do it all."

"I can't! The pain has started again." The edginess in his voice hinted at an impending breakdown.

"Since when?"

"Last week."

"You didn't tell me."

"I'm telling you now."

He's making excuses.

The voice was but a whisper, easy to ignore. His tone sounded so desperate. She couldn't be sure he wasn't telling the truth.

She softened. "Well, we still have a couple of months on the lease so let's see how you feel in a month's time."

He didn't reply.

❦

THEY FLEW TO QUEENSLAND, Elena still smarting at Garri's lack of respect. A week before they were due to fly out to Queensland, he had admitted he couldn't reimburse her for the flights or accommodation. He must have known all along that he couldn't afford the trip. If truth be told, something within her had known too, but she had wanted to believe him.

Garri turned the bacon on the grill, surveying King's Beach through the sliding door of the modern one-bedroom Airbnb apartment. "This is great! Awesome views, a good lifestyle right in the heart of the city, great apartment. It's small but for just the two of us, we wouldn't need anything bigger. This would be a good buy."

She had hoped this holiday would help improve their relationship but planning their long-term future together was jumping the gun.

"You want to move to Queensland?"

"The warmer weather is better for the arthritis in my hip and I'm sure we could get work here."

"I prefer this climate too, but we'd need a bigger apartment if we have children."

"We don't have kids yet. We can cross that bridge if and when we come to it."

Elena didn't want to buy a property and then have to sell and upgrade, paying government taxes twice. It made more sense to buy a bigger house to start with. She couldn't see herself living in a city high-rise, anyway. She needed space and greenery. The tiny balcony would struggle to house a pot plant. Plus she didn't want to uproot her life for the man who not long ago she was ready to walk away from.

She refrained from saying any of this to him because it had been so long since she had seen him this enthusiastic. "Let's see how things go with your Adelaide job first."

It was good to see Garri back to his enthusiastic and confident self.

That evening, overcome by a sudden flood of affection, Elena leaned over and kissed him.

He stared at her in surprise, grabbed hold of her and returned the kiss. He pulled her off the sofa and led her to the bedroom.

She wasn't in the mood for sex, but it might help them connect again.

Her foot started to cramp and she quickly changed position so she could stretch it. The cramp eased. She wasn't plagued by cramps like when she had been with Michael, but sometimes they still snuck up on her.

She regretted responding to Garri's advances though when, partway through their lovemaking, she experienced a sickening sensation in the pit of her stomach and a desire to push him away. But she persevered to the end, employing her now well-practised tactic of removing herself mentally from the physical act.

❧

RELAXING on the sun-kissed white sand on their last day, she realised that he hadn't once complained of pain. "How's your pain level at the moment?"

"Good. I'm not using any painkillers."

"That's great!"

Circumstances were improving and they were more relaxed in each other's company. Things were by no means perfect but they were moving in the right direction.

They returned to the apartment that evening to pack.

"Geez that's a lot of condoms," she blurted out as Garri threw a large stash into his suitcase.

"Well, I thought we might need them. But we're not exactly going for it."

His petulant reply enraged her. They'd had sex three times in the past two weeks, more than they'd had for almost a year, but it still wasn't enough for him. She was trying to meet at least some of his physical desires even though there was no desire on her part. What was he doing for her in return? Disrespecting her, keeping important information from her, potentially exposing her to dangerous people, then telling her he loved her, as if that made it all okay. She wondered for the millionth time what she was getting out of the relationship besides a growing sense of unease and a mounting pile of bills.

With her anger and distress on the rise again, she was glad she had a massage appointment with Jivan. She felt well overdue for a good dose of Jivan zen. Her shoulder was still giving her grief and now the tightness extended all the way down her left bicep. Jivan, as always, coaxed the muscle into submission but she knew it would tighten again within weeks.

"Have you figured out what's causing the shoulder problem yet?"

Elena shook her head. She knew he meant the emotional cause and she was aware there had to be an emotion at the root of it but it was evading her.

"The sensation is hard to describe, like my arm is in a vice and I'm trying to walk forward but it's stopping me."

"Hmm... you could check Louise Hay's book, *You Can Heal Your-self*. It lists the emotional side related to parts of the body and illnesses."

"Okay, thanks."

"How was Kings Beach?"

"It was good, beautiful weather and the beach is amazing!"

"Yes, I loved it there. Did you swim in the beachfront saltwater pool?"

"Yep... are you planning any holidays?" She wanted to move the attention away from her before he asked about Garri.

"I'm going back to India for a friend's wedding later this year. It's a traditional Hindu wedding."

"Is Lakshmi going with you?"

There was the slightest of pauses before his hands continued kneading the muscles surrounding her shoulder blades.

"Lakshmi and I have gone our separate ways."

"Oh, I'm sorry."

"It's okay, it was nothing like that. We're still friends. In fact I caught up with her last week."

"I didn't mean I thought it was a bad ending," she replied. "It's just sad when a relationship doesn't work out."

This comment was met with silence and she wondered if he disagreed. Maybe it wasn't sad for him. Come to think of it, he didn't sound at all sad. She allowed herself to indulge in a small spark of happiness that he was single again before scolding herself. It's not like she was free to date him. She had no right to feel that way.

Elena left the session relaxed and loose but no less perplexed by her own thoughts and feelings where Jivan was concerned, and tormented by the persistent hope that she could one day be with him when she knew it was ridiculous on so many levels.

At home, she played absent-mindedly with the mail on the kitchen bench while she told Garri of Jivan's travel plans, until she realised what she was holding—a final reminder for his overdrawn credit card. The blood froze in her veins.

"I thought you were on a payment plan for this?" She brandished the letter at him.

His eyes flickered surprise. Clearly he'd forgotten he had left it there. "I was… but Dad needed more money for treatment."

"Oh!" How could she berate him for that? "Why didn't you tell me?"

Garri turned away from her to open the fridge door. "Because you said you didn't want to support me anymore."

Memories of the day she had almost broken up with him flooded her and she blushed with shame. "I didn't mean that."

"That's not how it sounded."

She changed the subject. "I thought your dad was heading into remission?"

"No, I didn't say that."

"Yes, you did."

"I said the doc expected him to go into remission, but he hasn't."

"Oh. Well, I'm sorry to hear that."

She was sorry, really she was, but she couldn't shake her suspicion that something wasn't right. She was sure he'd indicated his father was all but cured, but she buried the memory of this latest worrisome conversation in the dark recess of her mind reserved for such things, and focussed on finding them a new home.

Within a week, Garri's pain symptoms returned and he refused to take part in searching for a new house. Determined to reduce their living expenses regardless, she researched properties and attended the open inspections on her own. She showed him pictures online of a modern western suburbs house which was as big as their eastern suburbs abode, had a garden and would save them one hundred and ten dollars a week.

His disinterest was obvious but he didn't object so she put in an application, which was accepted the next day.

"We've got the house!" she told him.

He nodded, regarding her with a dull stare.

"Don't worry, I'll hire someone to move furniture and I'll do the packing."

His shoulders slumped in deflated resignation.

He doesn't want to give up the eastern suburbs prestige.

A memory flashed into Elena's consciousness, of him advocating for the eastern suburbs when they first decided to live together. He'd told her that living in an area with successful people would enable them to attract the energy of success too. It was obvious he linked their postcode to his dream of being a businessman who could work from home while watching the dollars roll in. Such a dream was attractive to most people, herself included, and she wished he could realise it, but it was currently a dream with no basis in reality. Dreams didn't pay the rent and she couldn't afford to let him continue pretending while digging them both into a hole.

Elena ordered boxes and began packing. Garri's pain symptoms correspondingly worsened and he retreated to bed as soon as dinner was over each night. She plodded along, packing a little each night and crossing her fingers that it would be a move for the better.

The new house proved to be comfortable, if not as stylish as the townhouse had been. Elena indulged herself by planting flowers and pottering in the garden on weekends while Garri spent most of his time glued to the computer. When Garri's pain symptoms reduced and he gave up the dope again, Elena's optimism soared.

꙰

ELENA SAT LISTENING to the renowned mindset and emotional intelligence expert Brett Davis. It wasn't a cheap seminar, but she had sensed it was what she needed. Brett's ability to explain the connections between the mind and emotions in a simple, humorous manner appealed to her and the content about the subconscious mind and the buried beliefs which blocked a person's progress in life reminded her of the book Absolute Happiness.

As she listened to Brett, she realised that low self-esteem had prevented her from acknowledging her own abilities and achievements. From a young age she had wanted to write but, lacking confidence, had ensconced herself in research centres and libraries instead, doing the groundwork for other writers and hiding behind a physical wall of books in order to avoid facing her own fears and desires. Even after being steered into writing for children and getting good feedback, she still didn't see herself as a real author. She saw an imposter who had circumnavigated the established publishing model, snuck in the back door and was wandering around with a wine glass in hand, trying not to draw attention to herself, pretending she belonged but knowing she wasn't fooling those whose names were on the official guest list.

There was much scorn in the industry for self-publishers, who were considered sub-standard because their work wasn't evaluated by the industry and plucked out of a mediocre pile as a shining example of high quality craft. Her workplace had published on her behalf, but she hadn't been required to compete for the privilege, so in her eyes she hadn't been much better than a self-publisher.

Yet both her books had been popular with children and parents alike. Just how much more proof did she require that she could produce engaging stories for her audience? The thought coincided with a flash of inspiration for a rhyme about self-esteem. How many children might avoid the mistakes she had made if their self-esteem and emotional intelligence were cultivated from an early age? She grabbed a notepad, jotting down ideas until she had filled half a page with an outline. Distracted, she continued jotting notes during the breaks and had half the first draft on paper by the end of the workshop.

Elena decided to sign up for mentoring sessions with Brett to help her take this new idea through to a self-published reality. She would publish some poetry on her own, to prove to herself that she could produce a quality product without the endorsement of the traditional publishing industry or the support of her employer. An excited buzz overtook her entire body.

❦

"TELL me your top three goals for the next twelve months," Brett said.

"First is to successfully publish my poems, second to improve my relationship with Garri, and third to earn enough from writing to be able to give up my day job so that when I have children, I can spend more time at home with them."

"Okay, good, kids are something you're planning soon?"

"Well, no. I'd like to, but I can't have children with Garri yet."

"Why not?"

"He's had financial and heath problems. Now he's working again, but he's not in a position to support us yet and I can't trust him with money."

"Why can't you trust him?"

"He has a lot of debt. Actually, I'm not sure how much because he won't tell me. He wasn't working for a while because of his health and I tried to find out his financial details so I could budget but he wouldn't tell me. I only find out bits of information when the proverbial hits the fan so, even if circumstances changed and he developed a large income stream, I would have trouble trusting him enough to give up my own job and place my future in his hands."

"Honesty and trust are very important in relationships, Elena."

"I know."

"Do you feel you could to learn to trust him, and could he be more open with you?"

"I hope so."

"Then it sounds like our first priority is to work on your relationship goal. What about your weaknesses. Can you list them for me?"

"I'm a perfectionist. I fear failure and suffer from self-doubt. I struggle to know when my intuition is telling me something is not right compared to when fear is talking. I feel guilty if I can't or don't want to give someone what they want."

"Okay, and your strengths?"

"Um,… I guess I'm disciplined. When I do something, I follow through to the end."

"Good, what else?"

"Maybe being a perfectionist is a strength too. I put a lot of effort into doing things well."

"Keep going."

"Er,… I don't know."

"I want you to think about it and tell me at next session. I'm sure you have more strengths."

"Okay."

They met fortnightly, discussing Elena's history and significant life events to tease out unresolved issues. They set timeframes for each of her goals, worked through tasks linked to those goals and discussed ways to increase her awareness of her own behaviours and actions.

The work on writing and editing her poems ticked along but it continued to take a backseat to the issue of her relationship with Garri. Elena, eager to kick her poetry into existence in record time, was frustrated but agreed it was important to resolve the relationship issue in order to allow space for her writing to come to life.

Brett asked her to try a technique for learning to be present with a partner and connect at the heart level. He instructed them to sit facing each other, hold hands and stare into each other's eyes without speaking a word. Real connection came from simply being present and giving each other full and undivided attention.

Elena asked Garri to do it with her each morning upon waking. The first time surprised them both as they experienced a powerful connection that reduced Elena to tears. *This* connection was missing from their relationship. *This* was what she wanted. They practised each morning but, by the end of the first week, Garri no longer wanted to sit up and hold her hands. Instead, he heaved himself onto his side to face her. Elena found it harder to maintain eye contact from a lying position—she couldn't see his eyes clearly.

The following week, she sensed an increased reluctance on his part and, on gazing into his eyes, all she saw was two huge brown wells of sadness, a sadness so deep that she struggled to keep herself from being sucked into the abyss. By the end of the second week she could handle it no longer, so she stopped insisting they do it. Garri didn't once suggest it himself or even question why she had stopped asking him to do it.

❦

ELENA OPENED HER WORK INBOX.

Dear Elena
This may seem a strange email but I've wanted to tell you for some time. I'm
afraid Garri has a gambling problem. He has fought against it for many
years and had periods of breaking the habit, only to fall back into it again. He
has won and lost large sums a number of times over, often other people's
money.
You need to know that his father does not have cancer. He is fit and healthy,
living in his Tongan village and Garri didn't go to see him last year.
Sorry to be the one to tell you, but you deserve to know the truth.
From Distressed Observer

Elena stared at her computer, her heart palpitating. It couldn't be true, could it? Why would someone send her such an email? The sender's address was concerned@hotmail.com. After some time, with a sinking sensation, she typed a careful reply.

Dear Distressed Observer
Who are you? How do you know these things?
Garri sent me the attached photos of his father in hospital when he was visit-
ing, and with his family in the village. His father must be sick and Garri was
definitely in Tonga.
Elena

As she hit the send button, she prayed for evidence to prove this person wrong.

The next day she received a reply.

Hi Elena

I know it's hard to accept but his father is fine. He did have leukaemia seven years ago, which is when the photos you attached were taken. He was here in Australia for treatment, went into remission and has been healthy ever since. Here is a photo taken two weeks ago, and a photo of Garri coming out of the casino during the week he was supposedly in Tonga.

I'm sure Garri loves you, but you're also his latest cash cow who allows him to feed his addiction.

Kind regards, Distressed Observer

Elena opened the first photo of an elderly but more robust version of the man she had seen in the hospital bed. His dark skin glowed and his bare chest sported similar tattoos to Garri. It was date-stamped the tenth of May of the current year. Elena's shoulders slumped and she closed her eyes. Willing herself to continue, she hovered the cursor over the second attachment before taking a deep breath and clicking it open. Garri exiting the casino doorway stared back at her. The date stamp read the thirteenth of June of last year.

Distressed Observer said his father had had cancer treatment in Australia. Why not in Tonga? She opened a new Google browser and typed *cancer treatment in Tonga*. A line from the second result stood out: 'Cancer patients are sent abroad for chemotherapy. If they can't afford it, there's not much that can be done for them in Tonga.'

She sat at her desk, an immoveable rock, as images flashed through her mind—the shirt Garri wore in the photo he'd sent was one she hadn't seen before, his inability to video Skype the whole time he was away due to wifi problems, the multitude of reasons why she could never speak with his father, and seeing his 'doppelgänger' entering the casino. What a fool she had been to believe him.

She left the office and drove home in a trance.

While cutting vegetables for dinner, she wondered how best to raise the issue with him.

"How is your father?"

"He's doing okay."

"Can we Skype this weekend so I can meet him?"

"I think he's busy with village ceremonies this weekend. Let me ask him, sexy buns."

"He doesn't have cancer, does he?"

Surprise and panic flashed across his face for an infinitesimal moment then he regained control with a nonchalant shrug, his face closed and defiant. "He's in remission now, why?"

A searing anger surged through her and she stabbed the knife into the chopping board. The handle vibrated accusingly at her.

"*Why?* You borrow money from me to pay for treatment for a disease he doesn't even have and you act like it's no big deal?"

Tears of frustration sprang to her eyes and she ran into their bedroom to cry it out. She heard him move into the study where he stayed until he shuffled into the bedroom in the early hours of the morning. She was still awake, still fuming. Neither of them spoke and eventually she fell into a fitful sleep.

The next morning she thrashed it out with him.

"What did you do with my money, Garri? Did you blow it all in the casino?"

He hung his head. "I had to pay the rest of the business loan back. I didn't want to ask for help because you didn't want to support me but I couldn't find anyone else willing to give me the money. It was easier to ask you for money on someone else's behalf."

Shame engulfed her anew. "I'm sorry... But if you were working on the assumption I didn't want to support you, how do you explain me continuing to feed and house you or pay for our holiday? Why do you think I've been asking you for more than a year to provide your financial details so I can set up a proper budget for us? Why would I do any of that? Don't you consider that to be supporting you?"

Garri's shoulders sagged, "But you *said* you didn't want to support me."

"Because I felt I couldn't trust you. And once again you've proven my point!"

Their conversation went around in circles with Garri doggedly holding onto his belief that she didn't want to support him.

"And the money I gave you for Tonga? You didn't go to Tonga either."

His face registered astonishment. "How do you know all this?"

"I received an anonymous email at work, with photo evidence of you coming out of the casino when you were supposed to be in Tonga."

His eyes narrowed. "Any idea who sent the email?"

"No, the address doesn't give any clues and the person clearly doesn't want to be identified. So where did you stay when I thought you were in Tonga?"

"With a friend," he replied, avoiding her gaze.

"Which friend?"

"You don't know him. I told him we were having problems and needed time apart."

Elena glared at him. "And my money? Did it disappear in the casino?"

He nodded, looking at the floor.

An angry tic developed in the corner of her eye. "Your credit card debt, have you paid that off with my money too?"

"No… I still owe money on the cards."

"Great," she spat. A sudden, unwelcome thought occurred. "Was there really a business loan debt or did everything go on gambling?"

"Yes, of course there was a debt… *mumble, mumble.*"

"What?"

"… of forty-thousand," he muttered.

"And the other twenty-five thousand?"

"I invested it in Forex trading."

Her body trembled with barely contained anger. "How is gambling on foreign currencies more important than repaying your debts?"

"It's not gambling. I used proven methods which can be very lucrative. Ever heard of George Soros, who made a billion dollars in one day on Forex?"

Her anger threatened to escape in a molten lava rush. She tamped it down, gritting her teeth. "So where is the money, then?"

"I wanted to make enough to pay you back but I didn't have enough time to focus on trading. If I didn't have to work, I could have paid more attention to the market and responded at the right time."

"So you lost it all?"

"Yes." Panic widened his eyes. "But don't worry, I can get it back. I'll try again."

"NO!" Every fibre of her being shook with rage and her left shoulder spasmed. "The definition of stupidity is repeating the same mistake, and expecting a different result!"

"It's not stupid! I've made money on Forex in the past."

"When?"

"When I paid back the first half of the business loan. The creditor was pressuring me so I used Forex. I did well."

"If it worked so well, why did you only pay back half the debt?"

"I had a few setbacks and lost the money I had kept aside to keep trading. My divorce issues were distracting me and I was busy with the business. I need time to focus in order to trade. If I could stay home and focus instead of working, I could make enough now to cover your loan and the credit cards."

"What money would you buy more currency with?"

"Well,… if you could lend me a little, I'll make enough to pay you back with interest."

Elena's body shook with rage. "I've got a better idea. I'll pay your credit cards myself and you can go on a fortnightly payment plan to pay me back," she said through gritted teeth.

"No! I'll sort it out."

"With what?"

"I get paid this week."

"Enough to pay off all the cards?"

"No… but over the next few months I could do it if you cover my rent."

She regarded him with suspicion. "Do you owe anyone else money?"

"No." He shot her an angry look.

Her old friend guilt showed up, stopping her from berating him further. What had happened to her patience and self-control? She felt like such a bitch for getting so angry with him. But the warning bells in her mind were intensifying. If she stayed with this man, her life would be one unpleasant surprise after another, one dispute after another, the uncovering of one half-truth after another.

※

ELENA TOOK the afternoon off work and went shopping for some new work shirts. She was still in the city at a quarter to five and decided to surprise Garri by meeting him at his work. As she drew level with the corner shop, she glimpsed his back retreating down the side street. There was no point calling out to him—her voice would be drowned by the peak hour bustle. She picked up her pace. As she turned down the street, he ducked into a service lane behind the building. She followed, stopping short as she took in the sight of Garri with a reefer dangling from his mouth, another man in the act of lighting it for him, their heads bent close together, the man's free hand resting on Garri's bicep.

Garri looked up, his startled eyes meeting hers. Crushing disappointment quickly spiralled into anger that he had lied to her again. Without a word, she turned and stalked away. He called out to her but she refused to stop. She sensed him trailing along behind her.

He caught up with her outside the lift to the carpark. "I can explain, sexy buns," he panted.

She rounded on him. "For months, you've been telling me you haven't smoked!"

"Today was the first time that I've had one. I had a hard day and bummed one off a colleague. I promise it's a once-off."

"I don't believe you." She glared at him. The lift doors opened and she entered behind two women.

Garri followed. His face crumpled. "Look, I'm going through a rough patch at work."

The two women looked away, staring uncomfortably at the bare elevator doors. One repeatedly stabbed the button for level four as if to hurry the elevator along.

Shocked by his tears, Elena softened her voice. "What do you mean?"

"I'm not getting along with the boss because I challenged him on the way the shop is run and he overlooked me for a promotion," he mumbled, staring at the ground.

"Oh!"

He snuck a sideways look at her. "… and the pain has returned."

"So take painkillers instead of dope," she hissed in a whisper.

The elevator doors opened and the two women made a hasty escape.

"It's not that easy."

"Then I don't know what to suggest."

Even if it were all true, he should have told her, given her some idea what was going on in his life. Instead he had trundled home from work each day and sat in front of the computer, barely giving her the time of day.

She was both ashamed for berating him and annoyed with herself for continuing to accept his excuses. Withdrawing further from him, she spent long hours with Brett, talking through her heightened unease and distrust. Brett was attentive and supportive, asking questions to get Elena to examine her own feelings and beliefs and reminding her that she had to make the decision that felt right for her. But that was where Elena came unstuck. She was hamstrung, unable to decide what was right for her. Was it right for her to protect herself by walking away? Or should she be more patient with Garri?

"I need to give him the chance to prove himself."

"How many chances have you already given him? How many more are you prepared to give?"

Elena's shoulders sagged. "People can change and he's had a hard time lately..."

"Yes, people can change. He may change yet. But misrepresenting the truth has been a recurring theme from the beginning of your relationship."

"But partners have a responsibility to accept each other's faults, to support each other and allow each other the time they need to make changes within themselves."

"Yes, that is part of a committed relationship. But so is respecting your partner by being honest with them."

There was silence as Elena absorbed this undeniable truth.

Brett continued gently. "Garri has a responsibility to respect you and be honest with you. The choice is yours, but know what you are accepting in the choice you make. If you stay, make it crystal clear what you expect from him so there is no room for misinterpretation or excuses."

Elena knew deep down she'd had enough but she shied away from deciding. "Garri has agreed to come along to your workshop on Saturday. Maybe it will be a game-changer for us."

"Okay. Our time is up for today so I'll see you both there. Take care."

Chapter Sixteen

THE STORMY EAST-WIND STRAINING

As they parked outside the workshop venue, Elena's phone chimed. It was a message from Jivan, on holiday in India for the family wedding. He had sent a picture of the Ganga at sunset.

- To the special people. I'm enjoying my time here, currently in Rishikesh.

"It's Jivan," she gushed. "He's in Rishikesh!"

She tapped out a quick reply.

- Wonderful, enjoy!

"Why didn't you date Jivan when your marriage ended?"

She blinked, discomposed. How did Garri know she had once entertained that thought herself? "He wasn't interested in me... besides, he's way too good for me."

Garri didn't reply, only stared at her like she had grown a second head. But even his reaction couldn't stop her heart from singing. Jivan counted her among his group of special people!

The morning workshop covered common societal beliefs such as *money is the root of all evil* and subconscious belief patterns related to money, developed as a result of childhood experiences.

"Money itself is neither good nor bad," Brett told them. He waved a fifty dollar note in the air. "Money is just coloured paper that we agree has a certain value. The real value of money is in the choices and options it provides the holder. We choose to behave in good or bad ways in relation to our pursuit and use of money. But money itself is just a piece of paper."

Garri poured himself a coffee during the morning tea break.

"What do you think of the workshop so far?" Elena asked him.

"It's good." His reply sounded non-committal.

"Well, I was thinking back to an incident that occurred when I was fifteen. I was treated with scorn by a woman while door-knocking as a volunteer charity collector. I had thought I was doing something good to help people, but I felt humiliated by the woman's contemptuous response. It planted a seed in my mind that took swift and extensive root and I've believed ever since that I didn't deserve to ask for, or receive money, from anyone. The belief has extended to my work life, always taking on extra duties without requesting pay rises."

"There's nothing wrong with asking," Garri replied. "If you don't ask, you don't receive."

"I guess so. The trick is in learning when it is reasonable or necessary to ask as opposed to asking for things you don't really need. There has to be a level of responsibility attached, I feel."

Garri shrugged. "No harm in asking. People aren't obligated to give just because you ask." He downed the remainder of his coffee and they headed back to their seats.

She watched Garri closely throughout the remainder of the day to see if any of the content resonated with him but he seemed more intent on using the workshop to find new Forex trading partners than on examining his own relationship with money.

The afternoon covered relationship issues caused by conflicts over money.

"That's our problem," Garri said during the afternoon break.

"Which one?"

"We see money differently. I've experienced money matters in business, you haven't. In business I have to take some risks, but you don't take risks, you're conservative."

"Yes, but we need to talk about our financial situation, not just general attitudes to money. That's what I've been asking you to do."

"And I told you, I'm getting my situation under control again. Just trust me on this."

"What *is* your situation, Garri? That's my point. I don't know what it is exactly that you're getting under control."

"You need to speak to Joan," Garri directed her. "She'll explain what's important."

Brett's wife, Joan, was his backbone, the quiet nurturer to balance Brett's charismatic, pusher personality. Elena sensed Garri expected Joan to encourage Elena to embrace her own nurturer tendencies in support of Garri. Irritated, she itched to tell him to bugger off—but she did feel the need to speak to someone so she joined the line waiting to speak with Joan.

She became more jittery the longer she stood there. Would Joan persuade her to do what Garri wanted? The thought filled her with dread. She didn't know how much more support and forgiveness she could offer before it killed her. She had worked herself up into such a state that, by the time she had Joan's attention, all she could do was stumble over her words and burst into tears.

Joan took her aside and coaxed the story out of her before offering advice.

"Nurturers are good at keeping families and relationships going through the hard times. We all need nurturers in our lives. But the danger for nurturers is in denying themselves a life in order to support those around them. You are entitled to a happy life as much as anybody else on this planet. No law says we must live a life of complete servitude in order to be a good person! We all need to learn how to serve, and accept service, in equal measure." She gave Elena a pointed look. "If you are so focussed on supporting others that you ignore your own needs and feelings, in the end you become no use to either yourself or anyone else. If you don't respect yourself by acknowledging your own needs, others will not respect you. Care for yourself first. Only then will you have the energy and focus to care for others. If you force yourself to do or be what feels incongruent with your true self, nothing good will come of it."

A weight lifted from Elena's shoulders and she stretched her neck with an audible crack as the joints released their tension. "Thank you, I needed that," she sighed, giving Joan a hug.

With a clarity that had escaped her until now, she knew she had to put an end to her relationship with Garri.

❧

GARRI MADE a beeline for his computer when they arrived home.

Elena sat on the edge of their bed in a daze, wondering how to tell him it was over. Taking a notebook, she started writing her reasons for wanting to leave. Gathering her thoughts before they had the conversation should stop her from getting emotionally hijacked. She was still writing when Garri came to bed so she took the notebook into the study.

Garri had left a letter on the desk, from the tax office. He owed three years' worth of taxes.

She marched back into the bedroom. "Why didn't you pay your taxes?"

He replaced his startled expression with a well-rehearsed veneer of calm. "Does it matter?"

"I *asked you* if you owed money to *anyone else* and *you said no!*" Her voice shook with uncontrolled emotion.

He shrugged and held his palms out, his face a mask of bewilderment. "The government isn't a person. Besides, I planned to pay the outstanding back taxes, but when I couldn't work, I had to use my savings to live off."

Her whole body trembled with anger. "So you led me to believe you had savings but it was for your tax bill?! What else have you lied to me about?" This time her voice was dangerously quiet.

He glared at her. "I'm wary of telling you anything about my situation because you said you didn't want to support me."

"You're like a broken record! This isn't about money, it's about trust, honesty and respect. You were perfectly capable of telling me you had a tax debt, but you didn't. You told me about the business debt but insinuated Steve was responsible for paying it, then you invented a fantastical story about your poor father in order to get the money from me. You chose to mislead me and get yourself further into debt in the process."

"But how do you think I felt asking you for money when you said you didn't want to support me?"

"I'm sorry I didn't make myself clear but you can't keep using that as an excuse. There is evidence enough of my willingness to support you if you were honest with me."

"Well, it didn't feel that way."

"So why did you have a tax debt in the first place?"

He picked at a stray thread on the quilt. "I paid myself a wage from the business but didn't take out the income tax."

"Why not?"

He glared at her, harassed by her insistence on getting answers. "I was trying to pay Dad back..." he trailed off, looking like he wished he could retrieve the words.

"Pay him for what?"

"Er... some of the business loan," he muttered.

"Your *dad* was the 'friend' who lent you the money?"

"Yeah."

"Fantastic! That's why he's not speaking to you."

"I shouldn't have had to pay him back anyway," he sulked. "Tongan life is communal, we share everything in the family."

"Huh, yet when I reminded you children are important in the Tongan culture, your excuse was you're only half Tongan."

"That's different," he shot back, frustration written all over his face.

"We're getting off track. The 'friend' who kept messaging you, who you kept meeting with to discuss the loan? It couldn't be your dad if he's in Tonga."

Shame crossed Garri's features. "No."

"Then who?"

"It doesn't matter."

"WHO WAS IT, GARRIDAN?"

He put his head in his hands. "My lover."

Gob smacked, Elena opened her mouth to speak but nothing came out. Ashen-faced, her mouth opened and closed like a goldfish until finally an incredulous whisper escaped. "Who is she?"

"He..."

"What?"

"I'm... *mumble, mumble...*"

"What?"

"I'm bi-sexual."

Elena sat on the bed with a thud, her back to him. "You cheated on me... with a man?!"

Garri didn't answer.

"Why didn't you tell me you were bi-sexual?"

"*Why?* Because you're so bloody strait-laced, that's why! You freaked out when I smoked cannabis, when I got a tax-free chauffeur gig..."

"Who is he?"

"His name is Rob," Garri mumbled.

Rob, Rob, where had she heard that name? Ah, that's right, the man who had hung up on her when Elena had answered Garri's phone.

Realisation dawned on her. He had continued to tell her he was meeting with the creditor *after* she had lent him the money. She had been so incensed at him lying about his father, and so bamboozled with information about Forex, credit cards and whatnot that she hadn't twigged the timeframes didn't match up. He'd been going off for sordid liaisons while telling her he was in business meetings. Elena slumped with her head in her hands.

"He doesn't mean anything to me. It was just sex... I'm sorry, sexy buns."

She rounded on him. "Don't call me sexy buns!" Another flash of realisation hit her. "That man with you, behind the building... that was Rob."

"Yes." Garri hung his head.

She felt a surge of rage. "Being bi-sexual isn't an excuse to cheat." Fuming, she marched out of the room and prepared bedding to sleep on the sofa. She couldn't stand to be in the same room as him.

Rising early on the Sunday morning, she left the house without speaking to Garri and burned off her tension on the push bike, meeting Jane in Mile End and riding along the Torrens River. Elena poured out the happenings of the last few months.

Jane whistled. "What a mess."

Elena sighed. "You could say that."

"What are you going to do now?"

"I don't know—I'm too upset to think."

"I'd be upset too if I were you... but at least he *tries* to pay back his debts, I guess."

"I know he's not a bad person. I don't think he intends to hurt people, but he's a walking disaster and can't seem to get his act together. I can't deal with it anymore."

"Well, please... make sure you do what feels right for you this time. I'm here if you need anything." Jane gave her a fierce hug.

Tears pricked the corners of Elena's eyes. She was fortunate to have such a supportive friend.

At home, the sickening sight of Garri wallowing naked in bed, his face filled with shame, greeted her. She hated to see him like this.

"I'm sorry," his eyes pleaded for forgiveness.

"I'm sorry, too. Why couldn't you tell me the truth? You were misleading me even before I said I didn't want to support you, so please don't give me that answer again."

He held his hands up in helpless resignation. "I was embarrassed."

"I wouldn't have been surprised, you know. I suspected early on that your financial situation wasn't great. As for your sexual orientation, that's something you just can't lie to your partner about."

"I didn't lie, I just didn't tell you…"

"It's a lie of omission."

He apologised, promised to work on a budget with her as soon as he could organise his paperwork, promised to never cheat on her again, but she couldn't allow herself to hope that this time would be different. She didn't want to give him another chance. *But maybe he will change this time,* her conscience taunted.

The definition of stupidity is repeating the same mistake, expecting a different result.

She covered her face with her hands. "I need you to move out. I can't do this anymore."

"Can we talk about this?"

"I have nothing left to talk about." She raised her eyes to meet his. "This doesn't feel right for me. I'm sorry, Garri."

"So that's it… we're finished?"

She nodded. "Yeah."

Garri stared into space. He seemed to be taking it remarkably well, considering.

"You need to find somewhere else to live. I'm going to a green energy conference in Cairns in a weeks' time. I'll be away for a week and a half and I need you to be gone when I return."

He dropped his head. "Can we still catch up sometimes?"

"Yes, of course," she murmured.

THE COMPANY PAID for her airfares and accommodation during the conference and she added an extra six days onto the trip, giving herself a cheap nine day sanctuary.

Most of the sessions were interesting and she took notes when she was able to stop her mind replaying scenes of life with Garri. It didn't help that Garri frequently messaged and called, desperate to keep their contact alive. Like a hunted animal, she startled at every dreaded beep of her phone. Eventually capitulating to the guilt-ridden voice in her head, she replied.

- *I'm fine. Conference is busy but good.*
- *Are you free to talk this evening?*
- *I'm really tired, I need an early night.*
- *Okay, take care sexy buns and we'll talk soon x*

Her lip curled in distaste. How could he act like there was nothing wrong between them?

She crashed in bed and woke ten hours later with the weight of a nightmare pressing down upon her. She buried her head in the pillow, hiding from the mental imprint of a giant octopus chasing her through the ocean. No matter how far or fast she had swum, it had never been far enough to escape the enormous, suffocating tentacles which seemed to envelop the entire globe.

Drained, she decided to play hooky that afternoon, exploring the city with a couple of quirky, alternative thirty-something solar panel designers from New South Wales. They browsed the shops, watched a free dance performance at the Sound Shell, wandered along the esplanade, and then enjoyed a dinner of fresh local seafood. The fun company and conversations were a welcome distraction from her incessant, guilt-ridden internal dialogue, and she finally began to relax.

With her newfound energy and six days ahead of her to explore Cairns, she booked a full day bushwalking tour of the Daintree Rainforest for the next day.

Tropical Cyclone Lago crept closer as she lay unsuspecting in her room, not having heard the tv or radio warnings of its approach. She awoke to an oppressive, wet morning with ominous dark clouds rolling in. Waiting in the foyer for her tour pick up, a messenger arrived instead with news that the tour was cancelled due to the impending, unseasonal cyclone.

Elena moped around the foyer, casting longing glances out to the pool area as the rain intensified. Returning to her room, she worked on her poetry until interrupted by Garri.

- How are you? x

- I'm fine, in the hotel waiting 4 full force of cyclone 2 hit. The hotel staff say building is cyclone-proofed so we'll see.

- Can I call you now?

Elena's energy levels plummeted. She turned her phone off instead of answering him. It was only midday but she drew the blinds and collapsed into the billowing white pillows. She slept until the next morning, vaguely aware—during moments of wakefulness—of the awesome roar of nature outside her window but unconcerned by it. Opening the blind to observe wildly flapping palm trees, debris and minor floodwaters from her third-floor room, she wondered if there were something seriously wrong with her to be so unperturbed by the cyclone. The Elena she had known all her life would have been a basket case.

Sinking back into a dreamy haze and surfacing again at midday to continued wind and fierce rain, she turned her phone on. There was no signal and the battery indicator was down to twenty percent. She plugged it in, realised there was no power and turned it off again to conserve as much battery as possible. No power meant no hot water, so she dressed and opened her door. A note lying on the floor advised that the worst of the storm had passed, they were attempting to fix the failed back-up generator and would advise when it was up and running. A small portable generator was set up in the first floor conference room to provide tea and coffee and run a television. She could imagine nothing worse than sitting in a crowded room with a blaring TV, so she climbed back into bed. After another few hours of sleep, she tried her phone again. It picked up two bars of reception. A chorus of beeps signalled the missed calls and messages in the last thirty hours from her parents, Marcus and Garri. The battery was at seventeen percent so she sent a text to each letting them know all was well, the storm was passing and she was safe in the hotel. She would call them when she could charge her phone.

The clinginess of Garri's messages were smothering her. The

cyclone had been a godsend in terms of having a break from the relentless, demanding beeps of the phone and she realised that, if being in a cyclone was preferable to communicating with Garri, she'd made the right decision. This clarity gave her a sense of release and a surge of energy ran through her. Grabbing her laptop, she began working on her poems again. She continued writing until the battery went flat then descended to the conference room, torch in hand, to get a hot drink and some fruit.

When the generator was fixed and essential power restored, she plugged her phone in to charge and made calls to her family.

Over the next few days she tried to venture out on foot but fronts of bad weather continued blowing through and she was caught in sudden downpours and strong winds. The flooding had been minimal and was receding fast, with only low-lying areas of road still under water, but the tour operators were not resuming tours until the following week so she would miss out on the Daintree altogether. She passed the time reading and writing in her room or sitting by the pool in the humid sunlight in between downpours. She spoke to nobody. It was pure bliss.

❧

SOUNDS OF WATER trickling through a brook came from the overhead speakers. Jivan always played soft, relaxing music in the background.

"That's a nice CD," she commented.

"Yes, I thought it was a water day for you today. How was your trip?"

She laughed. "The conference was good but my week of R&R didn't quite go to plan thanks to the cyclone!"

"Ohhhh, were you in that? WOW!"

She laughed again, loving his animated response.

"Yep, I spent most of the week stuck in my hotel."

"Hmm, so maybe water isn't such a good choice for you today. I always choose music I feel will suit each client but I think you've had enough water."

"Yes, quite enough, thanks! I guess you picked up on the fact that I was surrounded by water!"

"True."

He worked a ropey muscle in her left shoulder.

"I went away saying I needed to be alone. Being completely alone in my room for days wasn't quite what I had in mind though!"

Jivan chortled. "You have to be specific. You should have put it into the universe that you wanted to be alone, enjoying the beach and beautiful weather."

"Yes, I know. Lesson learned."

"How is everything going with Garri?"

"We've separated."

Jivan nodded. "I think it's the best decision for you."

"Yes, there were many signs. Every time I made an excuse for him, another situation would pop up, another example of incongruity, until finally I couldn't ignore it anymore."

"That's how it works. We are given situations and people to learn from. If we ignore the lesson, another one comes, then another. They might start out as gentle taps on the shoulder but, the more we ignore them, the stronger they become. Sometimes we need a good smack from the universe to wake us up."

"Sometimes the universe has to use a baseball bat on me before I learn!"

"Oh well, at least you learn, that's the important thing. You know, the day I met Garri I didn't like his energy."

Elena propped herself on her elbows. "Really? But you told me he seemed gentle."

"Yes I sensed a gentleness to him but something about his energy made my hair stand on end."

"Oh! The same happened to me the night we met."

"Then you should have listened to your intuition. He wasn't right for you."

Why didn't you tell me you didn't like his energy? she thought. If only he had told her. She would have listened to him, would have trusted his intuition more than her own.

Another revelation hit her.

"You know, it's strange. Garri mumbles a lot, so I often had to listen very closely to work out what he was saying but I focussed so much energy on trying to decipher what he said that I wasn't paying attention to…"

"To what he wasn't saying," Jivan finished for her.

"Exactly!"

Their eyes met and they smiled. It was a nice feeling to be on the same wavelength as someone else.

"I'm coming back to your meditation class from now on. I always preferred your energy and the environment here."

"Thanks, that's nice to hear. I look forward to seeing you in class." He smiled again, radiating warmth and sincerity.

※

As ELENA ADJUSTED to being single again, her energy levels skyrocketed. Her sessions with Brett turned to focusing on polishing the draft of her small poetry anthology on the theme of self-esteem and emotions. Half the poems were aimed at children and designed to be used by school teachers, the other half for adults. She was in discussions with an illustrator about concept cover designs while working on the preliminary steps for preparing the book for publication, plus setting up a publishing label and website.

Her phone rang as she worked on her website at home.

"Hi Garri, how are you?"

"I'm doing okay. And you?"

"I'm fine."

There was a pause.

"What can I do for you Garri?"

"Can't we work things out?" he pleaded.

"I'm sorry, no."

"I'm getting myself sorted out. We could go to counselling." His frustration was audible.

"It doesn't feel right for me."

"It's all about money for you. When I hit hard times, you lost interest," he hissed. "There, I've said it," he huffed with a self-satisfied air.

She visualised him patting himself on the back for putting his belief out into the universe and therefore making it the truth in his world. This was how he operated. The more he repeated something, the more real it became in his own mind until he convinced himself that it was the truth.

Her anger bubbled. "It wasn't lack of money, Garri. It was lack of honesty and respect. But since we're on the topic of money, don't forget you still owe me sixty-five thousand!"

"I don't have the money to pay you."

"Two words Garri: payment plan."

"I'll get it to you when I can."

That will be never, Elena thought.

"I guess I'll see you around, then."

"Yeah, I guess," Elena replied, knowing it was unlikely they would cross paths again.

Chapter Seventeen

LIKE ONE BURNING FLAME TOGETHER

Elena walked through the city parklands on her way to work, engulfed by the heady scent of spring. Her phone chimed as she stopped to smell a crab apple blossom. The message was from Derek O'Malley.

- Hi Elena, My friend Channing saw our picture from last night on Facebook and wants 2 meet u. He's a nice guy.

Her instinct was to shy away. It was too soon, only three months since she and Garri had separated. She wasn't ready to get tangled up with anyone else, to trust anyone else. At thirty-two, Elena finally felt she was getting her life in order, but she wasn't confident she had resolved all her issues as far as attracting the right partner. She needed more time to become more grounded, so she didn't end up losing herself in yet another man.

Even so, something about the sound of his name sparked her interest. She had to be careful and sensible, but perhaps a coffee wouldn't hurt. It would be rude to refuse to meet him.

- I'm not ready 2 date. I'm happy 2 meet him 4 coffee so long as he is aware I only want friendship.

- I'll let him know.

The messages threw Elena into a philosophical frame of mind as she walked. Some people viewed the world as a random place, full of coincidence and chaos. Others saw a perfectly structured, ordered entity with everyone and everything intertwined, every event having a carefully orchestrated purpose. Elena was leaning towards the latter belief. She and Michael had met in a random manner but he had been the catalyst for her learning to respect her own needs. Not having sufficiently integrated the lesson, Garri then catapulted into the middle of her comfortable existence to reinforce the lesson.

Yet sometimes things seemed so random and their purpose so unclear. Her dinner with Derek last night was random. They had kept in touch since her separation with Garri but last night was the first time they had caught up. When Derek invited her to dinner, Elena had almost declined, but he had talked her around. She wasn't one for taking selfies but Derek had insisted, posted it on Facebook, and now Channing had surfaced. Was the universe trying to break her resolve to abstain from relationships until she had devoted more time to her own self-development? Did she need to learn something from Channing? Or was it just a random happenstance of a chaotic existence?

The ringing phone jerked her out of her reverie.

"Hello?"

"Hi, Elena?"

"Yes."

"This is Channing, Derek's friend."

"Oh! Hi, how are you?" She hadn't expected him to call so soon.

"Good, and you?"

"Great, thanks… Er, so this probably sounds a bit creepy, but I noticed your photo on Facebook and I wanted to meet you. I promise I'm not a psycho or anything."

"Ha! Well, I'm glad you're not a psycho," Elena laughed. "So tell me about yourself."

"I work at an art and craft supplies store, create sculptures in my spare time and I have just started accompanying Derek in his comedy acts."

"Derek does comedy acts?! He didn't tell me that."

"Well, it's just a bit of fun. I'm like his understudy and he's written a few duo routines for us."

"Huh! So what kind of sculptures do you create?"

"Mostly wood and metal. Some are on display at the Contemporary Arts Centre in Parkside if you'd like to check them out."

"Where in Parkside is it?"

"Porter Street. It runs parallel to George Street. It's not far from the Namaste restaurant, if you know that?"

"Oh cool, that restaurant name has always attracted me... but I haven't been there yet."

"Would you like to have dinner there with me on Thursday night? We could take a quick look at my artwork, then go to dinner."

Elena paused, considering. His passion for creative endeavours attracted her, and she wanted to check out Namaste. "Sure, that would be great."

"Awesome! The office is open until six and they will let me into the gallery space, so shall we meet at five-thirty?"

"Perfect. See you then."

Elena disconnected the call, surprised at herself for agreeing to a dinner date.

Between a busy work schedule, homework for her mentoring sessions, working on her new website and getting book printing quotes, Thursday night arrived fast. She was late leaving the office. Rushing into the Contemporary Arts Centre, it occurred to her she didn't know what Channing looked like. *I should have checked him out on Facebook before coming.* She faltered in the entrance. A lone man sat on a chair, squinting in her direction. She took a punt and smiled at him. He smiled back and rose to greet her.

Her first impression was of a well-built, nervous young man bent in awkward suspension, unsure if he should kiss her cheek or shake her hand. His faded blue jeans were a little baggy and his lime green linen shirt, sleeves rolled up to reveal muscular forearms, accentuated his breathtaking emerald eyes. His collar-length, untamed bleached blonde locks were a little greasy. Despite his obvious gorgeousness, there was no immediate attraction on her part. She breathed a sigh of relief and extended her hand in greeting.

"Nice to meet you, Channing."

"Likewise, Elena. Shall we take a quick look at my sculptures?"

"Sure." Elena followed him.

"I've only got a few items here. This is my friend's exhibition. He gave me some display space to help me gain exposure." His explanation seemed almost an apology for not having an exhibition of his own.

She surveyed Channing's sculptures, carved wood creations juxtaposed with ultra-modern iron designs. Some were painted in bright, bold colours, others featured raw materials. His diversity impressed her. In the corner closest to them, a one and a half metre wooden carving depicting a couple holding hands beneath an arch of roses caught her eye. The woman wore a long, flowing summer gown and the man a day suit and straw hat. Their inclined heads touched. It depicted such peace and beauty and the love between the couple was obvious. The placard next to it read *A Summer Outing*.

"This one is lovely! Is it for sale?"

"Yes." He nodded, shyly.

She understood how he felt. She would soon have to ask people to pay for her new anthology and the thought of it made her uncomfortable too. But with no prices displayed, how would anyone even know his art was available for purchase?

As she deliberated over whether to say something, she was struck by the thought that she had always avoided asking for money. She couldn't even ask for a pay rise when warranted—unlike Garri, who had no qualms whatsoever in asking people for money. A memory of Brett saying that opposites attract in order to balance each other out popped into her mind. A shy person and an outgoing person attracted each other so the shy person learned to be more open and the outgoing person cultivated a quieter side. Perhaps money had been another reason for her meeting Garri after all.

"Well, I think your work is impressive."

"Thank you." He blushed and cleared his throat. "The receptionist is waiting to close up. Shall we go to Namaste now?"

"Sure."

They drove their cars down the road and parked alongside the restaurant.

It was early still and the room was empty. A waitress showed them to a table tucked into the cosy front room.

"Excuse me while I go to the bathroom," Elena said.

"Of course." Channing shot out of his chair as she rose from her own.

She waved him down. "Sit, please. There's no need to stand for me."

When she returned, he rose again, but hovered in a stooped position, unsure if he should resume his seat or stand until she sat down.

Elena smiled in an attempt to put him at ease.

An open bottle of wine sat on the table.

"I chose a red, I hope that's okay?"

She suppressed her irritation that he had decided without consulting her. It was such a small oversight, not worth making an issue over. "Sure, I like red. But a whole bottle is too much. I can only have one glass when I'm driving."

"It will be fine," he replied, gesturing the waitress over to pour their glasses.

They chose some scrumptious Nepalese plates to share, Elena opting for vegetarian dishes. Her meat intake had plummeted since Garri had moved out and she didn't have to cater for a partner who thought his throat had been cut if there were no meat on the table. It wasn't a conscious decision, more of a natural turning towards a diet which suited her body and lifestyle. She wasn't a vegetarian, but she gravitated towards vegetables most days and was feeling much lighter and healthier for the change.

While waiting for the food to arrive, they sipped their wine.

"*A Summer Outing* is a beautiful piece."

"Thank you."

"I'm no artist, but I write books and poetry."

"I'd like to read your work."

"Really?"

"Sure."

"Okay, I'll send you some links." Elena picked up her wine glass, noting it had been refilled to generous proportions. The waitress had not come near them in some time, which meant that Channing must have refilled it and she, engrossed in the conversation, hadn't noticed. She didn't want to seem rude by complaining so she sipped slowly, promising herself to stop at the first sign of muddle-headedness.

During dessert, Channing moved to refill her glass again.

"No, I can't have any more. I won't be able to drive."

"Are you sure? Just a little more?"

"No thanks, I've reached my limit."

He shrugged and poured himself a third glass, filling it to the brim to drain the last drops from the bottle. It disappeared fast.

She hoped he wasn't driving.

He insisted on paying the bill, handing over his credit card and waving away Elena's proffered cash.

Could he, a struggling artist, afford to pay? She scolded herself for the thought. Just because he paid with a card didn't mean he was living on credit. Yet she was equally uneasy about letting him pay because now it felt like a date rather than two people meeting to discuss their creative endeavours.

"Okay, I'll get the next one," she conceded.

He tilted his head. "Maybe."

Her anger flared. It wasn't up to him to decide who paid! She was about to say as much when it occurred to her that perhaps he meant there may not be a next time. Maybe he didn't want to be friends with her. It had been presumptuous of her to assume. Uncertain which way to take his comment, she gave him a rueful smile and shrugged.

"Do you need a ride home?" She asked as they left the restaurant.

"No, my car's over there." He waved vaguely towards the street.

"But are you sure you're okay to drive? Do you have far to go?"

"Nah, just straight up Greenhill Road."

"Well, if you're sure… Thank you for dinner. It was lovely to meet you."

"You too." He kissed her cheek and turned away.

Elena drove home and stayed up late, working on the layout of her website and cursing the HTML coding that didn't want to behave the way she expected it to. She fell asleep with the laptop beside her in bed and awoke to the beep of her phone.

- Good Morning Elena I really enjoyed dinner with u last nite. Would u like 2 repeat?

He sounded keen—maybe too keen. Was she willing to go down that path? She thought about it as she showered and dressed for work. Perhaps she was being too rigid. Dating him didn't mean she was committing to a relationship. Maybe they would catch up a few times then decide to just be friends. Besides, she liked him. He seemed kind, humble, creative and talented.

- Hi Channing I enjoyed ur company 2. What days suit u best? I'm free next Thursday.

The reply was immediate.

- Next Thursday would be great.

CHANNING SEEMED IRRITABLE.

"Is everything okay?" Elena asked.

"Yes, I'm fine, just a bad day at work. I caught a colleague stealing and made a complaint to the manager, but the manager stuck up for her."

"Why?"

"Because they're friends."

"Do you want to talk about it?"

"No, let's go have dinner."

They wandered down Rundle Street and entered Cafe Michael 2 at Channing's suggestion.

"Are you sure you're okay?"

"Oh look, I've just got an upset stomach. You order what you want."

"I'm not that hungry either... just a vegetable Tom Yum please," she told the waiter.

"And two glasses of the Penfold's Shiraz," Channing added.

They conversed until the soup arrived, Elena working hard to maintain the conversation while Chan sat hunched over.

"You should be at home resting," she suggested.

"No, I insist. Eat your dinner."

She ate while Channing downed his glass of wine.

He jerked his chin towards her empty bowl. "Have you finished? I need to go home."

She nodded. "Sure."

His car was close by. "Hop in, I'll drive you to your car."

"No, it's okay," she protested. "I'm happy to walk."

"Don't be silly. Get in."

She conceded defeat.

He scrambled about in the centre console and pulled out a pair of glasses. "Nearsighted," he gave an apologetic shrug. "I hate these things but can't see more than six feet in front of me without them."

They gave him an air of mature sexiness. She tore her gaze away, wanting to look at him but afraid he would read the attraction in her eyes.

When they reached her car, she gave him a quick hug. "I hope you feel better soon."

She watched him drive away, feeling like a nuisance. It had been his choice to keep their date, but she still felt somehow responsible for his discomfort.

The following night, she met Jane and Dale at Casablabla, a restaurant and club offering a mix of Spanish tapas, indie music and live entertainment. Elena did a double-take. Channing and Derek were on the stage, ready for their duo-act. They waved to her. She smiled and waved back.

Their act was hilarious, self-depreciating and irreverent. Elena's belly ached from laughter. Afterwards, as she chatted to Jane and Dale at the table, a hand grazed her upper arm. She turned to find Channing gazing down at her.

"Hi." She flashed a bright smile and stood up.

"Hi Elena, how are you?" His deep, rumbling voice seemed so at odds with his boyish appearance but it was a voice that made her weak at the knees!

"I'm fine. Looks like you're feeling better."

"Yeah, I'm all good."

"Hi Derek." She kissed his cheek. "Great act, why didn't you tell me you were a comedian?!"

Derek looked bashful, "I'm just an amateur having a bit of fun. I started doing standup at the Rhino Room about six months ago and I got the gig tonight because I know the manager here."

"Well, I think you're really good!"

"Are you hanging around a while?" Channing inquired.

"No, Jane and Dale are leaving soon and I have to catch the last tram service to my car which is parked outside town."

"I can drive you to your car later if you want to stay."

"Okay, thanks!" She was surprised by her own response. Five minutes ago she had been ready to go home.

Two hours later, he pulled up beside her car in the early hours of the morning.

"Thanks for the ride." As she leaned over to give him a hug, she sensed a shift in his energy, a slight tension in the air.

He removed his glasses and leaned his head forward to kiss her.

She turned her head and the kiss landed on her cheek.

"Enjoy your weekend!" She jumped out of the car.

It was flattering that he found her attractive and—if she were honest—she was attracted to him too, but she wasn't ready for another entanglement.

Elena drove herself home and went to bed. Thoughts of Channing intruded, keeping sleep out of her reach. She got up and cleaned the house then went back to bed, falling into an exhausted sleep.

The next day, she planted petunias and a daisy bush for some summer colour, then pottered around inspecting the progress of the tomato bushes and herbs she had planted in early October, noting with excitement the first tomato flowers. The citronella she had planted when she first moved in was already waist height and covered in a mass of pink flowers.

In the afternoon she set up a mailing list function on her website, added her new logo, compared quotes from local printers then made an impulsive decision to go to Samoa for a five day self-development retreat offered by Brett. She brushed aside the feeling of self-indulgent guilt. *You're entitled to enjoy life as much as anyone else,* she told herself.

In the middle of booking her flight, Channing called to ask if they could have dinner again. Her schedule was full every night except Friday, so they agreed to meet at Semaphore after work.

෴

ELENA PARKED along the esplanade and checked her phone as she jumped out of the car. She was late again.

- *Elena I'm sitting outside Sully's on Semaphore. Chan*

"Hi, sorry I'm late!" She kissed his cheek.

"No problem, what are you drinking?"

"A glass of Moscato would be great." It was light, sweet and contained only five percent alcohol. She didn't like being drunk or even tipsy anymore. Her days of drinking for fun and excitement had been short-lived and her alcohol pendulum was now finding its balance point.

They chatted in the warm sunshine, sipping their wines, then strolled down Semaphore Road and found a restaurant where they shared a ploughman's platter and more wine. He was strictly a red wine drinker, so she relented and joined him in a glass of red. She still enjoyed the taste but not the heaviness that accompanied it, nor the fuzziness that was now taking hold of her mind.

"So tell me about your family," Elena asked.

Channing's face clouded over. "My parents died in an accident when I was five years old."

"Oh! I'm sorry, I didn't mean to pry." She cringed at her poor choice of questioning.

"It's okay, it was a long time ago." He hung his head, staring at the table. "My little sister and I were raised by an aunt and uncle. My aunt is a university lecturer in economics, my uncle is a company director and my sister runs a floristry business in Melbourne now."

Elena reached out and covered his hand with her own. Her heart ached for him. She suppressed the sudden urge to wrap him in her arms and tell him everything would be okay.

The waitress interrupted with the bill and Elena reached for her purse.

"No, it's my shout. Put that away," Channing ordered, handing over his credit card.

"But you paid last time."

He waved away her protest.

Insist on sharing the cost!

She squirmed, the jarring voice disrupting her mental peace. Would she ever again be able to accept a man wanting to pay for her meal without questioning either his intentions or his ability to afford it? Curse Garri for making her so distrustful of men. She really needed to work on that.

As they meandered along the almost deserted esplanade, Elena realised she was enjoying his company. Despite the darkness, she didn't feel at all unsafe. So she opened up and told him a watered down version of her marriage, what she had learned from it, her self-development efforts and mentoring experience.

"I had a mentor once."

She smiled through the darkness. He was interested in self-development! Another tick on her list. "What was the mentoring for?"

"Ah, just career stuff. I didn't know what I wanted to do. He was great. Sometimes I was such a mess because I didn't want to go to work. I'd call him and he'd talk me through it."

Elena nodded. He still had work issues if last week was any indication, but it sounded like he had made some progress in being able to cope with his emotional responses.

The air had cooled and Elena's summer dress was thin. Channing shrugged off his jacket and put it around her shoulders, reminding her of her first evening with Garridan. Channing's jacket was also too long but much lighter. Garri's had felt like a ton of weights cast over her slender shoulders, but Channing's jacket was light and cosy.

By the time they made their way back to her car, it was almost midnight. She handed back his jacket and gave him a hug. As she pulled away, he ducked his head and kissed her on the mouth.

"Goodnight, Elena." He backed away uncertainly.

In shocked silence, she wrestled with the strong reaction his kiss had sparked within her. It took all her strength not to call out to him. Don't go. *Please come back. Do that again!* But she knew she had to suppress those urges. She wasn't ready for a relationship.

She managed an eventual feeble goodnight in response.

❧

"HOW WAS YOUR DATE LAST NIGHT?" Jane asked as they hiked through the peaceful Onkaparinga Gorge bushland.

Elena smiled. "It was nice. He's easy to talk with, attractive. I like that he's so creative and he's interested in self-development. He once hired a mentor too."

"That sounds promising!" Jane enthused.

"Hmm." Elena ducked her head.

"But?"

"What?"

"I sense there's a but."

Elena sighed. "Oh, I don't know. I like him, I'm attracted to him, but I don't know if I should get involved with anyone yet."

"Why not?"

"It hasn't been long since Garri moved out."

"There's no rule on how long you have to wait between partners, Elena. You don't owe Garri anything."

"I know… but I'd rather be on my own than make another bad choice."

"So just take it slow. You don't have to make any commitment until you're ready."

Elena nodded. Her friend was making perfect sense. She really should stop worrying so much. The only problem was that she had a feeling Channing wanted to move things along faster than she did.

She shook her shoulders to relieve the tension creeping into them and smiled at Jane as she quickened her pace. "Come on, let's move!"

ON SUNDAY EVENING CHANNING CALLED.

"Hi Elena, how was your weekend?"

"Good thanks, and yours?"

"Great! What did you get up to?"

"I went for a hike with my friend Jane and worked on my website."

"Cool. I like hiking too. We should go together sometime."

"Sure that sounds nice. What are you doing this evening?"

"Watching a series called Rake… but I was thinking about you. I enjoyed Friday night."

"Me too."

There was an awkward pause. He cleared this throat. "I really want to see you now."

She flushed with pleasure. She had settled down to write for the evening but promptly lost interest in it. "I'd like to see you too."

"Can I come over?"

She paused. That would mean divulging where she lived, which was another step closer to letting him into her life. But she wanted to see him and to refuse him now might cause offence.

"Okay."

"Can I come now?"

"Sure, I'll text you my address."

"Cool. I'll see you soon!"

Thirty minutes later, she was a bundle of nerves as she let him in. After locking the security door, she turned to find him standing impossibly close, gazing down at her with an impish grin.

"So can I kiss you now?"

Despite trembling with apprehension, her hesitation lasted only a heartbeat. She had wanted him to kiss her again on Friday and nothing had changed. "Okay," she whispered.

His kiss was slow yet firm, but she was so full of pent up anxiety she was unable to enjoy the moment. It had been better when he had caught her by surprise, before her mind had time to question and analyse.

Pulling away, she led him into the living area and made cups of tea.

Chan inclined his head towards the open laptop. "Your writing?"

She nodded.

"I liked your books."

"Really?" It had been two weeks since she had sent him links to electronic copies of her books. He hadn't mentioned them and she had been too insecure to ask what he thought.

"Yes, your style is quirky and fun."

"Thank you!"

He leaned over and kissed her again.

Desire sparked, and she pulled away. "Would you like to see the draft cover designs for my poetry anthology?"

"Sure."

They looked over the sketches until he took the laptop out of her hands and sat it back on the coffee table. He kissed her with more intensity this time and her body responded with equal passion. He grasped her head in his hands, desperate and hungry. Her body betrayed her, responding even while that incessant voice within her was urging her to stop. Lost in the force of his desire, she was astounded to feel such a strong attraction to a man... but she had to stop this. She tore herself away and they slumped against the couch, chests heaving, staring at each other.

"Wow!" she gasped, "We'd better call it a night before we get too carried away."

He smiled, picked up her hand, entwined their fingers and kissed her forehead. "Okay, if that's what you want."

He pulled her to her feet and they walked to the front door where he kissed her swiftly, then left.

Leaning her forehead against the closed door, she exhaled. Even though she worried about moving too fast, she couldn't wipe the grin off her face.

She went to bed and the grin was still there when she woke up in the morning. She struggled to concentrate at work as her thoughts wandered to Channing. Late in the afternoon, she received another text.

- *Hi Elena I've been thinking about u.*

He was so cute with his messages.

- *Maybe u were thinking about me because I was thinking about u.*

- *Wow, thanks beautiful! x*

He had called her beautiful! Flushing with pleasure, she forced her attention back to work. She had only half an hour to finish the literature search she was working on before she had to go to her yoga class.

Emerging from the class more centred, she breathed in the warm evening air. She loved when she was able to focus on the poses and leave the mental chatter behind. She fished her phone out of her bag and saw that Channing had messaged her again.

- *What were you thinking about me today?*

- *I was thinking how much I enjoyed last nite but telling myself 2 not get carried away, even if u r attractive, talented & sweet.*

- *Thanks Elena. It's nice 2 hear good things from u! Please don't stress, things will take their course naturally if we want them 2!*

Thank God, he wasn't going to pressure her.

❦

"CHAN IS SO nice but I'm worried about getting involved with the wrong person again," she told Derek over lunch in the markets the next day.

"I've known Chan for a few years now and I don't think you could go wrong. He is a lot of fun, very considerate and creative. He likes you too. I think you'd be a perfect match!"

Elena was glad to hear such a good character reference so, when Channing asked her over after dinner to watch an episode of the Rake series, she accepted. His flat was at the back of his aunt and uncle's sizeable property in the hill zone of Burnside. Following his instructions, she walked past the double storey, cream-rendered Georgian house with its white grid style windows and manicured gardens and

230

located the tall side gate at the end of the wide driveway. It was locked.

She tried to call him but it went straight to voicemail. She dithered over whether to knock at the main house then decided to text him first.

- *Hi, I'm outside your gate. It's locked.*

A few minutes later she heard galloping footsteps on the other side of the gate which opened to reveal a smiling, playful Chan, his damp platinum hair dishevelled.

"Hi, sorry! I was taking a shower. Come in."

He led her up the cobblestone path which weaved through flowering jacarandas, over a small ridge and down a gentle slope to his secluded flat, which was surrounded by tall gum trees. A few tree trunks had been carved into various animal shapes—an owl, a cat pouncing, a dolphin leaping out of water. Angular, oxidised iron sculptures were scattered between the trees—a mother with an infant in her arms, a headless, naked female form.

"Welcome to my rusty forest of dreams," he said with an exaggerated sweep of his hand.

"These are all yours?"

"Yeah, I had an idea of opening an exhibition space here but it hasn't worked out so well…"

"It could still happen. Don't give up hope."

He shrugged.

The flat seemed large from the outside but inside was much smaller, just a bedroom, a bathroom, a kitchenette and a storage room. She stood until he urged her to sit on the only chair—a small, carved dark wood love seat with red cushions, facing the side of the bed.

He sat next to her and reached for the remote to turn down the TV that blared from the wall on the other side of the bed.

They sat together in silence, his thigh pressed against hers.

She adjusted her position, trying to create a little breathing space between them.

"Did you make this seat?"

"Yes."

"It's beautiful," she ran a hand over the polished arm.

"But uncomfortable to sit in for any length of time! Come, sit with me on the bed, you'll be more comfortable."

She perched on the edge of the bed while he sprawled across the superman duvet cover.

"So this is where I live. It used to be my grandma's flat."

"It's cosy. Do you use the main laundry?"

Chan nodded. "Well, my aunt does the laundry, but I help her sometimes."

Elena's uneasiness returned. She couldn't imagine still depending on her parents. She pushed the thought aside. It wasn't fair to judge him. Just because he lived on his aunt and uncle's property didn't mean he was incapable of looking after himself. It was no doubt a choice he made so he could devote more time to his art rather than have his energy consumed by long office hours like most of the population, herself included. She would never give up her independence now but who knows what choices she may have made earlier in life if other options had presented themselves.

"Does it bother you that I still live with my family?" He ducked his head.

Her heart went out to him. She didn't want him to feel that pursuing his passion was a bad decision. "No, if it makes you happy, that's all that matters."

"I wasn't sure how you would feel about it," he said, face brightening as he scooted over and gave her a hug, pulling her down onto the bed with him. They exchanged gentle kisses until Elena pulled away. This was too much, too soon. She had to find a distraction.

"What's the door at the other end of the kitchen?"

"It's my studio. It used to be a lounge and dining area, and a second bedroom but we converted it into a studio after Grandma died. Come, I'll show you."

He led her into a room twice the size of his flat. The minty scent of eucalyptus lingered in the air. Sawdust-covered benches flanked large windows on two sides. A variety of tools and materials covered the pine benches and hung on the walls. In the middle of the room, next to a part-completed metal sculpture, sat a large welding machine. Several posters of scantily-clad women in provocative poses hung on a third wall.

He followed her gaze. "They're for inspiration."

Elena nodded curtly, unimpressed.

"I like the visual effects in this one. What do you think?" he pointed to a woman in a black-and-white striped corset and fishnets, one stiletto clad foot slung artfully over the back of a wrought iron chair.

Elena considered it, trying to remain artistically objective. It didn't interest her but she could understand the artistic angle he would see it from.

"It's okay," she chose her words with care. "I can see how they might be useful to you."

He looked her squarely in the eye. "I guess I am a bit kinky, too."

She swallowed hard, fighting her embarrassment. Why was she embarrassed anyway? If liking a corset was as kinky as he got that wasn't so bad. What man didn't like lingerie?

She gave a nervous laugh. "Just as well I own a corset." Her mouth clamped shut and colour rose in her cheeks.

Oh God! Why did you say that?

He moved closer, wrapping his arms around her. "Mmmm, I'd like to see that."

She laughed again, moving away from him. "Maybe one day... so how about this Rake series?"

"Okay." He grabbed her hand and flopped back onto the bed, dragging her down with him.

The series had a predictable relationship drama storyline. Elena, never interested in television, soon tired of it and began to fidget, running her fingers along Channing's shoulders, kneading the muscles. He sighed and melted into her side. When she stopped, his head popped up, his emerald eyes sparkling playfully.

"Don't stop!"

She resumed her slow, gentle massage and he arched back towards her, purring with pleasure. He reminded her of a playful kitten and she smiled at his obvious pleasure. Whenever her hand came to a stop, he would grab it and tap it on his shoulder, demanding more please in a cute, childlike tone.

When the episode finished, he turned and rolled on top of her, covering her face and neck with little appreciative kisses. Amazingly, she felt comfortable being with him like this. He kissed her on the mouth, a long slow kiss that became more intense until they were rolling all over the bed, locked in a passionate embrace. Again the intensity of the charge between them surprised her.

They separated, chests heaving as they struggled to regain control of themselves. Chan snuggled his head into her side, twisting to focus his big playful eyes on hers, willing her to play with him. She chuckled and caressed his shoulders once more.

"Mmm," he purred.

At midnight she attempted to get up.

He grabbed hold of her wrist. "No! Stay," he demanded.

"It's late and I have to work tomorrow."

"Just a little longer," he pleaded.

She gave in and, as she continued to massage his shoulders, they talked of previous experiences, scars they each carried and what they would no longer accept in a relationship.

She checked the time and sat bolt upright. "It's one a.m.! I have to go."

He tried to pull her back down, but she resisted this time.

"I'd like to stay longer but I have to go or I'll be too tired to work tomorrow."

He pouted but got up to walk her out, holding her hand and kissing her three times before letting her get in the car. She drove home exhausted but happy.

- Hi Elena I wanted u 2 stay last nite. I really like u and I want u! Do I need 2 control myself as much next time? What do u think? x

It didn't sit well with her that he had chosen to have this conversation so soon, and to do it over text rather than in person. But she could understand him being nervous about broaching the subject of sex. She liked him too and found him very attractive. In fact, she had never experienced such a strong physical attraction before. The thought that he felt the same way about her sent a thrill down her spine. But it was too soon. Not wanting to upset him, she thought long and hard before responding.

- I really like u 2 Channing but I need more time. I don't mean 2 make things difficult 4 u. xo

- Okay beautiful x

She loved how he called her beautiful—much, much nicer than being called sexy buns.

- Come over for a cuppa tomorrow night x

Her living room would be a safer place to sit than his bed.

- *Okay! x*

❧

WHILE ELENA WAITED FOR CHANNING, she worked on a conference presentation for her boss which she hadn't managed to finish in the office and was satisfied to complete the notes and all but the last two slides before he arrived. His car purred as it entered the driveway, followed by a screeching of metal against metal.

Elena rushed outside to witness him backing away from her roller door.

"What happened?"

He joined her in front of the door, inspecting the damage in the fading daylight.

"Sorry, I misjudged the space."

"You're not wearing your glasses."

He shrugged, looking embarrassed. "They make me look old."

"I think you look good in them. Well, no real harm done, just a tiny dent in the door and a small scratch on your bumper."

She held the front door open for him. "How was your day?"

"Not so good. That woman at work blamed me for a mistake she made. I protested my innocence, but the boss stuck up for her again."

"She sounds like a nasty piece of work." Elena didn't know how to help him. She offered cups of tea and chocolate biscuits and tried to lift him out of his funk by telling him about her trip to Cairns and her upcoming trip to Samoa.

"Wow, you're a real jet-setter, aren't you!"

"No," she demurred. "It's not normal for me to travel."

"I've never been overseas."

"Would you like to go?"

"Definitely!"

Good, that was another tick on her list. Before long, he lunged at her playfully. Once again, Elena was overcome by both the force of her attraction to him and his intense focus on her. And once more, while her mind continued to chatter about whether getting this close to him was a good idea, her body was betraying her.

With practised deftness, he slipped his hand up her dress and into her panties. She froze in shock. The shock morphed into hurt that he would be so forward only one day after telling him she needed more time. It was so disrespectful... but her desire for him was strong. He was such a nice person, surely the disrespect wasn't intentional.

"Ah, I'm tired of being sensible," she heard herself groan.

"Good, me too!" he replied, pulling down her panties.

The abrupt shift from romantic to business-like sent her into a spin. An image of him rubbing his hands with glee popped into her mind. She struggled with her tumbling emotions even as she couldn't help but allow her body to respond. And respond it did, like it had never responded to anyone else. Before long, they were standing naked in her bedroom.

"Er, do you have protection?" she asked.

With a distracted shake of his head, he continued running little kisses down her neck. "Don't you?"

"No."

He paused, his expression hopeful.

She stared back.

"Where's the nearest late-night supermarket?" he asked, pulling on his jeans.

"There's nothing open after 9 p.m., you'll have to go to a petrol station."

Now is the perfect time to call it quits!

She ignored the voice.

He grabbed her by the shoulders and kissed her again. "While I'm gone, put your corset on for me?"

She nodded, watching him head to the doorway.

"And black stilettos," he called over his shoulder.

The front door banged shut.

She stood naked and indecisive. When he returned, she could tell him she wasn't ready for this. She picked her dress up off the floor, then hesitated, the dress dangling from her limp hand. It would be cruel to do that. He had left anticipating what he would return to. Besides, it's not like she wasn't attracted to him.

But the corset request made her uneasy. Sex should be about

connecting on a deeper level, not just the physical plane. He shouldn't need the trappings of lingerie, especially not their first time.

She shook her head to clear it. Why did she always over-analyse everything! He was artistic, the visual was important to him. She needed to relax and enjoy herself instead of being trapped in fear about whether it was the right time.

She dropped the dress back on the floor, dug out her heels and the little-used corset which had been a gift from Garri, struggled with the multitude of tiny hooks and finally got it done up just as she heard his car pull into the driveway.

It was not quite the experience she had hoped for. His intense lovemaking had an urgency bordering on desperation and she emerged from the encounter dishevelled, the survivor of a freak tornado, unsure whether she was distressed or elated.

She eventually fell asleep and overslept her alarm. He went home and she rushed out the door, late for work. The day was an annoying series of meetings that left her little time to get through her growing pile of work. She went to an extra yoga class after work but had trouble concentrating. As she moved through sun salutations, her mind replayed the events of the previous night. As she relaxed in Shavasana, Jivan's calming voice was interspersed with an internal debate over whether she should see him again.

At home, she started baking chocolate raspberry brownies for Jivan. Because she was going away, her massage appointment on Saturday would be the last time she saw him before Christmas. He had loved the brownies she made last Christmas, so she wanted to give him more this year, which meant making a special batch now, then another for her family when she returned from Samoa.

Channing called. "What are you doing tonight?"

"Baking brownies for a friend and I need to pack my bag for Samoa."

"What do you need to pack, beautiful?"

"Not sure. I wonder if I can get away with taking only a swim-suit!" she chuckled.

"Mmmm, I'd love to see you in a bikini."

She flinched. "I'm not an object, Channing. There's a real person inside this body."

"What? I know… I'm just saying I like how you look."

"But do you like my personality, my soul?"

There was a pause. "Of course I do."

"Good! That's more important. I've been wondering if we have let things move too fast between us. Maybe we need more time to get to know each other before we get serious." Her words spilled in an impulsive vomit.

"Er okay... We don't have to make any commitments yet, you know."

A wave of guilt washed over her. "Oh God, I'm sorry."

"It's okay. Well,... I guess I'll let you get on with packing. Would you like to do something this Sunday?"

"Sure, maybe we could have a picnic?" A public place would be safer.

"Good idea, see you on Sunday."

"Bye."

Fifteen minutes later, her phone chimed.

- Geez that was an awkward conversation!

Her shoulders sagged. Why hadn't he said what he wanted to over the phone rather than sending a passive-aggressive text now? Yet she was not blameless in the matter, she had overreacted.

- Sorry...

- I'm not like every other guy Elena! Sex is not the only thing on my mind. Guys talk about meeting someone special and not being able 2 live without them. Girls feel that way about clothes. I don't get that?

Her uneasiness returned. In Elena's experience, men had never seemed particularly focussed on romantic love and the statement contradicted his previous one about all other guys having one-track minds. Plus, he was the one interested in her bikini, she was the one who had said personality was more important than looks. He'd twisted the whole conversation around!

Not being able to live without someone was a worry, too. From what she had learned in the past six months, respecting someone, loving them, enjoying their presence and wanting them in your life could lead to a happy relationship, but to not be able to live without them was codependent. She didn't want that again, nor did she want someone clingy, suffocating and unhinged in her life. But how to respond without offending him?

- Actually, I'm not that interested in clothes. I'm sorry, the past has made me wary of men. It's not a reflection on u, please don't take it personally x

- okay I'm sorry if I got a bit sensitive x

She sighed in relief that they had sorted it out.

౼

"YUM! Thanks for the brownies, I'll enjoy eating these. So how is everything?" Jivan's magic hands got to work on her shoulders.

"Good."

She felt she should mention Channing but held back, embarrassed to tell him while she was still this unsure about the status or longevity of the relationship... liaison... whatever it was they were doing.

But Jivan wasn't just anyone, he was Jivan. Every time she saw him, she had the urge to bare her whole soul to him. It was crazy. He had done nothing to indicate he expected it of her, but somehow it was what she expected of herself. But, afraid of scaring him away, she held back, keeping a part of herself shielded from him even as she longed to do the opposite.

"How are you?" she asked, hoping to steer to conversation away from herself.

"I'm fine."

"How was India?"

The question launched him into an enthusiastic spiel and she breathed a sigh of relief. She was off the hook again. He told her about his visit to his spiritual guru and the amazing stories of perception and awareness he experienced with this man known only as Guruji. She wanted to meet this man and experience his awesome energy first-hand. It wasn't the first time Jivan's stories had sparked a desire in her to visit India, but fear of the potential dangers she may face there stopped her from considering it a holiday destination.

All too soon the hour had passed and she had to leave, with shoulders much looser but a wistful heart that wished to spend more time with this special person. Apart from that one text message while he was away, she didn't seem to exist for him outside the yoga studio. She would be forever grateful for his continued presence as a teacher and healer in her life but was there no hope for something more?

ON SUNDAY AFTERNOON, Elena and Channing lay on a rug, soaking up the warm sun in Veale Gardens in the southern city parklands until sunset. They returned to his flat and ate takeaway pizza, cross-legged on his bed while watching episodes of Rake.

Channing curled up next to her and put his head in her lap, giving her that impish grin which melted her heart. He lifted her hand to his shoulder, indicating that he wanted another massage. She massaged until her arm ached.

"It's my turn for a massage now."

"No, I want more rubs for me, babe!" he pouted.

"But you've had a long massage already."

He sighed and sat up, "Okay."

She settled into his lap and tried to focus on the relaxing sensation of his hands instead of the nagging sense of guilt that it was selfish of her to expect him to do something he wasn't keen to do. The rational part of her knew it was madness to feel guilty, but it was hard for her to dislodge the habit. After a short time, Channing stopped, rolled her out of his lap and flopped down beside her.

"My turn now," he demanded.

Unable to resist his boyish charm, she returned to her task with a sigh. This time her touch aroused him and it wasn't long before they were making out. She was conflicted. Should she put the brakes on until she had made a firm decision about him? But he was just so darn cute! Once again the combined intensity of their physical desires won and she left his place in the early hours of the morning, sneaking down the driveway so as not to wake his aunt and uncle.

He sent her sweet, attentive texts over the next couple of days before asking to see her again.

- Would u like 2 come over 4 a cuddle 2nite my beautiful? xx

His use of the possessive pronoun bothered her. Since when had she become his possession? But, despite her misgivings, she still wanted to see him.

- I'd love 2 but not sure I have time. Going 2 see my illustrator after work. Shall I call u when I'm done? x

- Yes, call me xx

It was after 8 p.m. by the time she left the illustrator and she didn't have the energy for another late night out, so she suggested Channing come to her place instead.

She devoured a toasted sandwich for dinner, finishing the last bite as Channing arrived. He was stressed after another bad day with his workmate.

"Want to talk about it?" she asked.

Channing shrugged. "She's just a cow. Don't worry about it, let's talk about your day."

"It was just a normal work day. I had a good meeting with the illustrator though. He's come up with some great sketches for the child section of my anthology! We've got a timeframe in place now so it should be ready to print soon." She stifled a yawn.

"Let's go to bed," he suggested.

She was caught out by the presumptuous ease with which the statement rolled off his tongue. He had none of the reservations she did. He was calling her all manner of endearments—beautiful, babe, sweetheart. Whilst it thrilled her every time he addressed her that way, she couldn't shake off the uncomfortable feeling that she had allowed him to become too familiar way too fast. But she couldn't backtrack now without offending him and harming their potential relationship. She allowed him to lead her into the bedroom once again and, after the hurricane of his love-making ended, curled into the arch of his body, more than ready for sleep.

But sleep evaded her as Channing tossed and turned.

He sat up. "I've got a headache. I need to go home."

"Why do you want to drive with a headache?"

"I need to be in my own bed when I'm sick."

"How about I get you some Panadol and try giving you some Reiki?" She wanted him to stay.

"What's that?" he snapped.

"It's an energy healing technique," she said, already heading to the kitchen to retrieve the Panadol. She gave him a hesitant Reiki treatment, nervous in case it didn't work and he thought she was a crackpot. But it was worth a try if it meant he didn't run away after sex.

To her relief, he settled down and was asleep before the Panadol had time to kick in.

Exhausted, she crawled back into bed, still smarting that he had wanted to leave as soon as the sex was over. She knew she was being unreasonable and that her reaction was because of the baggage she carried about men and sex. She was also aware that she had recently crept out of his house instead of staying the night—even if it was because his aunt and uncle didn't want him to have women stay over. Turning up to breakfast would not be the best way to introduce her to his family. Nevertheless, it was hypocritical of her to be hurt by him doing something she was guilty of herself.

The thoughts kept running around in her head until finally sleep came.

At yoga class the following night, she tried to focus on accepting the now and being non-judgmental towards herself in performing the asanas, hoping the non-judgement would translate itself to other areas of her life.

ॐ

ON FRIDAY NIGHT, Elena researched print-on-demand publishing. At first glance it seemed print-on-demand was not a viable option yet without selling each copy at an inflated per unit cost. After trawling through various sites to compare pricing, she found herself on a page for Sophie the Clairvoyant. A flashing red heart caught her attention.

'Find out what's in store for your love life. Now only $39!'

Elena couldn't recollect how she had arrived on the page and she had no idea who Sophie was. It could be an automated bot for all she knew. Despite her reservations, she was drawn to click on the link, fill in her details and hit send. She stared at the screen, surprised at herself for doing something so random and impulsive, then shrugged and turned off the laptop. She'd probably just blown her dough on a charlatan.

Channing was at a family function and had asked her to call him at midnight so he had an excuse to leave but she was struggling to keep her eyes open so she set an alarm, went to bed and woke up to the alarm two hours later. She called twice, but he didn't pick up the phone. When he hadn't called her back by one o'clock, she sent a message.

- R u okay Chan? x

There was no response. Concerned, she lay awake until her eyes refused to stay open any longer.

She awoke to her phone beeping and sun streaming through the window at half past nine.

- Good morning Elena. Sorry last nite is a blur! What did we decide 2 do 2day? xx

Suppressing her annoyance, she called him. Her annoyance increased when he told her he had drunk too much at the party then met friends afterwards and didn't get home until 4 a.m., at which time he'd noticed her missed calls. She had interrupted her own sleep at his request and he'd ditched her for some friends without even messaging her!

She drove to his house. By the time she arrived, she had calmed down enough to laugh at herself. Here she was—not even sure she was ready to commit to this guy—getting angry with him for not contacting her! He wasn't obliged to notify her of his every movement.

They drove to Waterfall Gully and climbed to Mt Lofty Summit and back. His family were out when they returned so he took her hand and they ran through the backyard into his flat, made frantic love in the shower, then drove their cars to her house. After dinner in Brighton and a moonlit walk along the beach, he stayed with her for the night.

Chapter Eighteen

I'M HALF SICK OF SHADOWS

E lena sat at the departure gate waiting for her flight to Samoa.

- *Goodbye beautiful have a good flight, I'm missing u already! xx*

He was too cute. She felt guilty that the thought of missing him hadn't crossed her mind yet. But she enjoyed his company and she was sure she would miss him over the next five days.

- *I'll miss u 2 xo*

She disembarked in Apia with the setting sun casting a gorgeous pink hue over the horizon.

- *What's Samoa like beautiful? xx*

He was sending normal messages instead of using Facebook messaging like she'd suggested. She pocketed the phone, planning to reply when she had wifi access, and found the meeting point where the rest of the workshop participants waited for transport to the resort. Her assigned roommate was Cat, a woman in her early thirties from Sydney who ran an interior decorating business with her boyfriend.

After settling into the room and connecting to the wifi, she replied to Channing via Facebook.

- *Warm & humid! Off to bed now, early start 2moro xx*

She awoke to his reply.

- *I bet it's beautiful there! I hope u have more rest and play than work! xx*

- *Thank u. I'm not here 4 work tho, it's a personal development workshop xx*

Personal development wasn't an easy process, but she had never equated it with work.

Their first session revisited the structure of the mind and how it connects with the feeling body. It didn't seem to matter how many times she heard or read about this stuff, she always picked up something new. There was always some definition or concept she hadn't quite grasped before that resulted in a subtle change in her perception. The mind was such a fascinating instrument and she was impatient to learn how to play hers more effectively.

During lunch she received an email from Sophie the Clairvoyant. Curious, she took her phone down to the beach and found a quiet spot to read.

Dear Elena,

At the risk of offending you, I'm going to be very blunt. You need to be more self-confident. Stop underestimating yourself! Don't feel obliged to accept partners who are not an age, intellectual or energetic match for you. I can see you have made this choice in the past because you felt you didn't deserve better.

I know that you are living under a cloud created by past events and you will have to make an effort to free your mind from the past. Shift that emotional baggage so you can move on. Three years ago, you missed out on an opportunity, do not let it pass you by again! Destiny will not happen by itself—you have to take action to help create your life the way you want it.

You are set to meet someone who is so different from the men you have met in the past and from the man you have in mind that you will have to react very differently. You need to listen to your heart and trust your intuition. When he appears you will feel a difference within you. You will feel an intense and rapid mutual attraction. Your first encounter will be brief. You will need to take the initiative to get back into contact again and, without you realising it, the relationship will intensify. For a while your contact will be virtual, then you will set up a physical meeting. The twenty-eighth of January stands out as a significant date. It is important that you just be yourself when you meet him. Don't over-analyse! You will react instinctively. Allow things to happen naturally. Try to relax and enjoy the relationship rather than seeing it as something to be always worked on and improved. Learning to have fun is one of your life lessons. At the same time, you need to learn boundaries in

your relationships. Being supportive and loving is not the same as being
submissive.

You and your partner will share the same opinions. He will be considerate,
give you a lot of affection and treat you with respect. All you need to do is
give the same in return. He is kind, loyal, trustworthy and reliable, with an
interesting personality. He is very open, with few preconceived ideas, so you
will need to get rid of some of your outdated ideas. Appearances are not very
important to him, he sees much deeper than the surface level.

Dialogue will be important in your relationship but you will have to accept
some concessions because he isn't someone who reveals his secrets easily.
While this is something to watch out for, you can trust him, he will not lie
to you.

He will be very sensitive about the attention you give him and if you have
any doubts about how you should proceed, ask him. Make communication a
priority to avoid any serious misunderstanding.

You need to react faster and be more ready to listen at the right moment than
you have in the past. Also you need to learn to control your emotions better.
Don't simply react according to the events you experience. Consider what
your partner might be feeling.

But overall, I see joy and happiness around this person and your relationship
together.

Elena stared blankly out to sea. She *had* always lacked confidence
where men were concerned. She *had* accepted partners in the past
who didn't feel right because she had felt she didn't deserve better or
that no better option may come along. She *was* living under a cloud as
a result of accepting Garri into her life. Three years ago she had
missed an opportunity, according to Sophie—just before meeting
Garri. She knew meeting Garri had derailed her from the path she
had intended to take. But how did Sophie know? Perhaps she was the
real deal.

The future partner Sophie described sounded exactly like the
partner she wanted. Two things puzzled her, though. Firstly, he was
so different to the person she had in mind, but to whom did that refer
—Channing or Jivan? She'd had Jivan in the back of her mind for so
long but Channing was now on her mind too.

Secondly, a virtual meeting was unlikely. She had never been
interested in online dating and never would be. Besides, that would

discount both Jivan and Channing, since she had already met them both, and neither had been online meetings. She walked back to the conference room still mulling it over.

Elena and Cat took a quick dip in the ocean before dressing to meet the rest of the group on the beach for dinner in the open-air restaurant. The diverse group included singles and couples ranging from early twenties through to mid-sixties, from across Australia. They came from all walks of life but shared one commonality: they were there to focus on their personal development.

Elena and Cat gravitated towards a small group of younger people who headed to the bar after dinner. More of the group joined them as they lounged on sofas to one side of the dance floor. The drinks flowed and, despite Elena's good intentions of having an early night, she found herself carried away by the group camaraderie. After the second vodka, she dug her phone out of her bag to check the time and noticed an earlier text from Channing.

- I miss u Elena! xx

She typed a hurried, tipsy reply.

- I miss u 2. Just had a beautiful dinner on the beach, it's like heaven here! xx

She stuffed the phone back in her bag as one guy, Anton, handed her a third vodka. Their group had grown to fifteen people. She sank back into the couch, content to watch everyone; the guy who ran a chain of adult shops, the nurse from Brisbane, the professional mentors, the EFT practitioner, the antiques dealer, the scientist, and the software engineer.

Suddenly half the group bounded onto the dance floor. Without hesitation, Elena joined them, bouncing to a local pop cover band. Her smile widened. She hadn't felt this carefree for at least three years.

The group slowly dissipated as people moved back to their rooms for the night, until only Elena, Cat, Anton and his roommate Felix remained.

"Would you like to try 'ava?" Anton asked.

"What's 'ava?" Cat asked.

"It's the Samoan name for kava. Felix and I have some in our room."

Mind-altering drugs scared Elena. But kava was considered a soft drug, nothing more than a relaxant, really. "Sure," she agreed, carried on the high of the night and the beverages she had already consumed.

The boys set a plastic tub on the floor and mixed a quantity of powdered 'ava root with water from the bathroom tap to create an unappetising, muddy concoction which they scooped into a coffee cup and passed between the five of them.

"You have to scull a full cup, it's the traditional way," Anton told them.

When Elena's turn came, she ignored the voice in the back of her head that told her drinking unfiltered tap water in a developing country might not be the smartest move. She cursed herself for being so distracted the last two weeks that she had forgotten to check for travel advice on water quality. Almost gagging on the bitter, gritty muck, she forced it down anyway.

The tub was still half full and the boys started round two. Elena glanced at her phone and saw Channing had replied to her message almost two hours ago.

- *Enjoy urself beautiful xx*

She wondered if he expected a response and decided she had better, lest he think she was ignoring him.

- *My roomie & I r drinking kava with 2 guys! Tastes awful, my mouth is numb xx*

His reply was swift, despite the lateness of the hour.

- *be careful but have a good time beautiful xx*
- *Don't worry I'm the definition of careful xx*

In the wee hours of the morning she and Cat stumbled back to their room. When the alarm sounded at seven o'clock, Elena felt anything but the definition of careful. Her head was fuzzy and her mouth dry. Her tongue felt swollen, her eyes gritty and glued together and her stomach made rumbling churns of protest. Cat wasn't much better. Elena groaned and rolled out of bed, stumbling into the bathroom. After a hot shower and drinking half a litre of water, she felt slightly more human. She took painkillers for the ache behind her eyes and laid down again while Cat showered.

The boys, fresh and chipper, were waiting for them at breakfast.

"Don't worry, you'll get used to it," Felix grinned, tucking into bacon and eggs.

Elena could stomach only a cup of peppermint tea.

"FEAR IS the single emotion at the root of most self-destructive behaviour and excuses for not taking action," Brett boomed, his amplified voice bouncing off the walls and echoing through the conference room.

"Fear of judgement, fear of failure, fear of success—how will my life change if I succeed and how will others respond to it—fear of making the wrong choice, fear of hurting ourselves or others. The list of fears in the human experience is endless!"

"But how many times does a fear prove unfounded? Think of something you were afraid to do but, once you made yourself do it, the outcome was nothing like you had imagined."

Elena could think of many. At different stages of her life she had been afraid of the dark, afraid of dogs, afraid to swim, afraid to live on her own, to drive a car, to change jobs, to voice her opinions in case they offended someone. She had been afraid to write a book, afraid no men would be interested in her, afraid to end her marriage in case an unseen force punished her for breaking her vows. She'd been a solid, rigid block of fear for much of her life yet, each fear had so far proven false. Life had become much more interesting, joyful and creative each time she had confronted a fear.

Her attention returned to Brett as he wrote a single line on the whiteboard: FEAR = False Expectations Appearing Real

She remained in the room after everyone adjourned to the lunch buffet. *Am I falsely afraid of getting involved with Channing or merely cautious? If it's a false fear, how can I move past it?* Her thoughts swam in circles until she gave up and joined the group for lunch.

Before heading into the afternoon meditation class, she checked her phone and saw she had missed a text from Channing an hour earlier.

- I'm worried! Last nite u were with strange guys! Please let me know u r okay xx

His need for her to check in every day was making her claustro-phobic. She had to admit though, from his point of view, her last message could seem a potential cause for worry.

- Hi Chan! No need 2 worry, I'm fine. I've been in workshop all day xxx

- thanks can u call me 2nite please? xx

Her annoyance level crept higher. Now she had to message *and* make international calls? She didn't even call her family when she was overseas unless necessary! Why didn't he offer to call her if he was so desperate to talk? It wouldn't be so bad if he'd use WhatsApp or Skype but he was a technology dinosaur… which was kind of cute, in an annoying kind of way. Plus now she felt responsible for making him worry and wanted to make up for it.

- *sure, I'll call b4 dinner xx*

- *okay xx*

As she moved to turn the phone off her thumb scrolled the screen upward to reveal two earlier messages.

- *How r u beautiful? xx*

- *Hello, how r u? xx*

Elena felt a stab of guilt.

- *sorry just saw ur other msgs. I had my phone on silent all day. Now I feel really bad! xx*

- *Don't feel bad, just don't make me worry! x*

Before dinner, she walked down to the water's edge and called Channing.

"Hello beautiful!"

"Hi Chan, how are you?"

"Great, how are you?"

"I'm good, thanks. So, what's up?"

"What do you mean?"

"Your message sounded like you wanted to tell me something."

"No beautiful, I just wanted to hear your voice!"

She rubbed at a stabbing pain in her left shoulder. He asked her to make an international call just to hear her voice? After being apart for only two days?

"I miss you," he continued.

Her heart melted in gratitude for his caring nature. But melted heart or not, warning bells sounded in her head at his accelerated clinginess.

"I miss you too," she lied, justifying it by the fact that she did enjoy his company and was sure they would have had a fantastic time if he were with her; therefore she *was* missing that opportunity even if she were having too good a time to dwell on his absence.

"It's nice to hear your voice, but I should go. Overseas calls are expensive," she hinted.

"Just a few more minutes, sweetheart?"

"I'd love to Chan but roaming charges are a killer! If you'd download Skype, we could talk for free."

"Yeah, but I don't know how to use it. Take care and I'll see you in three days, Mwah."

"Thanks Chan, Mwah."

Their group dinner began with a traditional 'ava ceremony performed by a local village chief. They sat in a circle on the sand while the chief's assistant prepared the 'ava, scooped it into a coconut shell, offered it first to the chief, then Brett, and then passed it around the circle. A traditional war dance followed, performed by ripped, tattooed young men, then they moved to the seafront restaurant. Over a long meal, Elena indulged in the free wine provided. People slowly drifted back to their rooms for the night until only Elena, Cat, Felix and Anton remained. Together they formed the fearless four, singing as they wandered along the darkened beach.

It was a glorious, balmy night, the most perfect kind of evening as far as Elena was concerned. Content, she sank into the sand.

Before long, the boys suggested another 'ava session. Returning to their room, they made a batch of 'ava and brought it down to where the girls waited on the beach.

They circled the 'ava bucket and scooped cups of the foul-tasting muck. She wondered why she was forcing herself to drink it. No sooner had the thought landed than it flittered off into the starry night. It was replaced by the thought that perhaps she shouldn't be mixing alcohol and 'ava. She would regret it in the morning. That thought too floated away to join the constellation of other sensible thoughts in the night sky. Her grin widened and she heard herself laughing at jokes she didn't understand. Her bones melted into the sand, which still retained heat from the daytime sun.

The conversation petered out. Cat rose and wordlessly shuffled back to the room. Not long after, Felix wandered off along the beach towards the sound of music drifting from the bar.

Elena and Anton looked at each other, both reluctant to leave the beach.

"Feel like a swim?" Anton suggested.

"Sure," Elena agreed, glad she was wearing her bikini under her short, white shift dress.

As they plunged into the inky ocean, Elena marvelled at her own courage. She had never gone near the ocean after dark. The fear of what may lurk beneath the darkened depths had kept her anchored to the shoreline even on the hottest summer nights. But tonight she threw herself with abandon into the tepid water, rolling around in the gentle waves then coming to tread water facing Anton.

He was staring at her with much more interest than before. He moved closer.

She arched backwards into the water, pushing herself away from him, but he caught hold of her ankles and pulled her towards him, wrapped her legs around his waist and his arms around her torso, then lifted her out of the water.

Oh God, how did you not see this coming?

She cringed in embarrassment and ducked her head. Anton ducked his head beneath hers and, bringing their faces together, kissed her. Floating in a state of languid suspension, her body responded to him while the voice in her head chided.

What are you DOING? Tell him to stop!

She tried to pull away but her floppy limbs wouldn't cooperate. She couldn't speak either, only giggle like a little girl.

Why don't you tell him to stop, you silly girl?

The voice had moved outside of her head and was suspended somewhere near her sensible thoughts constellation. It was a curious sensation, as if the disembodied voice was the real her and the body bobbing around in the water, connected to Anton, was somebody else.

When Anton grabbed her hand and led her out of the water, she obediently followed. On emerging from the water, an uncontrollable shaking took hold of her body.

"Are you cold?" He touched her goose-bumped upper arm.

She nodded, teeth chattering. What was happening? The outside temperature couldn't have dropped so fast.

"It's not that cold!"

She again nodded but her trembling body betrayed her. They scooped up their clothes and Anton ran up the sand towards the grassed area of the resort, dragging her along behind him. They were both giggling now and she was more focussed on avoiding the geckos she could hear calling out than on where he was leading her.

Don't squash the little geckos!

Their strange chirping calls were all around her so she ran on tiptoes to minimise the risk of landing on any which might be on the grass.

He led her, still shaking, into his bathroom, shoved her under the shower, turned on a torrent of hot water and disappeared into the bedroom. She sighed in relief, slumped against the wall and closed her eyes as the heat penetrated her rigid muscles and the shaking subsided. She opened her eyes when she heard him move back into the bathroom, watched him pull the screen door open and join her in the shower. He gathered her in his arms and rained little kisses all over her face and neck. He tugged at her bikini top.

Oh for the love of God! Tell him you're sick and get OUT!

"Let's go into the bedroom."

Elena stared at him, befuddled by the effort of trying to focus on his words while this 'other her' yelled down at her from above. He turned off the water and grabbed his towel. She took a nearby hand towel, trying to dry herself with the meagre fabric.

"What are you doing?" he laughed, then reached into the cupboard under the sink and tossed her a bath towel, "Here, use this."

She wrapped the towel around herself, grabbed her wet bikini off the floor and followed him into the bedroom, intending to don her dress and make a quick getaway. But when Anton took her clothes out of her hands and threw them on a chair, she let him. She let him lead her to his bed and she sat on the edge, watching him go back across the room to his suitcase to retrieve a box of condoms.

Wow, he had high expectations of this short holiday, she thought before allowing herself to become entangled in a mass of flailing arms and legs, while pelted by the relentless volley of dispersions cast on her mental capacity and moral character by her 'other self'.

"WHOA! Guys!" A shocked Felix stood in the open doorway.

Anton's reaction was swift, covering them with a sheet while Elena dissolved in an uncontrollable fit of giggles, thinking she should help with the sheet but unable to make her arms move.

Felix turned his back to them.

"Okay, you've got an hour then I'm coming back."

Elena and Anton laughed as Felix closed the door. The disgusted, disembodied voice spoke from above.

Who the hell are you? Elena wouldn't be laughing. Elena would be mortified.

She stumbled back to her room afterwards and collapsed into bed, willing for sleep to block out the night's madness.

The next morning she awoke with the same groggy, dehydrated sensation and forced herself to drink a bottle of water. She groaned upon recalling the previous night. Anton seemed a nice guy but, had she been in her normal state of mind, she wouldn't have slept with him. She buried her face in her hands, attempting to erase the memory.

"I slept with Anton last night," she confessed to Cat.

"Whoa! So are you going to keep seeing Channing?"

Elena groaned again. "I don't know." She began to dread going home. "I'll have a quick shower now," she said, escaping into the bathroom and letting the hot water cascade over her head. *How could I be so stupid?*

She dressed while Cat showered, then they walked to the dining room for breakfast. After a light breakfast, with some trepidation, Elena accompanied Cat to the meeting point for the group visit to a local village. To her relief, Anton behaved as if nothing had happened. His greeting was friendly but not overly familiar and he mentioned nothing of the previous night.

The village reception included an obligatory 'ava ceremony. Elena shuddered and sipped as little as possible from the communal cup. After a lunchtime feast, a muscular young man guided them way up into a mountainside jungle, along slippery muddy tracks and under large spiderwebs glistening with water droplets strung between lush green ferns.

On returning to the village, they were informed their driver had been held up and might not return for them for another hour. Their guide ushered them into a hut. While they settled down to wait, the guide mixed more 'ava.

Elena groaned inwardly. She had only accepted the ceremonial 'ava at lunchtime so as not to cause offence.

She refused the offered coconut shell. "It's not good for me."

Their guide raised an eyebrow. "It make you sick?"

"Yes," she replied, her cheeks reddening.

"But you had alcohol, too," Anton pointed out.

"Ah," said the guide, "Better no mix. But is okay today, no alcohol, only 'ava."

He handed her the cup.

Fearing offence, she relented.

When they finally arrived back to the resort, the others talked of meeting for dinner, but Elena excused herself and had an early night.

She had avoided her thoughts all day but now that she was alone in bed, they tormented her. She tossed and turned. A message interrupted her just as she was drifting off to sleep.

- *Hello beautiful how's sunny Samoa? xx*

- *Big day exploring. In bed now, speak later xx*

She turned her phone off, feeling like a royal jerk and escaped into her dreamworld.

❧

DURING MEDITATION, a shocking epiphany turned Elena upside down. The encounter with Anton was an amplified example of her entrenched behaviour pattern with men. She had always done what men wanted even if it wasn't what she wanted. She didn't speak up, didn't stand up for herself because she had been raised to obey those who said they knew better than her. The result was a tendency to believe everyone knew better than her. To the child who still existed within her, there was no distinction between her father, male teachers or religious authority figures telling her they knew what was best for her and a man who insisted that having sex with him would be good for her.

The 'ava-alcohol cocktail had put her into an altered state of consciousness where she was, for once, fully aware that she was taking actions she didn't want to take but still had no power to stop herself. It was a wake-up call, the latest in a long line of figurative slaps from a universe which by now must be exasperated with her.

Shaking her head in disbelief at the absurdity of her false logic, Elena left the meditation room and wandered along the beach alone. Relieved to have woken up to herself, she was however no more certain about where that left her with Channing. Why was she still hesitant? Was it because she knew she would have to tell him about Anton if she agreed to a committed relationship? She really didn't want to hurt him.

You're afraid of letting another man get close to you in case you get hurt.

The voice was quiet and subdued, not the indignant shouts of two nights previous, but it was no less jarring for its softness. She couldn't deny it. She had been afraid from the moment she'd met Chan.

Fear: False Expectations Appearing Real. Was it possible she was in danger of throwing away a chance at a good relationship due to fear of repeating past patterns?

Sitting on the pristine sand under a cluster of palm trees, she considered Channing's character. He didn't seem depressed and intent on avoiding human contact like Michael. He was much more affectionate and interested in having conversations with her. They were able to talk on a range of subjects and the conversation flowed in a way that had never occurred between her and Michael. Channing used his creative energy to produce beautiful art. It didn't provide him with a stable income but at least he worked to supplement his income. This was in contrast to Garri, who was more interested in get-rich-quick schemes using other people's money or ideas. Channing was in much better physical shape than Garri too. Plus Elena was genuinely attracted to both his personality and physical appearance. All things considered, perhaps she was being too cautious. She resolved to be more open to exploring where things might lead with Channing. She sent him a message.

- *My transfer 2 airport leaves hotel 5:30 a.m.! Looking forward 2 seeing u xx*

The reply was instant.

- *Enjoy the last night beautiful! Can't wait 2 c u xx*

Elena was careful to limit herself to a single glass of wine during dinner. Around ten o'clock, their little group and two other tables headed back to the main bar and took to the dancefloor for a final hurrah. Elena gyrated around the dancefloor sporting a massive grin. Dancing always helped her shake off lingering tensions. Before long it was midnight and she realised her good intentions of an early night had slipped through her fingers.

She checked her phone.

- *I can't wait 2 c u 2morro beautiful, sleep well xx*
- *I'm still up dancing! xx*
- *U party animal ;) xx*

"Time for me to get a few hours' shut-eye," she told the group in the lull between songs.

"I'll walk you back to your room," Anton said.

"Oh! Thanks," Elena said, surprised.

They hadn't spoken much the past two days and neither of them had mentioned what had transpired between them.

"Well, thank you…" Elena began as they stopped in front of her room.

Anton smiled and moved closer, reaching out to pull her towards him.

"Er, it was nice to meet you," she blurted, panic-stricken.

"It was nice to meet you too," he replied, bending his head and kissing her lightly.

With a nervous laugh, she inched towards the door. "Have a safe trip."

He smiled again as she fumbled getting the key in the lock. "You too."

Elena collapsed into bed with a relieved sigh, only to drag herself out again a few short hours later.

❦

ON ARRIVAL IN ADELAIDE, she checked her phone.

- Not long 2 go now, sweetheart! xx

Ashamed, Elena wondered if she deserved Channing. He was so keen to spend time with her and here was she, still dithering and indecisive. Her shame increased when he turned up on her doorstep that night holding a pale pink rose. Bounding inside like an excited puppy, he scooped her up and kissed her with a fierce passion. He dragged her into the bedroom and flopped onto the bed, trying to pull her down with him.

She resisted, hands planted on his chest, and opened her mouth to tell him what she had done, but her heart caught in her throat at the sight of those playful, innocent green eyes sparkling in eager expectation. She couldn't bear to hurt him. Better that she suffer in silence.

"Hey, I know I've hesitated to commit to a relationship..." she petered out as she saw a flicker of an unreadable emotion flash through his eyes. Their sparkle disappeared. He waited for her to continue.

She took a deep breath. "I realised while I was away that I am really scared. I've had some painful experiences with men and I'm scared of getting hurt again."

Channing nodded, his eyes now betraying a wariness, waiting for her to deliver the 'it's not you, it's me' line.

"But I can't live my life cowering in the shadows. So I'm willing to give us a go... if you want to?" she finished lamely.

He stared at her for an eternity of a moment before his face lit up again and that childish, playful glint returned.

"Yes, okay!" He pulled her towards him and this time she let him.

Chapter Nineteen

ALL RAIMENTED IN SNOWY WHITE

E lena was surprised at how quickly she had fallen in love with Channing. The jitters and doubts still danced in the back of her mind but she had to admit she had fallen for him nonetheless. They saw each other three or four nights a week. It was a good balance; he wasn't suffocating her by being around every day like Garri had been, but it was often enough for her to not feel she was missing out. He took her out for dinner, to meet his friends at the pub and attend art exhibitions. Even when fresh doubts arose, somehow his boyish charm seemed to win her over. Like the weekend before Christmas when he had wanted to exchange presents with her early because he was so excited he couldn't wait any longer. She had found his child-like enthusiasm so endearing until she opened the present to reveal a white lace corset.

He gets the benefit of this gift. No wonder he was keen to give it to you!

"Er… thank you," she faltered, trying to ignore her internal voice and the shoulder-slumping, pit-of-the-stomach heaviness that accompanied it.

"Put it on, babe," he urged.

"Open your present first."

He unwrapped the book of Frank Gehry's works, which she had bought after he had told her how inspiring he found the designs by the Guggenheim Museum architect, and held it in his hands with an expression of chagrin. "That's a very thoughtful gift," he whispered, and she understood his contrition to be because his gift was motivated by more base desires.

"You're welcome." She squeezed him tight, sorry to have robbed him of the satisfaction of presenting her with his gift.

When she let go, his cheeky grin was back.

"Put the lingerie on, babe, I'm sure you'll look beautiful!"

Elena held the soft, lacy fabric in her hands, "Okay, give me a few minutes."

༺༻

THE RINGING PHONE brought Elena back from the edge of sleep.

"Hi sweetie," she yawned.

"Babe, can you come stay at my place tonight?" Chan slurred. He was out with his friend Donna for the night.

"I can't. My parents are here for the weekend."

"So? They don't need a babysitter."

"No, but I hardly ever see them. When they come to town, I should spend time with them."

"You were with them today."

"Yes, but it's rude to leave them in my house alone. They're guests."

"They're your parents."

"Tonight they are guests in my home. I'm sorry but I can't come. I'll see you tomorrow, okay?" His insensitivity annoyed her.

"Okay."

Just as she was drifting off to sleep, her phone beeped.

- *wish I was with u right now! xx*

She glanced, blurry-eyed, at the message and rolled over in a futile attempt to reclaim her dream state. Twenty minutes later the phone beeped again.

- *At hotel n*

He was drunk, and she was out of patience. But just as she moved to turn her phone off, yet another message arrived.

- *Whoops at home now a bit drunk. But I miss u! xx*

She smiled. How could she stay angry with him when he was so darn cute?

- I wish u were here but please let me sleep now :) xxx

She turned the phone off, resisting the urge to invite him to come to her place instead. Turning up drunk would not be the best way to meet her parents for the first time.

He'd asked to meet her family only six weeks after their first date but she shied away from parading him in front of the family until she was sure she was making the right decision.

However, she'd had no choice but to meet Chan's family given they lived on the same property. His aunt was a down-to-earth lady whom Elena got along well with, but his uncle often worked late or was away on business trips so it was rare for her to speak with him.

Chan's aunt hadn't liked many of his previous girlfriends, so when she had kind words to say about Elena, he was quick to pass them on.

It pleased Elena to be accepted by his family although the possibility that she wouldn't be had not been weighing on her mind. Her problem seemed to be with maintaining a good relationship with her partners, not their families.

It wasn't long before Elena relented and took Chan to meet Marcus and Carla. He got along well with them but paid scant attention to Brigid, even when Elena was playing with her. It made her wonder how he felt about having children of his own but she didn't want to bring up the topic so early in their relationship. They were still getting to know each other. Besides, there was no time to think, let alone have a serious talk, in the whirlwind of activity that had become her life: work, website development, anthology preparation, mentoring sessions, art exhibitions, and hanging out at the pub with Chan and Derek. Not to mention squeezing in time to go to the cinema and watch the many DVDs Chan wanted to see.

❧

ELENA'S PHONE CHIMED.

- Have u gone to sleep sweetheart?

- no :)

- I wish you the sweetest of dreams you've ever had xx

- How can I have the sweetest dreams when u r not here with me? Peaceful slumbers my love xx

- oh u r the most beautiful girl in the world Elena, u make me feel wonderful xx

- And u r the most caring, sensitive guy I've ever met. It scares me how good I feel with u! sleep well xx

In the morning she awoke to find another message, received just before 4 a.m.

- Don't be scared! Our relationship is a wonderful thing xx

- yes, I know, just still scared of trusting myself 2 make good decisions. I'm looking forward 2 seeing u 2nite xx

- Okay, I'm looking forward 2 catching up with u 2nite as well beautiful. Have a good day. xx

She floated through the day, on a high that he thought their relationship so wonderful, and left work on time to walk into the city for their dinner.

Chan arrived in Rundle Street holding a bunch of pink tulips. They dined at Lemongrass Thai Bistro then walked back to Chan's car. A gift bag lay on the floor by the passenger seat.

"Open it." Chan nodded to the bag as he pulled out into the traffic, swerving to miss the car he hadn't seen coming.

"That's for me too?"

"Yes."

"You shouldn't spend so much on me, Chan, you're spoiling me!"

"I like to spoil my beautiful girl," he replied, caressing her cheek with his thumb, sending a delicious shiver down her spine.

A swathe of tissue paper obscured the bag's contents. Fishing through the paper, she extracted a piece of fabric which unravelled to reveal itself as a red, one-piece fishnet contraption with silver-studded leather fasteners.

More lingerie? At least the last set was tasteful. This is just plain sluttish!

She silenced the judgmental voice with a stern reminder that he had also given her beautiful flowers.

"Do you like it?" he asked eagerly.

"Er well… I'm not sure it's my style."

"You'll look great in it, babe."

Chan braked suddenly to avoid running a red light.

"Sorry, didn't see it change colour."

"Put your glasses on, Chan! You're like Mr Magoo on the road."

They reached her car and she jumped out, grateful to have made it alive. Chan followed her home and insisted she change into his latest purchase as soon as they walked in the door.

In her room, she struggled with the silly body stocking, getting tangled in the stockinged fishnet legs. She couldn't tell which side was the front as both necklines plunged to her navel. That it appeared to be crotchless only added to her disorientation.

"Are you ready?" Chan called from the other side of the bedroom door as she attempted to untangle the netting that had become ensnared by one of the thigh buckles

"Not yet," she replied, hopping on one foot while trying to unhook the other leg from the buckle, becoming more vexed and ill-humoured. Like a dolphin caught in a trawler net, the more she struggled, the more tangled she became. Eventually righting herself, she opened the door wondering, *How should I stand, where should I put my hands?* Posing in lingerie was way out of her comfort zone.

He whistled. "Look at you!"

She blushed as he sidled towards her.

After another tumultuous love-making session, she lay in the now familiar post-coital-tornado daze with Chan snuggled against her.

He cleared his throat. "Sweetheart…"

"Hmm?"

"Aren't I doing enough to make you feel good?"

"Yes, of course! Why?"

"Because you're scared of me."

Dejection settled on her shoulders and she wished she had never told him. "I'm sorry Chan, I didn't mean for it to bother you. It's nothing personal. With my track record with men, I'm bound to be jittery for a while. This isn't about you, sweetie." She caressed his cheek.

He gulped. "I want to tell you something."

She rolled over to face him. "What do you want to tell me?"

"I love you."

Her heart soared. The circumstances were not how she had imagined this moment, still clad as she was in the ridiculous porn star get-up, but it didn't matter because he loved her!

"I love you too," she squeezed him tight.

She was still basking in the afterglow of his declaration when he fidgeted beside her and she sensed he had something else to say.

"Hey babe, have you ever had a triple x wax?"

She recoiled, struggling to cope with the seesaw between trashy and heartfelt connection.

"No… Have you?"

"No, but I've heard it makes the sex better."

"Oh," she hoped the conversation wasn't heading in the direction she thought it was. "Really? I think it would be embarrassing to have it done."

"Probably… would you do it for me?"

There it was. Just as she had feared. What should she say? Her mind ticked over and came up with a cunning solution.

"Well, I'll do it if you do it."

She felt pleased with herself. He wouldn't be keen to do it himself.

"Okay, it's a deal."

You idiot! You should have just said no.

But she hadn't. Instead she had backed herself into a corner.

"When can I book us in?"

She tried a stalling tactic. "I'll be in Melbourne at the end of the month for the last of Brett's workshops. If you want to make the most of it, we should wait until after I get back."

"Okay, good idea sweetheart!"

ON FRIDAY NIGHT, he arrived at her house in a funk.

"What's wrong, sweetie?" she hugged him.

"Nothing." His deflated posture told her otherwise.

"Come on, it might help to talk about it," she cajoled.

"It's just my boss."

"Again? What happened?"

"He's got it in for me, that's all."

"Why?"

"I don't know! He likes the other worker better and ever since I complained about her, they've both had it in for me."

"Maybe it's time to find another job?"

"Do you know how hard it is to find a permanent job like I've got?" he snarled.

His reaction startled her, but she tried to remain calm, concentrating on her breathing so she wouldn't retaliate, trying to empathise without encouraging him to continue his emotional outburst.

"I know it's difficult sweetie, but there's no harm in looking."

"What would I do?"

"What about a carpentry apprenticeship? You've got a real talent for woodwork."

"I don't want to turn my passion into making boring furniture."

"Well, choose something else then. You never know, maybe your perfect job with a perfect boss is just around the corner."

"No, it's not."

"Then I don't know what to tell you. I guess you need to find ways to minimise the impact your colleagues are having on you." She knew that he was the only one who could change his circumstances, but that didn't stop her wishing she could save him.

He waved away her comment. "Come on, Donna is waiting for us at the Wheatsheaf pub."

Donna was a zany forty-something Amazonian with an enormous mane of black hair and a penchant for miniskirts that made her impossibly long legs seem even longer. She devoted her spare time to frequenting bars that supported live music and downing copious amounts of tequila.

Channing and Donna had had a short fling a few years' previous and remained friends ever since. Channing said she was still keen on him but he wasn't interested in anything more than friendship. Elena imagined it must be hard for Donna to settle for friendship and put up with Elena being around, but she seemed to have accepted the situation with good grace. She had been friendly towards Elena when they first met on New Year's Eve.

They found her in the beer garden with an ever-present cigarette in hand.

"Hello darlings," she said, showering them with tobacco scented air-kisses.

"How's life?" Chan asked, seating himself next to Donna so Elena could have the seat furthest from the smoke.

"Same old stuff—work and play. I try to do more play than work." She winked at Chan.

Chan laughed. "That's my girl." He signalled the waiter to bring another round of drinks.

"And you? How's tricks?" Donna asked Chan.

"Fine, fine—work and art, more art than work for me."

Looking at him, Elena thought, you would never know he was having work issues. Less than an hour ago, he had been miserable but now he appeared relaxed and carefree.

They stayed with Donna until well after midnight and flopped into bed as soon as they returned home. She was ready to sleep but Chan had other ideas. He cleared his throat.

"Um, can we talk about earlier please?"

"When?"

"You know, when I was upset about work."

"Okay, what do you want to talk about?"

Another throat clearing ensued. "Well, I didn't feel you were very supportive."

Confusion and depression descended upon her. "What did I do that felt unsupportive?"

"You kept going on about me finding another job. Can't you just accept me the way I am? I don't want another job."

Elena took a deep breath. "I thought I was being supportive. I wasn't saying you have to find a new job, just that if your current job is upsetting you so much then maybe you should change. But if you'd prefer to stay where you are, that's fine."

Chan looked unconvinced and unimpressed.

"I'm sorry if you felt I wasn't supportive enough. That wasn't my intention." She put her arms around him.

"But why couldn't you just listen instead of telling me what to do?"

She sighed inwardly, wanting to mend the situation yet unsure how to do so. "I wasn't trying to tell you what to do. I thought you wanted me to help you find solutions. But if you want me to just listen, I will. Okay?"

Chan nodded, still looking unconvinced.

She kissed him on the forehead. "Are you okay with that? Are we okay?"

The playful Chan suddenly reappeared and he threw his arms around her, squeezing her tight. "Yes, babe, we're okay."

❦

ELENA ENTERED CHAN'S FLAT, kissed him and flopped onto the bed. "Thank God it's Friday!"

"Babe, I spoke to Derek about our discussion the other night, about being supportive."

Elena rubbed a weary hand across her face, "But why? You said we were okay."

"Yes, but it was still bothering me a bit… Derek said he knows what happened between you and Garri and that, if I want a supportive partner, maybe you're not the right one for me."

Elena gasped. "Derek doesn't know the full story. Garri wanted to believe I was unsupportive because it was easier than facing the truth that I chose not to continue supporting someone who constantly lied to me!"

She stopped ranting to inhale shakily. Tears of indignation sprang in the corners of her eyes. How dare Garri continue to meddle in her life!

Chan, panic-stricken at her outburst, wrapped her in his arms. "It's okay babe."

"But you still think I'm unsupportive," Elena sniffed.

"No babe, it was just a misunderstanding, that's all." He hugged her tight, raining little kisses all over her face.

"I'll say it again, Chan, it doesn't bother me what you do for a job, as long as you're happy doing it. But if you're not happy with your situation, only you can change it."

Chan ducked his head. "I know. I'd rather sculpt for a living but it's not happening at the moment."

Elena's heart went out to him. "You're making progress. You've just sold a sculpture. That's something to be proud of."

"I guess so."

An idea struck her. "You know what? I'd love you to make a sculpture for me. I've been looking for something to hang on the wall under the patio. I've got this idea in my head but I can't find anything that matches it in the shops."

"Oh wow babe, I'd love to! Your wish is my command!"

"I want a wrought iron circlet of lotus flowers in both bud and full bloom, the flower heads painted a vibrant pink and some of them jutting out from the wall as small candle holders."

Chan nodded. "I see it. Let me work on some design sketches, ok?"

"Thank you, sweetie." She smiled, glad to see him animated again.

Channing hugged her. "Thank you, babe."

They lay in silence. She couldn't shift the niggle of worry that Derek thought her a bad person. "I should talk to Derek, explain things from my perspective so he doesn't have such a one-sided view."

"No! He asked me not to tell you. I had to talk to you about it babe —it didn't feel right not to—but please don't tell him I've told you."

"It's okay, I don't blame Derek. I know how persuasive Garri can be. I fell for his rhetoric myself. I just want to set the record straight."

"Please babe, don't say anything."

One look at his stricken face was enough to make her cave in. "Okay, I won't."

"Thank you, babe."

It galled her that she had to let Derek and God knows how many others believe Garri's spin, but she couldn't hurt Chan by bringing the subject to light.

☙

THE FIRST DAY of Brett's workshop in Melbourne lasted a marathon twelve hours with few breaks. It covered a lot of old ground about mindset and emotions and it amazed her how much she had forgotten from previous sessions. No matter how many times she poured this information into her brain, most of it seemed to leak straight out again. But she knew that each time she attended a work-shop, spoke with Brett, or read a book, a little more of the material was retained and she was hopeful that one day she would remember it all—remember it *and* put it into practice.

She messaged Chan during one break.

- Intense day so far, still 6 hours 2 go! hope u have a good nite xx

- Have a good nite, sweetheart. I've been thinking of u xx

She awoke early the next day to prepare for the 8 a.m. start, surprisingly alert and refreshed. Her phone chimed as she was walking into the conference room.

- I missed waking up with u. BTW, when can I book us in 4 xxx wax?

She groaned. He hadn't forgotten and now she would have to keep her word. She punched a hurried reply.

- Thursday nights or weekends are better. Going into workshop now, talk later xx

The energy buzzed in the conference room. She was with a group of motivated, like-minded people all looking to break through their own mental barriers and create their lives in ways that would enable greater flow, creativity and ease. Camaraderie in the group was strong, despite the short time they had been together, and it helped buoy her through the second long day. As she prepared for bed, Chan messaged her again.

- Babe I finished the Rake series 2nite. Sorry, I couldn't wait for you! It's like a blue print of how not 2 behave. I'm glad I am clear on what is wright and wrong in conducting urself in a relationship. I'm really looking forward to seeing u xx

It irked her that he had spelled 'right' the wrong way. She tried to ignore her irritation along with her prickling conscience which reminded her of her own bad conduct in relation to a certain 'ava-fuelled event.

- Just as well I'm not that interested in the series! I miss u xx

- I really miss u my 1 and only. It's nice 2 know u feel as I do, beautiful xxx

The following morning, Brett asked them to make a list of mental or emotional blockages they would like to break through and a list of goals for the next twelve months. Her list of blockages was easy to compile.

- Self-doubt
- Allowing others to control me

- Feeling guilty if I can't give others what they want
- The need to control outcomes
- Fear of failure
- Fear of success
- Not speaking my truth
- Fear of hurting others
- Fear of rejection
- Belief that wealth is bad

She thought back to the goals she had made almost nine months ago when she'd started the mentoring program.

1. Successfully publish my own book.
2. Improve my relationship with Garri.
3. Earn enough from writing to give up my day job.

Her anthology publication was set, the website build almost complete and a marketing plan started. That goal was close to a reality now, but she'd play it safe and include it, just in case. Goal number two was now defunct. She hesitated, pen poised above the blank sheet, conflicted over whether number three was a goal she should even aim for. Her eyes flicked over to the list of blockages and settled on the belief that wealth is bad. She felt guilty, selfish and greedy for wanting to earn a living doing something she enjoyed. Chiding herself over her stupidity, she wrote goals one and three before she could talk herself out of it. Should she replace the Garri goal with Channing?

What about Jivan?

Elena gritted her teeth in consternation, wishing the annoying voice would leave her alone. Channing was a nice, caring person who wanted to be with her, she loved him and had committed to a relationship with him so she should have a goal for their relationship development.

You're seeing Jivan on the twenty-eighth of January. The clairvoyant said that is an important date.

But Jivan isn't interested in me, Channing is! The argument in her head continued until Brett asked everyone to put their pens down, jolting her back to the present. Her paper still lacked a relationship goal.

Brett instructed everyone to copy their blockage list onto one inch thick pine boards which they would break with their bare hands. A surprised murmur rippled through the room. Elena's gut clenched. Her tiny little wrist couldn't karate chop a wooden board! He must be joking! It required years of martial arts training to do such things.

Brett demonstrated, using the heel of his palm to break a board held in front of him by an assistant.

"It's all about mindset, people," Brett assured them. "Anyone can do this with the right drive and focus. I've seen fifty-kilo women smash through a board like it was paper."

Dubious, Elena copied her blockages list onto her board. They were allowed three attempts at breaking their board, each time returning to the end of the queue if it didn't break. Standing in line, watching big, strong men busting their boards first go, didn't increase her confidence. They had much greater strength than her. When even some men faltered, her legs turned to jelly. Then she saw a woman, not much bigger than herself, break through the board. Elena's jaw dropped as the woman's expression turned from incredulous to joyful and she bounded across the room, hugging everyone in sight.

More women broke boards and Elena felt a twinge of hope that maybe she could do it too. However, when her turn came, she failed and trudged, crestfallen, to the back of the line, nursing her smarting palm.

"Use your voice. Yelling contracts the diaphragm and concentrates your power," Brett encouraged.

"Aaaahhh…" The embarrassing, tiny wail had no effect as her hand rebounded off the wood and she returned to the end of the line, more upset and disgusted with herself.

Those who had tried three times already were instructed to break it using a short metal jousting pole, getting a run up and using the force of the body behind the pole to crack the wood. Elena hoped she would not have to resort to that. She wanted to do it properly. But after her third failed attempt, she too was shunted into the jousting line. Under the impression that it was the easy option, she was mortified when her pole bounced off the unrelenting wood. By the third attempt, as tears of absolute desperation gathered, an unprecedented anger surged through her.

For God's sake woman, just break the bloody thing!

She charged at the board and smashed the pole into it with a desperate yell, bracing for the familiar jarring as it bounced, but instead lost her balance as the board broke. Elena's tears of frustration turned into a flood of relief. She picked up the two pieces of her board and endured many congratulatory hugs as she made her way to the 'winners' corner, feeling like a fraud amongst those who'd had enough focus to smash those suckers with their bare hands.

Brett's wife Joan put a reassuring arm around Elena's shoulders. "The most important thing is that you break the board, not the method you use."

Elena nodded but was unconvinced.

"The aim is to send a message to the subconscious mind that you've broken the blockages."

The explanation didn't reduce Elena's disappointment that it had been so hard for her to break through them. She inspected her board, noting she had broken it off to the side. In fact, the break was so far to the side that all but one of her blockage statements remained intact. Only 'feeling guilty if I can't give others what they want' was severed, and that only because it had taken up almost the entire width of the board. So after all that effort, her blockages remained intact, taunting her from their heavy, solid surface. In that instant, she resolved to repeat the workshop and teach the board who was boss!

❦

ELENA MADE a mad dash for the airport and passed through security just in time, still clutching her broken board, oblivious to the stares it elicited from the security staff until one of them informed her she couldn't take lumps of wood on the flight. Cursing herself for not having put it in her checked luggage, she left it with the guard and dashed off to find the departure gate.

Chan greeted her at the airport with hugs and kisses.

On the passenger car seat was a brass sculpture the size of her hand. She picked it up and stared, open-mouthed. It was an elaborate antique-style bird cage with a heart on the perch. Engraved on the heart were the words *You have captured my heart*.

"Wow… did you make this?"

"Yes, do you like it?"

She kissed him fiercely. "It's beautiful, thank you!" It was the most beautiful thing a man had ever done for her. In contrast, how ungrateful she had been, wavering on setting an intention for their relationship. All that silly anguish about a date mentioned by a clairvoyant, and a man who had never shown any romantic interest in her. Meanwhile, this gorgeous man had spent his time on a labour of love for her.

Elena held the cage in the palm of her hand. Something about it bothered her.

"Your heart belongs to you, though. It's a beautiful thought and you can share your heart with me but I want it to be free, not caged," she blurted out.

Chan nodded, looking chastised but said nothing in response. She worried that she had hurt him but the shadow passed from his features as soon as it had appeared and the moment was gone.

The next day from work she messaged him, wanting to make sure he knew how much he meant to her.

- *I love my sculpture & I love u! xxx*

- *I'm really glad u like it beautiful. I love u so much. I would really like 2 have dinner with my most favourite girl in the world this week xxx*

A tingle of pleasure ran through her body at the thought she was his most favourite person in the world.

⁂

ON THE TWENTY-EIGHTH, Elena attended her massage appointment with a slight trepidation, the clairvoyant's words still running through her mind. Jivan was his usual cheerful self and they chatted as he loosened the knots in her shoulders. It still amazed her that he could, seemingly without effort, make her feel so good. Other therapists had her gritting her teeth at the discomfort they said was necessary to soften muscles, but not Jivan—his touch was firm yet gentle and her muscles sprang into response at his magic touch.

She was hyper-alert for the slightest change between them but there was nothing. *The clairvoyant must have been referring to Channing,* she thought with a twinge of disappointment.

"I've met someone," she ventured.

"Hmm?"

"His name is Channing."

"The name has a nice energy about it."

She flushed with pleasure. His approval, she now realised, was important to her. But her pleasure was tempered by a nagging disappointment that he hadn't sat her up, grabbed her by the shoulders and begged her to be with him rather than Channing.

"He's a sculptor," she offered.

"Ah, a creative type. A good match for you."

"Yes, I hope so…"

The conversation moved onto yoga and the parasympathetic nervous system until it was again time for her to force herself to leave.

❦

ELENA TRIED to hide her embarrassment as the young girl explained the waxing process and handed her a pair of disposable underwear. What was the point? The girl would need to remove them in order to wax her, anyway. She cursed Channing under her breath and cursed herself for not saying no outright.

Mortified, she followed the girl's instructions about where to position her legs and responded to her small talk, avoiding eye contact. When the girl admitted she'd had her own pubic hair permanently removed with a laser so she wouldn't have to keep waxing, Elena relaxed a little. Knowing the girl had been in the same position gave her a sense of solidarity.

"Is triple x waxing common?"

"Oh yes," the girl exclaimed. "Lots of people do it!"

"I guess it's not something that comes up in conversation," Elena replied. "We always think we are in a minority until other people share their experiences and we find out we're not so different after all."

"Yes, can you imagine a workmate asking what you did on the weekend and you replying 'oh just some housework and a Brazilian wax'!" The girl giggled.

Elena giggled too, despite herself.

She messaged Chan when she got home.

- *All done, I hope the redness goes away soon! xxx*

- *I went this morning. My girlfriend is as bald as a badger! She likes 2 get waxed up! I love my naughty girl xx*

His reply was like a slap in the face, deflating her newly-buoyed spirits and leaving her feeling as debased as she had imagined she might have after the waxing ordeal. She didn't like getting waxed at all. She hated that he was creating a story about her based around what he wanted her to be. Disgusted, she didn't reply but, by the time he came over the following night, she had forgiven him.

They made love, Channing keen to explore the waxing results. He seemed particularly pleased but Elena couldn't fathom what all the fuss was about. The only difference she noticed was an uncomfortable post-wax itch and she resolved that, if he were to ask her to get waxed again, her answer would be an irrevocable no.

༶ఌ

AT YOGA CLASS, Elena noted her improvement. It was easier to sit cross-legged now, although the lotus position was still way beyond her reach. And her heels were getting closer to the ground in Downward Dog. Her body still had lots of restrictions but it was encouraging to see progress at last. *I really should practice at home too, she thought. It would speed up my progress.*

Elena inhaled sharply and collapsed out of pigeon pose as her right foot cramped.

"Are you ok?" Jane whispered beside her.

"Cramp," Elena groaned, massaging her foot. "It doesn't happen as often as it used to but sometimes it still gets me good."

Jivan came over and took hold of her foot, massaging it while giving further instructions to the rest of the class. He was such a caring person. When the cramp subsided, he returned to his mat at the front of the class and Elena gently stretched the foot. She had started doing foot stretches at home each night to loosen the tight, knotted muscles, but it was slow-going.

"You could check out what Louise Hay's book says about cramps," Jane suggested as they rolled up their mats. "I can lend you my copy if you want."

Jivan had recommended that book too, but she had forgotten to follow it up. "Thanks. It sounds like a book I should buy for myself though."

Channing sent her a message as they emerged from the studio.

- Hello gorgeous. I hope u had a great day! I'd like 2 come 2 ur meditation class tomorrow, it will be nice 2 meditate with the most beautiful girl in the world. Sweet dreams my love! xx

- Great! I'm glad u r coming & I love u lots and lots xx

His constant, sweet messages made her feel so special and appreciated. Never in her wildest dreams had she imagined a man saying such things to her.

She floated through the next day at work, then met Channing at the yoga studio.

After the meditation, she followed him back to his flat. They walked hand in hand up the garden path to his flat and cuddled up on the bed.

"How did you find the meditation?"

"It was practical and the more Westernised format easier to follow than the Buddhist meditation class I tried with my ex."

"I'm glad you like it!" Secretly, however, Elena longed to try Buddhist meditation classes. The eastern philosophy had long intrigued her and she wanted to investigate it further when she had time, but for now she still got the benefit of mindfulness from this practice and maybe it would help Channing deal with the emotions he was battling around his work and career path. Plus it was an extra opportunity each week for her to see Jivan.

"Let's watch a movie, babe."

Elena hesitated, "I should go home. I want to do a final check of the anthology before I give the file to the printer tomorrow."

"Just one movie first?" he pleaded and she caved in. Before long, it was midnight and Elena crept down the driveway to avoid waking his aunt and uncle and crawled into bed much later than she should have on a work night.

She dragged herself out of bed earlier than normal too, to give herself time to stop at the printer on her way to work. She worried that even after repeated proofreads, she may have missed an error and would end up with thousands of sub-standard books for her efforts. The perfectionist in her quaked as she handed the USB to the printer, but she knew she had to walk out and let it go. She had checked the file repeatedly, as had a freelance editor, Brett, and several friends. There was nothing more she could do. Procrastinating any longer was just prolonging the fear.

Walking back to her car with jellied legs and a churning stomach, she willed herself not to think about it again until she had a print copy in her hands.

Channing and Derek were doing a stand-up act at The Rhino Room but she still had homework to do for her session with Brett in the morning so she went home after work. Donna would be there to support them and they had landed a gig at The Garden of Unearthly Delights during the Fringe Festival so there would be another opportunity for Elena to see them.

She wondered if he would interpret her non-attendance as unsupportive. *But I just can't fit everything in,* she reasoned. Spending a few nights a week with him and going to sleep at the witching hour wasn't helping her energy levels either. She felt so tired and was noticing headaches and neck stiffness creeping back in.

"Any ideas as to the cause of the headaches and neck pain?" Brett asked her the next day.

"Tiredness, I guess. They're not as severe as I used to get, so I don't think it's emotional issues like with my ex-husband. My life is so busy and there's always too many short deadlines at work, plus my sitting posture isn't great."

"Okay, but do you remember our conversation about how the body acts as a reservoir to hold unexpressed emotions?"

"Yes."

"So do you think this could be related to Channing in any way?"

"I don't think so. I used to avoid crying because I thought it a sign of weakness and I didn't want to upset anyone. But with Channing, it's different. I tell him how I feel when important issues arise and he tells me when he's upset. It's still hard for me to enact, but we do talk."

"Then start with becoming more aware of your posture in front of the computer. Set a regular alarm to remind you. Perhaps you could also keep a diary of symptoms and daily events to analyse for any possible links. Subconscious behaviours can be hard to break."

CHANNING LEANED over the breakfast bar, watching her prepare dinner before they headed out to the opening of his friend's art exhibition.

"Hey babe…"

"Hmm?"

"Last night at The Rhino Room a girl slipped her business card in my jacket pocket and walked off without saying a word."

Elena, only half listening while concentrating on frying the chicken Chan had asked for, was jolted to attention by an intense constriction in her chest which took her breath away. She tried to keep her voice even as she struggled with her mental chatter over the meaning of her physical reaction.

"That's a bit odd, but it's very flattering for you. She liked the look of you."

"Yeah."

Elena waited for him to continue but he said no more on the topic. She was glad he was so open with her though. It made it easier to trust him.

At the Contemporary Art Centre, Elena stood quietly next to Chan, nursing a glass of Rockford Alicante that she managed to eke out for the entire evening. It seemed every time she and Channing went out together, it involved alcohol. She was drinking too much for her liking only in order to be sociable.

But she loved to watch Chan's face light up when he was talking art, even if she were unable to contribute much to the discussions. It was still a novelty to have such a creative partner.

They returned to Elena's house late and made love before falling into an exhausted sleep.

To his credit, Chan got up with her in the morning, even though he didn't have to work until the afternoon. As always, they showered together.

As she dressed, Elena checked the message on her phone. "Oh! My parents are coming to stay for a few days. Mum has a specialist appointment for her diabetes. They're worried she is developing diabetic kidney disease."

"That's not good, babe."

"I know. I hope they can get her sugar levels under control soon. Would you like to come for dinner and meet them on Friday night?"

He had been keen to meet her family almost from the moment they began dating and Elena suddenly felt comfortable enough to introduce them.

"Sure, babe."

❧

CHAN BOUNDED in the door bearing a huge bunch of flowers.

"More flowers for me? You're so sweet!" she kissed him and took the flowers to the sink while she looked for a vase.

"Sweetheart, I'm meeting the venue curator on Friday night to discuss my upcoming exhibition!" His eyes sparkled with excitement.

"That's the night we're having dinner with my parents. Is it possible to meet her another night?"

He had been so keen to meet her family but when she organised a meeting, he forgot their plans! His disinterest hurt. It was a big deal for her to introduce them.

"If your folks are down, the venue's not a priority then, babe!" He picked her up playfully and gave her a squeeze before setting her down again. Reassured by his answer, she kissed his nose and continued to arrange the flowers in the vase.

"What do you want to watch tonight, beautiful?"

"I don't know, you choose," she replied, sitting at the table to finish typing text into one of her new web pages. "Give me twenty minutes to finish this page, then we can watch something."

Chan loaded a DVD, paused it, then wandered around the room, fidgeting.

"Hey beautiful, you know that girl I told you about? The one who gave me her number?"

281

"Hmm," she replied. She wanted to get this page finished, but he wasn't going to make it easy for her.

"Well, I called her."

Elena stopped typing and turned to face him as another warning jolt surged through her chest. What was that? Jealousy? Fear? She wasn't sure but whatever it was, she didn't like it.

"Oh? Why did you do that?"

Chan moved from one foot to the other, swinging his arms. "I felt bad ignoring her. But I told her I was already seeing someone."

Elena's moment of uncertainty passed as she fell in love with him all over again. She also felt bad ignoring people. She remembered before meeting Garri, all the guys she hadn't been interested in had pestered her because she hadn't wanted to be rude by ignoring them. But even when she'd told them she wasn't interested, responding to their messages or calls had been enough for some of them to keep trying.

"That was very thoughtful of you. How did she respond?"

"She was okay. She works in an art gallery."

"Really?"

"Yeah, so I invited her to my exhibition opening."

"Okay," Elena turned back to her computer. She had nothing to worry about. If he were interested in the girl, he wouldn't have mentioned her at all. It was nice to know she could trust him and she would do everything in her power to ensure he could trust her in return... like avoiding 'ava. She pushed aside the unwelcome memory and the accompanying stab of guilt.

Channing put his arms around her. "You're my beautiful, perfect diamond!"

"No, no! I'm nowhere near perfect."

"To me, you are." He kissed her neck.

Elena put her hands either side of his head and pulled his face up to meet hers. "Thank you, but nobody is perfect, sweetie, least of all me."

"Geez, can't you just accept a compliment?"

Chastised, she cast her eyes downwards. "I'm sorry, I didn't mean to offend you."

"Don't worry about it," he turned away.

She finished what she was doing and sat down to watch a movie with Chan.

He put his arm around her. "Beautiful, the imperfections in a diamond are what make it so beautiful."

She was humbled that he saw her imperfections and thought her perfect, anyway. It was like a dream come true but words failed her to express how she felt.

"Aww, that's very poetic. I love you," she replied as she kissed him.

ʚϊɞ

THE REST of the week disappeared in a blur of work, yoga and hiking in Mount Lofty with Jane. She was so occupied that she barely had a chance to miss Chan, who was absent until he came to meet her parents on Friday. He left as soon as the meal ended, apologising that he had to meet the venue curator. Elena tried not to be offended by his eat and run performance. At least he had put in an appearance.

"A cuppa, Mum? Dad?" she asked, trying to sound jovial.

"That would be lovely, dear," her mother replied.

"How are you feeling tonight, Mum?"

"A bit tired."

"What did the doctor say about your kidneys?"

"He can't tell until the test results come back. He thinks I'll need to change my medication again. Don't worry, I'm sure it will be fine."

"Yes, I'm sure it will," Elena replied, trying to reassure herself as much as her mother.

Her father turned on the television while Elena and her mother cleaned the dinner dishes.

"I'm a bit tired," her mother said as she hung up the tea towel. "I think I'll go to bed."

"It's been a big day for you. Actually, I think I'll have an early night too." Elena kissed them both goodnight and retreated to her room.

She fell asleep quickly but awoke just after 4 a.m. and couldn't get back to sleep. When she heard her parents moving about at 7 a.m., she got up and made breakfast.

Her parents went to visit Marcus and Carla that afternoon and Elena met Chan and Derek at a pub. Avoiding meeting anyone's gaze, she entered the pub and searched the room for Chan, feeling a roomful of critical eyes on her. For as long as she could remember she had felt self-conscious entering a public venue on her own. She knew it was ridiculous, a hangover from her days of extreme shyness, but she couldn't help it. Locating the boys at the back of the room, she hurried over.

"Are you aware of men staring at you when you walk in a room?" Derek asked as he kissed her cheek.

Elena started. "Why?"

"When you walked in just now, every male head turned towards you. It's not the first time I've seen it happen. Do you notice it?"

Elena turned crimson and shook her head. Having avoided eye contact with anyone, she hadn't been aware that they were looking at her. It was a disconcerting moment as she realised that her gut feel had been correct. However, she had assumed the worst again—that she was being judged harshly—but Derek thought it was the opposite! She flushed with embarrassed pleasure until she reminded herself that every man in the room had a glass of beer in his hand and therefore were most likely seeing her through beer goggles. She was no ugly duckling, that she had figured out, but neither was she Miranda Kerr. Hence beer goggles was the only plausible answer.

"Sorry, I didn't mean to embarrass you. What are you drinking?"

"A glass of moscato would be great, thanks."

"How was your meeting with the curator?" she asked Chan.

"All good. We've decided the layout and the catering is organised now."

"Are you excited?"

"More nervous!"

She squeezed his hand. "It will be fine."

A moscato and two sodas later, they wandered down the road to dine in a Chinese restaurant, then she drove Channing home. "Sorry sweetie, my parents wouldn't be comfortable with you staying at my house because we're not married. They're conventional, like your aunt and uncle."

"Stay here with me, beautiful."

"I can't, I don't want to upset your family either. Plus, I can't leave my parents alone in the house. That would be rude." She knew she could have taken him home with her. It was her house. But sacrificing a weekend for the sake of her parent's peace of mind was something she was willing to do, especially with her mother's present health concerns.

"Marcus and Carla are coming for lunch before my parents go home tomorrow. Can you come?"

"I planned to work on a sculpture tomorrow. Can I take a rain check?"

"Okay, whatever you want." She tried to hide her disappointment at his lack of interest in spending time with her family. She couldn't figure him out. He had been super keen to meet her family but now he didn't want to see them at all.

❦

ELENA WAS WORKING on a new renewable energy research project when Chan called.

"Hi, what's up?"

"Sweetheart… I've been fired," he told her, his voice subdued and disbelieving.

"Oh no! I'm sorry, sweetie. What happened?"

"The boss is blaming the local economic downturn… but I know it's because he doesn't like me."

"That's shit! Are you ok?"

"I think so."

"Try to stay positive, sweetie. Something else will turn up… and, on the bright side, you can focus on your next exhibition now."

"I guess so."

"Where are you? Do you need me to meet you somewhere?"

"Thanks babe, but I'll be okay. I'm in my car outside work… I think I'll just go home now."

"Are you sure?"

"Yes."

"Well, drive safely. I'll see you at my place tonight?"

"Yes babe, see you tonight."

She returned to reading an article on the new idea of floating solar panels but had trouble concentrating. It wasn't long before her mother called to say they would be down again the following weekend. The test had confirmed early stage kidney disease and they needed to discuss further treatment options. Elena's gut constricted. She didn't want to show her concern in case it made her mother worry even more, so she tried to keep the conversation light and upbeat. She tried not to dwell on her lack of control over both her mother's health and Channing's emotional state.

It occurred to her there was something she could do to boost Channing's spirits. She had often thought of the beautiful sculpture she had seen the night they met but, at eight hundred dollars, had hesitated to commit. However, Chan needed both a financial and emotional boost right now.

- *Sweetie I'd like 2 buy A Summer Outing from u xx*
- *Oh wow! Thank u my wonderful girl. See u at 7 p.m. xxx*

His car pulled into her driveway not long after she arrived home. She heard him fumbling around, opening and closing doors, then he burst through the front door, staggering under the weight of the large sculpture. The joy on his face reassured her that her decision had been a good one.

"You brought it already? You should have said! I would have helped you carry it."

"It's okay beautiful, I can... manage," he groaned under the weight as he set the wood carving in a bare corner of the living room.

"Perfect!" Elena enthused.

Channing kissed her, lifting her off the ground in a tight bear hug. "I'm glad you like it gorgeous!"

"Give me your banking details so I can transfer the money to you."

"You can have it for four hundred, sweetheart," he told her.

"No! I should pay the full amount."

"But you're my girlfriend."

"Thank you, sweetie, but I don't want you to earn less just because I am buying it. Who knows, maybe someone else was considering buying it too. I don't want you to miss out on my account."

"Oh, you're lovely," he whispered, his face a mixture of disbelief and something else she couldn't quite put her finger on.

That night as they climbed into bed, Elena sensed a change in his mood.

"Babe..." he began.

"Yes?"

"I need to say something…"

She took his hand and waited for him to continue.

He wrung his hands together. "I'm not sure I want to have kids."

"Oh!" She made a hasty attempt to cover up her involuntary baulk.

"I know that you want them, but I'm just not sure…" His voice cracked and tears sprang into his eyes.

Her own tears of shock and disappointment welled in response. She still didn't trust herself to speak.

Great! What is it with you and baby-phobic men?

She squeezed her eyes shut to silence the voice.

"I'm sorry babe, don't cry! I don't want to hurt you. I didn't say I don't want kids, only that I'm not sure yet." He hugged her tight.

Crushed, she touched her forehead to his and whispered, "It's okay, it's still early days for us and having children is a big decision. Take your time. I can wait for you to decide."

Channing nodded and clutched her to him as they fell asleep in each other's embrace.

❦

SEVEN HUNDRED NEATLY BOXED COPIES OF her anthology lined the walls of the study. She opened a box and inspected a copy, breathing in its new book smell. The printer had done a good job.

Her parents' car pulled into the driveway.

"Look, my new book!" she ambushed them as they walked in the door.

"Well done, girlie," her father said, flicking through the pages and passing it on to her mother. Poetry wasn't really his thing. He dropped his Akubra hat on the table. He always wore it outside the house, even at night.

Her mother shook her head. "I don't know how you do it, dear! I could never write poetry. I wouldn't know where to start."

Elena smiled, both proud and embarrassed by the attention. "Now for the harder part—selling it! Do you feel like a cuppa?"

"Yep, that would hit the spot," her father agreed.

They chatted over a pot of tea then retired for the night.

In the morning, Chan arrived after her parents left to see the specialist. They sat under the patio, Chan sketching designs for new sculptures while she put finishing touches on her website. She found it hard to concentrate. Channing's look of intense, yet peaceful concentration was mesmerising. It was clear that the act of creating fed his soul.

"Dad loves *A Summer Outing*. He was admiring it last night."

Channing gave her a vague smile. "He's a nice man, your father. I'm glad he likes it." He turned his attention back to the sketch.

She continued to watch him, her heart filling with more love and affection than she had ever experienced. Watching him absorbed in his creativity was so inspiring.

Dragging her attention back to her website, she finished the last of the changes then wrote a post on her Facebook page. Her finger hovered over the post button. It was a daunting prospect to expose a creation so dear to her heart for the world to judge and criticise. Squaring her shoulders, she hit post then set up a Facebook advert—she didn't have much of a budget, but she figured she could start small with a five-dollar-a-day campaign for two weeks. She would need to do a lot of legwork with local bookstores and libraries but it was a huge relief to have the soft launch out of the way. She had shied away from a physical launch though—all those eyes on her, the venue and catering costs. It didn't seem worth it. Better to put effort into behind-the-scenes marketing.

Satisfied, she hugged Channing from behind and planted a kiss on the top of his head. "It's done! I've advertised the anthology."

Channing looked up and smiled. "Congratulations, beautiful, I'm proud of you."

"Thanks."

She could tell his mind was elsewhere, so she went inside to fix them some lunch. While she was preparing a salad, her parents returned with encouraging news. Because they had caught the kidney disease early, no damage would occur if her mother responded to the new medication. The Specialist wanted her to return to Adelaide every fortnight for check-ups until her sugar was back under control, of which he was confident would occur. It had been a great end to the week.

Chapter Twenty

THE MIRROR CRACKED FROM SIDE TO SIDE

C hanning's exhibition opened in Gallery M. Bursting with pride, Elena watched from the sidelines as Chan did the rounds, explaining his sculptures to friends and fellow artists. Elena joined Donna and Derek by the drinks table, selecting a glass of white as her prop for the evening. "How are you both tonight?"

"Good thanks," Donna smiled politely. She had been more distant with Elena of late. Elena wondered if Donna resented not being able to spend as much time alone with Chan since Elena had entered the scene.

Derek kissed her cheek. "What's your opinion of all this?"

"I love his work. Such diversity and beauty!"

"He's definitely got something. Let's hope the exhibition can lift him out of obscurity." Derek raised his glass in salute.

"Hear, hear." The three of them clanged wine glasses and lapsed into silence.

Elena was tense and tired after spending far too much time in front of computers; if she wasn't at work, she was doing stuff for her website, contacting bookstores, on Skype to Brett or completing homework for her next mentor session. In between all that, she had tried to fit in as much activity with Chan as her energy levels would allow but she felt she couldn't keep it up for much longer. She was looking forward to having more time for Chan and for relaxing now that the anthology was launched.

Channing's aunt and uncle joined them so she made a renewed effort at conversing.

"Where is Chan?" his uncle asked.

Elena craned her neck in search of Channing. She couldn't see him in the throng of people around the various installations nor in the gift shop. "Perhaps he's in the bathroom."

Twenty minutes later, he was still missing in action. Elena called his mobile but it went through to voicemail. "He's not answering his phone."

His uncle huffed in annoyance as he checked his watch. "He'd better turn up soon so we can say goodbye. I've got a business function tonight."

Elena tried a text.

- Where r u sweetie? Ur uncle needs 2 leave.

Still there was no response.

"He can't be far away," Elena said. "I'll go look for him."

His uncle stood up. "We'll come with you."

They headed out the glass doors, towards the cafe and toilets.

An invisible force slammed into Elena's chest, bringing her to an abrupt halt. Channing stood in the deserted cafe, previously obscured from view by a tall pot plant, locked deep in conversation with a petite, yet voluptuous red-headed young woman. He towered over her, head bent towards her, her head thrown back to meet his eyes. Their casual stance seemed somehow intimate. The way they smiled at each other made Elena feel like an intruder.

"Here he is," she said, forcing a bright smile. She read displeasure in his aunt's expression. *Here we go again, getting sidetracked by a pretty young thing.*

Bewildered by the barrage of strange, unspoken messages, Elena took some hesitant steps towards Channing. He looked up and slung his arm around her shoulder.

"Hey babe, we were just talking. Tennille meet Elena." He seemed so casual, so normal.

Elena relaxed and smiled at Tennille. "Hi, nice to meet you."

Tennille gave a small, lopsided smile, ducking her head as she returned the greeting and fiddling with the hem of her short green smock dress.

"So are you one of Channing's artist friends?"

Tennille shook her head.

"No, no she's not a friend," Channing replied.

There was an awkward pause.

"I should get going." Tennille batted her eyelids while fixing her big blue eyes on Chan, gave him that same lopsided smile and fled, having avoided any eye contact with Elena.

Channing turned towards his aunt and uncle who were waiting a few metres away, leaving Elena standing on her own. Then it dawned on her. That must have been the art gallery girl who had given Chan her number!

"Chan… was that the girl from…"

"Yeah," he cut her off, half turning back to her with a dismissive wave. "Don't worry about her."

❦

HER PARENTS WERE STAYING the weekend after her mother's checkup and Elena wanted to spend time with them. Chan wanted to lock himself away to work on her lotus flower sculpture, intent on finishing it soon and insisting he gift it to her instead of letting her buy it. They were like ships passing in the night until Wednesday evening when he turned up on her doorstep with a pizza. As he put the pizza on the table, his phone rang. He wandered into her bedroom, deep in conversation.

Elena got plates and drinks ready, turned the radio on low and found an '80s music station.

Chan re-emerged from the room, phone still attached to his ear.

"Hey, babe?"

"Yes?"

"You don't mind if I meet up with Tennille to plan an exhibition in her gallery, do you?"

Since the exhibition launch, it had become clear to Elena that Tennille was interested in more than friendship with Channing. However, Elena was also aware she was an opportunity for Channing to increase his artistic exposure.

"Sure, if that's what you want."

"She's okay with it," he said into the phone, throwing himself into the chair next to her.

Elena, helped herself to a slice of pizza.

"No, of course she won't care… What do you mean?… Yes, she's fine… Okay, sure… of course I'll be Facebook friends with you…. I'm not scoffing at you!… No, not at all… Yes, looking forward to it, I'll be in touch… bye."

"What was that about?" Elena asked as he sat next to her at the table.

"Nothing, she wants to design an art installation with me but is worried about what you would think of us being alone together."

"Seems strange that she would ask you to work with her then worry about what I think after you'd agreed to it."

"Uh yeah… well actually, I asked her."

Elena digested this new piece of information. "I'm okay with it, Chan. I know your art is important to you, but just be careful, okay? It's obvious she's interested in you."

"It's just business, Elena!" Chan scraped his chair back and carried his plate over to the sofa.

"I trust you, Chan. I'm just saying you need to be aware that she's interested in more than just your art, okay?"

"Okay," he mumbled around a mouthful of pizza, staring stonily at the floor.

☙

ELENA CHECKED HER PHONE.

- Hello beautiful, do u want 2 meet me at Carnevale at The Wayville Showground today? If we enter before 1 p.m. it's half price! Can I stay with you tonight? xx

- Yes, of course u can stay 2nite! I'll meet u there around 12:30? xx

- Great, c u soon xx

Elena arrived at The Showground just after 12:30 p.m. Chan hadn't arrived yet.

- I'm at the Rose Street entrance xx

Twenty minutes later, he still hadn't arrived or replied to her message.

- I'm guessing u r inside already but can't hear ur phone 4 the noise. I'm coming in now x

She handed over a twenty dollar bill, accepted her change from the ticket seller and wandered inside, passing the rotating Ferris wheel. In the large crowd before her, it wouldn't be easy to locate Chan. Perhaps he was at one of the other entrances. She made her way over to the Goodwood Street entrance, keeping her eyes peeled for Chan. When he wasn't there, she backtracked and headed towards the Leader Street entrance, dodging sugar-hyped kids sporting glittering Carnevale-inspired masks and face paint.

Chan was nowhere to be seen. Elena checked her phone. No message yet and now it was 1:30 p.m.

- Will you be here soon?

She received no reply. Trying to quell her disquiet, she wandered back to the food stands, bought a lemon gelato and found a tree to shelter her from the harsh afternoon sun.

When he had not replied by 2 o'clock she tried again.

- are you okay Chan? xx

He still didn't respond. Her mind began to conjure up horrible possibilities. Maybe he'd had an accident. She wanted to check whether his aunt knew of his whereabouts but she didn't have her phone number. *Perhaps I should drive to his house. Or should I call the police? No, don't overreact, Elena.* The volley of thoughts continued until 2:30 p.m. when she finally decided to drive to his house, dreading the prospect of encountering an accident scene en-route. She had just reached the showground exit when her phone vibrated in her hand.

- yes beautiful on my way c u soon! xx

- oh! Don't scare me like that! Was just about 2 drive over to urs, worried something had happened to u xxx

- Don't be silly I'm all good babe x

Her relief turned to astonishment then morphed into anger—the shaking, steaming, face burning kind of anger that made it hard to think straight. How dare he! He was two hours late without contact or an explanation and he had the audacity to call her silly for worrying about him!

She was still fuming when, twenty minutes later, he bounded into the Leader Street entrance, grinning from ear to ear. "Hi babe!"

"Hi." She glared up at him.

He stopped mid-stride, smile faltering. "What's wrong?"

"What's wrong? You ask me to meet you here at 12:30 p.m., then you disappear for two hours without a word, and you're asking me what's *wrong*?"

His face hardened. "I dropped a tool I'd borrowed back to a friend on the way over and he offered me a glass of wine."

"And you couldn't pick up your phone to tell me that, or reply to any of my messages?"

"I left my phone in the car so I didn't hear it."

"Two hours is a long time for one glass of wine."

"We drank a couple of bottles." He swayed a little, unsteady on his feet.

That explained the bright eyed excitement with which he'd bounded into the Carnevale. He was drunk. She couldn't believe how irresponsible he was.

"You didn't think to message me so I wouldn't worry?"

His face coloured but his eyes flashed defiantly. "I lost track of the time. I didn't expect you to worry…" he paused, swaying on his feet. "I'm not a child, I don't have to report to you," he slurred.

Her blood boiled. As the anger and hurt swelled to bursting point, she no longer trusted herself to speak. She turned her back on him.

"Do you want me to leave?"

She didn't reply.

"Because I can. I can go home *right now!*"

Elena was vaguely aware of the crowd swirling around them, the crazy-loud music and the tinkles of laughter. She didn't want him to go home, didn't want him to leave on bad terms, didn't want to be arguing with him in public like this. Nor did she want him getting behind the wheel of a car again while he was drunk.

She turned around. "No, I don't want you to go. But I need you to understand why I'm so angry. When you tell me you'll be some-where, I expect you to contact me if you're running late. A little late doesn't matter but two hours late and not responding to my messages is not okay. To call me silly because I was worried something had happened to you—" She stopped as her voice cracked.

Channing's defensiveness dropped away. He reached for her hand. "I'm sorry babe, don't cry."

Relieved that they were no longer fighting, she allowed him to draw her into his embrace, then trailed after him as he excitedly devoured a pizza, washed it down with a beer and drooled over the Ferrari display inside the pavilion.

"Let's watch the last fashion parade, babe!"

"Really?" Elena couldn't think of anything more boring but let him drag her over to the stage side chairs.

The first models were already making their way down the runway.

Chan wrinkled his nose. "Look how skinny that one is! I thought Italian women were supposed to be voluptuous."

Elena cringed and sank low in her chair, "Shh, just be quiet and watch."

He continued to drink beer throughout the evening. Relieved when the Carnevale closed at 10 p.m., Elena bundled him into her car. Still annoyed with him, she drove to his house. She wasn't in the mood for nursing his hangover in the morning.

His aunt answered the front doorbell, pursing her lips as she took in the sight of an inebriated Chan leaning against Elena.

"Hi, Chan's had a bit too much today."

"So I see."

"His car is still parked near The Wayville Showgrounds so he'll need to collect it tomorrow."

"Okay, thanks for bringing him home, dear."

"No problem, see you later."

Elena drove home and buried her nose in a book until she felt tired enough to sleep.

She woke late with the sun streaming through a crack in the blind and checked the time. Nine-thirty. Chan would still be asleep.

She pottered around the garden. When she heard her phone beep in the afternoon, she raced inside to retrieve it.

- Hello gorgeous, I miss you! I'm a bit busy this week, c u Friday night 4 Donna's party. xx

- U don't have any time 2 c me during the week? x

- I'll try, but probably not x

- Okay :(I love u x

❦

ELENA DROVE to Donna's house and Channing took the opportunity to drink again. She tried to ignore the growing sexual energy between Chan and Donna as they became more drunk. It was obvious that Donna still wanted him. She flung a perfectly shaped, stockinged leg over his thigh as they laughed at someone's joke.

Chan put a hand on her thigh.

Elena raised an eyebrow.

Chan caught her eye, sobered and lifted Donna's leg off his thigh. "Excuse me, I need the bathroom."

He was flattered by Donna's attention and less inhibited about showing it when he was drunk, but she knew he wouldn't do anything. But it made her uncomfortable to be in a house full of strangers, watching the dance play out in front of her, so she was relieved when he finally agreed they could go home.

Elena had the week off work to spend some quality time with Chan now that the anthology and exhibition launches were over. They spent the weekend in Port Elliott with Carla, Marcus and Brigid but when they returned to the city, Chan had a headache and preferred to sleep in his own bed.

The next day she took her laptop to his place and sat writing in a corner of his studio while he worked on her sculpture. She admired his biceps rippling as he worked the iron, the sweat glistening on his bare chest. She still couldn't believe he was her partner. But he barely threw a glance in her direction all afternoon. How could he be so focussed on his art and she so distracted whenever they were together?

"Sweetie, can you log into your Facebook profile for me? I'll set up that advert for your sculptures now." He'd been asking her to help him do it for weeks but she hadn't had time.

"Yeah, thanks beautiful!" He bounded over, logged himself in and planted a fierce kiss on her lips.

Within seconds of launching the advert, Tenille liked and shared the advert. Elena experienced a sudden, intense sensation of being pulled towards the screen. It was a most peculiar feeling, a desperate reaching out via the ethernet as if Tennille thought Chan was sitting at the computer and was willing him to connect with her. The grasping nature of the strange energy pulsated through Elena and she was transfixed by the screen. Imagining the girl's hands could emerge from the screen at any moment, she slammed the laptop closed.

"It's done…"

"Thanks babe," Chan interjected.

"… and Tennille instantly liked and shared it."

"Oh," Chan's hand paused mid-air before he continued bashing a piece of metal into shape.

Elena waited but he made no further comment. She couldn't articulate what she had just experienced. Every sentence she constructed in her mind sounded ridiculous.

The next day Channing had another headache and wanted to be alone. She was disappointed but put her free time to good use, turning her attention towards an issue that had been playing on her mind—deciding whether to pursue legal action against Garri. He didn't have the cash to repay her loan in a lump sum but she could force him to repay her in regular instalments. Some months ago, she had consulted a lawyer who said it was hard to prove a loan between family or friends in the absence of an official contract but, because Elena had some text message evidence which helped prove it was a loan rather than a gift, she had a good chance. She discussed the pros and cons with Brett, agonised for a few more days, and finally decided it was better for her mental health to forgive the debt. The stress and cost of legal action just wasn't worth it.

For the next few days, Channing was too busy to see her, although she wasn't sure why. It wasn't as if he had a job to go to anymore. She busied herself with tasks to keep her mind off her uneasiness: gardening, running, and walking the Hallett Cove coastal route. On Saturday she went to his flat, hoping to entice him out for a walk, but he continued working on her sculpture.

She turned on her laptop and flicked through her emails, opening one from Brett about his latest offer.

'My gift to you, free coaching audios. There are only a handful of issues stopping people achieving what they want in life. People find themselves in a huge variety of situations but the underlying issues are the same. So hop over to my website and listen to how I help real clients recognise and address these issues, then apply the same techniques to your own life!'

"This sounds good, Chan, Brett has some free coaching audios. I can send you the link if you like?"

"Okay," He mumbled, absorbed with inspecting a metal lotus

flower.

The next half an hour passed in silence.

"Why did you say I need coaching?" He suddenly blurted.

"Er… well, I didn't say need, I thought you might like it."

"Do you think there is something wrong with me?" His voice became harsh and angry.

"No, of course not! I thought the audios might help with your career decisions. There's nothing wrong with getting help. You used to have a mentor too, remember? I'm doing it, it doesn't mean there's something wrong with me, so why would I think there was something wrong with you?"

"But why do you have to do this self-development stuff? Can't you just be happy with who you are?"

Ominous warning bells sounded in her head. Michael had wanted to keep her locked into being exactly the same person, in exactly the same lifestyle, for the rest of her life. He hadn't wanted her to spread her wings, to discover what made her happy.

"I do it because I want to learn and grow and experience new things. I believe the point of our lives is to progress and challenge ourselves in various ways, not to settle for a limited experience," she replied, keeping her voice even.

Channing sighed. "But if there's nothing wrong, why change?"

Her frustration levels rose. "I guess we see things differently."

"I think you have major unresolved issues, Elena!" His tone was suddenly harsh and angry.

"Huh?"

"You have issues with your ex-partners that you need to sort out."

"I don't understand. You just told me I didn't need to do self-development."

"You need help Elena, not self-development. You need a shrink!"

Elena stared at him, open-mouthed. It took a few moments for her to gather her thoughts.

"Well, thank you for your opinion," she said, struggling to maintain her composure. "I think the mentoring is helping me, and I want to listen to those audios, but you don't have to listen if you're not interested."

"I don't want to talk about your mentor or workshops either."

"Okay, I'll keep that part of my life to myself."

"Good."

But it wasn't good. Her uneasiness grew. She loved him, but how could their relationship deepen if there were major parts of her personality he didn't like her showing and he thought she had psychological issues? She was trying hard not to over-analyse everything, trying to go with the flow and allow things to play out in their own time, but it seemed to be getting harder rather than easier.

Confused and hurt, she went home alone.

❦

ELENA ANSWERED HER PHONE. "Hi Chan, how are you?"

"Babe, my cousin Tom died in a horse-riding accident yesterday."

"Oh my God, Chan, I'm sorry."

"Thanks."

"Were you two close?"

"Not really... don't worry, I'm okay."

"But it must be a terrible shock."

"Yeah." There was a slight tremor in his voice.

"Can I do anything for you?"

"No, thanks, babe. But I should go to his parent's place tonight instead of coming for dinner with your parents. All the family will be there..."

"Yes, of course."

There was an awkward pause.

"Well, just call me if you need anything." She cringed at her own ineptitude.

"Thanks beautiful."

"Please pass on my condolences to your family tonight."

"Will do."

"I love you."

"I love you too."

❦

ON SATURDAY MORNING, Elena was with her parents after they had returned from her mother's latest checkup when Chan called.

"How did it go last night with your family?"

"It was pretty bad," he admitted.

"I'm sorry…"

"It's okay, babe, it's not your fault." His voice took on an edgy, accusing tone. "But you could have offered to come with me last night."

"Oh… ah, I didn't realise you wanted me to come." Her shoulders tensed. He'd had a huge shock on top of other recent bad news so she needed to be very careful what she said and did until his emotions settled down.

"I wanted you to come."

"I'm sorry. I thought you might need time alone with the family. Plus I've never met your cousin or his parents, so I thought it would be a bit weird to turn up with you at a time like this."

"It's okay, it doesn't matter," he replied, the edginess lessening.

She breathed a silent sigh of relief. "Do you feel like doing something today?"

"Not really. I'll let you know when the funeral date is set."

"Okay, I love you."

"I love you too."

ELENA SQUINTED against the afternoon sun and tottered gingerly down Channing's aunt's cobblestone driveway, cursing herself for wearing the black stilettos that pinched her toes. As she walked past the main house, heading for his flat, he called her name through the screen door, his tone sharp. He gave her a cursory peck on the lips, stood aside to allow her to enter, and grabbed a dark brown suede jacket from the coat rack, shrugging it over his shirt and tie.

Elena drove, following his uncle's car down to the funeral parlour.

She felt the awkwardness as she was introduced to Tom's grieving parents, just barely stopping herself from saying how glad she was to meet them. Glad was not appropriate for a funeral.

"So sorry for your loss," she murmured.

"Thank you," Chan's uncle replied, stoically, one arm supporting his clearly distraught wife.

Elena shadowed Chan as he greeted more family, mumbling subdued greetings as they were introduced to her.

The wake was held in a local pub, the room filled with young people. Tom had been a popular, fun-loving guy and the family's wish was to give him a fitting send-off—no sombre cups of tea in the funeral parlour for Tom.

Chan steered her towards a young guy standing at the far end of the bar.

"Elena, this is my cousin Jordan. He's back from America for the funeral."

"You live in America?"

"Yeah, been there five years for work. So where are you living now Chan, still in the granny flat?"

Chan nodded.

"I thought you might have moved out by now!" Jordan snorted, downing the remnants of his Shiraz and reaching for the full glass which awaited him on the bar. Elena suspected he had a few glasses under his belt already.

She gave Chan's hand a supportive squeeze in an attempt to lessen his obvious chagrin.

"So, what do you plan to do with your life?"

Chan squirmed, shoulders hunched, eyes downcast. "I'm not sure," he mumbled.

Elena put a comforting arm around Chan's waist.

"And what do you do, Jordan?" she asked, trying to take the spotlight off Chan.

"I'm a Wall Street stockbroker," he replied, chest puffing in pride.

"That must be stressful."

"Yeah, but someone's gotta do it!" He raised his glass in salute. "See you kids later."

Chan swapped his empty wine glass for a full one as the bartender appeared. He downed the glass, then another and another.

They were still there late at night with a small group of sloshed friends who were dancing next to the bar. Elena's feet screamed in protest after standing for hours in her tight, highly impractical but drop dead gorgeous stilettos. She pardoned herself to sit on a bar stool.

Channing appeared, slumping next to her. "You see that couple dancing over there?"

She followed his pointed finger, "Yes."

"He had an affair once. She found out about it." He revealed this in a slurred, triumphant tone.

"Really?" Elena tried to keep her voice even, hoping the couple hadn't heard him.

"Yeah." He waited for her to ask for details.

There was an uncomfortable silence. Elena didn't want to discuss the personal lives of strangers.

He doesn't want to talk about them. He's using them to raise the topic of affairs.

She felt it in the air, a tense expectancy, almost a challenge. Had he guessed what had happened in Samoa? It still weighed heavily on her mind. She had been on the verge of confessing many times, knowing their relationship could not progress any further until she came clean. The Samoan incident might be a deal-breaker for him, and that prospect scared her. But she needed the right time to tell him. So far, every time she thought she had worked up the courage, something happened that resulted in him being upset, stressed or angry, so she had continued to wait. Tonight was not the right time either.

"Well, I guess they sorted it out, since they're still together," she responded.

Channing shrugged and stood up. "Let's go home."

He fell asleep in the car, waking up as she pulled up outside his house. He stumbled out of the car.

"Get out babe. I want you to stay with me."

She hesitated. "It's not a good idea, Chan. Your aunt and uncle won't like it if I stay."

"They will be fine," he replied, his voice betraying a hint of anger.

Elena hesitated. It didn't feel right to stay when she knew it would upset his family, but it would upset Chan if she left. For weeks she'd contended with this jittery, tip-toeing on eggshells existence. Despite her best efforts, nothing she said or did was right.

"I can't stay, Chan. It feels wrong."

He didn't answer.

We'll talk soon, ok?" She watched him walk away.

☙

WHEN ELENA HADN'T HEARD from Chan by Monday evening, she called him.

"Hi sweetie, how are you?"

"Fine. Sorry I haven't called, it's been a crazy time."

"It's okay. What shall we do on Wednesday? It's a public holiday. I thought maybe a picnic, like when we first met."

"I'm going hiking with my cousin Jordan."

"The arrogant one?"

"He's ok. He was just drunk when you met him."

"I was hoping to spend some quality time with you. We barely see each other anymore."

"Yeah well, I haven't seen Jordan in a lot longer."

"Yes, of course."

"I'll call you when we've finished the hike, okay?"

"Okay, sure. Enjoy your day."

"You too."

Hurt that he hadn't asked her to join them, she spent the public holiday furiously pulling out weeds in the garden, cleaning the house until it shone, then distracting herself with a good book. He didn't call her. *Well, I'm not calling him either*, she thought.

She hated being suspicious of him but she couldn't shake the thought that his day had been spent doing something different to what he had told her.

ᘛ

A FEW NIGHTS LATER, Elena rolled over in her bed to face Chan. "I've been thinking I'd like to go to India one day."

"Why would you want to do that?"

"Because it interests me and I've heard about other people's experiences in India."

"You must be a selfish person to want to go there!"

"Huh? What do you mean?" Elena stammered, stunned by such an unexpected attack.

"To leave your family and friends and go traipsing all over India, enjoying yourself while they suffer at home, worrying about you!"

"Actually my thoughts were more about going to an ashram for spiritual and yoga practice rather than traipsing all over the country. How would that be any more selfish than visiting Samoa or Europe?"

"India is a more dangerous place," was his terse reply.

"I admit the possible dangers have stopped me going there until now, but travelling anywhere can be dangerous if you're not careful."

"My ex shaved her head and ran off to Dharamshala to become a Buddhist nun," his voice was almost inaudible.

"Oh! I didn't know… but I'm not your ex, Chan."

"You left your husband," he accused her, "and you do yoga and meditation. You're only one step away from shaving your head!"

"You think I'm selfish because I left my husband? Haven't you ever ended a relationship?"

"Yes, but I've never been married."

His words stung but she fought hard to control her emotions.

"So you think I should have stayed with my husband even though we had nothing in common, both of us were unhappy, I wanted children and he didn't, he wasn't interested in spending time with me and he got angry if I ever expressed my feelings?"

"I guess not." He stared at the ceiling in sullen silence.

She touched his hand. "I'd love to travel to India one day, but I won't leave you… and I promise not to shave my head."

He nodded, his features pinched and strained as her attempt at humour failed.

"Are you okay?"

He sighed, moving his hand out from under hers. "I've got a headache."

"Do you want to try Reiki?"

He shook his head, springing out of bed as if she'd prodded him with a taser. "No, I want to go home."

"I'll get you some painkillers."

"No, I just want to go home."

Elena watched him dress, walked him to his car and stood with a sinking heart as he drove away.

She contacted him as soon as she woke up the next morning.

- *I hope u r feeling better this morning xxx*
- *yes! How r u? xx*
- *I'm good. See u tonight xxx*

Elena got herself ready and drove to work.

Her phone chimed as she parked her car in the city.

- I think u should find ur own way home 2nite Elena. I want 2 sleep in my own bed again. Have a good day! xx

Chan and Derek had their Fringe gig at six o'clock. Elena was meeting Jane and Dale there after work.

Why did Chan keep pushing her away? She called him, desperate to put things right. His tone was harsh and angry and she dissolved in a flood of tears. As she struggled to regain her composure, he continued to harangue her.

"Stop it Elena!... Elena! It's okay... Where are you? Can people hear you?"

Her heart broke. As a numbness spread throughout her body, her sobbing subsided. What people thought concerned him more than the fact that she was distressed.

"I'm in my car... Maybe I shouldn't come tonight."

"You can come... I want you to come."

Elena drew a shaky breath. Perhaps she had overreacted again. That he still wanted her to come was encouraging. "Okay, I'll see you later."

She sat through their act in the pop-up tent, unable to laugh at Derek's jokes. She tried to catch Chan's eye, but he seemed oblivious to her presence.

Jane gave her a quizzical look as the show ended. "Is everything okay?"

"I don't know." Elena's lips quivered as she gave them a condensed version of the situation.

"Are you guys still okay to come to our place for dinner on Sunday?" Jane asked.

"I don't know... Can I confirm with you tomorrow?"

"Sure, we should catch up for a bushwalk soon too, maybe next weekend?"

"That would be great, thanks."

The tent had cleared. Only Jane, Dale and Elena still remained as Chan and Derek approached from the stage.

"Hi," Channing greeted them in that deep, sexy voice which had been her undoing from the beginning.

"Hi," Elena echoed.

They stood millimetres apart yet separated by an emotional gulf.

Should she attempt to hug or kiss him? He held back, so she took her cue from him.

"I'm going home now," Elena said.

Derek raised an eyebrow, "I can't tempt you to indulge in an unearthly cinnamon donut delight first?"

"I'm tired," she mumbled and beat a hasty retreat.

The next day Elena was afraid to call or message in case Chan felt smothered. He wrote to her at midday.

- It's a hard time 4 me right now but I do miss u! xxx

Relief flooded her.

- I miss u 2. I love u and I'm here whenever u want 2 talk xxx

- thanks babe, just in a bad head space xxx

Sophie The Clairvoyant's words sprang to mind: Try to consider how your partner might be feeling. He'd had so much emotional turmoil lately. She should be more understanding instead of taking it personally.

- Do u want me 2 cancel the dinner at Jane and Dale's 2morro? xxx

- no, I'll meet u at ur house at 5 p.m. xx

- okay xx

Despite his assurances that he missed her, something felt very wrong. She moped around the house all day, unable to shake the feeling. Five o'clock came and went. When he still hadn't arrived at 5:30 p.m., she called. His phone went through to voicemail. He turned up at 5:45 p.m., looking peeved and turned his head away so that her kiss landed on his cheek.

"I tried to call. Did you get my message?"

His eyes widened. "I was on the phone to Derek."

Something in his words, his expression, his energy felt incongruent. Nothing made sense. He didn't want to spend time with her, but he loved and missed her. He said he wanted to go to dinner but his tardiness indicated otherwise. There were always plausible explanations for failing to contact her or taking her calls, but she couldn't shake the feeling there was something he wasn't telling her.

When they returned home after dinner, Chan decided to stay the night and her heart quickened in hope. She was astounded when he rolled over and began to make love to her but her elation was short lived. There was a distinct lack of connection between them. He would kiss her fiercely on the mouth one moment, then pull away the next, making sure that their gaze never met. He seemed driven to connect with her body but lacked the desire to connect with her. Disconcerted but worried about angering him again, she said nothing. He needed her support to get through this difficult period.

In the morning, he stayed in bed while Elena showered. She watched him through the ensuite doorway, texting on his phone. Using his phone first thing in the morning and not wanting to shower together was out of character. He entered the bathroom as she exited, casting an irritated glance in her direction as he passed.

She dressed, resisting the urge to check his phone.

"Babe, can you help me?"

"With what?"

"Someone contacted me via Facebook. They're interested in one of my sculptures."

"That's fantastic!"

"Yes, but they're not my friend and the message has disappeared. Can you help me find it?"

"Okay but quickly, I don't have much time. Give me your phone."

"Can you use your laptop? I have to make a call."

"Okay," she turned on the laptop which was sitting on the coffee table and got him to log into his Facebook account.

He went into the bedroom, leaving her to search his messages. She heard him murmuring into his phone.

"I can't find it," she called out, checking her phone. Ten minutes until she had to leave for work.

He returned to the living room, phone in hand. "Maybe I deleted it by mistake."

"Sometimes the messages go to another part of your inbox if the person isn't your friend. It's happened to me before. I'll see if I can figure it out."

As she trawled through various messages, he repeatedly disappeared into the bedroom and re-emerged, each time seeming more agitated.

She was getting stressed too. This was taking longer than expected and she had to go to work. Then her laptop froze twice, ensuring that she would be late for work. Elena drummed her fingers on the table, watching the whirling coloured wheel of suspended time. She couldn't understand it. Macs were normally so reliable.

Just as she was about to give up, it started functioning again. The screen had dropped five months down the list to a curious conversation between Chan and Donna—*I think it's best if we are just friends*.

Without considering the ramifications, Elena opened the message. It contained a long communication thread which spanned three months, starting a month before Elena had met Chan. Donna had contacted Chan after meeting him at The Wheatsheaf pub and asked him to dinner. The relationship developed fast. Within a week she spoke of how perfect was the first time they made love. Chan replied that she was the most beautiful and sweetest girl he had ever seen and he couldn't wait to see her again. Then, the week that Elena went to Samoa, Chan asked Donna to meet him at the beach. He had something to tell her. A couple of weeks went by without any messages, then Donna suggested a catch-up. Two days later, Chan asked her to send him sexy photos of herself. More banter and flirting until Chan delivered the line 'I think it's best if we are just friends.'

A kaleidoscope of emotions tumbled through Elena—shock and outrage that he had called Donna the most beautiful, sweetest girl in the world while telling her the same thing; nausea and chagrin that he was still asking for near-naked pictures of Donna a month after Elena and he had committed to each other. All conducted through Facebook messenger, which he had told her he barely used and therefore didn't use it to communicate with her while she was in Samoa. He must not have wanted to risk Elena seeing him online while he was busy whispering sweet nothings to another woman. What a fool she had been!

You're not innocent either, Elena reminded herself. The thought brought the full shame of Samoa flooding back. Ah, the irony! She was in no position to be angry with him.

While he had been relentless in his pursuit of her, acting as if she, above all others, was whom he most desired, in reality he had been as unsure as Elena. True, he had continued to chase Donna after Elena said she was ready to commit but, in hindsight, she realised that she had been the only one to voice her commitment. He had nodded, accepting her declaration, but made no promise in return. In fact, if her memory were correct, he had actually looked a little frightened.

This whole situation—the computer freezing then dropping down the list, finding the messages while Chan was out of the room—was surely a sign that she was meant to find out the truth. While she had been beating herself up about Anton, Chan had been doing the same. They were no different to each other on that score and she now knew, despite whatever issues he was going through, she had to tell him about Anton. Perhaps Chan needed to clear the air as much as she did. Feeling sick to her stomach, she called out to him.

"Chan, can you come here please?"

Chan appeared in the doorway, overnight bag in hand. "Did you find it?"

"No, but I did find this."

She turned the laptop around so he could see Donna's messages.

Fear and surprise flashed across his face. "Oh!" His shoulders sagged.

She closed her eyes, her face a concentrated grimace.

"It's okay, I understand." She took his hand in hers. "I am a bit angry because you gave me the impression you wanted to commit to me at the same time you were seeing with her. You said the exact same lovely words to both of us, which diminishes their meaning for me, but I understand you were unsure where you stood with me because I wasn't ready to commit."

He shrugged. "It was nothing, it was just a bit of fun before I met you and, when you didn't seem so keen on me, I kept talking to her."

"Yes, I know. It hurts that you continued for a month after I said I was willing to commit to you, though. And I'm sure you said your relationship with Donna happened a few years ago."

Chan shook his head, refusing to look at her. "No, I didn't."

"Yes, you did."

His shoulders hunched forward and his hand went limp. "I think need to be on my own."

Elena's breath caught in her throat. "Do you mean you need time alone today? Or—"

"I mean I need to be on my own for a while. I don't know what I want. I don't have a job, I don't want to sculpt anymore because nobody wants to buy my work. We have nothing in common…" he mumbled, trailing off into silence, withdrawing his hand from her grasp.

Elena stiffened at a sharp pain in her chest and forced herself to take deep breaths until the pain reduced. Chan, wrapped up in his own misery, didn't notice her discomfort.

He was finding excuses not to be with her in order to hide from his shame. If she told him about Samoa, perhaps he wouldn't feel so bad about his actions and maybe, just maybe, there would be a chance for their relationship to continue.

"I need to tell you something." She picked up his limp and unresisting hand again. "I did something wrong too."

Chan gave her a sharp look but said nothing.

She began to explain, haltingly at first but soon the words were pouring out of her, stumbling over each other in their rush to be free.

He said not a word and she sat in agonised silence waiting for a reaction. "I'm sorry," she whispered, fighting back tears.

"I thought something happened in Samoa," he said. "It's okay, you were all 'avad up," he continued, still not looking at her.

"That's no excuse. I shouldn't have taken the 'ava in the first place, I shouldn't have mixed it with alcohol, and I should have told you what happened. I needed to tell you but it never seemed the right time. You always had something else to deal with and I couldn't bear to upset you."

"It doesn't matter."

She shuddered at the finality in his voice. Did it not matter because he was breaking up with her? Or did he mean he forgave her? She was afraid to ask.

"Can we just eat breakfast now please?" His harsh tone was like a physical slap.

"You want to eat *now*?"

"I'm hungry."

Elena moved to the kitchen, cut and plated some fresh fruit and yoghurt, and carried it to the table.

Channing tucked into his food.

Elena watched, her plate untouched, a lump constricting her throat. The tears she had fought to hold back suddenly burst out of her in uncontrollable sobs.

Channing exploded. "Stop it, Elena!"

His harshness shocked her into silence. Channing turned his attention back to eating while she sat, mourning the loss of the kind, gentle, charismatic Channing she had fallen in love with.

"Eat your fruit."

She winced. "I can't."

"Yes, you can. Just eat!"

Bewildered why her lack of appetite was making him so angry, she forced a mouthful of fruit around the hard lump in her throat.

Channing wiped his bowl clean. "You've hardly eaten a thing," he accused.

"I can't eat when I'm upset."

He scraped his chair back and took his bowl to the sink.

"Is there someone else, Chan?"

"What? No."

"Donna… or Tennille?"

"No, I could never be with Donna again. She's a smoker." His nose wrinkled in disgust. "I just need to be alone for a while."

"Are you breaking up with me or do you just want some time apart?"

He came over to her. "I need time apart. I'll come back to discuss it with you in a couple of weeks."

"Okay."

He kissed her cheek. "I'm going now."

Numb, she followed him outside and watched him get into his car.

"Can you give my house keys back please?" she heard herself ask.

He handed them over with a rueful shrug and drove away.

It was nine-thirty. She called in sick and spent the day wallowing in bed. In the afternoon, she worked up the courage to message him.

- Chan, I hope u r okay? I think we do have some common interests but differences can be good 2 because they force us out of our comfort zone and give us new experiences we otherwise wouldn't choose. I'm so sorry for everything. I promise I won't pressure u. U left some DVDs here. When would u prefer to collect them? Much love always x

He didn't reply.

A week later, Derek called to say how sorry he was about her break-up with Channing. Swallowing the incredible hurt, she took her time to construct another message.

- Hi Chan How r u? Derek thinks our break-up is final. If so, can u please tell me?

Her phone rang as she changed into her pyjamas. She looked at the screen—it was Channing.

Her heart in her throat, she answered the call. "Hello Chan."

"Hi Elena, how are you?"

"I'm fine, and you?"

"Good… Yeah look Elena, I think it would be best if we are just friends. I don't know what I want. You need someone who knows what they want."

Her heart contracted painfully. "Okay, thank you for making that clear." Her voice wobbled with emotion.

"I think it's too early to see each other. Can you drop the DVDs off with my aunt please?"

"Okay… well, take care."

"You too, Elena."

As she hung up, her eye fell on the brass cage sculpture on her dresser. Tears ran down her face as she hid it in a drawer—she couldn't bear to see it anymore.

Chapter Twenty-One

HER WIDE EYES FIX'D ON CAMELOT

H is aunt was kind and gracious when she dropped by. "I'm sorry it didn't work out, dear. He's a funny one, our Peter Pan."

"I was willing to give him time to work out what he wanted."

"You have enough in your life already, don't you?"

"Yes, but I made room for him... and I fell in love with him." Elena blinked back more tears.

His aunt hugged her. "You'll be okay. Don't look back."

It was advice Elena had every intention of following, but a week later, Channing texted her.

- *Hi Elena I was wondering if u would like 2 catch up? If u don't want 2, I would understand! x*

- *Of course I would like 2. When? xo*

- *What are u doing 4 lunch today? x*

- *I've got plans today. I'm free after work 2nite or 2moro nite.*

- *I guess we will be in touch Elena x*

He wants to tell you he's seeing someone else before you find out from other sources.

She felt the voice was right, sensing he didn't want to give up his evenings to see her because he'd reserved them for someone else. Well, she wasn't about to drop her plans to suit his needs, not this time. She would let him have his say but at a mutually convenient time.

In the afternoon, he messaged her again.

- *Elena I do have time 2nite after all, meet u at San Churro, Gouger Street at 6 p.m.? x*

- *Sure x*

Elena arrived first and sat at a corner table, steeling herself to hear his news.

He appeared, giving her a sheepish hug. Over hot chocolate, he kept the conversation impersonal. She waited for him to bring up the reason he had wanted to see her. He didn't.

"Shall we get something to eat?" He suggested.

"Sure," she was intrigued. What *did* he want?

They ambled down Gouger Street and chose a Chinese restaurant.

The waitress showed them to a table tucked away in the back corner.

"Yes, this is good," he mumbled to himself, surveying the restaurant.

He's worried someone will see us together, Elena thought.

They stared at each other across the table, feeling the strangeness of the shifted dynamics between them.

"I've been worried about you Chan. You seemed so stressed when you broke up with me. I know you've had some stuff to deal with. I just wish I was able to help." She reached across the table and squeezed his hand.

Chan crumbled under the weight of her words, shrinking back into himself as tears sprang in his eyes.

"I'm not over you Elena. You're wonderful!"

Elena's jaw dropped. Maybe her intuition had been wrong! "I'm not over you either. I didn't want to lose you as a friend too, so I tried to give you space but I do still love you."

"I've just had a lot of stuff going on."

The waitress interrupted with their food and the moment was gone.

He tucked into his meal with gusto. When Elena couldn't finish her meal, he finished it for her.

"You look fantastic," Chan commented as they rose to leave.

She would have been flattered had he looked her in the eye, but his gaze focused on her hips and she felt a need to raise her guard against the confused sexual energy emanating from him.

Outside, he planted a quick kiss on her lips then hurried away, shoulders hunched against the oncoming wind. He had reached the corner of the next side street before she recovered herself enough to move.

He turned to look back at her, gave a half-hearted wave and disappeared around the corner, leaving a void of unuttered thoughts in his wake.

Elena drove home and lay in bed trying to make sense of the evening's events. Hope quickened and she sent an impulsive text.

- *It was really nice 2 see u Chan xo*
- *It was great 2 c u Elena! I really have missed u! Sweet dreams x*
- *I've missed u 2. I love u xo*

He still hadn't replied by the following afternoon. In need of distraction, she accepted Robyn's offer to join her for Friday night drinks. They hadn't seen each other in such a long time but it only took a couple of drinks before Elena poured out her woes.

"I don't know where I stand. He keeps blowing hot and cold but I think we could work it out if he's willing..."

"Are you listening to what you're saying?" Robyn cut in. "He would hold you back. You need someone more suited to you, more settled."

Elena squirmed. Chan was a nice person. Saying he would hold her back seemed elitist.

"You should see Dawn, my clairvoyant." Robyn handed her Dawn's business card.

Her interest piqued, she pocketed the card for future reference.

⸙

ELENA HUNG back after yoga class to speak with Jivan.

"Thanks for the class tonight, it was great."

"You're welcome. I notice your trikonasana is improving. You're starting to open the chest more."

Elena smiled a shy smile. "Thanks, still a long way to go though."

"It's about the journey, Elena, not the destination."

She nodded.

"How is Channing?"

"He decided he only wants to be friends." All the rawness she was trying to suppress rose to the surface.

"It's nothing to do with you. I get a very strong sense it wasn't anything you did wrong. The anger, the yelling, those are his issues, him projecting onto you and wanting to be in control. Don't buy into it."

She had said nothing about feeling at fault or Channing being angry with her but Jivan, always so in tune, had picked up on it, anyway. She wished Channing were more like Jivan. Heck, she wished *she* were more like Jivan.

"I'm not blameless and I'm not perfect either," she countered.

"Nobody is perfect, but in this case the issue is not you. You're very hard on yourself, you know."

And sometimes I'm not hard enough, she thought.

"It all fell apart when I said I wanted to go to India. I didn't know his ex broke up with him to become a Buddhist nun in India!"

"Hmm, yes human emotions are very interesting… You've never told me you want to visit India!"

"Well, I've had it in mind since reading a book about a woman who travelled there, and your stories increased my interest."

"Be aware that it's not the easiest of places to travel, Elena. But I can give you some pointers if you decide to go. I sense you need to re-read that book, by the way."

"Which book?"

"The one about the woman who went to India."

Elena made a mental note. If Jivan thought it beneficial for her to read again, she would do so.

"Chan disappeared for a few weeks, but just when I reached the point of accepting his decision, he asked me to dinner," she said.

"That's because you let him go. You weren't smothering him with your energy and emotions, so he came back."

"Except that he's disappeared again now."

"He'll hold you back," Jivan blurted, echoing Robyn's warning.

"Yes, I know," she admitted. Jivan's opinion somehow carried more weight.

Jivan stood in the doorway watching her leave, concern lining his features. It tore at her heartstrings. She didn't want him to feel bad on her account.

She managed a wonky smile. "Take care."

"You too."

She glanced at her phone before starting the car.

- *U r the nicest girl but I struggle with ur self help obsession! I don't want to hurt u, u deserve a nice guy. x*

The spark of hope died and Elena's heart sank. She took a few deep breaths before replying.

- *Ok. Can we still catch up as friends? x*

- *Sure. I'm a bit busy right now though, I'll get back 2 u when I have more time. x*

So that was that. A sense of peace descended over her as she accepted the inevitable. In a way it was a relief after the rollercoaster of turmoil and anguish. In fact, their whole relationship had been a rollercoaster ride. The adrenalin rushes and continual anticipation of what lay over the hill or around the next corner had made it seem long at the time. But now that it was over, she felt the reality of the timeframe. A rushed beginning, tornado lovemaking, as many activities as they could cram into each week, then careening headlong into the finale. One blink and she might have missed the whole thing.

Similarly, Elena couldn't believe a whole year had passed since she had enlisted Brett's help. Despite the recent turmoil, she felt more stable and sure of herself so she decided not to continue the mentoring. It was time she learned to trust her own judgement without the constant reassurance of a sounding board. She also decided she would visit India before the end of the year and focus more on her writing. She applied for long service leave to begin in December. The business was moving into a major restructure period and word was the headcount would be decimated to make budget savings. There was every chance a lofty manager would see her absence as an excuse to get rid of her. But there were more important considerations right now. She was desperate to escape the daily grind and rejuvenate her soul. Three weeks in one of the peaceful Rishikesh ashrams Jivan had told her about would help to unleash her creativity. Then she would devote three months at home to writing. Unparalleled excitement grew inside her. She was going to India!

✦

ELENA STOOD AT TRAFFIC LIGHTS, mentally running through her to-do list for India.

Chan drove past, heading toward his aunt's house. It was eight-thirty in the morning. It had been a month since they had spoken and he hadn't tried to find time to catch up with her. As she watched his car disappear out of sight, her instinct told her he had spent the night with someone.

There was *another woman.*

Her hunch came flooding back along with a rising tide of anger. She silenced the hateful inner voice but it taunted her incessantly, reminding her that something wasn't right. Something about that girl, Tennille, had never added up. The night they had broken up, Elena had questioned him about Donna and Tennille and he had only denied involvement with Donna. Deep down she had known he wasn't being honest but she hadn't wanted to face it. There was no concrete evidence but her gut was screaming at her that she had been played a fool.

She punched out a series of hurried messages.

- *Chan, don't bother making time 4 me. U r clearly 2 busy with the new girlfriend.*

- *Hi Derek, hope u r well. I'm pretty sure Chan was seeing Tennille b4 he broke up with me so I don't think I can remain friends with him. Would love 2 keep in touch with u, but won't be joining any group catch ups. x*

Derek's reply was swift.

- *I'm sorry u had 2 find out this way Elena. It's good that u r valuing urself enough 2 take a stand. DO.*

Relief at having her hunch verified was combined with a sickening disappointment that her trust had once again been violated. At first Chan had seemed so different to both Michael and Garri, but now they all merged in her consciousness, taunting her with the similarities to which she had so willingly blinded herself.

Something else was teasing at the edge of her consciousness. She re-read Derek's reply. DO — Derek O'Malley... or Distressed Observer.

- R u the Distressed Observer??

- How did u know?

- Just a hunch.

- Sorry. Garri's a mate but I couldn't stand back and watch u get dragged down anymore.

- But Chan said u thought I was unsupportive of Garri?

- No, I told Chan that's what Garri told me. I haven't lived with u so I couldn't verify either way, all I knew was that both men said they didn't find u supportive.

Elena dropped her phone back into her bag, shaking her head in wonder. Was this all a coincidence, or a neatly structured plan?

꽃

THE PHONE CHIMED AGAIN as she got in the car to go home.

- Elena I'm sorry u feel that way. I value ur friendship.

What kind of fool did he take her for? Her entire body trembling with an anger she scarcely believed herself capable of, she punched an ill-considered reply.

- Think with ur brain for once, not ur penis. Grow up and treat people with respect.

- Says she who slept with a stranger in Samoa!

- Bullshit! At least I told u the truth — u had no intention of telling me.

- Actually I planned 2 tell u the last nite I stayed over, little miss self-righteous, but I didn't want 2 hurt u.

Elena sat in the car for a long time until the shaking subsided. Nobody had ever gotten under her skin the way he had—not even Garri. It rocked her to the core. Brett had once suggested physical methods for releasing anger: kickboxing, punching bags, throwing things.

She drove to a thrift shop, bought a box of old plates, drove to a deserted country road and hurled the plates down the side of a slope, one at a time, directing eruptions of abuse at the blameless crockery. Better the plates than a person, she thought grimly, watching the river of crockery pieces rush downhill. When she ran out of plates, she stamped her foot and ran through a field, screaming until she was limp and spent. Dragging herself to the car, she drove home.

The anger dipped into sadness and total disbelief at the loss of her sweet Chan. She struggled to accept and make peace with all these potent emotions and, as a last resort, went to the clairvoyant Robyn had recommended.

Dawn took Elena's hands and closed her eyes. "I see you travelling a lot for work, standing up in front of people. But first you are going somewhere with dirt roads and lots of people on bikes."

Elena started. "I'm going to India soon."

"Yes, that could be it. When are you going?"

"Probably December. I haven't booked the flights yet."

"Can't you go sooner?"

"No, I have four months leave beginning in December."

Dawn shook her head. "I think you'll be going sooner. How long are you going for?"

"Three weeks. I want to stay in an ashram then come home and spend the rest of the time writing."

"I feel you'll be spending much more time there than you plan."

Elena shook her head. "No, I want to focus on writing."

Dawn handed her a tarot pack. "Pick three cards for me."

She examined the cards. "I can see you've been through a difficult time. Someone you trusted didn't treat you very well, and you are struggling to let go of him. But he isn't right for you. You don't really want that kind of relationship, do you?"

"No, it's not what I want. But I'm struggling to get over the fact that he was so…" She stopped, searching for the right adjective, then gave a helpless shrug.

"Cruel," Dawn finished for her.

Elena's face crumpled. Yes, cruel was the word. How could her beautiful, talented, boyish, loving Chan have been so cruel? He had seemed so nice.

Nice! Michael seemed nice. Garri seemed nice. Channing seemed nice. Just because someone is nice, doesn't make him right for you.

She had spent her whole life accepting men who pursued her because she didn't believe she had the right to refuse them if they were nice, even if they weren't a good fit for her. The ridiculousness of it became painfully apparent. Letting 'nice' men walk all over her was no way to live.

Dawn's voice drew Elena's attention back to the present. "You're like a deer caught in headlights, sweetheart."

"Oh?"

"You need to stand your ground more, don't let others intimidate or control you. And learn to trust your instincts. This trip will be good for you."

Elena's shoulders sagged. "I thought I had learned to stand my ground."

"Life is a continual learning curve and you will be tested until your inner conviction becomes unshakeable. I do see a man in your future, and he's of Indian appearance. I don't know if I'm seeing that just because you've told me you're going to India. It might only be symbolic. Perhaps he follows an Indian philosophy, but the image I see is of a dark-haired, dark-skinned man wearing a turban. He is like an emperor, standing tall and proud, and he will be a mentor for you. I see the two of you standing together in wedding clothes."

"Oh!" What an unexpected, yet pleasant prediction!

He sounds like Jivan.

A sliver of hope illuminated her features and she went home feeling more peaceful and accepting than she had in a long while. She dug out her copy of *Eat, Pray, Love* and flicked through it. One dog-eared page contained a passage which she had forgotten—the Texan's definition of a soulmate as a person who is our own reflection, who smacks us awake and tears down the walls of protection and resistance we have built, thus enabling us to change our lives. And then they move on.

Had Channing been a soulmate? Garri? Michael? She had felt exposed, cosmically slapped around and forced to face her own human frailty with each of them. The idea was strangely comforting.

"You were right," she told Jivan during her massage appointment. "I needed to read that book again to find the passage about the reasons for soulmates and how they help us evolve. It has been painful, but Michael, Garri and Channing all helped my development."

"Then you should send gratitude to them for helping you wake up to yourself. Have you heard from Channing?"

"No, I'm not likely to either. He was already seeing someone before he broke up with me. I should have realised. The signs were right in front of me."

Jivan's lip curled in disdain.

"I thought I wasn't good enough for him."

"Oh, you're good enough," he replied. "Learn to trust the signs you receive."

Elena couldn't believe her ears! Was it possible that she was good enough for Jivan too?

Admit it, you want to be with Jivan!

Okay, I admit it! Now leave me alone! She scolded the pesky voice.

Tell him! Now is your chance.

I can't tell him while I'm half-naked on his table! I admit you're usually right but that would be completely inappropriate. Let me do it another day. She pushed the voice away.

❧

ELENA STOPPED FOR A BREATH, breaking a square from the Cadbury bar. The smooth milk chocolate melted in her mouth, exposing the fruit and nuts inside. She had needed to confide in someone and Jane was a good listener.

"I don't think you did anything wrong, Elena. You hadn't discussed being exclusive at that point, had you?"

"No, but sleeping with two men at the same time is not something that sits well with me. I shouldn't have done it."

"It sounds like you weren't in a state to make decisions at the time."

Elena shrugged. "Even not making a decision is a decision. More importantly, I should have told Channing when it happened."

"From what you've said, he wasn't exemplifying model behaviour."

"But I didn't know that at the time. I guess it was a recipe for disaster all 'round. At least I'm now aware of my tendency to let men control me and to feel obligated to give them what they want. I thought I had understood that after Samoa, but I hadn't yet learned that controlling natures come in many disguises, including niceness… and respect comes from within. Even a nice person won't necessarily respect me if I don't respect my own boundaries. I had learned to say no to some things by the time Chan came along but I was still making too many concessions. I told myself they weren't important things, but that means I didn't see my own feelings and needs as important."

"I think Chan also reflected your fear of hurting people. You were so worried about hurting each of your partners if you told them how you felt or made choices that were right for you. Then Chan told you he didn't want to hurt you."

"Oh, you're right! That hadn't occurred to me… thank you."

"Well, your stories amaze me, Elena. I love listening to how you make sense of your experiences and how it all fits together. Your life is like a jigsaw puzzle—you find more pieces that fit in every experience."

Elena laughed. "I hope to God I've finished this part of the puzzle! I'm not sure how many more pieces I can take!"

"Focus on your India trip. Tell yourself it's going to be amazing," Jane suggested.

"It's definitely shaping up that way. It has taken on a life of its own. First, I had to bring my holidays forward by a month to suit business requirements, so I'm taking leave from November to February. Then a friend of a friend told me about her own trip to India and the volunteer work she did in an orphanage. As she was telling me, I got so excited and I just knew I had to work there, too. I emailed the manager offering to teach English for a month and he accepted, so I extended my trip to seven weeks."

"Wow, that sounds incredible." Jane clapped her hands together. "I'm so excited for you!"

"That's not the end of the story. I caught up with my friend Robyn again, the one who suggested I see Dawn, the clairvoyant. Turns out her friend Swinitha lives in Delhi and she put me in contact with her to help arrange my travel and accommodation."

"Perfect! Someone is definitely looking out for you."

"It will put my parents more at ease, too. They're convinced I will return home in a body bag after being killed for cash by desperate beggars or becoming another victim in the latest string of violent Delhi rapes."

"You need to be careful, but don't let it stop you going. Bad things happen all over the world."

"Yes, that's what I told my parents." Elena's old fears had threatened to take over when they had pointed out these dangers, but she had suppressed them. She needed to take this trip. Nothing had ever felt so right. Whatever the risk, she knew it would be worth it.

"Swinitha talked me into staying with her for a week to do some Delhi sightseeing. So that makes eight weeks in total."

"Oh my giddy aunt! The clairvoyant was right!"

Elena gave a rueful shrug. "So it seems."

ELENA STAYED BACK after yoga class to update Jivan on her plans.

He was almost as excited as Elena. "I was worried when you first told me you wanted to go to India. Remember, I cautioned you it's not a place for the faint-hearted? But everything is falling into place for you so I can see this was meant to be!"

Elena beamed. "I know, it's incredible."

The only thing not falling into place is Jivan himself, she thought. *I want to tell him I'm in love with him, but I'm terrified he'll reject me. Maybe I should wait until I come back from India. Jivan said India raises your level of consciousness. If I improve myself more, he'll be less likely to reject me.*

"You should visit the yoga centre where I did my training. You can get good Ayurvedic treatments in India too!"

Elena had never heard of Ayurvedic treatments, but they must be good if Jivan recommended them.

She added an extra week to visit the yoga centre.

Six weeks before departure, another colleague put Elena in contact with her brother Ian, who was an English teacher in Bangalore. Ian gave her tips on teaching English in India and offered her his spare room if she wanted to volunteer in Bangalore too. Elena accepted without hesitation and amended her flights. The three-week trip was now twelve weeks, and she laughed at the memory of herself refuting Dawn's prediction.

"I'M interested in why you believed—for so many years—that you were unattractive." Jane wheezed with the effort of their climb back up to Mount Lofty's summit.

"I remember at nine years old believing I was ugly… Maybe it resulted from being teased… at school." Elena stopped to catch her breath. "I did go through an awkward phase, you know when your adult teeth are competing for prime place in your mouth and your limbs are as gangly as a colt."

"Haha, yes I remember it well!"

"Then the pimples appeared, rubbing salt into already painful wounds. As a teenager, when older women told me I was pretty, I assumed they were just trying to make the ugly duckling feel better about herself. My husband helped reinforce that belief for me but in recent years I've realised that it wasn't true."

"How did you reconcile that belief with the string of men who wanted to sleep with you? That must have taken some talented mental acrobatics!"

"Bizarre, isn't it? I told myself that they must have loved the person I was inside because they sure couldn't have loved what their eyes were seeing! When Isaac raped me, my coping mechanism was to believe he couldn't help himself because he was in love with me. What a crazy, mixed up outlook, hey?"

"Yet you seemed so level-headed in other areas of your life. Such complex creatures we are."

"We certainly are. Now I understand that lots of people use sex to make themselves feel good. They overindulge because, once the act is complete, the euphoric feelings subside and they have to chase the feeling all over again. They aren't considering the feelings or needs of the person they sleep with. It's a physical and chemical attraction, not a deep love and respect, which of course is what I was searching for. Deep down, it's what we all want."

"Hmm, yes I see what you mean."

They arrived at the summit. Elena gazed across the city, sparkling in the twilight. "A man who loves me for who I am will not pressure or cajole me into sex. He will take the time to get to know me first and develop that love and respect. The physical relationship should come after the mental and emotional connections."

"Well, it sounds like you've sorted that one out, so let's see who eventuates next. Maybe you'll meet someone in India!"

"I'm going to India to find myself, not to find a man."

"Fair enough!"

Elena sat on one of the metal benches. "Can you keep a secret?"

"Of course."

"I like Jivan."

Confusion crossed Jane's face but was quickly replaced with a dawning realisation. "You mean like, or *like* like?"

"I mean I'm in love with him. I think I have been ever since my first yoga class with him."

Jane jumped up and down, clasping her hands together in front of her chest. "Yes! You'd make a great couple!"

"But I don't know how he feels…"

"Are you going to tell him before you leave?"

"No! No, I think I need to go to India first. See what comes up for me there."

Jane nodded. "I can understand that." She sat next to Elena and hugged her. "Take care… and enjoy yourself!"

Chapter Twenty-Two

THE BROAD STREAM BORE HER FAR AWAY

E lena lay in bed, running over in her mind the dream she'd just
had of Jivan. She checked her phone.

- *May you be blessed with protection, love, good fortune & carry an
inward smile of satisfaction throughout your India journey. Will be thinking
of you. Much love Jivan xo :-)*

She beamed from ear to ear.

- *I just had a dream about u and woke up 2 your MSG. Thank u, that
means a lot 2 me :) plane leaves in 3 hours! The inward smile has been there
these past few months so I am sure it will remain. Look forward 2 sharing
stories when I return xoxo*

She got up, showered, gave the windows and doors one last check
and went outside to wait for the taxi.

Her phone chimed.

- *We are 20 minutes away from the airport, dear.*

Her parents had driven down that morning to say goodbye.

- *Me too. See you soon!*

"Be careful," her mother hugged her tight at the international
screening gate. Her sugar levels were stable again now, making it
easier for Elena to go away, knowing all was well.

"Don't go out on your own, girlie," her father added.

"Don't worry, I'll be careful."

How she could avoid being on her own when she was travelling
solo she didn't know, but it touched her that they cared. She didn't

want to worry them, but she couldn't back out now. She didn't want to back out! On the contrary, she wanted to run headlong into whatever awaited her on that vast, overpopulated, ancient land.

She cleared the security screening and sat opposite a group of Buddhist monks in saffron robes in the departure lounge. It was the first time she had been so close to a monk. *What is the etiquette?* She wondered. *Should I bow to them? Am I allowed to speak to them? Is it okay to make eye contact?*

She pulled out her phone and re-read Jivan's message. He had signed it with love but she had hesitated to type the word in reply. Why was she afraid to send him love in return? Agonising over whether she should, she became aware of a pair of eyes fixed on her. It was one of the monks. His face was an unreadable mask, but she had an uncomfortable conviction he was reading her thoughts. She squirmed under his gaze, exasperated with herself, and dropped her gaze back to her phone.

"First you tried to control everything in your life."

Elena looked up again.

The monk was still staring at her. "Then you tried going with the flow," he said.

Startled, Elena managed only to nod.

"But neither strategy worked. So what are you going to do now?"

Elena's brow crinkled as she tried not to cry. What was she going to do? "I don't know…"

The monk shrugged a shoulder and looked away.

Elena grabbed her phone, typed another message to Jivan and sent it before she could talk herself out of it.

- *And much love 2 u also xo*

Within minutes he replied.

- *Thank you… Good luck! xx*

Relieved, she looked up, straight into the eyes of the monk. His eyes bored into hers with a force that made it impossible for her to tear her gaze away. With an almost imperceptible nod, he looked away.

✤

ELENA ALIGHTED in Delhi some thirteen hours later. The excitement she felt couldn't be squashed, not even by the officious little man at the screening counter who seemed to take great delight in grilling her about her travel plans.

Unnerved by the row of AK47-bearing soldiers stationed at the terminal exit, she scurried out into the mild night and along the collection zone to pillar thirteen, the spot where Swinitha had arranged for them to meet. *Unlucky for some—but not for me*, she thought.

Three men approached her. "Taxi?" one asked.

"No, thank you," she shook her head.

"I do good price," another offered.

"I don't need a taxi."

A woman with a broad smile walked purposefully towards her. "Elena?"

"Yes! You must be Swinitha. Nice to meet you and thank you for helping me."

"You are welcome. My husband is with our car over here," she gestured towards a white, late model car of a make Elena didn't recognise.

Exiting the airport, a thick mist swirled around them, distinguishable from the darkness only when they passed by the sparse, dim streetlights. Total blackness lay beyond the small circles of light. They seemed to be on a freeway of sorts with a rough, pot-holed surface. Swinitha's husband Pedru focussed intently on the road and spoke little. It seemed to rub off on Swinitha who fell into silence too.

After a few failed attempts to start a conversation, Elena succumbed to the silence and sat in the back seat watching the swirling mist fly past the car's headlights. Fear resurfaced and she wondered if she had made a mistake. She didn't really know these people and she had no idea where she was. She was completely reliant on them. Her mind started to imagine a host of horrible scenarios which would result in the realisation of her parent's worst fears. *Get a grip*, she scolded herself.

They pulled into a military residential compound with an entrance guarded by another firearm-bearing soldier. Pedru worked as a military psychologist, screening new recruits. In the darkness, she could just make out the row upon row of identical houses separated by postage stamps of untamed grass.

"Please sit. I'll take your case to the bedroom," Pedru ushered her into the small, spotless living room, his manner courteous and self-consciously reserved.

"A glass of water?" Swinitha offered.

"Thank you." She accepted the glass of water Swinitha held out.

"It's bottled water," Swinitha assured her.

"Ah yes, my yoga teacher warned me to never drink the tap water."

"We drink tap water with a Reverse Osmosis filter, but better for you to not take the chance." Swinitha patted her hand.

Pedru returned, followed by their teenage daughter. "This is Priya."

"Nice to meet you," Elena smiled.

"How was your flight?" Priya asked.

"Fine. It was long but comfortable enough."

It was approaching midnight and Elena's strength was flagging but, not wanting to appear rude, she forced herself to converse.

"I'm afraid it is past our bedtime. We have work and school tomorrow," Pedru apologised, standing as soon as she placed the empty glass on the table.

"Oh yes, of course! I'm tired as well." Elena stood, embarrassed that her presence had shortened their rest, and allowed them to show her to her room.

The walls of her large, high ceilinged bedroom bore scars of past occupants. Elena closed the strange heavy duty bolt which replaced a door handle. There were bars on the window, which were covered by light blue curtains, thin enough that a stream of moonlight shone through. The room had an ensuite with a Western-style toilet, basin and shower recess, minus the shower head. In its place stood a plastic bucket of water and a jug. Perplexed by the missing shower head, she made do with a quick sponge wash then lay on the firm, single mattress and turned off the light.

In the darkness, a smile tugged at the corners of her mouth. It spread to a grin. She almost laughed out loud.

I'm in INDIA! she thought. I'm a lone traveller in a strange land; in a strange house with kind-hearted strangers; in a strange room that appears more like a prison with its bolted door and barred window, yet I feel freer than ever before.

Well played, Elena!

Thanks, she told the inner voice. *If only I'd listened to you earlier…*

Elena didn't know what the next few months held in store for her, but she was not afraid, for she knew that, whatever happened, she would be okay.

She had found a boat and down she'd lain, allowing the broad stream to carry her far away. With a song in her heart and a smile on her lips, she understood that she was embarking on a metamorphosis of the soul. With a blissful sigh, her eyes fluttered closed and she surrendered to the unknown future.

THANK YOU FOR READING

Please share your thoughts

Rate or review Peace of the Puzzle now

I hope you enjoyed Elena's journey!

I would be grateful if you could take a moment to rate or share an honest review via your favourite ebook retailer or Goodreads or LibraryThing.

Your review makes a big difference for indie authors like myself who don't have large marketing budgets or the backing of the marketing teams at publishing houses.

Thank you in advance. Namaste.

COMING SOON

Missing Peace - Peace of the Puzzle #2

Elena is on a mission to discover who she really is... and to find the courage to tell the man she loves how she feels.

The search for answers takes her to India—a land of ancient cultures and stark contrasts—which both test and support her. Buoyed by her new experiences and knowledge, Elena returns home full of hope... until a shocking development threatens to destroy all she has worked so hard for.

Join the mailing list on the contacts page of my website www.hayley-morton.com to receive a sneak preview before the publication date and be the first to know when *Missing Peace* is published.

One of my pet peeves is having my inbox clogged with weekly marketing mail so you will not hear from me very often. I promise never to spam you or give your details to anyone else.

ABOUT THE AUTHOR

When she isn't writing, Hayley may be found in her day job as a librarian, or teaching English as a Second Language, or practicing yoga. When she's not doing any those things, she's travelling or dreaming of travel. Her favourite kind of trips involve yoga, staying with local families, volunteering, and taking epic walks in nature.

She writes for both children and adults, has a Bachelor of Arts (English Literature major), a Graduate Diploma Information Studies and a TESOL Advanced Diploma.

Born in regional South Australia, she is now based in Adelaide — except when she is in Spain with her Spanish husband - olé!

facebook.com/HaymeadowStories

instagram.com/hayleymortonauthor

goodreads.com/Hayley_Morton

pinterest.com/hayleym0638

amazon.com/author/hayleymorton

ALSO BY HAYLEY MORTON

ThinkBeings (2012)

ThinkBeings is a fun, colourful, rhyming book which promotes self-esteem in children and highlights the connections between thoughts and feelings (an element of EQ).

Captain Plop series:

#1 *Captain Plop's water-saving mission* (2009)

Join Captain Plop, water-saver extraordinaire, on a flushingly wet adventure through the underworld of Emily and Luke's home!

This book teaches young children simple concepts for saving water at home, while entertaining them with a fun and engaging tale set within a household plumbing system.

#2 *Captain Plop: the desalination adventure* (2010)

Ahoy me hearties! Come aboard for more swashbuckling Captain Plop adventures as he journeys through a desalination plant. From the intake pipe in the ocean to your tap at home, learn how Captain Plop transforms from Salt water to drinking water.

This book assists young children to grasp the complex process of desalination by providing simplified explanations in the context of a fun, pirate-themed story.

#3 *Captain Plop and the tour de recycle* (2013)

Dust off your pushbikes and don your purple lycra for a water recycling adventure like no other.

Join Captain Plop as he races through three stages of water use and treatment —from the home to the treatment plant and back to the house and garden for reuse.

This book uses a bicycle race theme to introduce primary students to the concept of treating wastewater for the purpose of reuse.